Tess Thornton

A Heart
for the
Cowboy

 Walker Ranch Book 5

To request permission, contact the publisher at: EagleCreekPressBooks@gmail.com

Paperback ISBN: 978-1-957082-27-1

Library of Congress Number: Pending

First Paperback Edition January 2024

Cover Art by: GetCovers

Photography and Graphics Courtesy Of: Shutterstock.com, Depositphotos.com, Twenty20.com, Elements.envato.com

Editing and Layout by: Eagle Creek Press, Inc.

Printed in the USA

Publisher: Eagle Creek Press,

EAGLE CREEK
PRESS

Contents

Dedication

For Hula...
Yes, she's a horse.
But don't tell her that.

The Walker Ranch Series

Chapter One

Evan
July

"LUKE, THERE'S ANOTHER ONE!" I waved my brother down and held the gate as the last steer scampered through. He reined in that big black stud of his and circled around to scoop up the stray.

"How many is that?" he called.

"Twenty-seven. That's all of them. Can you guys take it from here?"

He tossed a gloved hand at me, then cupped it to his mouth. "Audrey, move on up to the left flank. Nice and easy, and we'll get these fellers pushed out to pasture. Wait, Lizzy, don't run! *Walk that horse!*"

I chuckled to myself as I latched the gate and turned my horse back toward the barn. Luke could handle the cows and the kid just fine without me. It was a sweet touch of irony that Luke was now parenting a teenager who was every bit as rowdy and reckless as he'd ever been. He was always in trouble and never slowed down at that age, and she was just like him. I often wondered how Audrey survived living in the same house with those two.

I cut through the broodmare pasture on my way back so I could take a look at the colts. They were all getting big, and some of them had already started to shed out their fluffy baby hair on their legs and muzzles. It was a hot and dry day, and the band of mares were all grouped under the shade trees, flicking flies off each other's faces and resting from the afternoon sun.

I halted my horse about fifty yards out and just gazed at them from a distance. When we had nursing foals, I came down here every day, without fail, and parked my horse in the same spot that I had for fifteen years. I came alone these days, but it hadn't always been that way. I sighed and rested my forearm on my saddle horn, scanning the group for any signs of trouble—lameness, sickness, anyone not thriving.

And, like always, one little face pushed its way out from the center of the herd to the outskirts. I grinned as I settled in to watch him. That little palomino colt of Goldie's tossed his head at me, then stood staring back with eyes bright and alert. A fly buzzed his nose, and he snorted, half-reared, and spun around. Then he whirled back to stare down my saddle horse. He was a picture, that one. Long, clean legs, chiseled muscles, and floating gaits, and all at just three months old.

"That's the age," my dad used to tell me. "You want to know what they'll look like as adults? Look at them at three months, and you'll see."

I'd said the same thing once to my daughter Emma. She was three years old at the time, and we were sitting in this very spot. I'd put her on in front of me that day so I could bring her down here to see the babies grazing, and she'd been captivated by a flashy buckskin colt she called Biz.

"See how he watches you?" I'd asked her. "He's curious and bold. He'll be friendlier than the others."

"He's special," she'd informed me. "Please, I want that one, Daddy."

I'd hugged her close, my heart swelling with pride. "Good choice, cupcake. I'd picked that one out for you, too. You guys are going to do amazing things together."

But the years hadn't played out the way I'd planned. Emma and Anne had left me to run down their dreams without them. I'd done my best, trying to check off the boxes and build the castles in the sky that we'd dreamed up together as a family. But without them to share the victories with, life was just hollow.

I watched that yellow colt for a few minutes more. He was so much like his uncle Biz in the way he would trot toward me with that springy stride, then stop and snort, then run off chasing butterflies like he wanted me to follow him. Emma would have loved this little guy, and I had my eye on him, too.

Finally, I picked up my reins and headed back toward the barn. I had to drive out to the hay fields this afternoon to decide when to harvest them, and I still had that one field sprinkler to finish repairing. I'd probably be working well after dark, but I'd take that over being bored. Keeping busy kept my mind from spiraling.

Cody was closing the door of the horse trailer as I trotted into the yard, and he tipped his hat to shield his eyes from the sun. "Oh, hey, Evan. I'm heading home. We're hauling out to that show in Tucson in the morning, so I'm going to go spend the evening with my wife before I go."

I gave a single nod as I hopped off my horse. "Fine. Say hi to Morgan for me."

"Yeah... uh, she's... she's not feeling well." He walked over and rested his hand on my horse's hip. "She asked me to pick up some ginger ale on my way home."

I was pulling my cinch, but when he said that, I stopped and stared at him. The smug look on his face said it all. I just grunted and finished loosening my saddle. "Anyone else know?"

"Not yet. She wanted to wait until I got back from this show, and then invite the family up for a barbecue to break the news."

"Well, cool. Congratulations."

"Thanks. I hate asking this, but would you mind stopping over there once or twice this week? Just to check on her. She won't ask for help, but she'd confide in you."

I looked up. "Why me? Why not Kelli or Jess or somebody?"

"Because you know how to keep a secret."

My mouth twisted into a frown. Yeah, he was right there. I was good at keeping secrets. I yanked the saddle off my horse and threw it over the wooden rail we had set up there. "Fine. What does she need?"

"Gosh, I don't even know." Cody pushed his hat up and scratched his head. "Any ideas? I've never done this before. Isn't she supposed to start craving pickle juice and watermelon?"

"Depends. She might start chowing down on Mexican food or ice cream, or she might not be able to eat hardly anything."

"See, I knew I came to the right guy. At least you know something. I'm completely clueless."

I blew out a sigh and untied my horse. "I don't know what you think I can tell you. Morgan's the one you need to listen to, not me."

"Yeah, and Morgan has a history of trying to do everything for herself and refusing to let anyone help her. She could be flat on her back with morning sickness but she'd tell me over the phone that everything's peachy. Just check on her once or twice, that's all I ask."

I shrugged. "Sure."

"And whatever you do, don't tell Kelli. Jess or Audrey, maybe, if you really need to. But Kelli would blast it on a loudspeaker in the middle of town, and then I'd have your dad calling me up to come home early from the horse show, Meryl trying to plan a baby shower in the first trimester, it would be a mess."

I smiled a little. "Sounds about right."

Cody stuck out his hand to shake mine. "Thanks, Evan! This means a lot to me."

"No worries. Ride 'em good and get your tail back home soon."

He started walking backward toward his truck. "You betcha. Maserati's on top of the world right now. You're going to have another champion this year, or I'll eat my hat!"

I pointed at him. "I'm holding you to that."

Meg

"DUSTIN, HERE'S A FRESH set of sheets. Please put them *on* your bed this time, okay? I don't want to find them crammed under the headboard again." My son was sitting at his desk with his back to me, his shoulders bent over something, and his feet swinging.

"Dustin, did you hear me?" I walked closer. "Please respond."

He straightened and meticulously set his carving tool aside. "Mom, I can't talk when... when I'm detailing. It's too squiggly."

"Fine. You're not detailing right now, so did you hear me about the sheets?"

"Yes." He picked the tool back up and resumed scraping at the block of wood on his desk. I couldn't tell what this one was going to be yet, but knowing Dustin, it would take my breath away when he was finished. He liked to work in sections, so while most of the block was still rough-cut, the corner where he was working had been carved away to reveal what looked like sweeping hair or waves or something.

I knew better than to touch one of his creations while he was working on it, so I leaned close and tucked my hands between my knees. "That's incredible. What is it?"

He sighed in exasperation and put his tool down. "It hasn't... hasn't told me yet."

My eyebrows raised. He had the oddest way of talking about his sculptures, as if they were living things. "Well, has it told you to clean up the shavings off the floor when you're done?"

He didn't answer this time. He just picked his tool back up and studied the corner where he'd been working, his tongue sticking out a little as he turned the piece from side to side. I shook my head and backed out of the room.

Nobody understood how Dustin could work the way he did. He started carving when he was two, with a kitchen knife on my dining room table legs. I still had that dining room table, and it was quite the conversation piece. By the time he was in preschool, he was creating chess pieces out of soapstone while most kids were still mastering the basics of Play-Doh. Oh, and he was beating all the local chess players down at the retirement center with his home-carved pieces.

At the time, his teacher thought he was a child genius—some kind of art prodigy descended to live among us mortal folk. Then, the next year, another teacher discovered that he couldn't read, and suddenly, he was no longer a genius. He was on the spectrum. A "special needs child."

But could you call it "special needs" when a kid could extract masterpieces from wood and clay and stone? He didn't start with a plan, he didn't begin on a large scale and hone in on the details later. The finished product just revealed itself bit by bit, and he spoke of it happening almost in spite of him rather than because of him.

Two years ago, I'd taken him to the university to ask an art professor to watch him work and help me decide how to guide his efforts. The art professor watched Dustin for an hour, then just shook his head and threw up his hands. "I don't even know what his concept is, let alone how to instruct him. You need someone trained in working with special needs students."

And so, there it was. Everywhere my brilliant, sensitive son went, he was labeled as different. A problem. That kid that no one understood and no one wanted to take the time to know because he intimidated them. Everywhere, that is, except for one place.

I made a pass through the kitchen and slipped three sandwiches into baggies. The same three sandwiches every week—turkey, turkey, and turkey. Dustin liked having choices, but he didn't appreciate variety, so this was my small way of actually getting him to eat his lunch instead of smashing it in the back seat of my car. I dropped my own sandwich in after them, zipped up the cooler bag, and walked back to Dustin's room.

"It's eleven-thirty," I said through the door. "Time to get ready to go up to White Pines."

There was the usual deliberate pause, then, "Okay."

I always held my breath until he said that "Okay." Because there was once a time when getting him to go anywhere at all was a fight—one I didn't usually win.

But then Morgan had come into our lives with her therapy horses and her love of people and her faithful troop of volunteers. And Dustin, the kid who didn't use to even get out of the car when we went places—assuming I could get him in the car in the first place—was now the poster child for the whole facility. It was the only place he went where he was made to feel equal and capable, and respected, just like every other kid.

He got in the car and put on his seat belt, and then asked the usual question. "Will Morgan let me ride Biz today?"

"I guess you'll have to see. Biz has lots of people who love him, you know. We have to share him."

"But I like him better than all the other people do," Dustin said. It wasn't up for debate. "I'm going to ride him today."

I sucked in a breath as I wrapped my fingers around the wheel. *Please let Biz be available today* was my usual prayer. "Okay. Here we go."

Chapter Two

Evan

"CAN YOU FIX IT?" Wyatt twisted a stem of hay between his teeth and glanced up at me as we stood over the control box for the big traveling field sprinkler.

I pulled my hat off and wiped my forehead. "I need parts. Gears are stripped out, and I used my last spares the other day." I put my hat back on and sighed. "Knew I should have ordered more."

He squinted against the sun. "So, this one's dead until you can mail order the parts? We gotta get it up and running Evan, or this whole corner is going to dry out before it's ready to harvest."

I nodded. "I'll check with the tractor store in town. They don't usually have specialty parts like this, though."

"What about the neighbors? Anyone else have some in their shed you can borrow?"

I scratched my chin. "Most everyone runs the center pivots, but this field was too sloped. Let's see... Brownings run a few of these."

"They're twenty miles away. Doesn't Cody have a couple up at his place?"

I blinked. "That's right, he does. I'll check with him." I pulled my phone out of my pocket. "I'll let you know. Mean time, go on out and check the flood pipes in that lower field.

Marshall hired some kid from town to set them, but he's new, so..."

Wyatt waved a hand. "Yeah, yeah. They never get the suction going before they just put it down and walk away."

I nodded. "Can't afford to lose ten acres of alfalfa on a hot week. I'll catch you later." I turned to walk back to my truck, sweat trickling under my collar with every movement. Criminy, but it was a hot one. The sort of weather where it almost does more harm than good to water the fields because the water droplets turned into tiny magnifying lenses for the sun's heat.

I started my truck and left the windows down until the air conditioning could catch up, then punched in Cody's number. After a few rings, he picked up.

"Yeah?" he called, and then there was a crash in the background. "Oh, dang. Hang on."

I held the phone away as muffled static filled the speaker. A few seconds later, he was back. "Need something?" Another loud bang.

I winced before I put the phone back to my ear. "You done? What's all that noise?"

"Sorry. I was packing the tack trunk in the trailer when you rang, and I thought I could hold it with one hand." His voice shifted as he moved the phone. "Hey, Cole! Come grab this, will you? Okay, Evan, I'm all yours. What's up?"

I thumbed the button to roll my windows up and tossed my hat on the passenger seat. "We have another field sprinkler down. I'm not sure I can find parts in town, so I was wondering if you had any spares at your place."

"Uh... I'm not sure. I'm still packing the show trailer, but you can run up there and look. Morgan can show you where all the parts are."

I put my truck in gear and rolled along the ditch bank bordering the hay field. "Yeah, I might do that if I can't find anything in town. Thanks, Cody."

"You bet. I'll be home in a while. If you're still up that way later, stay for dinner."

I swallowed and didn't answer for a few seconds.

"Oh, come on, Morgan's cooking isn't *that* bad. I know it doesn't compare to Meryl's, but—"

"No, it's not that," I broke in. "I need to get that thing fixed this evening if I can find the part."

"Okay. So if you don't find the part, you stay and eat. Deal?"

I allowed myself a little smile. "Deal."

"E VAN!" MORGAN WAVED AT me from across the White Pines therapy arena. "Cody said you might come up. Wait just a minute, and I'll be right there."

I nodded and shoved my hands in my pockets as I stepped up to the arena gate. She was busy, and I could wait. She was walking beside a raw-boned bay gelding, and a kid was walking between her and the horse. Once they rounded the corner and I got a better view of him, I recognized Dustin Truman. He was dragging his feet, his eyes were downcast, and his arms were hanging limp. I was pretty sure he was supposed to be taking part in the handling of the horse, but he looked like he would rather be anywhere else.

"Are you waiting for him, Dustin?" Morgan asked quietly. "He can't understand what you're telling him."

"I don't... don't want to do this," Dustin grumbled. "This is stupid. Why can't I ride Biz? I always, always ride Biz."

"Today, you're doing ground work with Badger," Morgan said. "He's trying to listen to you. Are you talking?" But Dustin crossed his arms and sewed his lips shut as they crossed the arena together.

"It's not talking when you don't use words. I want to ride Biz."

I heard a small gasp from someone sitting in the specta- tor's corner, and I craned my neck over the wall. If Dustin was here, his mom had to be here somewhere, too. And, yes, there she was—Meg Truman, with her dark blonde hair tied in a knot and her legs crossed in one of the plastic chairs of the spectator area. Her foot was bouncing unhappily, and she had her face in her palms. "Oh, good grief," I heard her muttering. "Not again."

I knew Meg and Dustin fairly well. And yeah... this wasn't the first time I'd seen her looking fit to tear her hair out, but she always pulled herself together pretty fast. I'm actually not sure how she managed it, but I always figured it was a sort of self-defense. You didn't get anywhere with a kid like Dustin if you showed your frustration, so she learned how to bottle it up. She could be biting her lip until it bled one minute, and smiling to beat the band the next.

But she wasn't to the smiling part yet. Well, there wasn't much else for me to do for a few minutes. Probably wasn't much I could really do, but I stepped up to the little raised seating area and waited for her to look up. She didn't.

"One of those days, huh?" I asked.

Meg started and jerked her head to me, her mouth falling into a little circle of humiliation. She blinked. "Ev-Evan?" She cleared her throat and tucked a lock of hair behind her ear. "I didn't... what did you say?"

I tipped my hat toward Dustin. "Doesn't look like it's going well."

She drew a shaky breath and rolled her eyes. "You have no idea. He almost wouldn't get out of the car, and then when he did, he was too late for the horse he wanted, and Morgan has had to deal with this his whole session."

I glanced over the arena wall. "She's got it handled. I wouldn't worry about it too much."

Meg's smile was thin and pained, and entirely forced. "I thought we were past this. I thought he... well. I should have known better." She moved her purse out of one of the other chairs in the spectator's box and pushed it a little toward me. "Care to have a seat?"

I thought about it for a second. Meg was one of the few people I would accept that offer from. She was easy to be around... didn't poke and prod where she ought to leave well enough alone, and she had a nice smile. When she used it.

But I just stepped back and shook my head. "Thanks, but I won't be here long enough for that. I just came up to raid Cody's tools."

Meg gave a small nod. "I see. What's broken?"

"Field sprinkler." I turned away, fixing my attention on Morgan as she came around to the gate and summoned a volunteer to walk with Dustin. "And there's my cue. Good seeing you, Meg."

"You too, Evan," Meg said to my back as I walked back down the steps. I paused for just a second, turning my head halfway back... Should I stop and say something else? But I just tipped my hat and moved to catch up with Morgan as she came out of the arena.

"I have to be quick," she apologized, leading me out of the barn and down the gravel driveway. "Kate is good with Dustin, but..."

"Not in his best mood today, I see."

She shot a grin over her shoulder. "You could say that. I would have just stopped his session early, but I kinda had a feeling this is the first time his mom has sat down all day, so we're still at it. Okay, here we are." She opened the door to a little garden shed Cody had brought in to serve as his temporary tool building until he had a proper shop built. "I don't have a light in here yet."

"That's fine." I doffed my hat and stepped inside. Cody never was good at organizing his crap, and even less so now, with everything in a constant state of construction and movement. Where was I supposed to even start looking?

"He said to tell you to check that blue tote down on the floor there," Morgan said, pointing to something in the corner. "And if not there, check that wire basket up on the top shelf."

Well, that was a start. I turned around to thank her, but when I did, I caught just the end of a heavy sigh. She was brushing the hair out of her face with one hand, and the other... it was resting on her stomach. Just like Anne used to do, when she was pregnant with Emma. I swallowed. Should I say something?

She caught me watching her and smiled brightly. "Anything else you need help finding?"

I shook my head. "No, uh..." Oh, heck with it. Luke and Dusty were always telling me I ought to talk more. Act like other people had feelings. I cleared my throat and gestured to her. "Cody told me your news. Hope you don't mind. Congrats."

Morgan was kneading her neck now, and a funny look appeared on her face. "He did? I asked him not to say anything yet."

"Aw, don't be upset with him. He figured I wouldn't tell anyone. Well... except for you."

An easy smile broke over her face. "I suppose not. Thanks, Evan."

I looked away, pulling that plastic tote out to the center of the shed to look for the parts I needed. "He said I should stop up here and check in on you while he's away."

"I figured as much. You don't need to do that. I'm fine, and he's only going to be gone for a week. Does he think I'm going to break or something?"

I shrugged and dug through the junk in the tote. "Yeah, well... I'll stop by in a few days. Just to keep him happy."

Morgan patted the frame of the door. "You're always welcome, but don't feel obligated. I'd better get back to my session. Are you staying for dinner?"

I grabbed a loose part from the bottom of the tote and held it up to the light. "Nope. Found what I need. Looks like I'm fixing a sprinkler."

"Well, don't be a stranger. Gotta go!"

I tipped my hat to her as she walked off. "See you."

Meg

M ORGAN CAME BACK TO the arena alone. I was watching behind her for any signs of that tall cowboy, but he never reappeared. Well... I really had no business thinking about Evan Walker, anyway. But sometimes, it was hard not to.

I'd known Evan Walker since his daughter Emma started first grade. She was two years younger than Dustin, but teaching at the school, I got to know all the kids, as well as their families. Small towns are nice that way.

Sometimes I'd see Dustin out on the playground with a pigtailed sidekick following along behind him. It annoyed him at first, the way little Emma Walker stuck to his heels and copied whatever he did. A couple of times, Dustin ran from her and hid, and I'd find him crying under the slide because she wouldn't leave him alone.

But then, one day, she drew a picture for him of a horse. After that, he softened. He even sat down with her on the lunch benches once or twice to try to "correct" her technique. And instead of ignoring his meticulous ways or being offended that he would want to fix her, she ate it up. So, for the rest of that year, they would just... sit together in the grass of the soccer field or at the picnic tables. They didn't talk much. Emma would draw, and Dustin would watch.

The next year, Dustin was a fourth grader, and his grade took their lunches at a different time than the younger kids. They never really saw much of each other anymore. I was always a little sad about that—Dustin didn't make friends easily, and he didn't relate the same way that other kids did. Emma Walker was the first kid to ever just... let him be himself.

I kneaded my eyes and let go a heavy sigh. I never could think of her without remembering... things I would rather not remember. And I was just her second-grade teacher—not even a close friend or a relative.

Sometimes I... well, I wondered how her father had survived it all. How he still got up in the morning, put one foot in front of the other, and even managed to smile once in a while. I don't think I'd have lived through it.

"I'M NOT COMING BACK on Thursday," Dustin announced as he got in the car.

I buckled my seat belt and looked at him in the rear-view mirror. "Why is that?"

"I don't like groundwork, and Morgan says I have to... have to do groundwork. I hate... *hate* walking. I'll come back when I can ride again."

I shook my head as my key found the ignition. "Skipping a session doesn't mean you get to skip what Morgan wants you to do. She will just have you do it the next time you come, no matter when that is."

"But I don't want to." End of conversation.

I rolled my eyes and just started the drive home. I couldn't reason with him when he dug his heels in like that. Morgan usually could, but sometimes, even she had no luck. And if he got really stubborn, so locked into his thoughts that he couldn't find his way back out, sometimes the whole day would spiral. *Please, not another meltdown...* not tonight... Maybe I could get him to talk about something else.

"Would you like spaghetti or baked chicken for dinner?" I watched him in the mirror. He always chose spaghetti... unless I didn't offer him a choice, in which case sometimes he wouldn't eat at all.

"Spaghetti."

I nodded and released an uneasy breath. Good. He was back to talking. For now.

I stopped and got the mail before I went into the house. It was the second week of the month, and I had bills to pay. John had never once missed a child support payment—never even by so much as a day. On one hand, I was grateful to him for that. I never had to pick up the phone and beg... at least, not for money owed... and I never had to fight him in court over Dustin's custody.

But part of me always wished that he *had* wanted to fight me, at least a little. That he hadn't just pulled up stakes and left because he couldn't take it anymore—didn't want to be part of our lives anymore.

I ripped open the envelope that held his check. Twelve hundred dollars. To the penny, dated for the fourteenth of every month. With a quick snap of my phone camera, the check was uploaded to my bank and already spent. There was never any leftover, but I counted my blessings that I had the money to pay the bills. John had never failed me there.

But a check once a month wasn't much company.

I marked the check as cashed and tossed it in my desk drawer, then went to the kitchen to start dinner. But I hadn't even opened the cupboard when someone knocked on the front door. Who could that be just before dinner?

I walked over and checked the peephole. I never used to do that, but after John left, and I was the only one here, well... I guess I got a little more cautious. I smiled when I recognized Kelli Walker, her nose magnified and her chin shrunken to nothing in the warped view of the lens.

"Kelli!" I pulled the door open. "To what do I owe the honor?"

She was wearing a ragged, sweat-stained t-shirt, and her hair was up in a high ponytail with a headband pinning her bangs back from her face. Her short sleeves were rolled up to her shoulders, and she looked like she'd been cleaning all day. She grinned and leaned on the door frame. "Whew! You don't have air conditioning in there, do you?"

I backed away from the door to let her in. "As a matter of fact, I do, but I don't usually keep it on. I have the fan running, though."

"Good enough." She plucked at her damp shirt and followed me inside, closing the door behind her.

"Iced tea?" I offered.

"Oh, you're a saint! Do you have like a whole gallon full?"

I chuckled and opened the fridge to pour her a glass. "Just a pitcher, but you're welcome to it. What have you been doing? You look exhausted."

She took the glass and gulped half of it down before she even drew a breath. "Getting my house ready to sell. Marshall and I are moving out to the ranch."

I pulled out a chair at the kitchen table for her and sat down at the opposite one. "Really? That's great news! So, your new house is done?"

She shook her head and finished the glass. "Not for a while. We have a foundation poured and power and water lines brought in, but that's about all so far. But Marshall went to the farm equipment auction with Evan last week, and someone was unloading an RV. He bought it without even telling me and drove that hunk of junk all the way back from Pocatello—without dying even once! I told him he should win a prize for that. Anyway, he wants to put it out on our property and live there while we finish building the house."

My eyebrows lifted. "And you're okay with this?"

Kelli laughed and shook her head. "Does it matter? But yes, I'm okay with it. We'd actually talked about doing that, but we didn't want to spend our ready cash on an RV when we still had my house to live in. But he got this thing super cheap, and he's right when he says that we'll get more money out of selling my house if we put it on the market in the summertime, rather than waiting 'til fall. So, maybe it's a wash on cost, and we get to live out at the ranch through the summer."

"That will make him happy, I'm sure."

"Yeah. He tries, bless his little cowboy heart, but he doesn't know what to do with himself with only a yard the size of a postage stamp to mow."

"What about you?" I asked. "You're giving up a real kitchen."

"Aw..." She waved a hand. "Trust me, I'll survive for a while. Someday, I'll have to take you up to the ranch and let you eat some of Meryl's cooking. We can mooch off her until I have my own house."

"Hah... uh, wow," was all I could think to say.

"I'm kidding about mooching off of her. We already worked out a grocery plan, and she's excited to be cooking for Marshall. We have a bet—she's determined to teach him to eat something besides steak, and I'm betting that she'll never get it done. So!" She clapped her hands on her thighs. "Wanna come look at some stuff we're getting rid of?"

I laughed, collected her glass, and went to refill it. "What kind of stuff? We have plenty of kitchen appliances, and Dustin doesn't really play with electronics, so—"

"Oh, I'm not talking about that kind of stuff. There's a lawn mower, and I remember you said yours died a while back. It's practically brand new. I'd just bought it last year. And a weed eater, some gardening tools, a really big book-shelf, and a lovely couch that Marshall hates because it's too short for him."

"Don't you want to take the tools up to the ranch?"

Kelli shrugged. "They have lots. I wanted to see if you could use them before I start donating things. I should do a yard sale, but frankly, Marshall and the ranch and the coffee wagon keep me busy enough."

I brought her glass back and eased into my chair with a frown. "Well, I'm... I'm flattered. Yes, I could definitely use the lawn mower, at least."

"Mmm..." Kelli gulped down the entire second glass, dipped her head while she swallowed, then looked back up with a big grin. "Great! I'll tell Marshall to hold it for you. Or are you free to just walk over with me now?"

I glanced over my shoulder at the empty hallway. Dustin would be lost in his carving until dinner time—six o'clock exactly. And it was only a little after five now. Kelli lived just a couple of blocks away—close enough that I could actually push the lawnmower from her house to mine, if I wanted to. "Sure. Let me tell Dustin."

Chapter Three

Meg

"HEY, MEG!" MARSHALL WALKER'S head popped above a heavy oak cabinet he was wrestling through the door into the garage. "How's it going?"

I hadn't talked to Marshall too many times. I was honestly surprised he remembered my name. Dustin, he knew—he'd broken his arm up on the mountain last winter, searching for my kid when he got lost in a snowstorm. No way he would forget Dustin after all that. But to lots of people, I was just "Dustin's Mom." I waved and smiled. "Hi, Marshall. I hear you're moving."

He grunted and gave the cabinet a twist to set it where he wanted it, then leaned against it with a grin. "That's the plan. Here to help get some stuff out of our hair?"

"I guess so."

Kelli patted my shoulder. "Honey, can you pull the lawn mower out for her? Come on, Meg, want to see the couch?"

"But I don't need a couch," I protested weakly... to no avail, for she was already marching through the garage door into the house and clearly expecting me to follow.

"Honestly, Kelli, the lawn mower is..." I stopped abruptly at the door, my gaze transfixed on the elegant deep burgundy couch that sat against the living room wall. My couch at home was ripped in every corner and leaking stuffing all over the floor because... well, Dustin had good days and bad days, and that was one of the bad ones. But I hadn't wanted to spend the money on a replacement yet, and certainly not on something *this* nice. How long would it take for him to start carving those modern-looking wood square legs into mere spindles?

But nice as it was, the couch itself wasn't what took my breath away. Draped over the back was an exquisite, hand-stitched log cabin quilt. The styling was something straight out of the quilter's catalogs from generations ago, but the fabric was crisp and brilliant as the day it was sewn. It was the kind of quilt you could tell had been crafted with love and deep thought. I sighed in awe and picked up the corner to admire it.

"It's beautiful, isn't it?" Kelli beamed.

"Oh, it looks like something my grandma would have made. Gorgeous! You didn't sew this, did you?"

"As if I could manage a needle without making myself bleed all over the fabric! That was made by Marshall's mom, Marci. She made one for each of her sons and tucked them away, waiting for the day they married—except, they kind of got forgotten for years. When Blake married Meryl, she discovered them all in a chest and made sure the guys all got their quilts."

My fingers brushed over the stitches, feeling the history and love sewn into every inch. "It's beautiful. Such a thoughtful gift."

Kelli nodded, a distant look in her eyes. "I know the guys all loved them... well, except for Evan. There wasn't one for him. Everyone assumed Marci had given it to him years ago, when he married Anne. But no one really knows. And no one quite has the guts to ask him about it."

I chuckled softly. "Evan? He seems so mild-mannered. Why would anyone be afraid to ask him?"

Kelli smirked. "Hah! You'd think that, wouldn't you? But you've never seen Evan at a branding. That's about the only time he says much, but trust me, he makes up for it when he's working cows. You don't cross Evan."

"I still have a hard time envisioning that. He always seems so nice, but I guess I've only seen him around town and... well... at the school."

"Oooh." Kelli's mouth puckered, then she winced. "Yeah, that's right. You were Emma's teacher, weren't you? Marshall said something about that. I'm sure he's got a soft spot for you just because of that. He'd be extra friendly to you."

I shook my head. "I guess I don't know him well enough to say, but I always felt like he walked on eggshells around me. Too many memories, you know?"

Kelli shrugged. "Yeah, maybe. Well, anyway, what do you think of the couch? Want to try it out?"

I sighed. "It's beautiful, Kelli, but I really can't..."

Kelli held up her hand, interrupting me. "I'm not asking you to pay for it, Meg. It would mean a lot to me if you had it. I know things have been tight for you, and we all love you and Dustin. Consider it a gift."

My cheeks flushed, feeling the weight of her generosity. "Kelli, that's too much. I know what this kind of furniture costs. I can't just take it."

She looked at me squarely. "Marshall hates this couch. Big baby thinks it's too short for him, and he keeps threatening to saw it down the middle and put a plank in it so he can fit. It'll be better off with you."

I crossed my arms. "Have you *seen* my dining room table legs?"

"They're works of art. Come on, what do you say?"

I looked from the couch to Kelli, torn. Her genuine offer tugged at my heart. "Alright," I finally whispered, "if you're sure."

"Perfect! I'll have Marshall load it up in the truck and bring it over to your place. It'll be easier that way."

I'D DIED AND GONE to heaven. The aroma of simmering spaghetti sauce filled the air—that would forever be comfort food to me, even if it was a hundred degrees outside. I had turned the heat down, letting it bubble a little longer so the flavors would blend, and I spared myself just five minutes to test out that new couch. So this was what it was supposed to feel like, not having furniture springs digging into your back. Miraculous!

Marshall hadn't just dropped off the couch, though. My garage was full of new tools—well over a thousand dollars worth of "stuff," most of which I'd actually been needing. I wasn't sure what to do or say to thank them. Maybe some people would feel offended, being given hand-me-down furniture and yard equipment, but for me... I guess it made me feel seen. Noticed. Cared for, at least a little, and that was a rare feeling these days.

I kicked my feet down off that plush piece of heaven and went into the kitchen to check dinner. The noodles were tender, and the sauce was as good as it was going to get. I turned off the burners and dumped the pasta water.

"Dustin!" I called out, "Spaghetti's ready."

Silence.

I probably shouldn't have taken his appetite for granted. If he really wanted spaghetti today, he'd have come running. But if he wasn't overly enthusiastic, I'd just shot myself in the foot by yelling for him across the house.

I walked toward his room and tapped gently on the door. "Dustin?"

"Not hungry," his muffled voice came through the closed door.

"It's your favorite. You said this was what you wanted for dinner."

"No!"

"Dustin, you need to eat."

The door suddenly flew open, and he stood in the gap, his eyes red, hands clenched. "I said no, *no*, Mom!"

I took a step back. I hadn't expected him to react *this* badly. "Dustin, what's going on?"

He looked down, avoiding my gaze, his fingers fidgeting. "I don't want spaghetti. I don't want anything."

My second mistake in as many minutes—I reached out, trying to touch his arm, but he pulled away. "Hey, it's okay," I whispered, attempting to soothe him.

"No, it's... it's not! I want macaroni and cheese."

I bit back a scowl. "You can't just change your mind after I've already made dinner, Dustin. You always like spaghetti."

He looked down, his feet shifting on the carpet. "It smells different."

"It's the same sauce, the same noodles as always."

He fidgeted with the hem of his shirt, a sign I had come to recognize as him grappling with how to express his feelings. "Just... feels different today. Not right."

"Different how? Can you explain?"

He hesitated. "Everything's just too... too big today."

I swallowed. "Fine. I'm going to eat dinner. You can come when you want."

"I want macaroni and cheese."

I was turning away, but I bit my lip and spun back to him. I tried... oh, I tried, but I screwed up, anyway. "I'm *not* making something else. I can't keep making five different meals every day just because you changed your mind. It's spaghetti or nothing."

"Then I'll starve!" he shouted. "Just go away. You never understand!"

The sting of his words hit hard—particularly because I *did* know better when that last retort shot out of my mouth. I knew that would only get his back up. And now, I blinked away the tears, forcing my voice to remain calm. "Dustin, I'm trying. Please, just tell me what's wrong."

But he'd already retreated, slamming his bedroom door behind him.

I STOOD ALONE IN the kitchen, the forgotten pot of spaghetti sauce on the stove and my stomach rumbling loudly. But eating just didn't sound good anymore. I took a deep breath, pushing back the tears.

I just wasn't enough. That was the reality of it.

For two years, I'd been able to convince myself that I could do this. That Dustin was better off... that *we* were better off on our own. If John couldn't cope with Dustin, they would just continue to fight every day, making things worse. I'd been broken that he didn't treat his marriage vows as seriously as I took mine, but the house... it got more peaceful after John left. Something I could manage, to create the environment Dustin needed to come home to when the world got to be too much.

White Pines had been my saving grace. I'd found Morgan and her horses by accident—ran into her in the grocery store the week after John left. She'd just moved back to town, all starry-eyed and hopeful for the big things she had planned. And I was just happy to talk to someone who didn't mind when I burst into tears at random things.

So, we went out to meet the horses the very next day. It was rough at first, but after we settled in, it was the one place where all the tools that Dustin's teachers and therapists from school tried to give him actually made sense. Truly, I don't know where Dustin and I would be if we hadn't met her.

But White Pines couldn't give him everything he needed. And neither could I—I needed help. I needed someone to talk to, someone who could step in when I was at the end of myself.

Without much thought, I found myself reaching for my phone, scrolling through the contacts until I landed on John's name. My thumb hovered over the call button. We didn't talk unless it was strictly about Dustin, and even then, our conversations were short and perfunctory. But I was desperate.

I pressed the button.

After a few rings, John answered. I could hardly hear him over the background noise. "Meg?"

I hesitated, "Hi, John. It's me."

"Yeah, I know. What's up?" His voice sounded distant—not just because of the background noise, but emotionally distant. That was nothing new.

"I... uh, I wanted to thank you for the check."

A pause. "You don't usually call for that. Everything okay?"

I sighed, trying to find the right words. "Dustin's having a tough time. He got really upset just now, and I just... I thought maybe you could talk to him."

John was silent for a moment and then, "Look, I'm not home. I have to go."

The brush-off hurt and my voice caught as I practically begged, "Could you call back later?"

There was a heavy pause before John replied, "Meg, I'm... I'm on a date."

It felt like the floor dropped from beneath me. "Oh," was all I could manage.

"I've uh... I've been seeing her for a few months now. Her name is Kirstin."

"Why didn't you tell me?" I didn't really want the answer to that. He wasn't obligated to share his life with me anymore... so he didn't.

He sighed, "It wasn't the right time. I have to go. I'll call Dustin tomorrow."

I nodded, even though he couldn't see me. "Okay. Thanks, John."

As the line disconnected, I dropped my phone with a shaking hand. So, that... that was it. I really was on my own.

Evan

I T WAS AFTER NINE by the time I hung my hat on the peg in the house. Dad and Meryl were probably upstairs somewhere, and the kitchen was abandoned, save for a single light over the stove and a sticky note saying there was a plate for me in the fridge. I flicked on the lights and went looking for my dinner—corn on the cob, salad, and some grilled chicken. I pulled a coke out of the door and settled down at the table with the paper to catch up on the local classifieds.

Sometime later, the stairs creaked, and I looked up to see Dad easing his way down. "Evan, there you are," he grunted. "Did you find your... oh, I see you did."

I speared the last bite of chicken on my fork and held it up. "Tell Meryl thanks for saving it."

"Sure thing. She was worried it would be too dry by the time you got in, but... aw, heck, we're used to over-done food, warmed up in the microwave, right?"

I shrugged. "I didn't bother warming it up. Makes the chicken chewy and the corn rubbery."

Dad rubbed his forehead and leaned over the back of his usual chair. "I won't tell Meryl you said that. Wyatt said you were working on that traveling field sprinkler again?"

I nodded and crunched down the last bite of my salad. "It's up and running again. Tomorrow, I'll drive out to the south fields and look them over. Should be ready to cut by next week."

Dad nodded. "What else did you do today?"

I picked up my plate and my empty can and got out of my chair. "Dropped a trailer off at the sale yard this morning, pushed some cow/calf pairs to fresh pasture, checked the yearlings on the upper forty with Luke. Looked at the broodmares on my way back, then had to go up to Cody's to borrow some parts."

"Nothing else?"

I rinsed my plate in the sink and opened the dishwasher to find a spot for it. "Got busy. I'll catch up tomorrow."

"Not what I meant." Dad followed me into the kitchen. "You gotta do something besides work all the time, Evan."

I turned around and leaned against the counter. "What do you suggest? Stuff still has to get done, doesn't it?"

"But you're not the only one who can do it. Everyone else was done for the day hours ago."

"So, what, should I have made someone come stand over me while I fixed that sprinkler this evening? Had to get done before tomorrow, and it was a one-person job."

Dad shrugged. "When's the last time you went out for the evening? Met up with some of your buddies after they got off work?"

"Just who would that be? Everyone I used to hang out with has..." I swallowed and turned around to brace my hands on the sink, my head lowered. "You know. Kids. Family stuff."

Dad's hand came to rest on my shoulder, and he squeezed lightly. He didn't say anything for a moment, but when he did, his voice was rough. "Sorry, Evan. I didn't mean..."

I shrugged away from him and shook my head. "It's alright. I'm heading to the shower."

Dad just stepped back and let me go.

The hallway to my old room hadn't changed much since childhood, though it felt narrower now—perhaps because I'd grown or maybe because the weight on my shoulders had grown. Each step echoed with memories; the floorboard creaks thundering as loudly in my ears as they used to when I was ten, sneaking out of my room at night.

The family photos still lined the walls—more faded now than they used to be. A hodgepodge of smiles, laughter, and tender moments... Dusty and me, covered head to toe in mud the day I helped him deliver his first calf. Luke, flying high on a bull back in high school, with his hat fanning the air and his heels dug in for the prize. Cody and Marshall when they were just kids, eating popcorn and watching movies all night because Cody was too scared to go back to his house with his dad home.

As I neared the end of the corridor, I paused, my fingers grazing the edge of a worn frame. This was one of my favorites—Dad carrying Mom over the threshold of this house the day they moved in. After five years of living out of a trailer next to the branding pen, raising Marshall and me out on the land they loved, and stretching every penny to survive, they built their dreams together. Dad was so proud, and Mom looked radiant. She was eight months pregnant with Luke in that picture, and her smile was the same as the one hanging right next to it. The one where she had one arm around my Annie as they held Emma together in the hospital.

And that was where I stopped looking at the pictures in the hall.

But it wasn't just the pictures. The whole house just didn't fit me anymore. It was better than living in the cabin Anne and I had built together, there was that. But this place was a time capsule of my youth, preserved like a shrine. The same old bathroom tiles with a slight crack in the corner, the worn-out shower curtain with its faded sunflower pattern, and the oak-framed lamp hanging over the mirror that Mom said was so stylish... almost thirty years ago.

The only thing new was the reflection staring back at me from the mirror. I tugged the skin around my eyes and peered hard at the lines starting to crack through my face. I looked... good grief, I looked like my dad. Craggy skin from weathering wind and rain, sun-squint creases around my eyes, and something else there that wore a lot like age. My reflection had altered drastically, that horrible day a little over two years ago, and it never really went back to what it used to be.

I started the shower, letting the water run until it was scalding. Steam filled the small room, blurring the mirror and, for a moment, scalding my mind so other things couldn't intrude. As I stepped under the spray, the water was near blistering. Each drop that hit my skin felt like an act of purification, as if I could wash away the past two years, cleanse myself of the guilt and pain. I rested my forehead against the cool tiles, letting the heat envelope me, trying to lose myself in its embrace.

The sensation of hot water cascading over my body usually brought a brief respite from the day, a chance to wash away the dust and toil. But today, the water wasn't just cleaning my exterior; it felt like it was trying to penetrate deeper, attempting to reach the places caked with grief. Memories of Anne surged forward, uninvited. The curve of her smile, the hint of mischief in her eyes, how her laughter had been the soundtrack of our best moments. And little Emma, her laughter echoing her mother's, ringing with innocent delight.

My fingers threaded into my hair, gripping the wet strands tightly. The pull at the roots, that sharp twinge of pain, became a lifeline—a desperate attempt to anchor me to the present, to keep the past from swallowing me whole. Every ounce of hurt, every shard of guilt, sought refuge in that simple act, like a grounding ritual.

But in trying to escape one set of memories, I inadvertently conjured up another. Today's visit to the therapy center came flooding back. There was something about that place that... no, that wasn't it.

There was something about the *people* there. About Morgan, the way her smile glowed with the fresh glory that everyone who's ever experienced it knows in an instant. It's a look you can't help but stop and stare at, once you know. You can't unsee it, and you can't forget.

And then, there was Meg. I'd avoided her for two years—one reason or another. Seeing her always made the memories ache a little more, and it would be a couple of days before I'd be right again. It wasn't that she was intrusive. She'd always been mildly friendly, no more, and I'd been the same in return... or, as friendly as I could manage. I knew she got it—she was the last one to see Anne and Emma, after all. The last person ever to have a conversation with them, that afternoon when Anne picked Emma up from school. It just seemed too... too raw to talk to her much.

Besides, she seemed to have her own problems.

I toweled off and crossed the threshold from the bathroom to my bedroom, wrapping the towel around my waist as I scrubbed my face with clean hands. I tugged open my drawer and pulled on some boxers, then turned to find my phone and plug it in for the night. Not much else to do, but climb into bed and stare at the ceiling for a while.

I grabbed the top covers and pulled them back but paused when they folded over that old quilt draped at the foot of my bed. I swallowed as my eyes skimmed over the red and blue, gold and green blocks Mom had salvaged from old bits and ends of other clothes. I remembered her sitting by the wood stove at night, rocking in that big wooden chair Dad had got her for Christmas one year, with her needle flashing in the firelight as she listened to Dad talking over his plans for the next calving season.

Bringing it to my face, I inhaled deeply, searching for the scents that defined my childhood. And there it was—the earthy aroma of freshly baled hay, the musky essence of horses after a long day's ride, and, under it all, the last traces of sweet, tangy Jasmine. Anne's favorite perfume.

I let it fall back to the bed, then my fist bunched, and I gathered it into a wad. Why did I still keep this thing? And why right *here*, of all places, where I had to look at it every day? I balled it up and tossed it in a drawer... out of sight, out of mind. Then, I hit the light switch and prepared to do battle with the darkness for the rest of the night.

Chapter Four

Evan

THE SUN BEAT DOWN on my back as my steps skirted the edge of one of our larger alfalfa fields. The green stalks reached my knees, with one or two purple dots speckling their tops. I'd turned the water off to this field at just the right time—too soon, and the hay would scorch before it was ready to harvest. Too late, and it wouldn't dry properly.

I brushed my hand over one of the feathery shoots, then stood with a grunt of satisfaction. I'd have Wyatt start cutting this on Saturday afternoon. That was promising—we'd get a third cutting off this field this year, and this first crop would be high yield without being too stemmy. Some years, first cutting turned out like that—so tough we could only feed it to the cattle because we had to wait on the weather. This crop was gorgeous in just about every way, and what we didn't keep would fetch a good price.

The familiar ping of my phone broke my train of thought, and I pulled it out of my pocket. Cody's name flashed on the screen with a quick update from the horse show.

-Maserati just knocked it outta the park in her herd work class.

A proud smile tugged at my lips. "That's my girl," I murmured. Maserati technically belonged to the ranch, but I sort of thought of her as mine, after I'd nursed her through that bad respiratory virus as a yearling. Luke usually doctors the horses, but... well, I had needed the distraction at the time. I spent a week bedding down outside her stall, hoping and praying she'd live to see another day. And now, she was a national Snaffle Bit Futurity Champion, on the warpath for more stars in her crown.

I thumbed a quick reply. -*Sounds like she's earnin' her keep. Keep it up.*

I could almost hear the Cody's cocky laugh. -*You betcha. Gotta run. Saddlin' up the next one. Check on Morgan for me?*

I chewed my lip. No, I hadn't... not since before he'd actually left town. I hissed a sigh as I slipped the phone back into my pocket, then I yanked it back out to type a quick answer. -*Heading up this afternoon.*

He replied with a thumbs-up, and I put my phone away. I guess it wasn't the end of the world if I had to squeeze something else into my day. Might actually feel good to take a short drive—do something where I wasn't bending over, picking something up, or trying to think very hard. Plus, my truck had air conditioning.

WHITE PINES WAS BUSTLING with activity—therapists leading horses around the arena, one of the volunteers giving a tour to a group of wide-eyed spectators, while those who had come to watch their loved ones looked on from the sidelines. My eyes scanned the faces, looking for Morgan's familiar features. I found her standing near the edge of the arena, talking to another woman.

"Hey, Morgan," I called out, my voice carrying over the sounds of hooves and laughter. She looked up and smiled, waving me over as she made her excuses to the woman she was talking to.

"Hi, Evan," she greeted me warmly. "How are things on the ranch?"

"Good," I replied, trying to sound casual even though we both knew why I was there. "'Bout time to start haying, so you know what that means."

She cocked her head and thinned her lips. "Do I ever."

I stuffed my hands in my pockets. "Cody told me Maserati won the cutting today."

"I know! It's great, isn't it?"

"Oh." I gestured to her. "Sorry. That's right, I guess he'd have told you first."

She snorted and rolled her eyes. "He's such a stinker. First, he texted me that they lost their cow, and she came in dead last. I saw his message in the middle of a session, so I worried about it for an hour until I could reply. It wasn't until I took the bait and texted him back that he fessed up and told me she won."

I chuckled. "That sounds like something he'd do."

"That's how you know he's in a good mood. Best score she's ever marked, he says. I think he likes showing her even better than Five Iron."

I shrugged. "They make a great team. She's touchy, but Cody's good with those sensitive ones."

Morgan smiled, her eyes twinkling with the sort of tenderness that a wife reserved for the man she loved. "Yeah. He would be."

I coughed. "Uh-huh. Well, uh... You're doing good? Everything going alright with the... the program?"

Morgan got a knowing grin on her face and shook a finger at me. "You can tell Cody that you did your duty. I'm just fine, Evan."

I shuffled my boots and looked at the ground. "Well, that's good. No, ah... no morning sickness? Sorry, but Cody made me promise to ask."

She blew out a breath, her eyes flicking away from mine before she answered. "Every day, to be truthful, but I'm doing fine. Just tired, but that's to be expected, right?"

"Right," I said slowly, not entirely convinced. "But if you need anything, you know you can always ask for help, right? I'll get my ears chewed out by more than just Cody if you get sick and don't say anything. Dad and Meryl will have my head."

"Thank you, Evan," she chuckled. "I appreciate that more than you know."

I nodded. "Guess I'll scoot, then." I started to turn away but stopped as my gaze landed on the crowd of people wandering the edge of the arena. "Say, what's going on? You guys giving tours now?"

Her face lit up. "Oh, you'll never believe it. Do you see that lady right there? The one I was talking to when you walked up?"

I glanced over my shoulder. "Yeah. Some big shot?"

"Only the dean of the university's occupational therapy department. She brought a whole group from the university—counselors and professors who specialize in teaching every kind of therapy and rehabilitation you can imagine. And they wanted to come *here* to tour our little program! Can you believe that? They drove over two hours to get here!"

I whistled. "Nice. So, what does that mean for you guys?"

She laughed, holding her arms out in a helpless shrug. "No clue! I'm just tickled to show them what equine therapy can do. Some of them have never seen it before."

To be honest, neither had I. I'd been here dozens of times, helping Cody with this or that, but I hadn't wanted to stick around to watch because... yep, there he was. That big buckskin gelding plodding around the arena—the one Emma had hung her dreams on when she was just three years old. She'd said he was special... and he was. Just special for other people now.

I sniffed and swallowed. "Yeah. Well, I'd better get back."

Morgan dipped her head with a smile. "Right. I'll go check on our tourists."

She walked away, and I followed as far as the door... then stopped and looked back at the figures walking across the arena. Maybe it couldn't hurt... I'd stay for a minute or three. I walked a little closer to the rail and let my eyes follow that familiar buckskin shape.

Biz looked good. Not just shiny and healthy—I'd have expected no less. But he also looked happy. His ears always had a funny way of flopping to the sides when he was content, and his lower lip made little plopping noises as he walked. He must have liked his job.

It took me a minute to register who was walking beside the horse, but then I recognized Dustin Truman. That must mean... I glanced over the rail and found Meg Truman's blue-green eyes ducking away from mine. Her cheeks were dusky, and she was trying to hide a little smile.

I stayed, watching her for another minute, and she flicked another conscious glance at me. This time, her eyes didn't shift away the instant they touched mine. Her smile widened, and she pushed the folding chair next to hers toward me. "Have a seat, Evan Walker?"

I cleared my throat. "I, uh... Just for a minute."

Meg

"THIS IS STUPID. I want to ride." Dustin's words carried up to me, his voice crackling with frustration. Part of me hoped he'd talk Amber into it for once—not that I wanted him to get his way all the time, but he was always so much more peaceful after getting to ride. There was something about that calming rhythm that made him not want to fight the world. And please, please, I didn't want to fight him all afternoon again.

But Amber knelt beside him, a kind smile on her face, as she waited for his breathing to calm down. "I know you do, Dustin, and you will. But before we ride today, we need to go back to something we haven't done for a while. It is *just* as important as trusting the horse to carry us."

Dustin scowled, his gaze darting to Biz's feet, then back to Amber's. "What is it?"

"The communication exercise," Amber explained gently. "We're going to talk to Biz without using words—just with our body language and presence. It's how horses talk to each other."

Dustin's scowl deepened. "But I don't... don't want to talk. I want to ride."

"I promise you, after this exercise, you can ride Biz. But this is about trust, Dustin. About knowing what he sees in you and making your connection even stronger. Can we make a deal? You help me with this, and then you ride. Deal?"

I watched the internal battle play out on Dustin's face, the longing to feel the rocking of the saddle as he let go of control in the only place he felt safe doing so, against the challenge being offered to him now. Slowly, his shoulders dropped, and he nodded. "Okay. Deal."

Amber stood. "Good. Now, let's start. Stand here like this." She demonstrated a confident stance. "Show Biz you're strong, and you're a leader."

Dustin mirrored her, standing tall, his chest puffed out slightly.

"Now, invite him closer without words. Use your body to ask him," Amber instructed, guiding him with her own subtle gestures, turning away just enough to be inviting.

With a deep breath, Dustin turned his gaze away from Biz, creating an open space between them. It was a silent request, a soft beckoning. Biz seemed to consider this wordless plea. Then, in a moment that seemed to stretch, he stepped toward Dustin, his movements slow and careful.

Dustin's eyes lit up, a sparkle of triumph and delight as Biz came closer until the horse's nose gently nudged against him.

"You did it." Amber's praise was soft but full of pride. "You see? He trusts you, and he understands you."

Dustin's hand reached out, stroking Biz with that tender sort of touch he used when he carved his sculptures. "Can I ride now?"

"This was very good, but there's something you have to accomplish in order to ride."

Dustin let Biz nuzzle his hand for a few more seconds without looking up, but he did answer. "What?"

"You need to get him *all* the way across the arena to where the saddle is, and you have to do it without any help from me."

His brow wrinkled. "But he's not..." Dustin gulped, like he was choking on the words. "Not w-wearing a halter. How do I lead him?"

Amber grinned. "Remember what we just did? That's how. You have to invite him to follow you."

This was almost too much for my son. I saw his shoulders start to shake, and the vicious swipe across his nose as he hid his head in Biz's neck. But then, a miracle happened. Without Amber saying another word, Dustin coughed and stepped gently away, holding out his hand.

And Biz followed.

Okay, I know it sounds ridiculous. It's such a small thing, after all. To most people, it would be second nature to walk across a pen or a corral and let an animal follow them. But the fact that Dustin had pulled himself back from that panic of "I can't do this," all on his own, and *tried*... well, I know *I* was tearing up.

They made it to the other side of the arena, where a saddle awaited, and I dusted some moisture from my cheeks. After the kind of week I was having, this was just the little glimmer I'd needed to see. I sent up a silent prayer of gratitude as I watched Amber helping my son saddle his favorite horse. But they were far enough away now that other things started finding their way into my attention. Voices, people... one voice, in particular.

Evan Walker had come to talk to Morgan again. I leaned forward in my chair, watching them. I couldn't hear what they were saying, but their manners made me study them for a second. Morgan laughed at something Evan said, but he wasn't laughing in return. He looked dead serious about something, and whatever it was, she was brushing it off.

And then, like a bolt of lightning on a clear day, I put it together. It was the way she unconsciously rested her hand on her stomach that caught my attention, confirming my hunch without a word. I'd been starting to wonder these last couple of weeks, when she seemed more tired than usual lately... So, *that* was it. Pregnancy suited her, and even from this distance, I could see the glow of impending motherhood.

Cody was away at a show, wasn't he? That was right—Dustin said the next sculpture he wanted to work on was Cody's show mare, Maserati. Last week, when we were up here, he'd badgered Cody to give him a "really good—really, *really* good action shot" from the show to work from when they got home. That wouldn't be until early next week, would it?

The rest of the puzzle clicked. Evan was here on Cody's behalf to check on Morgan.

That was sweet. Something a real family would do. What would *that* be like? I would have expected Cody to send Marshall or even Kelli—Morgan's best friend—to do the honors. They were all pretty close, but those four were practically inseparable. As I pondered, though, it made sense in a way only the heart understood. Evan's quiet way of taking care of things, his unassuming nature that didn't ruffle feathers or draw attention, was probably just what Cody wanted—what Morgan needed right now.

After a few more exchanged words and a shared laugh, Morgan excused herself, her hand still occasionally brushing her stomach. Evan turned, and I expected him to leave straight away. He had that look about him, the one that says he's finished with this place, ready to move on to the next task. But something made him pause, his gaze trailing back to the arena, and I felt a sudden flush of warmth creep up my neck when he saw me observing him.

I was embarrassed, caught in the act of watching him so intently, but as our eyes met, something in his look softened.

Well, so what if he saw me watching him? It wasn't like there was a lot else to watch, with Dustin on the far side of the arena saddling the horse.

Gathering my courage, I pushed the folding chair beside me towards him with my foot. "Have a seat, Evan Walker?" Would he accept this time?

He seemed to hesitate, and I held my breath. "I, uh... Just for a minute," he replied and made his way toward me.

Oh, dear. Now what? Did he want me to *talk* to him? Oh, what had I just started? I swallowed a hard lump in my throat and sat so tight in my chair that my knees started shaking together.

Evan eased himself into the seat, his eyes never leaving Dustin and Biz in the arena. That was some relief. I turned to watch as well. The saddle was on now, and Amber was asking Dustin to walk him back to the center to mount—without the benefit of holding on to the horse's reins. It was slow going.

Evan cleared his throat and tipped his hat toward the pair. "Doing good, I see."

I forced a nervous smile. "Yes. Dustin loves that horse. I think everyone does."

Evan was quiet for a few seconds. Then: "He's a good 'un."

My hands were clenched in a knot. Did I dare say it? I swallowed. "Morgan said you raised him personally? That he used to be..."

"Emma's horse," Evan said quietly.

Oh, heavens. I shouldn't have said it. I sucked in a breath. "Oh, Evan, I'm sor—"

"You don't have to apologize," he interrupted, his eyes flashing to me, then just as quickly, darting away.

I chewed my lower lip as I watched Dustin putting his foot in the stirrup. "I just didn't mean to bring up... you know."

He squinted and let go a heavy sigh. "So what do we do instead? Pretend she didn't exist?"

I blinked at him, my lips tight. "No. I can't, anyway."

Evan grunted and swung his feet out in front of his chair. I thought for a second he was going to leave, but he didn't. "You'd be one of the only ones. Most folks'd rather I didn't mention her." He sniffed and screwed up his mouth, his gaze growing distant. "Or Anne."

"I suppose some might feel like that." I studied him for a moment. "But I don't think it's for their own comfort. I think they'd rather not remind *you*."

His jaw shifted, his gaze still on Dustin as he rode the first lap around the arena on Biz. "*Remind*." He huffed. "It's not the remindin' that hurts. It's the forgettin'."

I turned my eyes from him. He was like Dustin in that way, it seemed—happier when he wasn't the center of someone's focus. More relaxed when he could slip behind the scenes. "Or being forgotten," I murmured.

"Come again?"

"Nothing." I shook my head. "I just thought what you said was... Never mind, it's just personal stuff."

His blue eyes narrowed faintly as he held my gaze, then he looked down and slapped his thighs. "Well, I'd better get back. Gotta change the oil in the tractors before we start hayin' tomorrow. Good seeing you, Meg."

I watched him go. "You too, Evan."

Chapter Five

Evan

I WIPED THE SWEAT off my brow with the back of my hand and walked over to Marshall's truck to dribble some water from the cooler into a cup. They'd been out here since sunup, and it was nigh on lunchtime now. But by the end of the day, we'd have Marshall's junky trailer all ready for him and Kelli to move into.

The roar of the trencher and the distant hum of the generator filled the air. Luke and Dusty were on one end of a hundred-foot-long trench, working on getting it deep enough for the water pipes. Marshall manned a pick and worked the delicate end, cleaning away the dirt from the power and water lines we'd already brought out to the corner of Marshall's plot.

"Feels like we're diggin' our way to China," Luke grunted as he shut down the trencher. "Hey Evan, think we'll need a translator once we get there?"

I just shook my head and finished my water cup, then splashed a little more on my face. "Are we ready for the pipe and cable?"

"I think so." Dusty grabbed a shovel to clear out the loose dirt that fell from Luke's trencher. "Is this where you wanted it to stop, Marshall?"

Marshall's hat tipped up from the hole he'd been clearing, and he turned around. "Well, where'd my flag go? Did you bury it?"

Dusty pointed at Luke. "He tossed it when the trencher got close. But this is the spot it was marking."

"You're sure?" Marshall called.

"'Course he's sure," Luke shot back. "Think I can't aim or somethin'?" He wiped his face and spat the dust from his mouth, then sauntered over to join me at the water cooler. "Don't see why we couldn't have just tapped into the main tee for his connections. Not like we're puttin' heavy water lines in for that crummy RV. All he needs is a hose and an extension cord for now."

"Because he needs to install a main power and water line to the house pad, anyway," I said. "Why put outlets out there where the driveway's going to be?"

Luke grunted and leaned on the flatbed. "Kelli sure must like that ornery cuss to put up with livin' with him out here in a rat-infested—"

"There aren't any rats," Dusty interrupted as he walked up. "We already checked it over. No mold, either."

"Huh," Luke snorted as he tugged on his ear. "I'll believe that when I see it."

I set my empty cup down with the others. "Well, you'll be seeing it in a few minutes. I'm driving over to Kelli's place in town to pick it up as soon as I unload the cable. Oh, and Meryl sent some sandwiches out for you. Ready for a break?"

"Don't know about them, but I sure am." Marshall walked up, mopping his face with a bandanna and reaching for a water cup. "I'd kill for a cold root beer right now, too."

"I'll see if your wife thinks you've earned one." I walked over to my truck, parked next to Marshall's, and dropped the tailgate so I could pull out the roll of power cable I'd just picked up in town. Beside it was a box full of hardware—outlet boxes, clamps, that sort of stuff, and behind it, a beefy roll of flexible conduit. I started hauling the big stuff over to the trench and dropped the box on the flatbed of Marshall's truck.

"Anything else?" I asked as I went back to close my tail-gate.

"Mmrf," Marshall mumbled around a mouthful of sand-wich. He gulped and held up a finger while he swallowed. "Make sure my wife didn't pack that motorhome so full that the axle busts driving it over this field."

I opened my truck door and chuckled. "I think it takes more weight than some blankets and clothes to break an axle."

Marshall shrugged and bit off more of his sandwich. "Your neck, not mine."

I DROVE BY THE lower hay field on my way out to the main road. Wyatt had the swather fired up and was halfway around the perimeter already. I checked my watch. He'd probably be cutting 'til after dark. I could have had him start earlier, but the hay was sweeter if we cut it later in the day, with all that hot summer sun turning into energy. We'd reserve this hay for the horses, especially the broodmares and the growing stock.

Speaking of which—I hadn't ridden out that way for a couple of days. I'd have to saddle up and take a turn through the mare pasture tomorrow to check on the babies. But no time for that now. I picked up my phone to send Kelli a text that I was on my way.

-*You're too fast!* she texted back. -*I still have some boxes to stuff in there!*

I decided not to answer.

She was running from the front door with a stack of plastic totes in her arms when I pulled up to her house. I put my truck in park and just shook my head. Maybe Marshall was right to fret about her overpacking that thing. I hoped there was still a spot for the driver to sit.

"Just a couple more loads!" she called as she dashed back to the house.

I got out and followed her. Might as well carry some of her crap so we could get this show on the road. What was she still packing? Kitchen stuff? Food?

Kelli met me at the door, her arms loaded again with a cardboard box that looked fit to bust. The bottom was sinking, the sides were collapsing, and her arms hardly reached halfway around it. "My mom just sent over some of my things from before I left home. I forgot I even had this stuff!"

My brow furrowed as I took the box from her. "You know, you guys have a spot cleared in the shop to store that kind of stuff. We don't have to take it now."

"I know," she chirped. "But if I let Marshall put it in the shop, I'll never get to sort through it. What if there's something in there I need?"

"You just said you didn't even know... oh, never mind." I sighed and pushed the squishy box through the narrow door of the old RV. There wasn't much room to set it down. In fact... there wasn't a single square inch. I'd have to hold it on my lap as I drove. What in blazes was the woman thinking? Wasn't the plan for them to live in this thing, not use it as a mobile storage unit?

"Oh, let me help you," she said from behind me. "I was going to take those things out and put them... here... and here... Oh! I didn't know there was still room in this box." She started pulling stuff out of the box and cramming it wherever she could find a spare square inch. "There!" She stood back and framed her hands on her lower back to give it a stretch.

I frowned. "You sure you've got it all?"

She waved a hand. "You sound just like your brother. Why make two trips? Although I was hoping for a little more time to get that bookcase emptied before Meg takes it. I have some..."

My phone went off, and I slipped it out of my pocket while she was talking. With any luck, it would be Marshall, and I could pass the phone off so *he* could fight this one. But it wasn't Marshall's name on the screen... it was Morgan's.

I squinted. She'd never called me before. Dusty or Marshall, or even Dad, but never me. Why would she now? Unless...

"Hey, what's wrong?" Kelli interrupted herself and was watching me, her head tilted. "You look like someone just stole your truck."

If Morgan was calling *me*, now, the only reason that made sense was that she was in some kind of trouble. The kind of trouble she didn't want Kelli or the rest of the family to know about yet. I blinked, held up my hand, and shook my head. "Hold on. I gotta take this."

I bolted back to my truck and got inside so I could talk privately, then swiped to answer the call right before it would have gone to voicemail. "Morgan? Everything okay?"

There was a muffled sound, like she was trying not to gag, and then a groan and a sniff. "Uhm... so, about that thing, where I said I didn't need anything?" Another gagging sound. "I... uh... might've lied."

"What's wrong? Do you need a doctor?"

She covered the phone, and all I heard was whooshing and static for a few seconds, then she came back. "I don't think so. I can't keep..." There was a groan, followed by some sounds that she probably wished I hadn't heard, and more static.

"Morgan, are you there?"

Her voice was scratchy when she came back. "Yeah, I'm here. I've been throwing up all day, and I can't even get out of bed. I didn't think... oh, my stars. Nobody ever said it was like this."

"That doesn't sound normal. I'm on my way over, and I'm bringing Kelli. I'm at her house now."

"No, please don't tell Kelli! I don't want her to worry, and..." Her voice disappeared again, but this time, I think she hit the mute button on the phone.

"Fine, I won't bring Kelli," I sighed, wondering if she could even hear me. "But I'm on my way. You sound awful. Can I bring you something to help?"

Morgan's voice came back on the line. "I didn't call to ask your help for me. I'll be fine. It's the chores. I don't have any volunteers today, and Amber has the day off—her sister's birthday or something. I haven't been able to get out to feed. I'm worried horses are going to run out of water if I don't..." She grunted in pain and muted the phone again.

"Right," I said, not waiting for her to come back on. "I'll be up soon." And I hung up.

Kelli was tapping her foot with her arms crossed, sending mischievous glances between the house and the RV when I got back out. She turned around when I walked up and offered a cringing grin. "I know Marshall's all hot to get this thing to the property, but do you think he'd let me keep it for just a *couple* more hours? I *really* wanted to get some more things done before you hauled it off."

"He's going to *have* to wait," I answered. "Emergency call, I gotta go."

"Oh." Her lower lip stuck out, and her eyebrows pinched together. "Everything okay?"

I shrugged and turned toward my truck.

"Well, how long are you going to be gone?" she called to my back.

I shrugged again. "No idea."

I heard a loud sigh. "Because if you're going to be a *long* time, I'll see if Meg is free to come help me."

I'd reached my truck by now and gotten the door open, but I stopped and peered at her through the open window. "Meg Truman? Why?"

"Just to get her out of the house. She just lives on Second Street and doesn't get much company."

I grunted and got into my truck. "Can't say how long I'll be."

She frowned. "Well, tell Marshall it's not my fault. He'll say I overpacked and made you wait."

I just nodded and put the truck in reverse. If I hurried, maybe I could swing by and pick up some ginger ale. Didn't Cody say she liked that? And maybe... oh, heck, I wasn't a woman. I'd watched Anne carrying Emma, but she'd never been that sick. What could a guy even do to help?

Wait a minute.

If Meg Truman was close, maybe I could swing by her place. She'd know what to do. Morgan trusted her, and Cody hadn't specifically forbidden me to say anything to someone *outside* the family, had he? I wondered if I could spot her house. Second Street was right around the corner, and I knew what her car looked like. It was worth a shot, anyway.

Meg

I LOWERED THE PHONE at the sound of a heavy diesel engine pulling into my driveway. "Hang on," I said to the lady scheduling Dustin's speech therapy appointment. "I have a delivery driver or something. Let me see if they need me to sign for anything."

"Take your time," she replied cheerfully. "I'll just pull up the schedule while I wait."

"Thanks." I held the phone away from my face as I peeked through the window. It wasn't a brown delivery truck or even a white van like I usually got, but a silver pickup. And my stomach crashed into my shoes when I saw that straw cowboy hat and those broad shoulders ducking out of the door. I blinked and rubbed my eyes to see if they were working properly. *Evan Walker?* I had to be imagining things.

But when his hat brim lifted, those clear blue Walker eyes snatched a glance at me through the window, and I almost dropped my phone. His lips thinned to a tight smile, and he made his way to my porch.

My hand was shaking when I put the phone back to my cheek. "Excuse me, but I think I have to go. I'll call and schedule later."

"Sure thing, Mrs. Truman," the receptionist answered. "Just remember we close at 4:30 instead of five now."

"Right." I nodded blankly, entirely missing her last sentence as I hung up the phone. *Mrs. Truman*... that was who I was, and I'd do well not to forget it.

I had the door open before Evan could knock, but his hand was in the air already. "Evan?" I backed away from the door, inviting him in. "Something I can do for you?"

He pulled his hat off and held it in front of his chest like a shield or something. He cleared his throat. "Sorry to bother you. Wasn't sure if this was the right place."

My eyebrows raised. "For the last ten years. And it's no bother—I don't go in to work for a few hours yet."

"Oh." He nodded and looked down at his boots as if making sure they didn't stray over the threshold to the house. "I'm... uh..." He sucked in a breath and blew it out. "Well, might as well tell you, but I'd rather you didn't say anything yet. I wasn't supposed to tell. Morgan's expecting."

"Ah." So, *that* was what this was about. "I kind of already knew that, but it's nice to hear. I'm happy for her."

"Uh-huh." He tugged on his ear—something I'd seen a couple of his brothers do when they were trying to think of what to say, but I'd never seen Evan uncertain enough to display that mannerism. "Yeah, so... you know Cody's still out of town, right?" His eyes flashed up to mine for a second, waiting for me to confirm it with a nod. "Anyway, she's sick. Called me asking for help with the horses, but I was just over at Kelli's, and she didn't want me to tell her anything yet, and I was wondering..."

"You want me to come with you and look in on Morgan while you take care of her animals?"

His hand twitched on his hat. "Something like that."

I pushed the door open a little more. "I'm free, but I need to check on Dustin to make sure he's okay alone for a couple of hours."

Evan shrugged, his eyes roving the interior of my house in a way that seemed like he was trying to look like he wasn't being nosy. "He can come, too. I got a crew cab. If... you know... you guys don't mind riding with me. Either way."

I blinked. Most people didn't invite Dustin to tag along. Especially if it was *my* help they wanted. They never said as much, but if I forced them to admit it, most folks figured he kind of got in the way. "Dustin doesn't always appreciate sudden invitations," I ventured cautiously.

"Well, if it doesn't work, I understand. Sorry I can't wait around long, though. I need to get up there, but I just thought—"

I put up a finger. "Hold on. If we're going up to White Pines, he'll probably agree. Can you wait just a minute?"

His mouth pushed into an agreeable frown as he nodded. "Sure. Would it be better if I waited in the truck?"

I stopped and studied him. He almost sounded like he understood... some of it. "I don't think so. He knows your face. I'll be right back."

I STILL COULDN'T BELIEVE how easy it had been to pull Dustin away from his carving. No warning at all, completely deviating from our usual schedule, and he even agreed we could ride in Evan's truck with him! I hoped he didn't change his mind later when it was time to go home. For now, though, he just acted like this was part of his normal routine, climbing in the back seat of some cowboy's truck without a firm plan of what we were doing or how long we'd be there. I prayed silently for it to last.

Evan wasn't saying much—not that he ever did, but his cheeks were red, and he was avoiding looking at me as he drove. Once in a while, his eyes would shift to the rearview mirror to look at Dustin, who had his head out the back window reveling in the feeling of wind on his face. Then he would act like he thought about glancing my way, but stopped himself.

There had to be some way to break the uncomfortable silence. I sniffed and looked out the passenger side window, but that didn't do anything to make it seem less awkward. I might as well try to talk.

"So..." I bent to rummage through a paper bag that held a few things I'd grabbed from home. "I don't know what Morgan has, or what she's tried, but I brought some frozen electrolyte pops, a blister pack of dissolvable ginger tabs, some crackers, tea, and a watermelon I just picked up from the store yesterday. Think we need anything else?"

His shoulders lifted, and he dropped a look at my bag of goodies. "Search me. That's why I asked for your help. I don't have a clue what to do for her."

"I'm sure just knowing she could call you when she needed help is huge."

This time, he did look me in the eye. His expression was unreadable, but he held my gaze for several seconds. "Guess so," he said as he turned his eyes back to the road. But his voice was curiously hoarse. "You'll help her more than I can."

"I don't know about that, but I'll do what I can."

I saw Evan's throat bob as he swallowed, then his fingers flexing a little on the wheel. He was relaxing a little. "Wondering if I should call Cody."

"Did Morgan ask you to?"

He shook his head.

"Then let's just wait and see how she is when we get there. She might just need a little rest and she won't want to worry him. This *is* why he asked you to check on her, isn't it?"

He glanced sharply at me. "How'd you figure?"

I chuckled. "It wasn't hard. You coming up to the ranch twice in a week and looking at her like she was ready to break? And when I took a closer look at her, it sort of came together."

He swallowed and nodded again. "Guess I'm kinda obvious."

"You're just lucky Kelli wasn't there instead of me. She'd have been onto you in a hot second."

Evan's face split into a grin, and I think I even heard a faint chuckle in his throat. "Probably. Lucky it was you." Then, the flesh around his eyes cracked, and he started blinking as if he wasn't sure how those words had come out. He cleared his throat and fell silent.

"I'm going to clean Biz's stall," Dustin announced from the back seat. "You can do the rest," he said to Evan.

Evan's eyes flipped to the mirror again. "That so, son?"

Dustin shrugged as if it were the most obvious thing in the world. "I'll brush him, too, while I'm w-waiting for you and Mom."

Evan shook his head as a smile found his face again, and turned his attention back to the road. "We'll see about that. You sure like that horse, don't you?"

"He's pretty much my horse," Dustin declared matter-of-factly.

Evan was fighting a real grin now, and he sent me a quick glance. "I see. You know, I have a nephew of his up to the ranch. You might like him. Just a baby, but he's gonna be friendly and kinda quirky like Biz. I'll have to show him to you someday."

Dustin frowned, mulling it over. "You can. But I'll still like Biz better."

Evan laughed as he put on his turn signal to pull up the White Pines driveway. "That's fine, then. Suppose I can't fault your taste."

Chapter Six

Evan

D USTIN'S FINGERS LINGERED ON the wood grain of Biz's stall, his eyes fixed on the big buckskin as he filled the water bucket. Biz was happily lipping at a rattle toy hanging from the rafters, and Dustin's head bobbed in sync as the horse played. I swiped at my forehead and stopped shoveling to catch my breath. The fans and water misters in the barn helped—it was cooler in here than out in the blistering sun, but the horses were damp with perspiration, and so was I. Dustin, however, hardly seemed to notice. I rested against my rake, feeling the slow drip of sweat trickling down my spine, and watched him.

"It's a hot one," I mused, partly to acknowledge the suffo-cating atmosphere, partly to just hear a voice in the dense silence.

He gave a small nod, his gaze not leaving the wooden door. "Biz gets thirsty."

"That he does." I looked over the wall to see how he was doing. "But he's not the only one. On to the next stall with that hose when it's topped off, okay? I'll finish up with the bedding."

Dustin watched the water rise, a wrinkle appearing be-tween his eyes. "They... they need water too?"

"With this heat, every last one of them. You got this? It's important."

He didn't look at me, but he nodded. I watched for another minute to make sure he was paying attention, but he let the water swell exactly to the edge, then shut the nozzle off and carefully withdrew it, not even letting a drop of water splash over the edge into the stall. Well, he looked like he knew what he was doing. I shrugged and carted a load of fresh shavings into the stall I'd just cleaned.

How had Morgan intended to do this all by herself today? Ten stalls indoors to clean, plus fifteen or sixteen outdoor paddocks, horses to rotate, troughs to clean out and fill, and probably a dozen other projects she'd try to tackle on her own. Why wouldn't she have asked someone to help sooner? I guess that was what Cody meant when he asked me to look in on her. She'd be on her deathbed before admitting she needed a hand.

I spread bedding in the rest of the stalls and put the wheelbarrow and fork up. When I turned around, Dustin was coiling the hose into meticulous loops. "You got them all watered?" I asked.

He wiped his hands on his pants. "Yes."

It wasn't that I didn't believe him. It just seemed really fast, and there were no drips in the aisle from a dragging hose, and... well, you just didn't take chances with dehydration on a hot day. "I'll, uh, just check to see if everyone is drinking."

We went from stall to stall, and sure enough, he'd done the job perfectly. I frowned, impressed. "Right. Nice work. Time to go take care of that bunch down in the other pens."

Dustin's face darkened, and his eyes dropped to the ground. He didn't say anything, but he didn't have to. He was digging his heels in. Guess he'd been serious when he said he'd groom Biz and let me do all the rest.

Well, why would that matter? I didn't bring Meg and Dustin up here to get help with the chores. He could hang out here, didn't bother me at all. I headed for the door. Then, I stopped. Morgan said it wasn't necessary, but I *could* put a few of the therapy geldings out for a while. I should have done it earlier, honestly.

I'd already done a once-over down at the pens that held the rescue horses. They all had hay and water, so it was just an hour or so of clean-up. Nothing too emergent. I glanced at the whiteboard where Morgan had laid out all the details of each horse's care, so literally anyone could walk into the barn and know what needed to be done at any given moment.

"Hey," I said, gesturing to the wall. "Looks like some horses need pasture turnout today. Wanna help me move them?"

Dustin stared at my belt buckle, and his jaw worked. "Biz has a r-run off his stall. He doesn't..." He gulped and stopped, so I just waited for him. "...n-need to go out in the big field."

"Not today," I said, nodding to the schedule again. "But another group should be out by now. They like getting that break. Makes 'em feel good to roll in the grass."

He didn't say anything.

I cocked my stance so I wasn't facing him quite so squarely and turned to tip my hat toward one of the other stall. "You know Badger there, don't you?"

"I like Biz better."

I shrugged. "Doesn't really matter what *we* like all the time. I'll just bet you that Badger likes his time out in the field as much as Biz does. And it's his turn today."

Dustin just blinked at my belt buckle. I shrugged and grabbed a couple of halters. Looked like I'd be doing it myself. However, by the time I got back from walking Badger and his buddy Duke out to the field, Dustin was slipping a halter on the face of a big Paint whose stall plate said "Mick." I glanced at the board—that left just Trigger and Ben.

"They shouldn't stay out very long," Dustin said as we slipped the halter off the last horse and closed the gate.

"Why not?" I asked as I hung the halters on the post.

"It's too hot. They'll get sick."

I grinned as I looked away, but addressed his concerns with due seriousness. "That's good thinking. But..." I squinted out at the horses rolling on the turf. "You know, it's cooler out there in the grass than it is here by the gravel. The sprinkler was on last night, so the grass is nice and lush, and it helps keep them cool, just like the fans in the barn."

He considered this, but didn't appear convinced.

"Anyway, we'll bring them back inside before we leave," I said. "Those chores down below will take another good hour, so they'll get some time to play and stretch their legs. I don't want Morgan to have to worry about things after we go home."

"So they just get a little extra care today?"

I was already walking down to the lower pens, my head low and hands swinging like I could reach for my next task before I even got to it. "How do you mean?

Dustin caught up, walking just behind my elbow. "The board says they have their own runs to play in. This was just... ex-extra for them?"

"Right. Exercise and a change of scenery while we finish up. Just a little extra, like you said. Everyone needs a bit of extra care on days like this."

He paused, and for a moment, I was afraid I had overstepped, but then he spoke, his voice soft but solid. "Mom says that. She says everyone needs help sometimes."

"She's right. And you've been a big help today."

Dustin's eyes shifted up to my face, but then he dropped his gaze just as quickly and lengthened his steps to surge ahead of me. Guess he was coming to help with the other pens.

Meg

I DIPPED THE CLOTH into the bowl of cool water, wrung it out, and gently laid it across Morgan's forehead. She was lying on the couch, pale as the pillowcase, a sheen of sweat still glistening on her upper lip.

"Here," I said softly, "try to take one of these." I offered her a ginger tablet, hoping it would ease the relentless waves of nausea that had hijacked her morning.

Morgan opened one eye, a shadow of her usual fire flickering within. "Thanks, Meg," she managed. She let the tablet dissolve on her tongue, grimacing slightly at the taste.

I sat down beside her, armed with an arsenal of remedies: Pedialyte popsicles that Dustin refused to eat last time he was sick, a freshly cut watermelon, crackers, and tea, all lined up like soldiers on the coffee table. Morgan had her ginger ale and lemon already within reach, but it remained untouched.

"Morgan, you're looking really faint. Have you thought about seeing a doctor?"

She shook her head weakly, a hand fluttering to her stomach. "No, no, I just need to get something down. If I can keep some crackers in, I'll start to turn a corner."

I thinned my lips and surveyed her. "How far along are you?"

"Barely. Like seven weeks. I just found out right before Cody left town, and it was only because I woke up heaving one day."

I crossed my arms and sat back. "You're about in the middle of it, then. Well... hopefully."

"Ugh." She cast her elbow over her face and tried to sigh, but caught herself because it made her gag slightly. "I just wanna die. Tell me it gets easier!"

"It should start tapering off in a couple of weeks, but... Morgan you don't look good. How long has it been like this?"

She waved a hand. "I know where you're going with this. I saw a doctor last week, and she says it's to be expected."

"But not being able to get out of bed? I'd call that the deep end of the morning sickness pool."

She massaged her neck and squinted her eyes against the sunlight filtering in through the windows. "Hangry-sick, morning sick—apparently it's my lot. I always feel queasy when my stomach is empty, and my blood sugar gets low, so it's like a vicious cycle. Did I ever tell you about throwing up in the driveway at Walker Ranch because I had a headache and no breakfast ... Well, it was a bad day all around."

"Never heard that story."

"I'll spare you, then." Her eyes squinted open, and she put on a brave smile. "Really, I'll be fine. Let this ginger settle for a minute, and I'll try some crackers."

"Alright," I agreed reluctantly. "But if you're not better by tomorrow, I'm taking you in. And I know better than to just check on you over the phone because you'll just swear everything's peachy."

"You know me too well." She grinned weakly, and I could see the effort it took for her to swallow the saliva building in her mouth to stave off another wave of sickness.

To distract her, I reached for a lighter topic. "So, when was the last time you talked to Cody? How's he doing at the horse show?"

"I talked to him last night. Maserati's doing great, but there's this sorrel colt, Rust, who's having a tough time. He's stupidly talented—Cody swears he can turn himself inside out, he's so agile—but he just can't settle down in the show atmosphere. Cody's got his hands full trying to keep the colt focused."

I couldn't help but chuckle. "Sounds like a horse version of Dustin." I blew out a sigh and couldn't help craning my neck to peer out the window—not that I could see anything from where we were. "I probably should have left him home," I mumbled. "I didn't mean to saddle Evan with my kid."

Morgan let out a careful laugh, which she stifled with a hand to her mouth, her body tensing to ward off the nausea. "Are you kidding? If anyone can just hang out with Dustin and not get his feathers ruffled, it's Evan. He's so level-headed and mild-mannered. And you know what they say about the silent ones—they listen and feel more than anyone else. Evan's fine."

My gaze drifted to the window, the sun blistering down on the barns outside. I could picture Dustin out there, quiet and focused, with Evan guiding him. Could it really be? *Nah*, that was too much to hope for. But maybe Evan wouldn't have steam coming out of his ears by the time we were ready to leave, like John used to. That was something worth hoping for.

"You're right," I said after a moment. If I tried to believe it, even for a few minutes, I'd be easier. Morgan didn't need my stress on top of her own. "Evan's... Evan's good with him."

Morgan squinted one eye at me. "Nice guy, too. The kind of guy you can count on when you really need him."

"He is," I mused, my eyes straining for the window again.

"Easy to look at as well. Tall, square jaw, and those *eyes* of his..."

I sent her a look that was swift and accusing. "I'm not getting mushy over Evan Walker, Morgan Haskins. He's about as unavailable as a guy can get, and I'm..." My brow wrinkled. What was I? My divorce was final a year and a half ago, but... well, Dustin still needed his dad, didn't he? I guessed I'd always hoped we could give it another try. But...

"Evan's as lonely as you are, Meg," Morgan said softly.

My gaze focused on her again. "You're serious." I laughed. "Me! And Evan Walker? No. No way."

"Why not?"

I stared at her. "Because Anne Walker, that's why. She was my friend, and she was beautiful and kind and so capable, and everyone adored her. She and Evan practically grew up together." I looked down and turned over the cloth I'd used on Morgan's forehead. It was all warm and useless now. "A man just doesn't forget his wife like that. The kind of marriage they had. Who could measure up to that standard?"

Morgan shrugged. "Have to be someone pretty amazing."

I scoffed and shook my head. "Nobody I know, that's for sure."

Morgan let her eyes drift closed, and she grunted softly, with a faint smile on her lips. "Maybe not. You're right, it's a crazy idea."

I raised an eyebrow. "You know, I may not have a counseling degree, but I recognize reverse psychology when I see it."

Her smile deepened, but she didn't open her eyes. "Can't blame me for trying. Hey, that ginger is helping. Think I should try a cracker yet?"

I blew air through my lips and opened the package to pass her one. "Should I fetch your bowl?"

She sat up a little and grinned. "Just to be safe."

Evan

DUSTIN AND I MADE our way to the lower pens, the quiet only broken by the sound of our boots crunching on the dry earth. I glanced at him once in a while but mostly left him alone. He wasn't hiding his face like he had at first. Not turning his shoulders away from me. He was just working.

"Your mom's going to be real pleased, knowing you're helping out so much," I ventured. "Makes her job a little easier."

He continued to work, nodding slightly, his expression unchanged. "She likes it when things are done right."

"She's not the only one," I added, glancing over at him. "Taking care of animals, it's important to see things done well. They depend on you. Seems like you've got a good handle on things around here."

"Morgan shows me, and Amber, too. When I come to ride Biz."

"They're good at that," I agreed, pausing to lean on my pitchfork for a moment. "Your dad must be proud too, hearing about all this, huh?"

He stopped then, the pitchfork in his hands coming to a rest. "I don't... don't talk to him. He's in Seattle."

"That's quite a ways off."

Dustin nodded, turning his fork over and raking the paddock sand with meticulous strokes. It was easy to spot the runs Dustin had cleaned because he finished them all with a perfect herringbone pattern. "Dad hasn't come back since he moved."

"Must be tough, not seeing him around," I probed gently, watching his face for any sign of discomfort.

He shrugged. "I don't like talking on the... the phone. We don't talk much."

The matter-of-fact way he said it made it clear this wasn't a door he liked to open. "I get that. Phones can be impersonal sometimes."

He glanced up, a flicker of something passing over his features. "Biz doesn't like l-loud noises. He gets scared."

I chuckled softly. That was a rather sudden change of topic. Where'd he get the idea that Biz got scared of loud noises? That horse showed in some of the noisiest coliseums in the western U.S. back in his competition days. But if it pleased Dustin to be considerate of the horse's sensibilities, who was I to discourage him? "Sounds like you and Biz have a lot in common. You both appreciate things being... peaceful."

"Yeah," he said, a hint of warmth finally creeping into his voice. "It's better when it's quiet."

"I can agree with that. That's why I like working on the ranch. I can just get out and think."

Dustin nodded and fell silent. And that was fine with me. Just getting a job done together, you don't always need words to make yourself understood.

By the time we finished with the pens, the sun was starting to slant in the sky. It was after three, and the day's heat was at its peak. And I needed to get Meg home in time to get ready for her shift at the restaurant. Dustin and I walked back to the field to fetch the horses we'd turned out.

"They seem happy out there," I said, leaning on the fence, watching the horses graze and saunter about.

Dustin stood beside me, his eyes following the animals with a sort of quiet contentment. "Yeah, happy."

The simple word hung between us, filled with unspoken understanding. We watched in silence for a few more moments before I dropped my arms from the fence rails. "Let's get them back in. Don't want them to overdo it on that rich grass. Morgan doesn't need one of these old fellas foundering on her."

He nodded, and together we moved toward the gate, ready to round up the horses. One by one, we caught the gentle old pensioners. This time, Dustin thought he'd be okay to lead two at a time while I took the remaining three.

As we finished up, I turned to Dustin. "You know, you're pretty good at this. Maybe you could consider helping out more often, and not just with Biz."

"I already come up twice a week. Mom says she can't m... make time... for more sessions. And my therapist says it won't... it won't do any good."

"I don't mean sessions. Just helpin'. Morgan always needs volunteers. Heck, I don't think there's a ranch in the whole world that couldn't use more help."

He considered my words as he turned away. After several steps, he gave a small, decisive nod. "Maybe."

I smiled, clapping him on the back as we headed out of the barn. "Well, that's something to think about on the drive home. Come on, let's go find your mom and tell her what a great job you did today."

Dustin walked beside me, his posture confident, a quiet pride in his step. Only after the fact did I realize the enormity of what had just happened. I'd patted Dustin on the back like he was one of my brothers, or... well, if I'd had a son, I might have given him a friendly jostle like that.

But I'd always heard Dustin didn't like to be touched. And he certainly didn't like to be taken by surprise. But this time, he didn't seem to mind.

Chapter Seven

Meg

I'VE ALWAYS LOVED RIDING in a pickup. I suppose it goes back to the summers I spent with my dad, after my parents got divorced. He made a living working on the ranches around here as a hired hand. He never had much money, but he always had a pickup—usually one on its last legs, with a smoking catalytic converter and bald tires. But the feeling of being rocked to sleep in that stiff old pickup frame had never really left me. Apparently, it worked its magic on Dustin, too, because his face was smashed against the window in the back seat, and he was probably drooling.

Hopefully, Evan Walker wasn't the kind of guy to get frustrated with fingerprints or face smudges on the glass. John used to hate it. It got to the point that he didn't even want Dustin riding in the back seat of his car because of how mine always looked—like Dustin had tried to flatten his sandwich under his pants and fingerpaint all over the glass in the steam from his breath. I swallowed and glanced at Evan.

His eyes were occasionally shifting to the mirror to look at my son, then transitioning easily back to the road. He didn't *look* annoyed... but with Evan Walker, it was hard to say *what* he was feeling, if anything at all. How did you talk to a guy like that? I couldn't tell if he was really as contented as he seemed, or if he had compressed all his emotions into that tiny flicker around the corners of his mouth.

He caught me looking at him once, and that mouth turned up a little more. "Glad you could come out today. Sounds like Morgan was in pretty rough shape."

I blinked and turned my gaze back to the landscape rolling past my window in a tranquil blur. "Worse than she wanted to let on. She was keeping the crackers down when we left, but I'm going to call her later just to make sure." I fumbled with my phone in my lap—just nervous energy, and tried to decide if I should say it... well, why not? I pressed my lips into a smile and looked at him again. "I'm glad you thought to ask me."

He turned his head my way, gave me a real smile—one of the biggest ones I'd ever seen on his face, frankly—then pulled his attention back to the road. "Lucky it worked out."

"So, why *did* you ask me?"

There was a tick in his cheek, and he kept his eyes forward, but his reply was casual. "Cody and Morgan didn't want the family knowin' yet. Figured it'd make a fuss before they were ready." He shrugged. "You were close to hand."

"Convenience?"

He squinted and adjusted his sun visor as the road took a turn. "I wouldn't've asked if I didn't figure Morgan would appreciate it. She knows you. She'd listen to you."

"And I can keep a secret?"

A smile shadowed his cheeks again. "Guess so. That's exactly how I got wrapped up in it, you could say."

I watched him for a second... and had to tear my gaze away because now that Morgan had put me on to admiring Evan's profile, I just wanted to keep staring. I'd never *let* myself look at him like that before, and... well, it was... it was hard to think straight, that was what it was. And a little hard to breathe properly.

I should try to say something. The silence hadn't seemed awkward before, but now it was almost excruciating because my brain was playing with stupid, dangerous ideas. I needed the distraction of conversation.

I swallowed and rolled my eyes up to the roof of the pickup, biting my lip. *Just get home.* I could fix my head once I got out of this truck and once I wasn't sitting beside that cowboy.

"How long have you been working at Beaufort's?" he asked out of the blue.

Oh, thank heavens. Words—easy words. I cleared my throat. "Since last winter. I needed a little extra income—teacher's salary, you know?"

He nodded. "What does Dustin do while you're out?"

"That's the problem. It's too long of a shift for me to be comfortable leaving him alone yet, so I started paying Kate or Missy to come sleep on the couch. Dustin knows them from White Pines, and they understand him. But they're still students, so they can't be out every night. I only work weekends, usually. And holidays. I worked Valentine's Day."

A funny smile cracked his face. "Heard about that one. That was when Conrad proposed to Jess, wasn't it?"

I groaned. "Oh, I'm terribly glad she didn't marry him! She's so much happier with Dusty. You can just see it in her eyes."

He smiled and let his eyes touch mine. "They're good together."

Uh-huh. Okay, *that* conversation wasn't helping my brain, after all. I shifted in my seat and stared at the front window, blinking fast and thinking even faster. "So, it sounds like you guys are pretty busy building houses this summer? Marshall and Kelli's house and Dusty and Jess's, and... are Luke and Audrey building, too?"

He shook his head. "They'll wait 'til next year. Luke wanted to help Dusty and Marshall first. Plus, Audrey wasn't sure if she oughta move Lizzy so soon. Kid's had a lot of upheaval this year."

"I imagine if anyone were to ask Lizzy about it, she'd say she wanted to be living out on the ranch already."

Evan's smile widened. "Probably. Secretly, I think Luke just doesn't think he can keep up with her yet. This way, she still depends on him to drive her out there instead of being able to sneak off on her own whenever she wants."

I laughed and took hold of the hand grip by the window. "I bet that's it, exactly! I can almost picture her galloping over the hills before Luke's even out of bed for the day."

Evan's head had whipped around, and he was giving me a funny look—somewhere between scandalized and sentimental. There was a swift sheen over his eyes, and his throat was working as his breath caught. Then, his jaw clenched, and something... I don't know, something broke behind his eyes, but he didn't look away.

I blinked, my hand easing down from the hand grip. Why would he be looking at me like that? Had I done something wrong? I swallowed and stared through the windshield again.

He was quiet for a few seconds. Felt like several minutes, but it couldn't have been because we didn't drive that far. At last, he mumbled something about Lizzy keeping Luke on his toes, and I wasn't sure if I dared reply.

Had I offended him somehow? I'd spent years learning subtleties in my son's expressions—discovering what he was feeling even before he knew himself—and there was something in Evan's look just a moment ago that made me think even he wasn't sure what to make of his own thoughts.

Thank heaven we turned onto our street right after that. It wasn't so much that Evan made me uncomfortable... not that at all, actually... it was more like he made me want to reach for his hand and just hold it. No words, no explanations or questions—just a quiet reassurance that I saw whatever was battling inside him, and I respected the complexities of all the emotions he must keep bottled up.

And that was insane because what did I know? Wishful thinking—I seemed to be good at *that*. But I wouldn't trust me to know anything else.

He pulled into my driveway and dipped his head in a crisp nod. "Thanks for comin' out today."

"I told her I'd come tomorrow, but I have a tutoring appointment at nine. I can go later, though."

Evan shrugged. "Or I can let you know how she is. I'm going up early. Tutoring, huh? That's a good summer gig."

"It could be if I did more of it, but..." I gestured to the back seat, and Evan nodded in quick understanding. "It's just one student. A boy who was in my class last year and had some trouble reading, so his mom asked me to work with him once a week through the summer to help him be ready for third grade."

He nodded. "'Just one kid,' you say, but something like that might make a world of difference for that kid's whole life. Don't undersell it."

"Right." I smiled as I leaned over the back of my seat. "Dustin?" I murmured. "Time to go. Wake up, please."

Dustin stirred, swatting my hand away at first until the drowsiness faded enough for him to realize where he was. He lurched, grabbed at his seatbelt buckle, and tumbled out of the truck. He slammed the door and ran into the house without even saying goodbye to Evan.

I sighed. "He means 'thank you for the ride.' Just... doesn't always say it."

Evan was smothering a chuckle. "I got it."

"Right. Look, I really do appreciate being asked."

He squinted, a question in his eyes.

I shrugged. "Morgan's done so much for me. It was nice to be able to do something for her, for a change."

He nodded. "Know what you mean. Hopefully, she'll start feeling better soon."

"Hopefully." My hand found the latch, and I eased the door open. "Bye."

I was halfway to the house, and Evan had already backed onto the street when I heard his voice again. "I'm gonna head up there first thing tomorrow to feed stock. Figured I'd get up there before she had a chance to run me off. Think Dustin would want to come help?"

My mouth wasn't working. Was he really asking for Dustin's help? *My* Dustin? I just gaped at him for a few seconds, then shook myself. "Uh, sure! I mean, I'll ask him. He'll probably want to go. But sometimes he changes his mind."

Evan lifted a shoulder. "I'll swing by on my way up tomorrow. He can decide then. See you."

I lifted a hand, but his window was already rolling up as the truck shifted into forward gear. "See you," I murmured to the tailgate.

I was a little numb when I opened my front door. I couldn't make sense of half the things that had happened in the last ten minutes—Evan's smile when I actually got him talking, his ease with Dustin, the strange way he'd looked at me... and the realization that my house wasn't even close to the route he would normally take from Walker Ranch to White Pines.

He'd really come this far out of his way just to invite my son to help with chores? Dustin wasn't *that* much help. He probably slowed Evan down. And there was no guarantee that Dustin would even agree to go tomorrow morning! But Evan hadn't seemed to mind.

I leaned against my front door, closing it with my body weight as the familiar shapes of my house registered again in my brain. But even then, forcing myself back into what I knew and making myself face my realities—what was *true* about my life—didn't help. I couldn't stop thinking about my afternoon with that cowboy, who seemed, somehow, to get it.

"You're being stupid, Meg," I hissed to myself. "Evan Walker... It doesn't even make sense!" I brushed the hair out of my face and went to my room to get ready for work.

Evan

"'B OUT TIME YOU GUYS got here!" Marshall met me at the window of the RV as I rolled it to a stop near his building site. "Thought you took my rig out for a joy ride."

I put it in park. "Not this thing. You oughta see the stuff your wife crammed in here—not a square inch anywhere to even stand up. Looks like you're sleeping out under the stars tonight, brother."

He growled. "I told you not to let her do that!"

"It was too late by the time I got there." I gestured to a new gravel parking pad that someone had put down while I was gone. "I assume that's where you want it?"

Marshall nodded and stepped out of my way. "Hookups are all ready. Now all I need to do is build a barn for all our junk so we have a place to sit down."

"Better plan for a big one." I rolled the window up and drove the RV toward the pad. He hadn't told me which way he wanted it facing, but if I put the nose to the north, they could have a gorgeous view of the sunrise over the mountains from the biggest windows. And since he didn't say anything different when I started driving up on the gravel spot, that's what he was going to get.

By the time I had struggled my way to the door to get out, Kelli was bumping along over the fields in my truck—gunning the engine and slipping the tires, of course. She slid it to a stop on the grass beside Marshall's truck and hopped out to duck under my brother's arm. "Wow, honey! It looks amazing there!"

She had a peculiar idea of "amazing," but that was none of my business. I set my hat back on my head and went to stand beside Dusty and Luke. "Anything left to do?"

Luke had a stem of grass in his mouth, and he shook his head. "Was just about to head out. Finish chores and go home for the evening."

"Oh, hold on, Luke," Marshall said, turning Kelli with him as they both walked toward us. "We wanted to thank you guys for the help, and... well, it doesn't look like we have anywhere to make dinner... yet." He sent a wry look down at his wife, but Kelli just grinned. "Anyway, want to go out? Our treat."

Dusty and Luke glanced at each other. "I was thinking of taking Jess out," Dusty said.

"Same." Luke tugged a fresh orchard stem from the tall grass growing beside his boots and bit into the sweet end. "Lizzy got invited to stay at a friend's house, so..."

Marshall put both hands up. "Well, I don't mean to ruin your special evenings, but there are precisely three restaurants open in town, and only one is really suitable for a 'romantic' date night. So, unless you all want to get separate tables and pretend you don't know each other, you might as well come with us. I'm buying." He pointed at me. "You too, Evan."

"I didn't hardly do anything," I protested. "They're the ones who put all the sweat in."

"We couldn't have done it if you hadn't picked up all the supplies, kept things on the ranch running, and brought the RV out," Marshall pointed out.

"Yeah, because I won't drive that thing," Kelli added. "I like living. Hey, what was that emergency you had to take care of? Everything okay?"

I stuffed my hand in my back pocket. "Fine. Look, you guys go ahead. I'll just go up to the house and find something."

"I already invited Dad and Meryl. You might as well come, Evan."

I felt my shoulders sag. "Fine."

"WELCOME TO BEAUFORT'S, MAY I..." Meg Truman was rushing up from the seating area, grabbing a stack of menus to greet us at the door, but she stopped dead when she recognized Marshall and Kelli. Her menus drooped, and she grinned. "Well, fancy seeing you here!"

"Right?" Kelli bubbled. "Remember that thing about how I was losing a real kitchen? Now you see the method to my madness."

Meg laughed and let Kelli hug her—it was decidedly all Kelli's idea—and I watched her eyes widening as they traveled over our heads to count us. I was in the very back, and her gaze skipped over everyone else, two by two until they got to me. A faint lift of her brows, and she turned back to Marshall and Kelli.

"What's the occasion, everyone?" she asked with a smile as she led us toward a table.

"Saturday night," Marshall answered. "Do we need a better excuse to come eat steak?"

Meg's laugh floated to me as I trailed in the back. Everyone paired up as they clustered around the table Meg led us to—Dad and Meryl easing into the bench along the wall, with Dusty and Jess sliding in beside them. Marshall took the head of the table, since he figured he was our host this evening, and Kelli plopped into the seat at his elbow. Audrey sat beside her, then Luke.

That left two chairs and only one of me. I smiled tightly at Meg as she cleared away the extra set of silverware, and then I took the chair at the foot of the table, close to Meryl.

"Aw, man, we should've invited Morgan," Luke realized. "I bet she'd appreciate a chance to get out and eat someone else's cooking."

Meg was dropping water glasses, and I saw her hand freeze on the one she set before me. I glanced up and caught her eye, but only for a second before she moved on. And something there...

It was like that moment in my truck earlier, when she'd grabbed the hand grip by the window and laughed so easily... like she belonged there. Like there was history and comfort and connection that I'd never noticed before. It was there in her eyes again now, when she asked me that unspoken question about Morgan, where we both understood each other so clearly... and it made my heart stop for a second. Just like it had earlier today. *What was it?*

"I called her," Kelli piped up. "She said she's really busy. I tried getting her to come anyway because she's got to eat, too, right? But she said she couldn't, so..." Kelli sighed and pouted a little. "Next time, I guess."

Jess sipped some water and smiled. "Yeah, I texted her, too. She wouldn't budge."

"Me, too. I wish she could have made it, but at least she won't feel forgotten." Audrey folded her menu and put it down. "I know what I'm having."

Luke chuckled and squeezed her knee. "Cowboy Bill's smoked chili?"

She gave him a prim look. "How'd you guess?"

"Lucky." Luke tossed his menu on top of hers. "Guess I'll get the same, with a baked potato."

Meg had hardly finished putting water glasses in front of everyone, but she came back to stand beside me at the end of the table and whipped out a note pad. "Are you ready to order already?"

Everyone looked around the table and nodded at each other. It wasn't like the menu at Beaufort's was a mystery to any of us. It hadn't changed in twenty years. Meg didn't even bother taking notes—everyone got what they usually got, including me. Sirloin, medium-rare, every time. Easy, minimal seasoning, less expensive than Marshall's porterhouse, and simpler than Dad's massive chiliburger.

Meg left us to put our order in, but not before giving me one more questioning glance. I wasn't sure what it meant, but maybe it was her way of asking about Morgan, since she'd overheard all the girls saying they'd tried to invite her. I slipped my phone out of my pocket and sent Morgan a quick text to make sure she was still doing okay, then I turned my phone on silent so only I would know if she replied back.

A few minutes later, I did get a buzz in my pocket. Meg had brought us a round of chips and salsa—Cowboy Bill's Southwestern salsa was almost as famous as his chili—and as soon as she disappeared in the back again, I made an excuse of needing to use the restroom. I stopped in the hall outside to read Morgan's message.

-Thanks for asking, but I'm fine. And this time, I mean it! I'm eating the watermelon Meg left, and I even sucked down one of those Pedialyte popsicles. Starting to feel better. Cody will be home on Monday. He said

*he's scratching his Sunday classes, but he didn't say why.
I'd better not find out that you ratted on me and messed
up his show, Evan! (Just kidding. I really do appreciate
everything.) Enjoy dinner. If I had to smell a steak right
now, my stomach would act up again and they'd be kicking
me out of the restaurant.*

I chuckled a little at the text, and sensed someone approaching in the hall. I looked up and smiled at Meg carrying a tray of drinks, who arched her brows and grinned back. "Still keeping secrets from everyone, I see?"

I showed her Morgan's text, and her grin widened. "Kelli is going to barbecue her for not saying something sooner."

I shrugged as I put my phone away. "It's their business, I guess. Cody said they wanted to tell everyone together, make it a big surprise. Not my deal."

Meg's smile softened. "I wouldn't want the stress of making a big family announcement. When I found out I was pregnant with Dustin, I literally sent my dad and a couple of my teacher friends a text message."

I swallowed and chewed my lower lip. I wasn't even sure how Anne had broken the news to a lot of people. I was probably out working at the time. "Yeah," I mumbled. I swiped a hand over my jaw and looked down. "Never figured there was much need to make a fuss. But to each his own."

Meg was quiet, and I risked a glance up at her eyes. There was a line between them that wasn't there a minute ago, and she was tilting her head. "Evan, are you..." She looked over her shoulder at the crowded tables, where we could hear Luke and Marshall laughing about something over the rest of the din.

"What?"

"Are you okay?"

I shrugged. "Sure. Why wouldn't I be?"

Her lips pulled into a smile, and she shook her head. "Of course. Sorry." She lifted her shoulders and gestured to the tray she was carrying. "I'd better get these drinks taken out."

I stepped out of her way and watched her go.

And kicked myself for not saying... I don't know. Something. Not sure what I'd have said, but something.

Chapter Eight

Meg

I PULLED THE DRAPES aside as Evan's truck rolled up in front of my house the next morning. He'd really come, all the way out of his way, at six-thirty in the morning for my son. Dustin wasn't even out of bed yet, and I doubted he would be anytime soon. I opened the front door, wondering if Evan meant to just wait in the truck or...

No, he was getting out. And walking my direction, his hands tucking the back of his shirt deeper into his jeans and his hat shading his eyes so that he didn't see me until he was almost to the door.

I stepped out on the porch. "I don't think he's going to be interested, but I haven't asked yet today. I didn't think about it being so early."

"Wanted to get up there before it got hot."

"And before Morgan could get out there?"

He grinned. "You caught me."

"Dustin's not up yet, and you probably don't want to wait for him, so..."

Evan shrugged. "I don't need to rush, if you think it's worth asking."

"Whew." I blew air through my lips and shook my head. "I don't know. I can check, but my chances of success are higher if I wake him up slowly. Care for a cup of coffee while you wait?"

His eyes brightened at that. "I've already had some, but I'll always take a second cup."

"Yeah?" I nodded and invited him inside. "I got rid of my big coffee pot... well, actually, it broke. With a little help... ahem. But I have a little stovetop espresso maker. It's metal with no moving parts, which is exactly what I needed! But it makes just enough for one cup. I really like how the coffee tastes from it, but it takes a few minutes. I'll get it started and show you how to watch for when it's done while I check on..." I stopped myself, clenching a fist and closing my eyes. "I'm babbling, aren't I?"

Evan was hanging his hat on the back of a chair, and he just gave me a mild little smile. "I don't mind. Is that the pot? I can start it."

"You're sure?"

His chin puckered into an agreeable frown, and he nodded. "Go ahead. I'll be fine."

"Right." I clenched a fist again and tried to make myself breathe. I hadn't had a man in my house since John. Unless you counted the guy who came to fix the kitchen drain after Dustin decided to feed a bucketful of his wood shavings to the garbage disposal. But I hadn't left the plumber to find his way around my kitchen on his own. Make his own pot of coffee and settle in at the kitchen table like the kind of friend who could raid my fridge.

Just a bit... unnerving, really. And not in a bad way.

I knocked on Dustin's door, starting softly and gradually increasing the volume. He never actually woke up to that, but it gave him a little subconscious warning before I cracked the door open and pushed my head in. "Dustin," I whispered.

He looked dead to the world. His face was half hidden by the pillow, and his mouth was hanging open, with one arm wrapped over his head and the other hanging off the mattress. I came closer and touched his shoulder. "Dustin," I said gently. He stirred a little.

I didn't want to keep Evan waiting longer than necessary, but if I rushed, it would just kick the day off badly all around.

I turned the stick that adjusted the blind, letting in a little more of the morning sun, and he winced, shielding his eyes.

"Dustin, Evan Walker is here. He wants to know if you want to help him at White Pines this morning."

He rolled away from me, grabbing his pillow and piling it over his face.

I shrugged. "Okay, then. I'll tell him he can feed Biz by himself."

That did it. I saw the heavy flinch, and he went completely still. That meant he was alert and thinking, but wasn't ready to answer me yet.

"He'll be leaving as soon as he finishes his coffee," I said. "If you want to go with him, you can get in his truck while he's drinking."

Dustin didn't really respond, but I didn't expect him to. I left the door open and went back to the kitchen.

Evan was just pouring his coffee into a cup he must have found somewhere—because I'd forgotten to get one out for him—and he looked up as I came into the kitchen. "Any luck?"

"We'll see. Cream and sugar?"

"I'm not picky. If you have it handy, fine, but I'm good with black."

I reached into the fridge with a chuckle. "Are you always this agreeable?"

"No point in bein' otherwise. Saves a heap of trouble, not worrying over things that don't matter."

I passed him the jug of half and half, then found the sugar jar. "But some things do matter. Surely, there are some things you'd be particular about."

He finished dressing up his coffee and blew the steam off before taking a sip. Then, savoring it, his brow clouded in thought. "That's good coffee."

"It's just a generic brand."

His shoulders lifted as he took another sip. "Tastes good to me. Better than the stupid pods Dusty had us all drinking for a while when he was trying to get Dad down to one cup a day."

I put the half-and-half away and leaned on the fridge. "Ah, so you *do* have some opinions," I teased.

"Sure I do. I'm pretty particular when it comes to stuff like work. The ranch." He sipped again. "You don't take shortcuts."

"Because it's your livelihood. And you care about your animals."

He nodded as he stared down into his cup. "I'm picky about doing things right the first time. Being on time—I won't waste another man's time just because I can't manage my own." He frowned. "That's about it."

I crossed my arms. "You ordered your steak medium-rare last night. Usually, the guys who ask for that are pretty particular about it."

"Nah." He shook his head. "Just takes them less time to cook. Plus, I know they'll probably get it wrong when they're trying to time it to come out with everyone else's food when it's a big order. Saves me from getting something on my plate that could pass for a brick of charcoal."

I laughed. "That's quite the trick. I'll remember that next time."

Evan smiled and looked like he was going to say something, but Dustin's door banged from down the hall, and we both turned to watch. A second later, Dustin was running through the house, his shirt inside-out and only one shoe on.

"Slow down!" I called, but he didn't listen as he hopped through the living room, tugging another shoe on. I went over to him. Same shirt he'd worn for the last three days, and his hair was matted in about three places and sticking out in two others. "Do you want to eat?"

He brushed my arm away and finished putting his shoe on.

"Fine, but at least stop and comb your hair."

Dustin hid his face—he wasn't listening—and wormed away from me to run out the front door. I sighed and turned around to Evan.

He was rinsing his cup in the sink, but when he finished, he looked up with a funny little smile. "Don't worry 'bout his hair. Horses don't care. They figure anyone who feeds them is a-okay."

"Well... thank you. Thanks for offering to take him. It looks like he's looking forward to it."

Evan paused as he walked by me toward the door. "Sure thing. Thanks for the coffee."

"You'll let me know how Morgan is? I can go up and help her out around the house later today if she needs anything."

He stopped and gave me a wink that sent shivers right down into my socks. "Best plan on just going up there, if you have time. You know as well as I do that she won't admit how sick she is unless she's at death's door."

I chuckled. "Right. Tell her I'll be up at about eleven-thirty, then."

Evan dipped his head and gave me another one of those mouth-watering smiles as he reached for his hat off the hook. *Oh, dear...* that wasn't even *fair*. "Sounds good."

I followed him to the front door and watched as he got into the truck. It was then that the realization struck me—I'd never let my son go anywhere with someone else. For one thing, no one had ever invited him. But I'd also never quite been able to let go of my terror... the *"what if"* that every parent has to answer at some point or another. The question probably comes up later... or at least differently... when that parent has a special needs child, but it comes up all the same.

I thought it would be a lot more terrifying when that day finally arrived, but for some reason, I wasn't worried for my son. Evan would keep him safe. I was more worried about Evan's sanity.

Dustin was already in the back seat—he didn't like riding in the front—and I saw Evan turn around to say something to him. Then, he put the truck in reverse and lifted a hand to me as he pulled out.

And I just stood there, watching them go, with my heart beating outside my body.

Evan

C ODY ROLLED INTO THE driveway the next afternoon with the horse trailer. I was in the round pen when he pulled up, throwing a saddle over a young colt I was planning to take out to check the herds. The colt was a big, rangy type—just the kind I liked for spending all day in the saddle—but he still wasn't used to all the noise from the stable yard. He jumped and skittered a bit as the horse trailer swept right by the pen we were in.

"Whoa," I said quietly, giving a little pressure on his halter and just moving with him until he turned to face me. His eyes were bulging, and his muscles quivered, but he stood and let me approach again. "Good lad." I stepped close and rubbed his neck as I watched the truck park.

Cody's road crew, Emily and Cole, both piled out of the truck almost before it got stopped, stomping off in opposite directions. Emily was the first to the back door and the horses, and Cole, seeing that, did an about-face and went for the tack room. He started yanking out wheelbarrows and pitchforks like he was trying to throw them at someone while Emily was rocking the trailer with the way she slammed open the dividers.

Cody was shaking his head, and he wandered over to me, lifting his hat off his brow and closing his eyes like he was getting a migraine.

I tipped my chin toward the pair at the horse trailer. "What's all that about?"

His teeth clenched, and he dragged his hands down his face as his eyes rolled. "Great gobs of goose grease. Tell me we were never that young and stupid."

I tugged the cinch on the colt and tossed my stirrup fender down. "I wasn't. You were. What's going on? A little competition between those two?"

"Or something. You know, when I hired Cole on this spring, I thought he was about the easiest-going kid around. Got a bit of a jokester streak in him, but he's smart and got a good bead on things. He's the youngest Langton boy—you remember Gage and Chase and those guys from Skyview Ranch, right?"

I nodded. "Gage was in Dusty's class, right? Or was he a year older?"

Cody shrugged. "I don't know. Don't really care, actually. I was looking for someone good with the horses who might want to learn and was willing to do some heavy lifting, since Blake's staying home this season. Cole was perfect. Hard worker, handy with the colts, learning like gangbusters, and hungry. He's going to be good, and I'd like to see him stay with me for a few years and learn things right."

"Yeah, so?"

"And Emily's kicking tail in all the novice classes I enter her in. You should see her—I think she rides some of those colts better than I do. I'd be stupid to let her go."

"So, don't."

Cody growled and sent a dark look over his shoulder at the pair unloading the trailer. "Yeah, no problem. Just keep them both on. Sounds easy. Until they're at each other's throats. Constantly. I swear, I don't know if I'm running a training stable or a kindergarten."

I chuckled and unhooked my bridle from the saddle horn to slip it over the colt's head. "Sounds like a fun trip home."

"Oh, it wasn't just the trip home. Every chance they get, they're trying to one-up each other. It's enough to drive a man insane. That's why we came home a day early—I couldn't take it anymore." He settled his hat back where it belonged and heaved a sigh. "How are things here?"

I was tugging the reins from side to side on the colt, making sure he remembered what they meant before I climbed aboard and took him out to the fields. "Fine. You need to get home, though."

I heard the edge enter his voice. "Why, what's wrong? Morgan?"

"She was pretty sick the other day."

He hissed. "I made her promise to tell me if she wasn't feeling well, and what does she say? 'I'm fine, honey, just enjoy your show,'" he mimicked in a high-pitched voice.

I laughed as I put my foot in the stirrup. "For what it's worth, she did call. Not for herself, mind you, but for the horses."

"Tell me something that would shock me."

I gave the colt a little nudge and sent him moving into a circle, just testing... sometimes they still blew up in these early weeks of riding, no matter how well-prepared you thought they were. "I had to spill the beans a little. I was over at Marshall and Kelli's place when Morgan called, and she wouldn't let me bring Kelli up, so I drove over to Meg Truman's house to see if she was free. She helped Morgan out while I did the chores."

Cody rubbed the back of his neck. "Wow, she must have been really sick. Have you seen her today?"

"Yeah, I went up yesterday and today to do chores early before she could get out and run me off. She looked a little better when I saw her this morning, but she's probably jonesin' to have you back."

He nodded. "Right. I owe you one, Evan."

I shrugged, my eyes down on the colt's head. "Nothin' to it."

"No, really, it was a big relief to me to know she'd have some help. I really appreciate it." He glanced over at the trailer. The last of the horses were walking to the stable beside Emily, and Cole was on top of the trailer at the cargo rack, tossing down the remaining hay bales they'd taken to feed at the show. He sighed, shaking his head again.

"Sorry if I had to spoil your surprise a little by dragging Meg along," I said as the colt circled back toward him.

Cody turned around to face me. "I'm a lot more worried about my wife's wellbeing than ruining any surprises. Meg, huh? That was actually pretty brilliant."

"She was close. Said she was happy to do it."

Cody leaned through the bars, resting his arms on them and peering up at me. "I like her a lot. The first time I ever saw her, she'd had a horrible day. I'm not sure, but I think she'd been crying—so stressed out, you know? And then, like three seconds later, she was smiling and cheerful, and you'd never know she was even upset. She knew what she needed to be in the moment, and she made herself pull it together for her kid."

"You do what you have to," I reasoned.

Cody leaned a little farther through the rails. "It's just a rare person who can do it so well, for so long."

I glanced at him as a shiver ran down my spine. I wasn't ready for anyone to be speculating about stuff like that. "You tryin' to say something?"

He frowned and shook his head. "Nope. I'm trying to go home and see my wife. Thanks again, Evan."

"You got it."

Cody stopped off at the rig and gave Cole some instructions on how to put the truck and trailer away, and then he was gone only a minute later. I stepped the colt over to the round pen gate and opened the latch. Time to go check the herds.

As I passed by the runs off the main stable, I paused to study the old brown gelding in the farthest pen. Pistol, my old bulldogging horse. He'd been fresh of an NFR championship season when I bought him a little over ten years ago. That horse and I won a lot of buckles, and then when I retired from competing, he settled into ranch life along with me. He was my most reliable partner when I needed to doctor a wild mama cow or cover a lot of miles in a day.

And then, the navicular disease hit. I'd seen it coming for a while, but a couple of springs ago, he just got more and more tender-footed until I had to get Doc Burns involved. And no matter what we did, it just kept getting worse. I pulled the colt to a stop and sat there for a minute, watching Pistol.

He was standing rocked back, with his toes pushed out a little—trying to take weight off his front feet. When I whistled to him, his ears went up, but he refused to step up to the gate to lobby for head scratches like he used to.

Doc was right. It wouldn't be long now, and I'd have to make a tough decision. Better a week early than a day too late, they say... but I never was easy with just brushing it off like that. I knew he was just a horse, and horses don't think about the future like we do. They don't cling to hope quite the same. Not that they don't have feelings and can't look forward to stuff—they absolutely do—but it's not the same as the desperation of a person, willing to suffer for the pleasure of seeing another sunrise.

One of these days, Pistol would look at me and tell me he'd had enough. And I'd have to honor that. I sniffed a little and lifted my reins to turn the colt away. That day wasn't today, and I sure hoped it wouldn't be tomorrow.

Chapter Nine

Meg

"I HATE TO BE the bearer of bad news, but he's just not progressing, Mrs. Truman. I think it might be in Dustin's best interests to discontinue speech therapy."

My fingers tightened on the phone, and I fought against the tremble in my breath as I blinked up at the ceiling. "Well, what standard are you measuring him with? I know he still repeats things, and his diction isn't really improving at present, but he *has* improved his expression, and he's been learning to *try*. A little frustration is actually *good* for him, just like it's good for everyone else when they're learning and growing. If everything is comfortable and easy, we never get better at anything."

"What I'm concerned with, Mrs. Truman, is that we may be adding stress where it is not helpful. And, also..." She sighed. "I didn't want to tell you this, but Dustin tried to hit one of our therapists last week."

I swallowed. "What?"

"He wanted something she had on her desk—I think it was a framed picture of a dog or a horse or something, I don't know. I understand he just grabbed it and became agitated when she informed him that was not appropriate."

I pinched the bridge of my nose. "He wanted to sculpt an image of it. He carves... wood, you know? And right now, horses are his favorite things to carve."

"But his behavior was problematic, and the safety of our staff members is paramount, Mrs. Truman. We are not equipped to handle patients who become belligerent. I'm sorry, but—"

"What if we continued over a video call?" I suggested. "Because, truthfully, it's a long drive for us every week, anyway. Wouldn't that solve the problem?"

The office manager sighed heavily on the other end. "I'm sorry, Mrs. Truman, but we don't feel comfortable continuing at this time. Dustin has no confidence in his therapist, and the relationship has grown increasingly antagonistic. We would like to encourage you to take a break—at least for a while."

My hand was shaking on the phone, and my eyes were burning. "Of course," I said in my clearest, most civilized voice. "Perhaps that is for the best."

"Thank you for understanding, Mrs. Truman. I will cancel his upcoming appointments. Please feel free to reach out to us if things change. I'll keep his chart filed with our present clients."

"Yes, thank you. Goodbye." I hung up and dropped the phone on the table, then covered my mouth and tried to stifle a sob.

It wasn't about speech therapy. And I sure wasn't going to miss driving two hours each way every week to get him there, nor was I going to miss the fights we had about getting in the car to go, or getting out of the car for his appointment.

It was just... one more place that gave up on my son. Not that I blamed them. They weren't paid to wrestle or get punched by kids who got a bit... overzealous. That wasn't in their job description. But couldn't they have just given him one more chance?

Well... they probably already had. How many incidents hadn't they told me about? For the last year, Dustin had been more willing to attend his sessions if I sat in the waiting room or even out in the car, so I hadn't been with him every second. What else had he done when I was in the next room?

And if that *was* the problem, why wouldn't they have said something sooner?

The phone rang again, and I snatched it up, my finger hitting the answer button before I even really looked at the caller ID. I suppose I thought it was still the speech therapist's office, so it was with a wary tone that I said, "Hello?"

"Meg, it's Morgan."

Her voice was low, like something was troubling her or like she didn't want to be overheard, and a sense of foreboding filled my stomach. "Hi," I answered as lightly as I could. Either she was sick again, or she was also calling me to say that Dustin wasn't progressing... wasn't worth the time spent... *Please, not White Pines.* Dustin couldn't care less about missing speech therapy, but White Pines was where he'd come alive. I swallowed and waited for the worst.

"Can you hear me okay? Amber is working with a client, and I don't want to interrupt them, but I need to stay close to observe this one."

I closed my eyes. If she was calling during a session, it must be important. It was Tuesday, which meant we were scheduled to go up there today. Was she canceling? "Yes," I said, my teeth grinding, "I can hear you fine. How are you feeling?"

"Oh, good. Much better today, thank you. Hey, you don't work tonight, do you?"

My jaw slackened, and I started breathing again. That didn't *sound* ominous. "No. I picked up a shift tomorrow evening, but not tonight."

"Great! Cody and I were wondering if you'd like to come over for a barbecue this evening."

I froze. Pulled the phone away and stared at it for a second. "A... a barbecue?"

"It's just family. Nothing too special, but we wanted to invite you, too, because... well, you know everyone there, right? And I don't know what I'd have done without you last week. I really appreciated your help, and I'd love to have you there this evening."

"Uh... I don't... I don't have anyone to stay home with Dustin."

Morgan paused, then laughed. "Meg! You don't think I'd exclude Dustin, do you?"

I drew shaky breath and stared at the kitchen table. "Right. No, you wouldn't."

"By the tone of your voice, I'm guessing someone else just did that?"

"It's not really worth talking about."

"Uh-huh..." She didn't sound convinced. "About six, does that work?"

I was finally breathing normally, and my brain was actually turning over on the pleasure of being invited. "Sure! What can I bring? Salad, dessert?"

"Nothing, please. Really, it's not a big deal. We just wanted to get everyone together to tell them... well, you know," she whispered into the receiver. "I have to keep it down because I haven't even told Amber yet. Family gets to hear first."

I smiled. "Well, I feel honored. I'll be there."

"See you then!"

She hung up, and I dropped my hand to the table as I stared at the darkened screen of my phone. I couldn't think of anything that would have turned my frustration about Dustin's speech therapist around quite so quickly as a personal invitation to something fun.

I didn't really have many friends. I'd lived with my mom in Oregon during the school year, and then I came back here after high school to be with my dad. That was when I met John, and we'd had our handful of "couple's friends." Then Dustin sort of changed my life, Dad passed away, John left, and there wasn't much to build from after that. I couldn't even remember the last time someone invited us to a family barbecue. And I wished Morgan would have said I could bring something, just to help out a little.

Evan ought to be there tonight. I bit into my lower lip and put my phone down. It was getting harder and harder not to think about that cowboy, whenever my thoughts wandered in search of something... I don't know... *better*. He'd made me smile so often in the last week, and I didn't think he'd even meant to, or realized he was the reason my day got a little brighter. It was just who he was, and I was starting to crave more.

That would only end in heartache for one or both of us. The dumbest thing in the world, really—setting your heart on a man who no longer had anything to give in return. If I was smart, I'd give Evan Walker a wide berth.

But I've made plenty of dumber mistakes than to lose my heart to a sweet cowboy.

Evan

I LOWERED MY HAND and let the colt I was on rest for a minute. He'd been a little jumpy yesterday when I first got on him, but today, he'd settled right into his work. I always made a point of trying out the new ranch colts sometime in that first month we had them on the job—mostly so I could keep my finger on the pulse of our breeding program and know just what sorts of colts we were turning out. But also, I wanted to make sure my guys had good, solid horses to do their jobs on. This one was just fine.

Better than fine, actually. I'd decided to add him to my personal string and bring him along myself, and that meant I needed to come up with a name for him. But the only name that stuck in my head was Pistol, and I couldn't use the old man's name over again like that. I'd have to put a few more rides on him and see what fit. I settled in on the little rise to look at the broodmare band—heads down in the shade, tails swishing against the afternoon flies, with most of their foals curled up at their feet.

But of course, there was always one that had to be up playing. I smiled at that little palomino colt as he braced his forelegs and watched my horse and me with a wide-eyed sneeze. That one, I'd picked a name for. I don't know why—chances were, he'd go to the show barn, and I'd probably never even throw a leg over him. He'd be the next Five Iron or Maserati, hitting the circuit and making a name for the ranch.

But the name just seemed to fit, and I couldn't look at him without saying it. I'd call him Forge. Reminiscent of his daddy's name, with all the "Iron" references in his sire's name tree, and it touched on that flaming gold color of his. But more than that, it rang to me of the crucible one must walk through to come out on the other side—reborn and ready to be reshaped by the Master's hands.

I looked down at my own hands, the way they curled lightly around the reins. That was the only way to hold things, they said—with a light grip, ready to let them go when the call came. But how do you let go of something that's part of you? How do you open your palm when the thing being ripped away is your very soul?

I sniffed and blinked up at that yellow colt again. I'd heard it often enough—the pain would just keep eating me unless I found some way to make my peace with it. And until I found something else to hold on to. That was what everyone said, but I couldn't see how it would solve anything.

My phone buzzed in my pocket, and at first, I ignored it. But then it buzzed again, and again, and again. I rolled my eyes and sighed. Someone had added me to a stinking group text. I pulled it out just as another reply landed and thumbed open the message thread to see what it was.

And then, I did smile a little. It was a group text from Cody, letting us all know that they were having a barbecue this evening. "*No special occasion*," he'd replied when Dusty asked what the reason was. "*I figured Marshall and Kelli didn't have a kitchen yet.*"

Nice. They didn't waste much time getting that planned, which was good. I didn't like being the only one in the know.

I chuckled and tapped out a quick answer that I'd be there. But there are few things I hate more than being spammed by a thousand replies and emojis from a chat with twenty people on it, so I turned off notifications to the thread and put my phone away. If I was going to be at their place by six, I'd better get out to the hay fields and then into the shower.

"**W**ANNA RIDE, EVAN?" MARSHALL stopped in the driveway and rolled the window down as I was hopping in the side-by-side to head up to the house.

I shook my head. "Couple more things to finish, then I'll go clean up." I held my arms out—my shirt clinging to me with sweat, my hands grimy from the steer I'd just doctored on my way up from the fields. "Can't show up lookin' like this."

"It ain't your looks that'll get you booted from the dinner table," Marshall said, waving his hand in front of his face. "It's how you smell. Don't be long, now."

I snorted and walked off as he rolled up his window and turned down the driveway. I was almost to the house when my phone rang. It was Brandon, and he was out with Wyatt this afternoon, doing ear tags and vaccinations on some of the young stock today. I blew out a sigh and answered.

"Yeah?"

"Evan, we've got a problem. Can you come down to the sorting pens?"

I did an about-face. "On my way. What is it?"

Brandon hesitated for a second. "Got a calf that's drooling all over himself. Depressed, not a good doer."

I narrowed my eyes and kicked into a run toward the side-by-side. "Any fever or lesions in his mouth?"

"Checking his temp now, but he don't look good, Evan."

"On my way, and I'm calling Doc Burns." I hung up and called the vet as I jumped into the side-by-side. Cody and Morgan's barbecue would have to wait.

Meg

"HEY, DUSTIN, WANNA RACE to the tree?"

I stood back and watched as Lizzy, Audrey's niece, tossed her soda cup aside and bounded up to Dustin as soon as we got out of the car. He shrank, and his eyes scanned the ground. "No. Racing is... is stupid. I know you'll beat me."

She scoffed. "I will if you don't run. Come on!"

He flinched and recoiled when she made a grab for his hand. "Stop! I don't want to."

Lizzy rolled her eyes and heaved a melodramatic sigh. "Whatever. I'll just go run by myself." And she did, kicking up a cloud of dust as she went.

I bent low to murmur in my son's ear. "Why don't you find a nice place to watch for now? There will be food soon, so come up when you're ready."

He blinked—didn't nod or say anything—and I left him to think over where he wanted to be while I glanced at the faces gathered in the yard. Well... it was sort of a yard. They hadn't gotten around to seeding an actual lawn yet, but there was a swath of thin, spiny meadow grass cleared near the house, with a couple of newly-built picnic tables and some lawn chairs scattered around. Cody was at the grill with a pair of tongs while Marshall stood at his side and poked whatever he was cooking. They were bickering like a couple of kids about how to cook the meat. Dusty and Luke were on the tables, sharing drinks and laughs with Jess and Audrey, and Blake was stretched out in a reclining lawn chair under a tree, his hat covering his face.

I didn't see Kelli or Meryl, and I didn't see... well, I didn't want to be caught looking around for Evan, so I went inside to search for Morgan. I found her in the kitchen, rinsing a salad. "Anything I can do?" I asked when she looked up.

Morgan beamed. "Sit down under the shade trees and put your feet up for once. We're almost ready to eat."

I slid my purse off my shoulder. "You're sure?"

"Yep. This is the very last of it." Morgan turned the water off and shook the salad bowl to make it drain faster. "Did you get yourself anything to drink yet?"

I shook my head. "No."

Morgan poured the fresh salad into another bowl, gave it another toss, and then threw a paper towel over it to carry it out to the picnic table. "Well, come on! We're just waiting on Evan, I think."

I glanced over my shoulder as we stepped outside the house. Kelli and Meryl were at the picnic tables now, sorting the side dishes and utensils. I grabbed my elbow with my opposite hand and hugged myself a little nervously. We'd have been here in time to help if I'd planned ahead a little better. I should have known Dustin wouldn't want to leave his carving this afternoon, and now I looked like the flake who showed up just in time to eat and run.

"Anyone know where Evan is?" Morgan asked the group at the table. "I don't want to start without him."

Blank looks greeted her. "He said he was taking a shower and heading up," Marshall offered. "Should'a been here by now."

I glanced down at my toes, trying not to look too interested in the answer. It was already far too obvious that I was the odd one in the group. Everyone else was married and paired off at the picnic tables. No matter where I sat, I'd be the fifth wheel in a group of happy couples. I thought I'd gotten over being uncomfortable about that, but apparently not. But if Evan came, at least we could be... alone together, I guess.

Besides, I liked being around him. He was soothing company.

Dusty held up his phone. "He's not answering his texts, but I just tracked his location. He's almost here."

I stared at him as I took a seat. "You track your older brother's location?"

"Sure." He put his phone away. "We all share locations. Makes it easier to find each other when we're out working because sometimes the signal isn't good, but we can at least have a rough idea of where the other person was heading before they dropped off. Pretty handy."

"Huh." I frowned. "I never thought of it that way. I always thought it sounded stalkerish."

Kelli laughed and sat down beside me. "That's exactly what Marshall said when I called him at the *precise* moment he got to the barn this afternoon."

"Wasn't complaining, baby," Marshall said, winking at his wife. "Nice to feel missed."

"That's what he thinks," Kelli whispered, leaning close to me. "I really just wanted to make sure he didn't forget about dinner."

I snickered, then scanned the yard for Dustin. I'd already told him that he was not to disappear and that he shouldn't try to wander off to the barns this evening. Hopefully, he remembered, but where was he now? I craned my neck to peer around a couple of trees, and that was when I saw Dustin lying on the grass beside Jess's dog. Dakota, I think his name was. They both looked comfortable and peaceful, and I let go a sigh of relief.

"Heads up, everyone." Cody came over to the table with a platter of steaks and waited for us to clear a spot for them. "Blake, come and get it!"

Everyone found seats except for Cody and Morgan, who remained standing. This would be it—their little announcement. I clenched my hands together under the table, trying to hold back a cheesy grin so I wouldn't give it away. But Cody just doffed his hat and nodded to Blake.

"Your house," Blake said, shaking his head. "You ask the blessing."

I blinked and shifted on the bench. Cody waited for everyone, then bowed his head and asked a humble blessing over the food. I didn't close my eyes like everyone else. It wasn't that I was irreverent—far from it. I was just a little in awe, I suppose, watching this family of tough cowboys, every one of them, holding hands with their wives and thanking their Maker for a simple meal. Nothing taken for granted.

After Cody closed his prayer, heads lifted, and we all heard the sound of tires crunching on gravel. I twisted around to see the driveway, and the silver pickup that was just cresting the little knoll. Evan Walker parked his truck beside Marshall's and got out, sending a casual glance at each brother who waved at him. But when his eyes got to me, they stopped, and he stiffened.

And suddenly, it didn't seem like it had been such a good idea for me to be here, after all.

Chapter Ten

Evan

"YOU DIDN'T TELL ME Meg was coming," I hissed to Cody as he passed me a plate.

He gave me a funny look. "Dude, she was on the text thread with everyone else. Don't you check your messages?"

"Not all fifty of them. I turned the notifications off because I hate my phone blowing up when I'm trying to work."

Cody shrugged. "Well, I guess that's on you, then. She was on there just like the rest of us. She even asked if we wanted her to pick anything up from town before she headed up. You really didn't see any of that? Geez, now I know why you never answer my messages."

I scowled and followed him back to the grill. "I thought you said this was just family," I whispered.

"Yeah, well, Meg nursed my wife last week when she had her head in the popcorn bowl all day. That makes her family in my book, not sure about yours. Good grief, lighten up. Wasn't it your idea?"

"It was, and... would you stop for a second?"

Cody halted and turned around, pointing his grill tongs at me. "What's wrong with Meg? Is it her kid?"

"No! I like both of them just fine. More than fine, actually."

"So? Why are you so upset that they'd be here?"

"I'm not upset," I clarified. "But don't you know how it looks?"

He raised his brows and shook his head. "What are you talking about?"

I clenched my jaw and rolled my eyes. "Think about it. Every single one of you guys are newlyweds. That leaves me... and it leaves Meg... You see?"

"Mm-hmm." His face was deadpan. "So? I don't follow you."

"So, I'm not ready to be set up on some weird 'family date'. You're putting her on the spot, and you're making me look bad if I don't—"

"Evan! Hey." He held up a hand. "It's just a barbecue. Find a hole on the bench and eat some steak. That's all."

My shoulders drooped, and my eyes fell to the plate he'd handed me. It just wasn't that simple.

I *did* like Meg. A lot more than I wanted to, and a lot more than I was ready to confess. The last thing I was in the mood for was to have all those love-drunk newlyweds, including my *dad*, for Pete's sake, ogling her and me and trying to set us up for more than I was ready for.

I turned around and made my way back to everyone else. They were all laughing and talking, didn't seem like anyone had even paid much attention to me yet. I hesitated, looking for a spot to wedge into. There was an open end next to Marshall... directly across from Meg. I swallowed and sniffed my shirt. Well... at least I wouldn't be sitting right beside her. Maybe she wouldn't notice that I hadn't gotten a shower after all.

"Dude," Marshall said, wrinkling his nose as I slid in beside him. "Thought you said you were going to clean up. You're supposed to use soap."

My eyes shifted helplessly to Meg across the table. She met my gaze, then blinked bashfully away.

"I was," I confessed. "Got a call from Brandon at the last minute. He had a calf that was drooling and not looking good."

"What's this?" Dad's voice raised from the next table over. "Did you check it out?"

I nodded and picked up my steak knife. "Doc Burns came out, too. I was worried about foot and mouth, after that bad outbreak a few years ago. But it turns out he was choking on a ball of feed. Doc got him fixed up."

Dad nodded and turned around, and I found Meg's eyes on me again. I offered a thin smile. "Sorry, I probably don't smell like roses. I didn't want to miss..." I bobbed my head. "You know. Looks like I was too late, anyway."

A hesitant smile appeared on her lips, and she darted a glance at Marshall, who was already ignoring us. "You didn't," Meg mouthed. "I think Morgan was waiting for you."

"Oh." I cleared my throat. "Still, if I'd known—"

A clanging sound interrupted me. Cody was standing between the tables, and he had this little dinner triangle he was banging for attention. Everyone stopped eating, and Meg and I shared a glance.

"Everyone, Morgan and I want to thank you for coming up to our little housewarming barbecue. And..." He reached for Morgan's hand as she came to stand beside him. "We have a surprise for you!"

Meg

I KNEW IT!" KELLI said again. "I *knew* when she said she was too busy to come to Beaufort's the other night, something was up. Morgan *never* passes up a chance to eat someone else's cooking."

"I suspected today when I saw her eating salad," Meryl chuckled. "Morgan's never been a big fan of 'health food'."

Audrey shook her head and surveyed Morgan with a little smirk. "I think I'd have put it together on my own before too much longer. Girl's giddy and glowing, but I *think* I caught her napping in the house the other day when I came up for my volunteer slot."

Morgan laughed. "I was not! It just was a thirty-second shut-eye."

"That turned into half an hour?" Audrey said with a teasing grin.

Morgan shrugged. "I'll never tell. I thought I had you fooled into believing I'd just gone in for a snack."

"Not a chance," Audrey said. "You had pillow creases on your cheek."

Morgan sighed and shook her head. "Well, what about you, Jess? When did you figure it out?"

Jess held up her hands. "I never did, but then, we all know that observation isn't my strongest suit. Nothing personal, but I think you'd have to be six months along before I'd have noticed you put on a couple of pounds."

I laughed and sipped my soda. "You'd have spotted it before that, Jess. She's too obvious."

"And you were in on it!" Jess accused, laughing. "No fair at all!"

"Only because I was conveniently close," I objected. "Just lucky."

Morgan reached to squeeze my shoulder. "I was the lucky one. And Evan didn't stop by your house just because you were close, you know."

I blinked and lowered my soda. All five of them had some kind of funny look on their faces—Kelli was puckering her lips and arching her brows, Meryl had a sentimental little smile, and Jess was starting to bounce on her toes. Morgan and Audrey, however, were pinning me with expectant stares.

"I'm not sure what you're looking for," I replied helplessly. "I live close by, and it didn't technically spoil the surprise since I'm not direct family, so I guess he thought—"

"He'd have hauled *me* up there no matter what Morgan said, if he hadn't thought of you first," Kelli retorted. "So, he likes you."

I shook my head vehemently. "It's nothing like that! Evan and I have... history, I guess." My brow furrowed. "That doesn't sound right. It's not like *that*."

"And it's none of our business, anyway," Meryl inserted firmly. "Don't worry about it, Meg. No one is going to nag you."

Kelli and Audrey looked disappointed, but Morgan sighed and smiled. "You're right, Meryl. Sorry, I didn't mean to make you uncomfortable about Evan."

I shrugged and tried to look casual. "I'm not uncomfortable," I lied. Evan hadn't exactly seemed pleased to see me when he arrived. What had that been about? And he wasn't precisely welcoming of conversation when we were eating, either. Not that he was normally a talker, but he'd been more reserved than usual.

Kelli got that arch look again, but she rolled her eyes and hid her mouth behind her Dixie cup. In fact, everyone was suddenly looking away—at their shoes, at each other—and a second later, I found out why.

"Meg?" Evan's voice sent a tingle down my spine, and put a knot in my throat. I sucked in a breath, then narrowed my eyes at Morgan, who was trying to hide a smirk. They could have warned me!

I turned around to see Evan rubbing the back of his neck, his hat in his hand. "Yes?" I asked innocently.

"Hey, uh... Dustin wandered off. He isn't in the therapy barns—I just checked. I was going to go to the lower pens to look for him, but I figured I'd better let you know."

I suppressed a groan. "Not again. I told him to stay close!"

Evan stepped to the side, gesturing with his head. "He probably just went down to see the rescue horses. Cody lent me his utility quad. Wanna hop on and run down there with me to see if that's where he went?"

I couldn't exactly refuse. And I didn't exactly want to, either, but that meant climbing on the back and putting my arms around Evan Walker. Someone coughed—probably Kelli—and someone else shuffled their feet. My guess was Morgan, shushing her with a physical shove.

I smiled, my eyes locked on Evan's face. "Sure."

Evan

I REALLY, *REALLY* WISHED I'd gotten to take that shower.

To Meg's credit, she never flinched when she had to shimmy up against me on the quad. She didn't cling to me for dear life, but she also didn't act like I was a leper, even though my shirt was far from fresh.

"You said you checked the barns?" she asked over the roar of the engine. "He usually looks for Biz."

I gestured to the new pole buildings standing on the rise near the house. "Yeah, he's not in there. But I've a pretty good idea where he went. Hang on."

Her arms tightened a little as I gunned the engine, and I spared a quick glance down. Her hands were locked together over my chest, and her warm body was pressed against my back, with her chin bumping my shoulder. And I didn't hate it.

We rolled down to the bottom of the long driveway, about three-quarters of a mile, and the whole time, my heart was hammering almost louder than the quad.

"How could he could have gotten this far without someone noticing he was gone?" Meg shouted. "I swear, I just saw him a few minutes ago."

I turned my head back a little. "All I know is Lizzy was looking for him to play fetch with Jess's dog with her, and she said he'd been gone for a little bit. I guess he could've been in the upper barns, but I sure didn't see him. Does he ever hide?"

Meg was quiet for a few seconds. "Not for a long time."

I felt her arms tighten a little more—probably not because the quad sped up suddenly. There was a little tremble in her hands, too, so I grabbed both of them with one of mine and gave them a quick squeeze. "He can't have gone too far. We'll find him, Meg."

I didn't hear any more as the quad coasted down to the open turnaround area where Morgan quarantined the new horses that came in from heaven-only-knew-where. I just let off the gas, and the quad coasted a few yards until I pulled the brake and cut the engine.

"I don't see him," Meg said. "Really, he can't have come this far. I know I saw him—"

"Right there." I pointed.

Meg's arms dropped from around my chest, and she leaned out to look where I was pointing. "Where? I don't see..."

"By the trough. See that little pinto colt? He's got his head down inspecting something."

She squinted doubtfully. "It looks like he's drinking."

I shook my head and swung my leg over the side of the quad, then offered my hand to help her slide off. "He's got his head outside the trough, on the far side, and I saw a tuft of hair poking up a second ago. Come on."

Meg's eyes were wide, but she let me tug her by the hand until we got a better angle. And sure enough—Dustin was there laying on the ground in front of the trough, bopping the colt on the nose with a wildflower he'd picked somewhere.

"How...? *Oh*, he's grounded now." Meg started forward, but I pulled her back.

"He ain't hurtin' nothin'. Only problem is if he gets stepped on. Just hold up for a second."

She crossed her arms and gave me a cynical look. "What are you going to do?"

I held up a finger, begging her to stay put, and wandered casually over to the pen where Dustin and the colt were. Dustin didn't move, but I saw his shoulders tense when he heard me approach. I leaned over the railing and just watched the colt for a minute.

"I'm not... not hurting anything," came his defensive voice. "I'm not leaving."

"Didn't say you were."

Dustin flicked the wildflower against the metal trough. "Mom said I couldn't go see Biz in-in the barn. She didn't say I c-couldn't come down here."

I nodded. "Makes sense."

"I don't want to go back up there. There's too many people."

I turned around and leaned my shoulder against the rail. "Not here to take you back."

"Lizzy won't... won't leave me alone," he continued, his voice starting to crack. "I hate how she's always bugging me!"

"You don't like crowds, huh? Yeah. Me either."

He didn't have much to say to that.

I pushed my hat back on my head a little. "But you know, we have a rule up at the ranch, and Morgan has the same rule here."

Dustin didn't answer, but his eyes were shifting my way every few seconds, so I guessed he was listening.

"The rule is," I went on, "that you always say something when you're going somewhere. You never know when you'll need a hand, and if no one knows where to find you, you're in a heap of trouble."

He blinked and ducked his head into the side of the trough. "Like l-last winter."

"Yeah, like that. And there's another rule, too, but I don't know if you can remember two new rules on the same day."

Dustin's head came up. "I can remember rules. I'm good at memorizing things, ask my mom."

I shrugged. "Well, if you're sure. See, this other rule is that you never sit on the ground in front of a horse. They can step on you. But I'm not sure you can remember all that, so..."

"I can. Always tell someone where you're going, and never sit on the ground in front of a horse," he recited with the precision of a robot.

I nodded toward him. "But you're still sitting there."

Dustin scrambled to his feet and hunched his shoulders as he dusted off his backside. "Do I have to go?"

"Not if you can remember the rules. Think you can do it?"

Dustin's head bobbed jerkily. "I nev-*nev*er forget rules."

"Well, it's a deal then." I smacked the pipe railing and tipped my hat to him. "I don't want to go back up to the barbecue, either, so I'm going to be over there for a while. You good?"

Dustin looked uncertain, his eyes roving over to where his mom stood, then back to me. And then he smiled. "Good."

Meg

I CAN'T BELIEVE YOU got him to do that. He didn't even argue with you!"

Evan pulled his hat off and wiped his forehead with a rag. "He likes rules, doesn't he?"

I tipped my head. "Yes. He always has. I think they make him feel safe. They're predictable."

He replaced his hat. "Well, I just told him the rules. He seemed okay with that. But we probably shouldn't leave him down here alone. Did you want to go back up? I can stay with him."

"Don't you want to be with your family?"

He offered a shy grin. "Oh, I see them often enough. And I don't mind being alone."

"You don't have to be."

He blinked, and his eyes shot to mine. "How's that?"

I swallowed. *Had I said that?* "I just meant that I don't plan on leaving you down here to watch my son by yourself."

"Oh." He nodded and leaned against the handlebars of the quad, his gaze turning back toward the pens of horses.

"Are you okay with that?"

Evan lifted his shoulders. "Sure. Why wouldn't I be?"

"I don't know. It's just that you didn't seem very comfortable when you got to the barbecue and realized I was there. I'm sorry if I made it awkward for you."

His eyes widened as he turned back to me, and his cheeks even blistered red. "I didn't mean that the way it might've sounded."

"Sounded?" I crossed my arms. "What did you say?"

His jaw clenched, and he swallowed. "Nothing. Well... nothing worth repeating. I just didn't want anyone... never mind, it's stupid."

My eyes dropped as he looked away again. "Evan, I know that... that we only met because of..." I broke off.

He tipped his head toward me. "Because of Emma? Is that what you're saying?"

I thinned my lips. "What I'm saying is that I might bring up some bad memories for you. I didn't mean to intrude on your family and make you—"

"It's not that." His hands found the grips of the handlebars as he leaned against them, and he squeezed them until his knuckles were white. "We've each had a... a bad spell, you could say. And that's a nest of matchmakers if you ever saw them. I don't like being put on the spot like that, and I figure you might not be too fond of it, either."

Something in my stomach squeezed, and my heart kicked into another gear. Evan wasn't looking at me, so I couldn't read his feelings on the matter. But something in the way he said it made me think he wasn't happy about even the suggestion that some in his family might be looking at me, and at him, like that. I swallowed.

"I didn't think of it that way. I'm sorry, Evan. I'll go—"

His head snapped around. "What? No, I didn't mean that."

My breath caught, and I raised an eyebrow. "You didn't?"

"I mean, unless it bothers you."

I studied his face. My thoughts were a blur—I couldn't even make sense of them. And I certainly couldn't make sense of what he was saying. Maybe he couldn't, either, because there was a flicker in his cheek, and it looked like he was holding his breath.

"It doesn't bother me," I whispered.

Evan's chest lifted in a shaky sigh. "No? I figured it might."

"All I meant is that I didn't feel like I was under a microscope," I blurted. "The rest..."

"Well, they sure as heck made *me* feel a little awkward." He got a funny look on his face as he plucked the front of his shirt and held it out. "I'm not exactly presentable."

It took me a few seconds to understand that he wasn't talking about me, but his appearance. I flicked a glance over his sweat-stained shirt and the dirt that had been rubbed into the thighs of his jeans and laughed softly. "I don't think anyone minds, Evan. They'd rather have you here, sweaty and dirty, than not have you at all."

He smiled at that—a slow, gentle smile as his eyes fixed on the gravel beneath his boots. He drank in a long sigh and shifted his feet. "Suppose I *was* able to get a shower in? Hypothetically."

I let a grin tug at my mouth. "Showers are hypothetical things now?"

"Before dinner, sometimes they are." His hands twisted around the grips of the quad, and he lifted his face to gaze at the trees on the horizon. "But if I got that shower... wasn't worried about how I smelled or looked, and didn't mind being dragged out in public... would you want to come with me?"

He turned to look at me again, and something in his eyes tugged a part of me I'd forgotten I even had. I think in that second, I'd have given up everything I ever owned to help Evan Walker learn to laugh again. Could I do it? Be that first person he reached out to after his world had crumbled? Because that first person, whoever it ended up being, would bear a terrible responsibility. She would be the one who had to help him make peace with what he couldn't change, and to teach him that just because his future couldn't be what he'd wanted, didn't mean it couldn't be what he needed.

And if she was a decent human, she'd have to make a promise in the beginning not to hurt him. It would be all or nothing with Evan Walker, and how could someone *know* that kind of thing right from the get-go?

Evan was blinking now, and his gaze was starting to drop again. Before he could turn away and take back his question, I hurried to say something. "Hypothetically...?"

His eyes lifted once more, and his lips parted slightly. "Yes?"

I swallowed. "Would you be willing to take that early shower on a night when I could get someone to stay with Dustin? I mean that just as an academic question, really. I mean... I guess you could take a shower whenever you want, and Dustin's not..."

I quit blabbering when his hand left the grip of the quad, and he held it out to me. My brow clouded, and I took his hand, instinctively shaking it like we were forming a pact.

"I think we can make that work," he said quietly.

I smiled. "Then we have a deal."

Chapter Eleven

Evan

I STEPPED INTO THE house at four-thirty to grab a shower, and the familiar warmth and the scent of something cooking made me pause for a moment. "Hey, Evan," Meryl called cheerfully without turning around, her focus on chopping what looked like fresh herbs. "I'm torn between corn on the cob and baked potatoes for dinner. What do you think?"

I hesitated, hovering in the doorway. I hadn't mentioned anything about going out tonight, not even a hint. The thought of explaining it made my stomach twist oddly. "Uh, actually, Meryl, I won't be home for dinner tonight."

She paused, her knife hovering over the cutting board, then resumed chopping. "Oh? That's a change. Got plans?"

I rubbed the back of my neck, feeling the prickly heat rise to my face. "Yeah, something like that." I didn't meet her eyes, hoping she wouldn't probe further. I wasn't sure I could handle a barrage of questions about Meg and what this dinner meant—or didn't mean.

Meryl glanced over her shoulder, giving me a small, knowing smile. "Well, that sounds nice. It's good to see you getting out."

I fidgeted with the keys in the pocket of my jeans, feeling suddenly awkward standing there. "Yeah, I guess so."

The silence stretched for a moment, filled only by the sounds of cooking. Meryl set down her knife and wiped her hands on her apron, turning to face me fully.

"I hope you have a pleasant evening, Evan," she said, her voice warm and devoid of any prying tone. "You deserve it."

I managed a small smile, grateful for her tact. "Thanks, Meryl. I appreciate it."

I PARKED MY TRUCK outside Meg's house, the rumble of the engine dying as I turned the key. For a moment, I just sat there, staring at the closed curtains of her front window, my stomach a twisted ball of nerves and resolve.

She had to know I was here; the sound of my truck was unmistakable in the quiet neighborhood. Yet, I hesitated, my hands gripping the steering wheel. A part of me was still grappling with the idea of being here, of moving forward. I found myself whispering a silent apology to Anne. "I haven't forgotten you," I murmured, my voice barely audible. "I'm just trying to... to live."

I closed my eyes for a moment, feeling an almost tangible pressure on my chest. But as I sat there, something shifted inside me, a sensation like a gentle hand on my shoulder, easing the burden. I didn't believe in ghosts or supernatural mumbo-jumbo, and I'd never fancied she could hear me from heaven. But for a second, it felt like Anne was giving me a nudge, a silent reassurance that it was okay to step forward.

Taking a deep breath, I opened the truck door and stepped out. The weight that had been pressing down on me seemed to lift, and I breathed just a little bit easier. I reached the porch and hesitated just a second before pressing the doorbell. The sound echoed slightly, a clear, definitive chime that broke the silence of the evening. I straightened my shirt and ran a hand through my hair, waiting for Meg to answer.

Meg was... well, she was great. More than great. She wasn't Anne—I knew that. But I didn't expect her to be, and I think I'd finally gotten to a place where I was sort of okay with that. Meg was a remarkable person in every sense of the word, and that made it a little easier, I suppose. I hadn't asked her out just because I was lonely. I really did see something there that was worth investigating—maybe worth taking a chance on—but that always came with a risk. Someone could seem pretty normal until you got to know them a little, and out of nowhere, the crazy would bite you.

I shook my head and snorted at myself. I'd known Meg for years—I knew she wasn't crazy, at least. Okay, so that was a pretty low bar, but at least she wasn't covered in red flags.

No, Meg was someone I'd always admired. Liked talking to, could be comfortable just spending time with her. For quite a while now, actually, I'd been perking up just a bit when she was around—just listening to what she had to say, seeing what she was doing. And I always wanted to keep looking, so that was... well, that was good, right? I might not be in love with her, but I liked her a lot. And more than my brain seemed to like her because my senses always hummed and tingled whenever she was around. Had to start somewhere.

But when Meg opened the door, it was like seeing her anew. I usually saw her when she was in survival mode, but tonight, she'd taken some extra pains with her appearance, and the effect caught me by the throat. Her soft, dark blonde hair framed her face, the layers flipping playfully at the ends, and those blue-green eyes of hers held a mix of warmth and bright energy. She'd always looked and moved like someone who had some native athleticism, and that, combined with the flattering cut of her simple cotton dress, made a pretty picture this evening. She tugged occasionally at the hem, like she wasn't accustomed to wearing it, and there was a nervous edge to her smile when she greeted me.

It was the lines around her eyes, though, probably etched by stress and sleepless nights, that drew me in the most. Meg was one person who knew what it was to paste a smile on like a band-aid, and maybe, around her, I wouldn't have to pretend to be... whole, I guess. Something I hadn't been for a long time.

I dipped my head and took off my hat. "You look nice this evening."

Meg's cheeks brightened, and she held her breath for a second before letting it go in a gush. "Thank you. You too—I mean, you look—"

"Like I got a shower?"

She relaxed a little and laughed. "Yes, that. Won't you come in? I'll just be a minute. I just want to make sure Missy has everything she needs."

"Take your time," I said, my voice softer than I intended. I followed her inside, hanging my hat on a hook by the door. The house was filled with the smell of fresh marinara sauce and Dustin's low, monotone singing from down the hall. I nodded briefly to the girl in the kitchen as Meg rushed back in to dump a pot full of noodles into a strainer.

"I wouldn't fight him if he doesn't want to eat," Meg was telling the girl. "He's been hit or miss lately, but I think spaghetti is still his favorite. He's been working on a new sculpture this week, so he probably won't even notice you being here, but watch that he doesn't come in here and start sharpening his carving tools over the sink. He jammed up my garbage disposal last time, so make him use the trash can." She clapped her hands on her thighs and looked around. "I think that's all. You know where everything is, right?"

Missy assured her that she did, and Meg whirled around the kitchen twice more, picking up this or that, grabbing for her purse, flipping the hair behind her ear, and glancing unconsciously at me. "Okay. Well, I don't know when we'll be back, so you have my number. Call me if you need anything."

"I will," Missy promised as she pulled a plate out of the cupboard and started serving noodles. "Have fun."

Meg blew out a huff, patted her sides down one last time as if she was looking for something, and then turned to me with a bright, nervous look. "I guess I don't need my keys, but I keep thinking there's something I'm forgetting."

I shrugged. "Not like we can't come back if we need to."

Her face softened fractionally, and her brows drifted up as she let go an easier breath. "Right. We can."

"You ready?"

She swallowed and turned around once more, then visibly forced herself to let go of whatever was nagging her. "Yes, I think so."

I pulled my hat off the hook and held the door for her, enjoying that giddy little smile she made when she passed by me. Then, I closed the door and gestured to the passenger side of the truck.

Meg nodded, as if just then understanding that I meant to get the door for her. "Th-thank you. You must think I'm a goose. I wanted to be ready before you got here."

"It's fine," I replied, offering her a reassuring smile. "You're a good mom, Meg. It's natural to worry."

She blinked, and the corner of her mouth lifted faintly. "Thank you for understanding. I guess I'm... a little out of practice."

I didn't say anything to that. What was I supposed to say? That the last "date" I'd been on, if you wanted to call it that, was my high school prom? That was the night I'd blurted out that half-witted proposal to Anne, and she'd shocked me by saying yes. I guess I figured our dating life ended there, and everything after that was just... *us*. I was never an expert at this stuff. I just walked to the door of the pickup and popped it open for her.

Meg smiled bashfully and stepped around me to climb in, but then she froze. "Oh, no. I almost forgot. Dustin's favorite night shirt is in the wash." She squeezed her eyes and pressed her fingertips into them. "It sounds stupid, I know, but he hates going to bed without it, and I didn't want Missy to..."

"Hey." I tugged one of her hands down from her face and waited for her to open her eyes.

She drew her lower lip sideways between her teeth and sagged a little. "I'm sorry. I just thought of that."

I smiled a little, then asked, in a low voice, "Are you sure you want to do this?"

Meg looked slightly taken aback, her eyes flicking momentarily toward the house. "You know what? Dustin will be fine. Missy's great with him, and he's comfortable with her. He's got his spaghetti and his carving, and they'll probably watch a movie or something. Well—he doesn't *watch* them the way most people do, but sometimes he likes to play twenty questions about the plot. It's kind of annoying, really, but Missy tolerates it, and anyway, I doubt he'll even want to go to bed until I'm home."

But I kept my gaze steady on her, conveying without words that there was more to my question than concern for Dustin. In the silence that followed, I saw the realization dawn.

She took a deep breath, her eyes not leaving mine. "Oh. You were talking about..."

"If it's too fast, we can try for another night. Or..." I hesitated. "Not at all, if that's... too much."

Meg tightened her fingers through mine. "Yes, Evan, I do. I want to do this. Like you said, we can always..." She tipped her head toward the house. "We can always come back if we need to."

That, I wasn't so sure of. A date was a date, and once we got into this truck, it had to end up some way or another. Failure or success—whatever that meant. But if we didn't get in, then nothing happened, and we could go back to tomorrow with nothing changed and nothing risked.

But something inside me was awful glad she'd said yes.

"Alright then." I opened the truck door for her. "Let's go."

Meg

A S EVAN HELPED ME into his truck, I couldn't help but notice the slight tremor in his hand. I hadn't even noticed until now that *he* was as nervous as I, but there it was. He kept it all so tightly wrapped, I doubted anyone noticed half the things this man felt. After closing the door for me, he walked around to the driver's side and got in, but instead of starting the engine, he just sat there for a moment, staring at the steering wheel. What was going through his mind? I didn't think I had a right to ask quite so soon.

Trying to inject some cheer into the moment, I asked, "Where are we heading tonight?"

Evan finally looked up, his eyes meeting mine briefly before shifting away. "I thought about Beaufort's, but you work there, and it didn't seem..." His voice trailed off, then he cleared his throat and continued, "The tavern's an option, but it's not... well, it's not as nice, and I..." Again, his voice faded as if he was contemplating another idea.

I leaned forward slightly. "What are my choices?"

"Would you... would you mind just going for a drive? We could pick up some burgers and just... drive. Watch the sunset from the overlook, maybe. No one watching us, no schedule. We can turn around whenever you want."

His suggestion caught me off guard, but in a good way. A drive sounded perfect—simple, no pressure, just the two of us and the open road. "I like that idea, Evan. It sounds wonderful."

Evan's face relaxed into a relieved smile, and he finally started the truck. As we pulled away from my house, I felt the butterflies in my stomach starting to settle a bit. This was new territory for both of us, but with Evan it wasn't as scary as it could have been. It seemed like we wanted the same thing—no fancy restaurants, no expectations, just us and the opportunity to talk, to learn about each other in the quiet spaces between.

"Y OU NEED AN EXTRA pair of hands there?" I teased, reaching over to help steady the wrapper.

Evan took a bite and let me take the messy burger, but some of the contents fell out before I could catch them in the wrapper and plopped on the napkin he'd draped over his leg. I handed him another napkin, but I wasn't sure what to do about that one in his lap. Did I dare...?

"Thanks," he grunted with an embarrassed laugh as he tried to wad the fresh napkin around the messy one. "I didn't think this part through."

"I think there's a law somewhere about onions on a burger when you're driving."

He blinked. "Onions... dang, I didn't even think about that, either." He turned his face away and switched hands on the steering wheel as he checked his breath. Then, with his eye edging my way, he toggled the switch to roll his window down a little. "Sorry. Closed space and all."

I laughed and handed him back the rest of his burger. "I had onions on mine, too."

"Oh, so you're immune! In that case, is it too noisy for you, or is the... ah... fresh air necessary?"

"I'm fine either way." I propped my elbow on the center console, my chin resting on my knuckles, and waited to see if he needed any more help with his messy burger.

"Then maybe I'll roll it up so I can hear you talk." With a grin, he managed to get the burger under control and took a big bite, finishing it quickly to avoid further mishaps. He took the napkin I offered and wiped his mouth, then let me cram it all in the paper sack with the rest of the garbage.

"Not exactly the most elegant supper you've ever had," he apologized.

"Yeah, but the view is worth it." I pointed through the windshield at the mountains dominating the landscape. "Better than any restaurant wall."

Evan nodded, ducking his head to peer a little further up the rise of the peaks. "Looking pretty brown this year. Dry as a bone."

I caught the worry in his tone and studied him. "Are you having problems with grazing this summer?"

"Not yet." He pointed to the right. "But we have a herd grazing up in those hills in the distance. I'm thinking I'll have to bring them down early this year so they don't run out of water. We usually ride up there the last week of August, head them down the mountain, and get the weaning done, but we might have to go up a couple weeks sooner this year. I'll say something to Marshall and Luke about that when I get..."

He stopped himself and turned back to me with an apologetic look. "Sorry. You didn't come out to listen to me rattle on about the ranch."

"I don't mind. I like how you talk about your ranch and your family."

He took a sip of his soda and glanced at me as he drove. "Speaking of family, you were saying something a minute ago about your dad being from around here? I thought you were from Oregon originally."

"That's right. Dad moved here after they divorced. I lived in Oregon with my mom during the school year, but every summer, I'd be here with Dad. He was a ranch hand, hired out to different outfits. Never to Walker Ranch, though. Those summers were some of my best memories."

"And then you moved here for good?"

"Dad got sick the summer after I graduated high school, so I moved here to help him. A year later, I met John, so... I stayed."

"But you have a teaching degree," Evan pointed out, a slight frown creasing his brow.

I sighed, the memories flooding back. Those were tough years—the sorts of years that are supposed to galvanize you, put you through the fire so you can withstand anything. It just didn't turn out like that. "Yes, I was commuting two hours each way to Pocatello to finish school. It was rough. Dad wasn't able to work anymore. Dustin was born before I finished, and then... my dad passed away shortly after that."

Evan drove in silence for a moment. "That must've been tough. You were juggling a lot."

I gave a small, resigned smile. "Still graduated with a 3.8. You do what you have to, right?"

He nodded, his eyes back on the road. "Right. What you have to. So, John... is he...?"

"Lives in Seattle now." I waved a hand. "Don't ask me why. The rain would kill me, but he's a lineman and got a good job with the power company. You wouldn't believe what those guys can make."

"Oh..." He nodded, his eyebrows jumping. "I have an idea. I had other buddies go into that. Union jobs."

"Yeah." I fumbled with the edge of my seatbelt and looked out the passenger window. "My lawyer said I should push for higher child support, considering the kind of money John makes, but... well, I'd rather keep it amicable. For Dustin's sake."

Evan narrowed his eyes as he stared at the road. "He ever see his son anymore?"

I dropped my eyes and shook my head. "He's... you know. Far away. And has no intention of coming back."

Evan's jaw tightened. "I'm sorry."

I lifted a shoulder. "He wasn't exactly his best when he was here. It wasn't good for Dustin anyway."

"But it's a lot on your shoulders."

"Well." I smiled tightly. "Like I said. You do what you have to."

Evan turned to study me. He didn't say anything, but there was a crease around his eyes that wasn't usually there. And then, he just gave a single nod. It was like a gesture of respect, like I imagined he'd give to another cowboy after a job well done. And something deep inside me warmed just a little more.

He put on his signal—not that there was anyone else on the road to see it—and turned off at the overlook. From there, we could see the town down in the valley and the deep gash cutting a divide through the mountains beyond. Slowly, he turned the truck around so we faced west and slid the gear shift into park. But he didn't turn off the engine.

Butterflies were rioting in my stomach. The overlook was practically legendary for all the couples who had begun their romance here. I'd even heard rumors that Kelli and Marshall were among them. But Evan didn't look like a guy who was eager to be beginning any romance. He was holding his breath and tapping his finger on the steering wheel.

"So..." He stared at the horizon below us—pink streaks just starting to swirl across the glaring blue of the evening sky—and his hand started to drift toward the ignition to shut the truck off.

"Evan?"

His head snapped my way. "Yeah?"

I reached for his hand and stopped it from hitting the key. "I'm not expecting anything. You don't have to 'show me a good time' or feel obligated to... you know. Anything. I'd be happy just to sit here and watch the sunset with you."

Some sort of tension eased from behind his eyes. "You won't think I'm boring? Letting you down?"

"From what? My other option this evening was listening to Dustin singing in his room and eating dinner alone again."

A shy twist turned his mouth into something like a smile. "Okay, then." His hand dropped to his lap... then, shaking slightly, he forced himself to pick it up and drop it on the center console between us. He blinked for a few seconds, staring at our hands, where they rested several inches apart, then lifted his eyes to me.

Oh, dear. Better women than I had lost themselves in those expressive Walker eyes. Every single one of those men knew how to work the smolder, and pair it with the clear blue heartache in Evan's... well, I might be lost before I even knew I'd begun. Is there anything more like Kryptonite to the heart of a feeling woman than *that* sort of look in the eyes of a man who's had his heart broken?

Slowly, I let my hand slide under his, wondering what he would do about it. His cheek flickered; he looked down for a second; and then he smiled. And his fingers curled lightly over mine.

"Beautiful evening," he murmured. But he wasn't looking out at the sky or listening to whatever birds might be calling outside. He was looking at me, and I was smiling back.

"Yes," I agreed. "It is."

Chapter Twelve

Evan

"PUSH UP ANOTHER ONE, Dusty!" I pulled the lever on the doctoring chute, releasing the cow I'd just vaccinated and tagged. I wiped a rivulet of sweat off my cheek and waited for my brother to funnel another calf my way.

It was only ten in the morning, but the sun was already high in the sky, its heat beating down on us mercilessly. Dusty was on foot in the sorting pen, moving the calves into the chute one by one with a long pole. Dad was beside me, preparing shots and tags, his hands moving with the speed and precision honed from years of experience. And I was doing the actual work of vaccinating and tagging each calf.

"Should be done in less than an hour," Dad said as he stood back and counted the remaining calves in the pen.

"That was the plan," I grunted as the calf in the chute tossed himself around, pinning my arm momentarily against the bars. "I'd rather not be out here when the temps get up over a hundred. Too stressful on the calves."

Dad nodded and handed me the ear tag for this calf. "Meryl and I planned to take a ride out to the lower eighty this afternoon. Where will you be? Care to join us?"

I shook my head as I reached inside the panel to tag the calf. "Making rounds with Brandon, then I was going to ride ditch, check the irrigation pipes. Wyatt said the upper third of one of the fields isn't getting enough water." I pulled the lever and released the calf, then closed the gate and waited for Dusty to send me another one.

"Well," Dad said, "s'pose we'll catch you at supper, then. You'll be home, I guess?"

I frowned at my dad. He had that look in his eye again—that same look he got last winter when he assured Marshall he wasn't betting on him and Kelli. The same look he got whenever he'd "disappear" to go have coffee with Meryl back when he was seeing her on the sly. "I might be," I said slowly.

"Alright by me if you're not. Not like you need to check in or anything." Dad grinned and passed me the vaccination gun as Dusty clinked the gate behind the calf he'd pushed in.

"You know, for someone who wants to act like he's minding his own business, you can be pretty nosy," I muttered.

"What? All I said was—"

"Fine." I reached through the bars to administer the vaccine and waited for him to hand me the next ear tag. "I picked up burgers with Meg Truman last night. It was no big deal."

"I never said it was. You're the one acting all touchy. You know me, I never pry."

I snorted. "No. You just get that funny look on your face until we can't stand it anymore and fess up."

"You act like you're doing something wrong."

I stopped what I was doing, freezing in my tracks, and looked up at him. "I'm not."

A little tug pulled at the side of Dad's mouth. "Now you're gettin' it. You're not doing anything wrong, Evan. So stop worrying about what other people might think."

I braced my hands on my knees and nodded. "Sure. Pass me that ear tagger."

Dad raised an eyebrow, reaching for the tagger, and closed his mouth.

We finished the job in silence, and after the last calf was released, I nodded to Dad and Dusty. "I'll see you guys later." I grabbed my hat, dusting it off before settling it on my head.

As I walked towards the barn, where Brandon was already waiting with the horses, a sudden impulse struck me. My eyes drifted towards the far end of the ranch, where my old house stood—a place I hadn't visited in a long time. "Brandon, you mind if I take a detour? I'll catch up with you down in the coulee."

Brandon nodded. "Sure thing, Evan. Take your time. I'll check the bunch up on the ridge first."

Hoisting myself onto the saddle, I gently nudged my horse toward the northern edge of our ranch—that quarter that had been sectioned off more than ten years ago, and edged up to the shadow of the Bitterroot Mountains. I hadn't ridden this loop for a while, and for a reason. The distance wasn't far, but with each step, the house I had built for Anne loomed larger. Everything had changed around it, yet it still stood there, a silent testament to a life and love that once filled its rooms.

Reaching the crest of a small hill, I pulled the reins, bringing my horse to a standstill. From here, I could see the herd grazing peacefully near the fence bordering the house. Pedigreed Angus—top genetic specimens, every one of them. This was the herd we raised our breeding stock from, and the bull alone cost over ten grand when I bought him last year. But he'd been worth it for what he brought to our program. Raising stock is a long game—you don't see results in a year, or sometimes even five years. It's a generation or two later when the payoff happens, and the wise ranchers are the ones who spend those years investing in something worthwhile—something that will build a legacy that outlives you.

And that... that was why I hated looking at that house, because I'd lost everything it stood for. It looked just as pretty as it ever had, nestled among the trees, its windows reflecting the bright morning light. It stood just as Anne had left it that day, a picture-perfect image of our family home. But now, it was like looking at a photograph from another life—one where laughter echoed in the halls, and the smell of Anne's cooking wafted from the kitchen, where Emma's toys were scattered in the yard.

A lump formed in my throat. I could almost hear Anne's laughter on the wind, see Emma running through the fields to pet the calves nosing at the fence. It was overwhelming, a tidal wave of emotion that threatened to pull me under.

Taking a deep, steadying breath, I nudged my horse forward. With each step toward the house, my heart felt heavier, but it was past time I faced this. I'd been avoiding it for so long. I needed to walk through those doors and confront the ghosts of my past. It was the only way I could hope to find peace and maybe, just maybe, allow myself to embrace a future that suddenly didn't seem so impossible anymore.

I tied my horse to a post outside and hesitated at the door, my hand trembling slightly as I reached for the knob. Giving it a twist, I was engulfed by the silence of the house. It was as if time had stood still. Anne's favorite vase still sat on the mantel, her books lined the shelves, and Emma's sketches still hung on the refrigerator.

Anne's presence was everywhere—in the carefully chosen curtains, in the pictures of our family on the walls, in the kitchen where she'd cook while humming her favorite tunes. And Emma, with her bright, infectious energy, seemed to linger in the corners of each room, in the spaces where her toys used to be scattered, in the echoes of her giggles that once filled our home.

I brushed my hand over the back of the sofa, recalling evenings spent here, curled up with Anne, talking about our days and dreaming of our future. A future that was cruelly snatched away, leaving me in a void I thought was permanent.

Yet, as I stood there, surrounded by these ghosts of my past, my mind inevitably wandered to my evening with Meg. Her laughter—so genuine and free—echoed in my mind, and I found myself smiling, recalling the way her eyes lit up when she spoke. Her warmth and vitality had somehow reached through the numbness that had enveloped me for so long.

For the first time in what felt like forever, I had felt a flicker of something akin to happiness—a feeling I thought I had lost. The realization was both terrifying and exhilarating.

Meg was different, her presence bringing a new kind of light into my life, one I hadn't expected to find again.

But how could I move forward with these reminders of my past all around me? The house was a shrine to a life and love that was no more, yet stepping into a future with someone else felt like betraying the memory of my wife and daughter. It was like a tug-of-war between clinging to the past and reaching for a new beginning. If... things ever changed... this was still my house, my little piece of Walker Ranch. I didn't want that to go away—that was family, heritage, and it was around long before Anne ever entered my life. But how was I supposed to hang on to it while trying to build something new at the same time?

You have these conversations with the one you love—ridiculous little talks where you ponder what would happen if one of you were to... You always assure your love that if something ever happened to you, you'd want them to find life again. Anne had said that, and so had I. I guess I just never figured, with the life a rancher leads, that she'd be the one whose words would end up being put to the test.

I used to wrestle steers for fun, for crying out loud! My horse could slip and fall on the ice, or a hay bale could fall on me, or a utility vehicle could flip over. A wild kick from a cow I was doctoring, a slippery slide into the river on a cattle drive, or a brush fire. Any number of freak accidents could have been my end long before now.

It should have been me to go first.

But it hadn't been, and now, I had to decide whether Anne had really meant those words she whispered to me, so long ago on this very couch. And if she did—I know she did—I owed it to her to believe them.

I swallowed and made another pass through the house. I wasn't sure why, but something made me pause back at the fridge, staring at Emma's sketches. The biggest one was one of her riding Biz, of course. It sure didn't look like anything I'd have drawn at age seven. There was already sophistication of shade and shape in her work that someday might have developed into something remarkable. I'd never know, now.

Blinking back the sting in my eyes, I sniffed and slid all the aging papers out from their magnets and arranged them in a neat stack. I'd like to take these back to the main house and look at them a little more... but later, maybe at night when I couldn't sleep. Right now, Brandon was waiting for me down in the coulee, and I'd best tuck these into my saddle bag and get moving.

But before I got too far away from the house and the cell service, I stopped my horse and pulled out my phone. Maybe Meg would be up for dinner again sometime soon.

Meg

M Y PHONE PINGED AT eleven the next morning. I was just putting away groceries, and I closed the fridge to check the message. It was my boss, "Cowboy Bill," from Beaufort's.

-Hey, Meg, we're short for the lunch shift today. Can you come in early?

I bit my lip and thought for a few seconds. I could sure use the extra hours. But what to do with Dustin? "Who can watch him?" I muttered under my breath, scrolling through my contacts for a potential babysitter. Missy, my usual go-to, was out of the question, busy at White Pines until four. I considered a few others but doubted their availability on such short notice. And Dustin wasn't the kid you could leave with just anyone.

As I hovered over the button to text Cowboy Bill back that I couldn't make it, my phone vibrated with a new message. It was from Evan. My heart did a little somersault. He was reaching out so soon after last night? That had to be good, right?

I abandoned the message to my boss and opened Evan's.

-I had a good time last night. Thank you for saying yes. Would you want to do it again sometime soon?

I might have done a little dance, my hand covering my mouth in shock. He was asking me out again? He'd been so quiet last night when he dropped me off.

I honestly wasn't sure if he was sorry he'd asked, but he did offer that little smile when he walked me to my door. No good night kiss, but I wouldn't have expected that. The more time I spent around him, the more I started to see rippling under that quiet surface, but it would be a while before I could actually read his feelings.

But this was more than I'd hoped for. I almost couldn't reply fast enough... and then I wondered if I'd answered *too* quickly. I didn't want to look desperate, after all. I wasn't. But I'd thought the world of Evan Walker for as long as I'd known him, and lately, I'd started thinking even more. *What if...?* That was the question I was aching to find the answer to.

I stared at Evan's offer for a few more seconds, then thumbed back to the text from my boss. Maybe I'd look through my contacts just one more time. But even as I touched the app for my contacts, another message popped up from Evan.

Well, that was too good to pass up. I smiled as I opened the thread again.

-Busy day today? You're working tonight, aren't you?

I leaned against the counter as I typed back. *-Yes, but my boss asked if I could come in early. I'm trying to find someone to stay with Dustin, but it's not looking promising.*

What had made me say all that? A simple yes would have been sufficient. But I sent the message anyway, and his reply was almost instantaneous.

-I could put him to work here. Get him out of the house and keep him busy.

I blinked. He couldn't possibly! No. I wouldn't do that to him. My thumbs moved almost automatically as I tapped out a quick reply. -*Oh, no. I wouldn't want you to go to that kind of trouble.*

-*No trouble. He's a good worker, and I'm riding ditch later this afternoon. Good work for someone young and nimble. He might save me from throwing my back out.*

A smile crept over my face, and I stuck my tongue between my teeth in a little cringe as I replied. -*This is Dustin. He's not always cooperative.*

-*Neither am I.*

Stunned, I stared at the screen. Evan's offer was both thoughtful and immensely helpful. It also showed a level of comfort and familiarity that surprised me. Was he really stepping into our world like that, all of his own accord?

-*Are you sure?* I replied.

-*Absolutely. I'm on a horse right now, heading up to the barns. Meet you at the restaurant in half an hour.*

My hands trembled on the phone as I typed a final -*Yes.* Then, I almost collapsed against the kitchen counter in pure, utter shock.

And maybe a little terror.

As I HUSTLED THROUGH the dinner crowd, balancing a tray laden with drinks and a notepad crammed with orders, I caught sight of Evan and Dustin entering Beaufort's. They approached the seating hostess as if they came in every day and requested a table. My heart raced with apprehension. How had their day been at the ranch? They didn't look fit to strangle each other, so that was probably good news.

I'd made arrangements for Missy to meet Evan after she got done at White Pines to take Dustin home, but he'd brushed it off, saying they would be working until late and he'd bring Dustin to town himself if that was okay with me. And here they were, strolling in like any other pair of cowboys. Dustin was even wearing a hat that looked just like Evan's, and he was adopting the air of conscious nonchalance we usually saw on the younger guys who came in here, wanting to impress a date. He looked two years older than he had this morning.

I delivered the drinks on my tray, then snatched up a couple of menus and made a beeline for them as they settled into their booth. "Hey. How was—"

But before I could finish, Evan looked up with an easy grin. "We'll start with a pizza and..." He inclined his head toward me, his brows lifting. "*Two* sodas?"

"Mom says I can't have soda this late at night," Dustin piped up. "She says the sugar makes me vibrate like this." He grabbed the table and proceeded to demonstrate in a violent tremor that rattled his teeth and sent the silverware jangling all over the surface.

Evan laughed. "Okay, no soda then. Two waters and two pepperonis, please."

I blinked, taken aback. "Pizza? Here at Beaufort's?" Our restaurant was famous for its steaks and homestyle dishes, not pizza. We did have one on the menu, but it was a small, gourmet personal pizza cooked in a wood fire pit—more a novelty than a meal. "You know that takes about forty-five minutes to cook, right?"

Evan's grin didn't falter. "Sounds perfect. Dustin tells me he likes pizza."

I hesitated, glancing at Dustin, who was looking around with interest. How long would he be willing to wait for the pizza? But Evan seemed confident, and his relaxed demeanor suggested he had everything under control. Well... why not? Maybe this was Evan's way of bringing Dustin back to me and keeping him busy for the rest of my shift.

"Okay, two gourmet pepperoni pizzas, coming right up," I said, trying to match his confidence. I scribbled the order onto my pad with a wink at each of them.

Half an hour slipped by, and I made several trips to Evan and Dustin's table, ensuring they had an endless supply of Cowboy Bill's chips and salsa. Evan ate most of those because Dustin was absorbed in creating intricate designs with piles of salt on the table. To my surprise, Evan seemed completely unperturbed by the mess, only gently steering Dustin to keep the salt contained rather than sweeping it onto the floor every time he wanted to start over.

The man must have some magic gift. Either that, or he'd been taking lessons from Morgan. How did he seem to understand what not to do? He didn't demand eye contact, didn't push when Dustin put up a wall. Instead, he kept his tone even and calm and somehow got Dustin to do most of the talking. It was fascinating to watch—Evan eating chips and nodding along as Dustin rambled on about... well, I didn't even know what—without breaking his concentration on his salt art.

Once, as I was approaching to refresh their water glasses, Evan leaned in slightly. "So, what are you drawing this time?"

Dustin continued his drawing, not looking up. "It's a maze. For the horses."

"What, like you make for rats, to test their intelligence?

Dustin's hand paused, and a small smile appeared. "Yeah. Biz is sm-smarter than rats, though."

"I'd just bet he is. Prettier, too."

"I'm going to carve him next," Dustin announced. "I've been waiting for the r-right piece of wood, and I met... met it yesterday."

"You don't say. The wood cares what you make from it?" Evan looked up as I approached and gave me a short smile. "I never knew that."

I hid a smile and a shake of my head in return.

"Well, I know *I'd* care if someone wanted to turn *me* into something else," Dustin stated, as matter-of-factly as if he were reporting the time of day.

"Makes sense," Evan agreed, with another smile at me. "So, what, do you take pictures of him home to study before you start working?"

Dustin shook his head, continuing to trace the salt. "I know what he looks like. In here." He patted his chest. "I just need the right pose. It hasn't told me that yet."

"Maybe Evan has some pictures of Biz from his showing days that you could look at," I suggested as I slid the fresh glasses onto the table.

Dustin looked up, and Evan nodded agreeably. "I do, actually. As a matter of fact, I have a whole portfolio on him. I'll drop it by some time."

Dustin thought about this for a minute, then shrugged. "I guess."

Evan chuckled as he picked up his water glass. "Don't get emotional, now," he muttered with a grin.

I winced. "He doesn't mean—" I started to whisper, but Evan stopped me by touching my hand.

"I know. I was kidding. He's fun to listen to."

My eyes narrowed faintly. Was he really serious? People didn't hang out with Dustin because they thought he was fun. I cleared my throat. "Uh... the pizzas should be up in a minute."

Evan nodded. "Sounds good. Thanks."

As I was hurrying back to the kitchen with my empty tray, Cowboy Bill waved me over. "Hey, Meg, wait a second."

A knot formed in my stomach. Was he going to comment on Dustin being here, causing a distraction, or perhaps the mess he was making with the salt? I folded my empty tray over my stomach like a shield. "Sure. Is everything okay?"

I was getting fired. I knew it, I was getting fired for bringing my kid to work and letting him make a mess.

He glanced at the table, a small smile growing as he watched Dustin. "Everything's fine. Why don't you take the rest of the night off? Business is quieting down for the night, and you hardly ever take a break. You've been here since morning, and I haven't seen you sit down for more than five minutes."

I blinked in surprise. "But, I can finish my shift—"

He raised his hand to stop me. "No, I insist. I'll pay you for the full night. Just hang up your apron and enjoy your evening."

Before I could protest, he motioned to another server carrying a tray with a third pizza, identical to the ones Evan and Dustin had ordered. "I had an extra one made for you. Take it to your table, sit down with that cowboy over there, and relax for a change."

My mouth fell open slightly. "I'm not sure what to say."

"Say you'll be in tomorrow evening." He leaned in and whispered loudly. "We have a reservation for thirty people for a birthday party. I could really use you to help prep."

A smile broke on my face, and I chuckled. "Thank you, Bill. That's really kind of you."

He grunted, a twinkle in his eye. "Don't mention it. Now go on, get out of here."

I grabbed the tray with the pizza and approached the table with a newfound lightness in my step. "Looks like we have an unexpected addition to our dinner," I said, setting the pizza down.

Evan looked up, a curious expression on his face. "Everything okay?"

I nodded, unable to keep the smile off my face. "More than okay. My boss just gave me the rest of the night off, and this pizza is on the house. So, it looks like I'm joining you two for dinner."

Dustin looked up, his expression brightening at the sight of another pizza, and Evan's eyes met mine with a warm, inviting gaze. "Well, that's great news," he said. "We're glad to have you join us."

As I sat down, a sense of contentment washed over me. The evening had taken an unexpected turn, and for the first time in a long while, I felt like I could truly relax and enjoy the moment.

Chapter Thirteen

Evan

DUSTY WAS REALLY TERRIBLE at "minding his own business." Marshall was worse. And Luke... he didn't even try.

I pressed down on the chop saw and kicked off the boards I was cutting, letting Dusty pull them away and cart them toward his "house." It was starting to actually resemble a house by now. The exterior walls were framed, there was sort of a roof, Luke was threading the main wiring through the wall studs, and Marshall and Dusty were getting the interior walls framed. I was manning the chop saw, handing them the cut lengths they needed. I liked running the chop saw because I got to wear ear muffs, and I didn't have to talk to anyone.

But that didn't stop all of them from looking at me funny, or from acting awkward whenever they had to come ask me for something. I lost count of how many times Dusty and Marshall traded guilty looks whenever I called one of them over for another cut. Luke was working alone with his typical stem of sweet grass tucked in his cheek—we all figured it was an improvement on that old tobacco habit he'd kicked—and grinning every time he happened to look my way.

This was ridiculous. I sighed and switched off the saw. "Break time," I announced. I pulled off my work gloves and made my way over to the water cooler as my brothers stopped what they were doing, one by one, to follow me.

Dusty was eyeing me strangely as he pushed the spout to fill a cup. Marshall wasn't looking at me at all, and Luke took a big swig of his ice water and smacked his lips with a satisfied gasp and a grin as big as the whole outdoors.

"So," he said, staring and grinning at me like a moron. "Nice... day."

"Sure is," Marshall piped up. "Mmm-hmm. Nice day. Don't you think, Dusty?"

"Oh, yes. Yep. Puts me in mind of a poem I wrote for Jess last week. Blue skies and all. Nothing like it, right?"

I shook my head. "You guys are pathetic."

"I'm telling Dad," Dusty complained in a mock-childish voice. "Evan said something mean."

I rolled my eyes. "I know you're all itching to say something. I'm tired of watching you act like a passel of middle-school girls, so spit it out."

It was Luke who spoke up first. Predictably. He tugged on his ear and made a scrunched-up face. "Well, see, it's like this. We're all... uh... what was the word, Dusty?"

"Concerned."

"Right. We're all *concerned* that you, ah... no, doggone it, that's not the right word."

"Cautiously optimistic," Marshall supplied.

"Right! What he said," Luke rejoined, pointing at Marshall. "Oh, heck, I'll just ask. You good, brother?"

I finished my water. "I should have known you all would be blabbering sooner rather than later. I've been out with her twice."

"And had her kid at the ranch all afternoon. And from what I hear, that's not the first time you've taken care of him on your own." Luke saluted. "Dude. That's serious."

"What do you mean, 'that's serious'? She was stuck for someone to watch him. I've seen him work. He's a detail-oriented kid who loves the job, and he was more help than trouble. Mostly. What's the problem?"

"No problem," Dusty cut in, with a dark look at Luke. "All he means is that... you know, the single mom thing. Stepping in for her kid..."

"Right," Luke added. "Been there, done that. You fall in love with the kid, you get the woman, too. That's what happened to me."

"Sure it is," I retorted dryly. "Tell me how much you hate it."

Luke flashed all his teeth. "Never said I did. Matter of fact, it worked out pretty well for me, but... what was I saying?"

"Dustin's not an ordinary kid," Marshall interjected. "I saw him with you the other day. One minute, he was getting frustrated with the irrigation pipes and yelling at the dirt clods, the next, he was running after you like a four-foot soldier and looking up at you like you were some sort of a king. You can't mess around with that kid's feelings."

"And you're afraid I'll let him down?"

Marshall and Dusty both looked at their boots, refusing to answer. "That ain't it," Luke replied for them. "Marshall's convinced that you'll jump all in, whether you really want to or not, just to *keep* from letting the kid down." He shrugged. "And his mom."

I dropped my cup back on the flatbed of the truck next to the cooler and pointed at each of them. "I'm going to say this one time. I asked Meg out because I like her. That's all it is for now. If any of you goons want to make something out of it, go do it somewhere else and leave me alone."

Dusty's eyes widened, and he blinked. Marshall made a face, then nodded. But Luke never did know when to shut up, and he was opening his mouth to say something when Dusty grabbed him by the arm. "You heard the man. Back to work. I'm not paying you to stand around drinking water."

"You're not paying me squat to begin with," Luke argued as Dusty dragged him away.

"That's right, and I don't have to help you on *your* house if you're a pain in my rear," Dusty shot back.

Marshall was rubbing his jaw, still standing beside me. "For what it's worth," he mumbled, "Meg's awesome."

I leaned against the flatbed and squinted at the horizon. "I know she is."

"And it's not like you have to ask anyone for permission, you know. You can just do what you want, try something new. Take your time and see where it goes."

I raised my eyebrows and crossed my arms. "That's what I figured."

"Not like you can change the past, you know. And... well, gosh, we'd all like to see you happy."

I turned toward him with an exaggerated nod. "Thanks for that."

"Uh-huh. So... Yeah, Meg's pretty great. Kind of like you, now that I think of it. Never hear much out of her, but she sure gets it done."

I sighed. "Any more pearls of wisdom you want to drop, or can we get back to work now?"

Marshall's hand fell from his jaw, and he gave a slow grin. "Naw. I'm good."

"Good, because I'd like to get done before next winter. Besides..." I paused, waiting for the curiosity to build in his face. "Meg's coming over this afternoon, and I wanted to get a shower before she gets here."

Meg

I HELD THE PHONE to my ear, bracing myself for a conversation that was taking a much more difficult turn than it should have. "He's not getting any better, Meg," John's voice crackled over the line. "Why do we keep throwing money at this?"

I pinched the bridge of my nose, fighting frustration. "He *is* progressing, John. It's just... not in the way you expect."

"Progress? He got kicked out of speech therapy. What kind of progress is that?"

I squeezed my eyes shut, trying to find the right words. "It's not about the therapy. It's about him learning to communicate, to express himself. There's more to it than just speaking."

"Yeah, apparently hitting is on the menu, too. Look, I agreed to split the costs of anything the state wouldn't cover, but this... it's pointless. If it was going to help, we'd have seen something by now."

"I *have* seen things. You would have, too, if..." I bit back the rest of the words.

"Oh, so now it's my fault for leaving? You know, this is *exactly* why I left. I couldn't take him being out of control and you always making excuses."

I swallowed and leaned against the refrigerator. "I'm an educator, John. Not to rub it in, but I've been trained in things you haven't."

"You're a waitress, Meg. What, you thought I wouldn't hear about your little moonlighting gig? You're out killing yourself to make all this work."

I ground my teeth. "Someone has to step in the gap."

"And who's watching him while you're working? How much are you paying for that? Come on, this is pointless. You always said he needed stability, but now you're dumping him with a babysitter every night?"

"She's someone he knows from his therapy program, and it's not every night," I retorted hotly. "And even after I pay her, it's still worth it for what I make in tips. Look, John, I'm doing everything I can. That should prove to you that I'm not asking for something I don't believe in myself. All I'm asking is that you don't cut off your half of the speech therapy. I'll find a way to get him back on the schedule."

John sighed. "I'm not there, Meg. I don't see this 'progress.' If you think it's worth it, fine, but I think you're just causing yourself more headaches."

His words stung. Not because of the bitter tone but because he sounded like he just didn't care what I did. Shouldn't he care, at least a little? "I know him, John. I see the changes, the growth. It's there, even if it's not always obvious."

There was a pause on the other end, then, "Do what you think is best. I just... I don't know. If you can get him back on the schedule, I'll keep sending them a check for six more months, but if by the end of that, you can't put him on the phone and expect him to hold a normal conversation—"

"*That's* your measurement?" I scoffed in dismay. "You know he hates the phone. He converses just fine if you're face to face."

"No, he doesn't. He rambles on about random crap, he won't look you in the eye, he has absolutely zero context for social cues. He still stammers sometimes! You call that 'fine'?"

I set my teeth. "Well, then maybe you should come out here and see him yourself. He's still your son, you know, and you haven't seen him in over a year. You could come out for Christmas break, and—"

"Meg..." He hissed into the receiver.

"What?" I felt a prickle run up my spine. This was a different tone of voice, and one that never came with good things.

"I'm... I'm getting married. It's set for December 18."

I heard his words, but I didn't actually *hear* them, as he was speaking them. They echoed, cold and hollow, until I wasn't sure if I was standing up or sitting down. I felt vaguely around with my hand and braced it on the counter beside the fridge.

"Meg. Say something."

I shook my head. "What am I supposed to say? Congratulations? That's a little much to ask."

"I'm not asking for that, but I need you to be okay with this. I'm moving on. We talked about this—I'm not coming back, and you said you understood."

"Oh, I do. I understand perfectly. And you know what? I'm not bitter about losing you for myself. I'm *not*. You can divorce me and find another wife, and I'm just fine with that. But you're still the father of my son, and a piece of paper doesn't make that go away."

He blew out another sigh into the phone, and I could almost see him rolling his eyes and shaking his head. "Look, I have to go. Bye, Meg."

The line went dead. I kept listening for a few seconds, stared at it for several more, then tossed it on the kitchen counter.

I should probably be crying. I should probably pick up the phone again and beg him to reconsider, to fight for our family. Or, at least, I should want to fight for my son's father.

But what was the point? Even if I managed to force John to come back, maybe live in the same town again so he could see our son, it wouldn't fix anything. He'd still be distant. Still wouldn't understand how to talk to Dustin, or even want to. So why should I make everyone miserable? Much as I hated it... maybe we were all better off this way.

Besides, there was no point in making my mascara run or my eyes puffy. Evan had asked us to dinner out at the ranch, and that sounded a lot more appealing than crying alone in my kitchen.

I HAD PLANNED TO leave on time, but things didn't work out that way. It was always a gamble, and today, I lost. If I started moving toward the car too soon and Dustin came right away, I'd be obnoxiously early for dinner and I'd feel like I had to drive around town for half an hour before actually going where we were supposed to. But if he decided to be more stubborn than usual, we'd end up an hour late... like we were right now.

"Dustin," I repeated, trying to keep my voice calm, "we need to go to Evan's for dinner. Remember, we talked about it? You said you wanted to go to the ranch again."

Dustin sat on his bed, his knees bunched to his chest as he continued to shake his head. "But I just went there, and I d..." He gulped on the word. "Don't w-want to work."

I knelt down beside him. "It's okay, sweetheart. Evan's ranch is fun, and we'll see horses. You like the ranch. You don't have to do therapy or work. It's just for fun."

Dustin started shaking his head. Maybe that was the problem— "fun" sounded too unstructured, too nebulous. What other kids found enjoyable was stressful to him because he couldn't control it. He made two fists and began to bang them together, a self-soothing behavior I hadn't seen for a while, and let out a high-pitched noise of frustration.

That had sure escalated quickly. What was this all of a sudden? Was there some other trigger I'd missed? I tried to remain patient because pushing too hard would only make things worse, but it was tough when I wanted to go so badly. "Come on, Dustin. Let's get in the car, and we'll take your iPad with us. You can watch your favorite videos."

He shook his head. I should have known the iPad wouldn't work. Tears welled up in his eyes as he continued to vocalize his frustration, some of his words unintelligible.

The clock on the wall continued to tick away, and my anxiety grew. We were running out of time, and Evan was expecting us. I was going to have to cancel, and I really... *really* didn't want to do that. I'd already texted him twice that we were running late. He'd offered to come to us instead, but I hoped it wouldn't come to that. I couldn't explain why, but I ached to accept Evan's invitation to see a bit of his world, and I had to fight back a sensation of near-panic because it looked like it wasn't going to work out tonight.

After an hour, I excused myself to go have a quiet fume in the living room. Of all the nights for this to happen! A childish, bitter part of me tried to whisper that I'd already lost one man because of my son, and I was about to miss out on my second chance, too. But even as the tears leaked between my fingers, the sensible part of me tried to rally.

Evan wasn't John. He didn't owe us anything, and he wasn't reaching out because he had to, but because he wanted to. He knew what he was getting into, and he didn't spook that easily... I hoped. I closed my eyes and repeated that to myself before I picked up the phone to call off the evening.

That was when I heard the click of Dustin's door. I turned around and saw him, hunched and hesitant, as he shuffled into the living room. I lowered my phone.

"Are you ready to go?"

His eyes shifted to the door, then back at the floor as he nodded.

I blew out a sigh. Well... hopefully, Evan wouldn't mind it if we still came.

E VAN WAS WAITING IN the driveway, holding some kind of file folder, and he came over to open my door for me. I offered him an apologetic smile as I stepped out of the car. "Hey, Meg," he said softly. "Is everything okay?"

I nodded, hoping he didn't notice that my eyes were still puffy from frustration. "Yeah, just a tough day. I still don't know what started it. I'm so sorry."

"Don't be. I was late getting cleaned up anyway." Evan glanced at Dustin, but he didn't kneel down and try to wheedle him like most people do. He just kept his distance, respecting Dustin's space, and acknowledged him. "Hey there, bud. You can come inside if you want to. Take your time, okay?"

Dustin looked at Evan briefly, his eyes flickering with uncertainty, before he turned away, his attention drawn to the pebbles on the ground. The car door was open, but he hadn't decided to step out yet.

Evan's hand found its way to the small of my back, and it was like some of the tension drained from me at his touch. I smiled at him. "Thanks," I murmured.

"Hey. It's okay." He tipped his head toward the house. "Meryl just put dinner in the fridge. Nothing fancy. Corn on the cob and barbecued chicken. Are you hungry?"

I sighed. "Famished. I'm so sorry you guys had to wait for us. Really, it would have been fine if—"

He held up a hand. "It's okay, Meg. Look at them." He gestured to the front porch, where Blake and Meryl were rocking away in the swing, swatting at the evening bugs and talking in low voices. Meryl smiled and waved when I looked her way, and Blake tipped his hat to me.

"Do they look impatient to you?"

I chuckled and shook my head. "They look like it would take a natural disaster to unsettle them."

"Well, let's not try to make one. Dustin?" Evan asked, lowering his head a little to meet Dustin's eye inside the car. "I've got something for you that I thought you might like." He laid the folder on the car seat beside Dustin. "You were asking the other day about pictures of Biz. Here's everything I have—including a..." I saw Evan hesitate. "...A sketch of him. You might find it useful for your carving."

Dustin didn't look up, but he swallowed, and his features softened. That, there, was the evidence I needed to see that he was starting to relax. Soon, he'd be wanting to explore the pages, but not until we left him alone.

Evan seemed to realize the same thing. "We're going to be right over there on the porch. We won't leave your sight, so you know right where we are. Come on and join us when you're ready, okay? Meryl made you your own pot of spaghetti, just like your mom makes it, so I think you'll like it."

I looked at him as he straightened. "You got Meryl to make him a special meal?"

"She asked. I told her what brand of sauce I'd seen at your house." He shrugged. "Hope it's good enough."

I smiled. Could this cowboy get any sweeter? "Thank you again," I mouthed.

Evan just grinned back. "Come on. I see Meryl's already gone in to fetch dinner, so I'll go help her, and you can get comfortable. Ready?" He held out his hand, and I took it—probably smiling like a star-struck goofball.

"Yeah," I murmured. "I'm ready."

Chapter Fourteen

Evan

"ALRIGHT, BUDDY, THIS IS June Bug," I said. Dustin's eyes fixed on the saddled horse, doubt, and uncertainty creasing his young face. He shifted on his feet, his hands clutching the reins I passed him. He'd spent the first forty-five minutes of the evening in the car, and we'd seen him shuffling through the pictures I gave him. Then, about half an hour ago, he'd come out and asked if he could go down to the barn. A visit to the barn had quickly turned into a sunset ride, and Dustin had been eager and excited until I presented him with the horse I had for him.

"She's not Biz," Dustin replied. "I only like riding Biz."

I crouched down to Dustin's eye level, my gaze meeting his. "You're absolutely right, Dustin. June Bug isn't Biz, but you know what? She's pretty special in her own way. Did you know that she knows her way home from anywhere in the woods? One time, she led a whole string of pack horses to safety when they got separated from the rest. And riding her is the only way I can take you out to the field where all the mares and foals are."

"But I saw... saw an ATV," he objected. "You can drive me in that."

"Well, sure," I agreed. "Except those new baby horses don't know what to do with a loud engine like that in their field. The mares would be fine, but you don't want to spook the babies, do you? It's hard to get up close to them like that."

His eyes dropped, and he made a nervous gesture with his hands. "Is she f-fast?"

"June is one of the horses we pack supplies on when we go up in the hills. She's as gentle and steady as they come, and she'll do exactly what I ask her to do. Let's take it slow, okay? Just like you do with Biz. You can have the reins, but just to be safe, I'll be holding a lead rope the whole time."

Dustin looked at June Bug, then back at me, still not entirely convinced. "What if I d—" He swallowed. "Don't like it? What if... if she's not nice?"

I squatted a little to bring myself to eye level. "You don't have to do anything you don't want to do. If you don't like it or if you're not comfortable, you can tell me, and we'll stop. No pressure, okay? It's your choice."

Dustin considered this for a moment, his uncertainty slowly giving way to a tentative willingness. "Okay," he finally replied, his doubt still lingering but with a bit more openness. It wasn't the enthusiastic response I had hoped for, but it was a start.

I nodded and offered a warm smile. "That's the spirit. We'll go at your pace, and if you ever want to stop or get off, just let me know. We're a team, remember?"

Dustin nodded. "Okay."

"Okay." I helped him on, then turned around to check on Meg. I'd asked Dusty if Meg could borrow Duchess, his gray mare, because I wanted a gentle mount with smooth gaits. Duchess was carrying a foal herself, so Dusty had quit training hard on her, but she still enjoyed getting out to stretch her legs.

"Ready?" I asked.

Meg's mouth moved like she was trying to say yes, but no words came out. She just blinked—was she trying not to cry?—and gave me a brave smile. I stepped closer, checking her tack and making sure the stirrups were adjusted right for her. "Are you comfortable?"

Meg took a deep breath. "It's been a while since I was on a horse—probably since I was about seventeen. Kelli's right—it's kind of like riding a bike. I'm probably pretty rusty, but it feels good to be back in the saddle."

I patted Duchess's neck, then stepped away to scoop up the lead rope for Dustin's horse and grab the reins for that young ranch horse I'd been training. "We'll just take it easy. We should have time to get back before the sun sets."

We rode at a leisurely pace, the horses' hooves muffled by the soft earth beneath them. The ranch stretched out around us, bathed in the warm hues of the setting sun. I pointed out landmarks and areas of the ranch, explaining a bit about our operations. Meg listened, her eyes scanning the landscape with genuine interest.

As the evening painted the sky with shades of orange and pink, we reached the area where the broodmare band grazed. The mares lifted their heads as we approached, watching us with mild curiosity. "They're beautiful," Meg said, her gaze lingering on a mare nuzzling her foal. There was a softness in her voice that echoed the tenderness of the scene before us.

Dustin's eyes lit up with excitement as he took in the sight. "Baby horses, Mom!"

Meg gave an expansive sigh, her admiring gaze wandering over that handsome herd of young stock. "Yes, lots of them. They're so playful!"

"Do they have names?" he asked.

I shook my head. "No. We don't usually name them until we bring them in as weanlings and start handling them more. They're papered stock, and I already sent off for registered names on all of them, but a horse's official name and what he's called around the barn are often different things. It's nice to get to know them a little before you hang a name on them."

Dustin's brow clouded. "But my mom didn't know me before she named me, and she named me just fine."

Meg and I both chuckled quietly. "It's different with people, isn't it?" I asked. "I guess if you want to know, I did name one colt—the one that's Biz's nephew. Think you can pick him out?"

Dustin didn't have to scan the herd. He never even hesitated. "That one. The palomino one that's looking at us."

"Spot on! How'd you guess it so easily?"

Dustin made an exaggerated shrugging motion. "Well, I just thought he looked like Biz."

"Yeah," I agreed softly. "He kind of does. I decided to call him Forge. What do you think?"

Dustin wrinkled his brow. "Like you make horseshoes in?" He frowned and thought about it. "It's okay, I guess."

"Glad to hear you approve," I said dryly.

Meg leaned a little closer to my horse with a low voice. "He doesn't care too much about names. To him, it's just a handle. He didn't mean any offense."

I tipped my face so she could see my eyes under the brim of my hat. "Meg, it's okay. You don't have to apologize for him."

There was a fine line between her eyes, and she fought for a smile, but couldn't quite make it. "It's just that eventually, everyone gets exasperated by him somehow."

"And you think I'm next?"

She closed her eyes, drawing her lower lip between her teeth, then cleared her throat. "So, Forge, is it? Will he be your ranch horse when he grows up?"

That was a pretty rapid change of subject, and it told me a lot more than she probably meant to let on. I just shifted in the saddle. "No, I think Forge is destined for something greater. Cody will add him to the show string, and with any luck, he'll be as famous as his daddy someday. But we'll just have to wait and see, won't we?"

"Yes," she whispered, her eyes fixed on my face. "I guess so."

"Can I pet him?" Dustin asked.

I turned and nodded. "Of course, Dustin. Just walk up to him slowly and be careful. Babies are unpredictable."

Dustin rode his horse closer to the herd, making straight for Forge. The colt struck a pose—head high, snorting at the air, then approached them with a springing trot. After a moment's hesitation, he nuzzled Dustin's outstretched hand. Dustin's eyes sparkled with delight as he gently stroked Forge's soft muzzle.

"That's pretty good," I said. "I haven't even petted him in the pasture. Last time I handled him was when we brought all the mares into the corrals for hoof trims."

Dustin was petting the colt's little tuft of white forelock, then he let out a yelp. "Ouch! He bit my boot!" With a sudden burst of energy, Forge wheeled around, kicking at the air before darting off.

I probably shouldn't have laughed, but at least I kept it quiet.

We continued our ride, the fading light lending an enchanting quality to the rolling fields I loved. Meg's eyes sparkled, and I couldn't help but admire her against the backdrop of the serene landscape. She looked more peaceful here than I had ever seen—like the brittle edges honed by fighting battles every day had not precisely vanished, but found a purpose. The soft, golden rays of the setting sun cast a warm glow on her features, highlighting the genuine wonder in her expression. It was as if she had found a piece of her past that had been long forgotten, and it resonated with the present moment in a beautiful way.

It made me wonder for a moment what she'd been like, back before life knocked her around. What hobbies had she loved? Who was Meg...? I didn't even know her maiden name. But I had a powerful hankering to find out.

"What's that over there?" Meg asked, pointing.

I followed her finger to the lone house sitting quietly amidst the fields. A lump formed in my throat, and for a moment, I hesitated. "That's... that's my house," I admitted. It felt strange acknowledging it out loud, especially to Meg.

"Your house?" Her voice was soft. "I didn't realize you had a separate house on the ranch."

"I don't, not really. Not anymore," I said, the words tumbling out. "I built it with Anne, but I haven't stayed there since..."

Meg nodded, her expression softening with understanding. "Do you want to ride closer? Or, we could walk the other way, if you prefer."

The offer hung between us, and a part of me wanted to show her the place that had been my home. But the thought of walking through those rooms, filled with memories and ghosts of a life that was no longer mine, made me uncomfortable. "It's fine. You don't need to see it. There's nothing much there anyway," I said, trying to keep my voice steady.

"Okay," she said simply, giving me a reassuring smile. "I understand."

Relief washed over me, mingling with a pang of something else—regret, maybe, or just the ever-present weight of the past. We turned our horses around and headed back, the quiet comfort of the ride giving me space to think, to feel. Meg rode beside me, her presence a gentle reminder that life was still moving forward, even if I wasn't quite ready to leave everything behind.

Meg

THE PHONE BUZZED ON the kitchen counter, interrupting the lesson plan I was writing out for my tutoring student. Evan's name lit up the screen, bringing an instant smile to my face. We'd been seeing each other every few days for the last couple of weeks, each encounter easy and relaxed, like the unfolding of a long, comfortable conversation. Today, we'd planned to pick up burgers on the way to Dustin's therapy session at White Pines, and Evan was going to stay and watch with me. I picked up, eager to hear his voice.

"Hey, Meg." Evan sounded apologetic. "I've got some news."

I leaned against the counter, a flicker of concern sparking within me. "Everything okay?"

"Yeah, it's just... I have to cancel our lunch today. The trusses for Marshall and Kelli's new house are being delivered earlier than expected, and Marshall needs me there to meet the driver. He's thirty miles away, and won't be back in time."

I felt a twinge of disappointment, but I smothered it quickly. There would be another time. "That's alright. These things happen."

There was a pause on the other end. "I really didn't want to let Dustin down."

I chuckled softly. "Honestly, Evan, Dustin probably doesn't like having an audience for his therapy sessions anyway. It's fine, really."

"I'll make it up to you," he promised earnestly.

The words slipped out before I could think. "Oh? How about taking me dancing then?" I teased, half-joking.

There was a moment of silence, and I imagined him gawking and maybe choking on the other end of the line. "Dancing?" he finally said. "Really?"

A blush crept up my cheeks. "I was just kidding. But I used to go swing dancing quite a bit. I loved it."

"You did?" He was quiet again for several seconds. "Well then, it's a date. I'll take you dancing at the tavern tonight. No promises that I won't step on your toes."

My heart did a little somersault. Dancing with Evan? Really? The thought sent a flutter of anticipation through me. "Oh, don't worry about my toes. I've got more."

There was a low chuckle from his end. "That's good to know. I'll pick you up at seven?"

"Perfect. See you then." I hung up, grinning like a little girl. *Dancing with Evan.* This was going to be interesting.

I STOOD IN FRONT of the mirror, the red flowy dress clinging to me like a second skin. I'd lost count of how many
times I'd taken it off, only to slip back into it again. The
dress, a relic from a time when I danced more and worried
less, seemed out of place in my current life. I wasn't even
sure why I still had it in the closet, but... oh, I did used to
love dancing in it. Its lightweight fabric twirled effortlessly
around my legs, making me feel light and flirty. Was I too
old to care about such things?

I studied my reflection with pursed lips. No... I couldn't do
it. It was just too much, and Evan might think... well, I wasn't
sure what he would think, but it was too soon for it, whatever
it would be.

As I reached for the zipper, a knock on the door startled
me. I guess that settled it. I was wearing the dress.

I opened the door to find Evan standing there, his usual
calm smile in place. But as his gaze fell on me, something
shifted. His eyes widened, and I caught the faintest hitch in
his breath. In all the time I'd known him, he'd never shown
this much unguarded emotion.

His smile grew, slow and genuine, transforming his entire
demeanor. "Meg, you look... incredible," he said, his voice
filled with an awe that sent a warm flush across my cheeks.

"Thank you, Evan," I managed, my voice steadier than I
felt. "Shall we go?"

"What about Dustin?"

I crooked a finger and led him silently down the hall, then
pushed open Dustin's unlatched door. Missy was standing
over my son's shoulder as he babbled an endless stream
of words, describing how he was going to transform that
huge block of sugar maple wood into the most magnificent
sculpture she'd ever seen. The poor girl's eyes were probably
about to glaze over.

"He's not moving for the rest of the evening," I whispered.

"Doesn't look that way," Evan murmured back. I glanced up at him, and only then did I realize that he had bridged an arm across the bedroom doorway and was leaning over my shoulder so closely that I was almost wrapped in his arms. I could feel the heat of his body through that thin dress, and that lazy, cowboy smile of his was almost close enough to kiss.

His eyes dropped to mine an instant after that realization struck me, and something in him stiffened. "Well?" He stepped back and crooked his arm for me to take, like an old-style gentleman. "Ready, Meg?"

I smiled as I took his arm. "Yeah. Let's go, cowboy."

T HE JUKEBOX BLARED JOHN Denver's "Thank God I'm a Country Boy," setting a lively rhythm that brought boots to the dance floor. Evan and I joined about six other couples—most of them about ten years younger than us—as they stomped and twirled around to the silly old song. We were less lively and tended to get lost in the center of the floor as everyone else swarmed the edges.

Evan's hand tentatively grasped mine as the other rested lightly on my waist. "Okay, I think I've got this," he said with a cautious grin, his eyes fixed on our intertwined hands.

"Just follow the beat and enjoy. Dancing is easier if you don't think too hard."

"Must be why they sell so much beer," he muttered.

I laughed. "Breathe, Evan. I don't think I'm strong enough to drag you off the floor if you pass out."

He nodded, not even cracking a smile at my joke, and attempted a basic step. It was a bit stiff, but he managed to keep in time with the music. Mostly. I matched his movements, letting him lead. As the song picked up, he started to relax, a genuine smile replacing his grim concentration.

"Ready to try a turn?" I asked as the tempo started to sweep us along with it.

"Sure, but fair warning, I might mess this up." As the final chorus hit, he gave a gentle push, signaling me to turn. I spun under his arm, feeling the skirt of my red flowy dress flare out. Evan's timing was slightly off, causing a minor stumble, but we found our rhythm again.

"Sorry about that."

"No harm done," I laughed, patting his chest playfully. "You're doing great."

He smiled, a hint of relief in his eyes. "Thanks. I'm actually enjoying this."

"Could've fooled me. No one's watching us, Evan."

He glanced over his shoulder as if to verify my words. "It's not that. I was just never much good at this. Don't like being center stage, you know?"

I thinned my lips and nodded. "I know. You like being in the background—the guy who makes things happen without much fuss or fanfare, while others get the limelight."

A slow turn appeared at the corner of his mouth. "You got me pegged, alright."

"But don't you see how you really are center stage? You may feel like you're just quietly going along, getting things done, but you're the one guy everyone would miss like crazy if suddenly you weren't there anymore. You're the one lots of people don't even notice until they realize you're the one who keeps it all together."

His gaze narrowed, and a crease appeared in his brow as he blinked at me. His chest rose, and his hand on my waist tightened.

"Evan, I'm sorry, I didn't—"

He shook his head. "It's nothing. Just..." He wetted his lips and took a breath. "You're not the first person to say that to me."

I closed my eyes. "Oh." That was the last thing I'd wanted. This cloud was hanging over us—the elephant in the room. I couldn't replace his wife—I don't think either of us wanted that, anyway—but how was I supposed to fit with him when half the things I said reminded him of her? What were we supposed to do with that?

"Meg, it's okay," he said softly.

I opened my eyes and found his staring intently into my own. "What is?"

"I mean, you don't have to get spooked off just because you happen to notice the same things as... I'm sorry. Maybe I shouldn't have said that. I didn't mean to make you think..." His shoulders sagged, and our step had slowed from a lively swing to an almost stationary slow waltz.

"I'm not sure what to think, Evan," I whispered. "I can't tell what you feel when things like this come up. Should I not say them? And how am I supposed to know what they are before they come out of my mouth?"

"You can't. And I don't want you to." Evan lifted his gaze across the room, and a little kink appeared at the corner of his mouth. "See that young couple over there?"

I twisted to look over my shoulder, and Evan obliged by turning us both so I could see them better. "The ones who can't stop staring at each other?"

He chuckled. "Yeah. I remember that feeling."

"Me too," I murmured. "A lifetime ago."

He tightened his grip around my waist, pulling my focus back to him. "I still feel like that. When I look at you."

I felt my forehead crease and my heart kick into another gear. "You do?"

"But it's more now. I've felt deeper things since I was a dumb kid. I can't unfeel all that, and I bet you can't, either."

I shook my head, and my lips quivered a little as something stung in the corner of my eye.

"I guess what I'm saying is..." He screwed up his mouth, his gaze turned inward as he led me through a few more slow steps. "You say whatever you want. I like it. I like being reminded that..." He chewed on his cheek. "That someone else gets it. That you get *me*... And... oh, blast, I'm saying it all wrong, aren't I?"

I shook my head and sniffed. "I think you're saying it just right, Evan."

He let go a breath and lifted his hand to brush my cheek with his thumb. "I didn't mean to make you cry."

I laughed and dashed the rest of it away. "You know what, cowboy? Maybe we should leave the dance floor to the ones who want to really cut a rug. I think I'd rather just watch with you."

Evan smiled and pulled me closer into a tender slow dance while everyone else was bouncing to something with a heavy beat. "Nah. I'm enjoying myself too much to clear out. They can just dance around us."

Chapter Fifteen

Evan

I T WAS THE SECOND week of August, and in our town, that meant one thing: the county fair.

I hadn't missed a year since I was in plastic pants—even those years when I had to come alone. It might not have been my idea, but I always got dragged out for some reason or other.

Two years ago, Dad and I just came together for the Friday night rodeo. We sat behind his buddy in the announcer's booth, watched the rough stock events, and went home. His idea to get us both away from the ranch and out among other humans for a few hours, I guess. Then, last year, Cody wrangled all of us so we could make a show of support for Morgan at the White Pines booth.

But this year, for the first time in a while, it had been *my* idea to come back. And I'd invited Meg to come with me.

As we walked through the gates, I couldn't help but feel a surge of nostalgia. The fair had always been a highlight for me, a symbol of the close-knit community we had here. It was a time when the agricultural roots of our town were celebrated, where farmers and ranchers came together, and the whole community got involved. I loved the fair for what it meant—a celebration of hard work, family, and community spirit.

The sights and sounds of the fairgrounds were a lively mix of colors, music, and the chatter of people. It was an atmosphere that brought back memories of my own childhood, and of walking these same grounds with my Anne by my side and Emma on my shoulders. I thought I'd be a lot more emotional when those memories slammed into me, but I weathered it okay.

Now, walking here with Meg and Dustin, I felt a new kind of joy. The idea of sharing this part of my world with them, seeing the fair through their eyes, gave me a sense of anticipation I hadn't felt in years. I wanted them to experience the best of what this day could offer, to create new memories here together.

But Meg's smile was starting to fade rapidly. "I'm not sure this is such a good idea," she murmured in my ear. "I've never brought him to the fair... for... reasons."

I tucked her hand into mine and glanced down at Dustin. He walked just behind us, his fists banging together rhythmically, humming to himself. She'd told me it was his way of coping with the sensory overload. "Do you want to leave?"

Her teeth sank into her lip as she watched her son. We'd stopped to watch a guy swing a big hammer and ring the bell, and when he struck it with a loud clang, Dustin flinched and covered his ears. But he didn't do much more than that.

"I think he's okay for now," Meg said slowly. "But sometimes there's no warning before a little becomes way too much."

"You'll have to tell me," I said. "We can leave if you think it's best."

Meg shook her head and squeezed my hand. "I'm trying to just relax and let life happen around him. I can't keep him in a bubble forever. So, I'm going to just smile for now. See?" She bared her teeth in a grin that looked more like a grimace.

I chuckled and touched her cheek with my free hand. "You're supposed to breathe."

"Is that how you do that?" Her smile warmed under my fingertips, and for a few seconds, I'm pretty sure my heart stopped.

And that right there was the answer I'd been looking for. Yes, it *was* possible for lightning to strike twice. And I'd just been electrocuted.

Meg's pupils had dilated, even in the midday sun, and I saw her throat bob. Her lips parted, and she drew another deep breath, her eyes still locked with mine.

Whatever this was... or could be... now wasn't the time for it. Dustin was weaving from one foot to the other, his humming picking up tempo as he wheeled about, then covered his nose with his t-shirt at the assault of exotic aromas from the food row. "Ew!" he cried, ducking his head and trying to turn away from the smell. So, we walked the other way for a bit.

A magician was walking along the pathway, drawing a small crowd as he performed tricks with counting cards and disappearing coins. Dustin watched, fascinated, as the magician pulled a seemingly endless scarf from his hat. "How does he do that?" he demanded. It was not a rhetorical question, and he was not going to take "magic" for an answer, so we stood there for fifteen minutes as Dustin stared, trying to work out the secret.

After a while, Meg pulled him away to an informative booth on honeybees, where I explained to Dustin the importance of bees in ranching. "We wouldn't have grain for the horses or seed to plant for hay if..." but he wasn't listening to that. It was just too big, too nebulous. I tried a visual a little more concrete and picked up a display apple they had at the booth. "You know that tree we have in the back yard at the ranch? You and Lizzy were climbing on it at Dusty's wedding."

He nodded.

"Well, that tree can't make apples like this without bees in the spring. They kiss the flowers so they can make fruit."

Dustin's humming stopped as he marveled at the apple. "I'm going to keep this," he announced.

"Well, it's not ours to keep," I explained. "That's here for other kids to—"

"I'm keeping it!" And he took a big bite out of it.

"Dustin!" Meg began in a dangerous tone, but the lady at the booth interrupted her.

"Oh, that's okay! We have lots more. He's welcome to keep it. They're good, aren't they? Would the rest of you like one, too?"

From the corner of my eye, I saw Meg gritting her teeth, but she just thanked the lady and took me by the elbow. "Let's go," she whispered. Once we'd gotten a few steps away, she slowed and glanced back.

"That was real nice of her," I observed.

She let go a sigh. "It was. I know she was just trying to be helpful, but sometimes it doesn't *help* when people do stuff like that. He needs to hear 'no' once in while, just like every kid, but it takes longer to get through to him. And when people see it and think I'm losing the argument, they just step in. I think they're trying to keep me from losing face or keep from having to watch a public screaming match... I don't know. But it didn't help."

"Is there something I could have done?"

Her eyes widened, searching mine. "Well... No! I mean... I don't think... you can't just jump in. Not with Dustin."

"I know that. I'm not asking that. I'm asking how I earn the right to help you instead of just standing back to watch."

She blinked, then clapped a hand over her mouth as her eyes clouded.

"Meg? Are you okay?"

She shook her head.

I pulled her fingers from her mouth and just cupped her hand. "Let's talk about this later, okay?"

She sucked in a breath and nodded. "Okay."

I dropped my hand, and Meg cleared her throat, tucking a lock of hair behind her ear. I offered a tight smile. "Uh... Hungry?"

"I thought you'd never ask. Hmm... Dustin likes..." She winced. "Maybe he'll just want the apple he stole. I probably shouldn't have let him keep it, but at least he's getting food into him that he'll eat. We can get something else for ourselves, though. Turkey drumsticks?"

"Lead the way." I caught her hand again as we wandered down the row, the food stalls selling everything from cotton candy to barbecued ribs, the game booths with their enticing prizes, and the laughter of children running around. Meg was still casting worried glances at Dustin, then looking guiltily away whenever she saw me noticing the direction of her gaze. I hated that.

Not that she was worried for her son—I'd have expected no less. But I didn't like that she seemed to feel like she was doing something wrong by watching him. Like she expected me to get tired of it, or demand all her attention for myself. How could I tell her that was the furthest thing from my mind?

I guess I could see why she'd fear that. She'd told me about John—why he left, why he was never coming back—but hang it all, I'd spent a lifetime rolling along with the unpredictable. With the "not quite" and the "almost" and the "maybe next year". That was just life on a ranch. This wasn't really any different, and to be honest, I was a lot more worried about whether she could put up with *my* world than I was about stepping into hers.

But there just didn't seem to be words to prove it, so I just put my hand on the small of her back and nodded. She sent me a nervous glance, then a heavy sigh left her—a breath she'd been holding for too long. "Okay?" I murmured.

She leaned into my shoulder, and I let my arm drape around her a little snugger. "Better than okay," she whispered back.

Dustin couldn't take the smells from the food row, and I wasn't all that hungry. Meg said she'd rather have ice cream anyway, and I knew just where to get it. I steered them both toward the livestock barns, where Dustin's humming subsided as he became engrossed in the sights of various animals. This was where we should have started out. His eyes widened with wonder at each new pen we passed.

"Here we are," I announced at last. "The dairy club, led by none other than... well, I guess she's my step-mom." I poked my head in the ice cream shack and found Meryl bent over a cooler, helping one of her clubbers learn to use the electric ice cream maker.

"Hey, Meryl," I called through the window.

She straightened and turned around. "Evan, Meg, Dustin!" Meryl greeted us with a warm smile. "You guys look like Fudge Sundae lovers."

"Nailed it," Meg laughed as she pulled out her wallet. "Three, please?"

Meryl moved to the cash register, dragging one of her little cloverbud kids over to teach her how to make change. Meg was counting her cash, but I beat her to it and laid a bill on the counter. "Keep the change for the club," I told her.

Meryl reached through the window and patted my cheek like I'd seen her do to Luke when she was teasing him. "Bless you, Evan. Did you see we won the herdsmanship award again this year?"

"When have you ever lost?" I put my wallet away, catching Meg's grateful smile.

"Once!" Meryl laughed. "And if you want to know, it was Morgan's senior year. I won't say who it was, but '*someone*' forgot to clean their stall the morning of judging."

"No prizes for guessing, huh?" I chuckled as we took our ice creams.

Meg checked her watch. "Speaking of Morgan, it's almost time for her presentation at the White Pines exhibit. We should head over."

"You should," Meryl agreed. "She talked the fair board into letting her bring a therapy horse this year for public relations, so guess who she brought?"

"Now that one, I can guess for sure," I replied. "Dustin won't want to miss Biz. Right, Dustin?"

The kid slurped up a chocolatey banana, smearing fudge all over his face. "Right."

I heard Meg's breath sucking into her lungs, but she just gave me a tight smile. "Well, cowboy? Let's go."

Meg

A S WE EDGED CLOSER to the White Pines booth, the
buzz of the fair seemed to crescendo. Morgan had a
captivated audience crowding the bleachers, and she was
just beginning her presentation. I could see Dustin's unease
growing amidst the crowd's excitement, his hands taking up
their rhythmic tapping once more, his gaze low and evasive
as he ducked around the crowd.

But he paused for a moment when Morgan's familiar voice
cut through the background noise as she launched into her
speech. She started by welcoming everyone to the fair and
thanking them for giving her a moment of their time. "At
White Pines, we believe in the healing power of connection,"
she began, her eyes scanning the crowd, alighting on familiar
and new faces alike. "That's why we are so lucky to have with
us here today one of our most popular therapy horses—Biz,
the equine ambassador of our program."

I swear that cheesy gelding picked up his head and twirled
his ears when he felt people's gazes on him. And they say
horses don't understand English... Biz sure seemed to, and
he preened like a peacock when he heard his name. I heard
Evan laughing quietly as Morgan continued.

"I'll talk more about Biz in a minute, but first, I'd like you
to see a little of what we do at White Pines, all thanks to
our generous sponsors." She gestured towards a screen set
up beside her, where a video started playing. It showcased
different individuals at the therapy center, interacting with
horses, their faces alight with joy and triumph. The crowd
watched, visibly moved by the stories unfolding before them.

Finishing the video, Morgan shifted the focus to Biz, who
stood beside her, a gentle giant with a clownish way of

demanding her attention every time she looked away. She explained his journey, how he transitioned from being a competitive horse to a one-eyed therapy animal, his resilience a beacon of hope.

"With his loss, Biz gained an even greater ability to connect," Morgan told the crowd. "He's worked with wounded veterans, aiding their physical and emotional recovery, facilitated family and marriage therapy sessions, helped individuals with PTSD find peace, and even assisted in rehabilitation after surgery."

Her voice softened as she glanced at Dustin, now visibly more agitated by all the noise and attention. "And perhaps closest to my heart," she added, "he's become a voice for children with autism, helping them express themselves in ways they never could before."

As the crowd erupted into applause, cheers, and whistles, the sensory overload became too much for Dustin. His humming escalated into a distressed vocalization, his body language shifting from anxious to panicked. I saw the signs of his impending meltdown, my own heart rate spiking with concern for my son.

"Evan, we need to get out of here," I implored. But even as Evan turned to act, Dustin's behavior escalated.

Covering his ears and chucking his apple core at some lady's head, he made a beeline for the fence enclosing Biz. "No, Dustin, stop!" I cried out, but it was too late.

Morgan tried to defuse the situation, welcoming Dustin over in an attempt to calm him. But I couldn't stand it. The crowd's astonished stares bored into me.

"Dustin, come down this instant!" My son, however, was fixated on Biz, his hands gripping the fence as he tried to climb over.

Morgan, attempting to maintain calm, gently called out, "Dustin, it's okay, you can come over. Biz is here for everyone."

But I couldn't let it go that easily. I knew it was the wrong tactic—I *knew* it, but of all the times I've ever screwed up with him, I could usually stop myself before I drew a boundary I couldn't defend.

Not this time, though.

"Dustin, get down from there right now!" My tone was sharp, and my mind was scrambling for a consequence for when he refused.

The crowd watched in stunned silence, their eyes darting between Morgan, Dustin, and me. I felt their judgment, their curiosity, and it only fueled my frustration. "*Now*, Dustin."

He had hopped over the fence now and was clinging to Biz's neck, hiding his face in the horse's mane.

"Dustin!" I hissed. What was I going to do now? I'd chosen the battle, and I was losing fast.

"Dustin, listen to your mom," Evan interjected, his voice firm yet calm. And for the first time, I wasn't sure if I wanted him in the middle of this. He was trying to help, and so was Morgan, but they didn't get it! Dustin knew better. He *knew* better! We'd been working on this very sort of thing for how long? Morgan contradicting me and Evan escalating things wasn't going to help.

Dustin, predictably, was unyielding. "No! Biz is *my* horse! I won't go!" he shouted, his voice breaking.

Morgan kept trying to pacify the situation. "It's all right, Meg. Let's just let him be for a moment."

"No, Morgan!" I shot back, my patience wearing thin. "This is not the time for coddling. He needs to learn."

She drew back, her eyes wide, and held up her hands. "Okay, then."

"Dustin," I warned, "not this time. This is not the place."

Dustin's fingers tightened around Biz's mane, his knuckles white. The horse, surprisingly calm, nuzzled Dustin gently, but my son's agitation only grew. His body shook, a mix of fear, defiance, and overwhelming emotion coursing through him.

Evan had climbed over the fence and approached slowly, his movements cautious, almost hesitant. I could see him assessing the situation, weighing his options. There was a tenderness in his approach, a careful balance between authority and empathy. "Dustin," he called out softly, "it's time to let go, buddy."

But Dustin's response was immediate and frantic. "No! He's mine!" And then, it happened. Dustin kicked out, his foot swinging wildly in the air until it cracked Evan in the stomach. His other leg pushed against the fence as if trying to climb back out of the enclosure, dragging Biz with him.

Evan didn't hesitate. In one swift motion, he reached out, snagging Dustin by the waist. He pulled him back into a bear hug, pinning Dustin's arms to his side so he couldn't swing his fists.

"Okay, Dustin, let's ease up," he said... how *did* the man sound so calm? I was fuming and shaking in anger and humiliation, and I wasn't sure who I was more angry with—Dustin for acting out, Morgan or Evan for getting in the way... or myself. For letting it happen.

Dustin squirmed and shrieked in fury, his body twisting and turning, trying to break free. His arms flailed, his legs kicked, but Evan held him steady like he'd been wrestling things much bigger than Dustin most of his life. He probably had.

"I got him, Meg," Evan said, glancing over at me. "Let's get him somewhere quiet to *yee-ouch!*" Evan pried his hand out of my son's teeth with a grimace, and Dustin jumped the fence and sped away, arms pumping. I could hear him sobbing as he ran.

Evan looked at me, fear and hurt sickening his expression. "I'll take care of this. I'll bring him back."

My fists balled, and I was fighting back tears. "I think you've done enough."

His face blanched white, and he stepped closer. Dimly, I was aware of the crowd dispersing with mumbles and laughter at my son's expense. "Meg..."

"Just... don't. Don't, Evan." I crossed my arms and started to march away from him. "I'll go find him myself."

"Alone?" he called to my back.

"Meg," I heard Morgan pleading. "Just wait a minute. He can't have gone—"

"Stop!" I clapped my hands to my head in exasperation and turned to face them both as the tears washed down my face. "He can't just do whatever he wants, Morgan! He ruined your talk and refused to listen to me, and you were just going to let him do it! And you—" I sniffed and faced Evan. "You can't grab him. Not like that. You'll only push him further over the edge."

He bristled, and I swear, his shoulders got wider and taller. "You wanna tell me what I shoulda done? He was going to hurt someone—probably himself."

I folded my arms over my chest and tucked my face down to swipe at some tears. Evan wasn't wrong. I'd had to immobilize Dustin myself when things got dangerously out of hand, and for some reason, in that tight arm lock, the kid who usually didn't like being touched would relax like a baby in a blanket. But Evan hadn't done it right... or he should have let me... or *something*. I couldn't even rationalize what I was feeling.

"Just stop," I pleaded, my voice beginning to crack. "I'll go find him myself, and I guess..."

What? *"See you later?" "I'll come find you for cotton candy?"* That was all stupid. I couldn't remember the last time I'd felt such anger, humiliation, and disappointment all at once, unless you counted the day John left.

Evan and Morgan. They were staring blankly back at me, their eyes wide and mouths slightly agape in astonishment. Of all people, I had to snap at Evan and Morgan, the two people in town I'd learned I could lean on more than any others.

I didn't know what to say, so I shook my head and walked off, wiping the tears as I went.

Chapter Sixteen

Evan

"WELL?"

I spun around and glared at Morgan in annoyance. "Well, what?"

"Aren't you going to go after her?"

"You heard her. She doesn't want me to." I tugged my hat down a little farther and climbed out of Biz's enclosure.

"That's just what she said. What she *meant*—"

"Now, how is that fair? I'm supposed to hear one thing and understand it means something else?"

"Now you're getting it."

I rolled my eyes. "I'm not doing drama. I won't chase after that kind of madness."

"I'm not asking you to chase drama. I'm telling you to chase *her*, Evan."

I turned away, staring at the horse in the pen and clenching my jaw in thought. "She's just maxed out. I pushed too fast, assumed too much. She's right—I shouldn't have jumped in like that. Probably scared them both. Maybe in time..."

"The time is now."

I turned around. Morgan had pushed her ball cap a little higher on her head and was sucking on a straw—she was always drinking water these days, it seemed. "Just what're you saying?"

She waved her steel mug, the ice rattling around inside. "This a test, bud. Whether you know it or not, that's exactly what it is. So, are you going to pass or bail?"

I shook my head. "Meg's not the kind of woman to set a guy up like that. And if she is, I'd rather... well, she's not."

"*She* isn't, but life sure is. She needs someone who can be that tough guy beside her in *these* moments, without tucking his tail between his legs and choosing the easy way out. And *you*..." She dragged again on her water. "Well, you haven't smiled so much since I've known you. Cody always swore you had teeth, but I never believed him until this last month or so. She brings the life out in you."

I gestured toward the fair crowd. "If I go trotting after her now, with Dustin's hackles up and her at her wit's end, I'll just be stepping into a hornet's nest. Best to let it settle a bit and talk to her later. She's not ready for..." I let my arms drop and growled.

I scratched my chin, scuffed my boot heels on the pavement. Morgan just watched me, her lips puckered around her straw and her eyebrows raised.

"You sure she wants me to follow her?"

Morgan shrugged. "She will, once you find her."

"That doesn't make any sense. What if you're wrong? What if I go hot on her heels after her and make it worse?"

"What if she turns around, hoping to see you, and you don't show up?"

I blew out a sigh. "I sure hope you're right about this."

Morgan grinned and gave a little jerk on her ball cap. "Oh, don't worry. I am."

"WHERE *WOULDN'T* DUSTIN GO?" I muttered to myself as I paced the fairgrounds, trying to think like him. The noise and chaos of the midway were definitely out. He'd steer clear of that. The livestock barns were a possibility, but a quick pass through them revealed nothing but animals and a few scattered 4-H kids prepping for shows.

I headed over to the rodeo arena, its stands empty and quiet at this time of day. Scanning the area, I hoped to catch a glimpse of Meg or Dustin, but it was like looking for a needle in a haystack. Nothing. I let out a sigh and walked back past the honey bee stand, half wondering if Dustin might have circled back for another apple. No luck there either.

With a growing sense of unease, I finally made my way out to the parking lot. My truck sat there empty, the only familiar thing in a sea of vehicles. Meg's car was home, where she'd left it when I picked her up. So unless someone gave her a ride... "They're still here," I murmured to myself. Where could they be?

I retraced my steps, heading back toward the livestock barns. Something nudged me towards the dairy exhibit, a hunch or maybe just hope. I found myself walking faster as I approached the ice cream booth run by Meryl's club. She always had a knack for knowing things without being told, and right now, I was banking on that intuition.

As I approached, I saw her before she spotted me. Meryl was standing like a sentinel outside the ice cream booth. The window was shut with a sign in it that said "Back in 15 minutes," and Meryl was munching on a corn dog, her gaze scanning the meandering patches of fairgoers. She lifted her chin when she saw me, and I raised my brows in reply. She tilted her head, gesturing to the inside of the booth.

I looked inside, and there they were—Meg and Dustin, huddled against the thin plywood wall of the ice cream booth, sitting on the cool concrete floor. Meg was crouched down beside Dustin, her posture protective yet giving him space. He was curled up, his arms wrapped tightly around his knees, his head buried against them. The scene hit me hard, a mix of relief and heartache swirling inside me.

I went around to the door and gently pushed it open. "Meg?"

Meg looked up, her eyes red-rimmed but relieved. "Evan," she breathed out.

I slipped through the door slowly, glancing once at Meryl, who was blatantly "ignoring" us, then I crawled inside and crouched down beside Meg. Not too close to Dustin—not so close that I might scare him—but close enough to be there for them. "I've been looking everywhere," I said. "I should've known you'd end up back here."

Meg nodded, her hand reaching out to gently touch Dustin's back. "He just needed a quiet place. I didn't know where else to go."

"It's okay," I assured her, my gaze shifting to Dustin's tense form. "You found the perfect spot."

She rocked her head against my shoulder. "Evan, I'm sorry. I shouldn't have..."

I touched my finger to my lips and shook my head. "It's okay. Maybe later, you can tell me how I can help instead of making things worse."

"It wasn't you. And I don't think it was me. It was just... too much of everything, I think. Sometimes it's just that way."

I nodded and let my arm slip around her a little more. "Okay."

"Look." She turned her head to whisper into my ear. "You don't have to stay. You've never seen him like that, and I know it can be... what I'm saying is that I wouldn't blame you if you—"

"Meg?"

She leaned back, a wounded crease appearing on her brow as her teeth clenched and her eyes fluttered in dread. "Yes?"

"I'm not going anywhere. Well... unless you're thirsty. You look thirsty. Lemonade to cool off?"

She sighed and chuckled. "No, thank you, Evan. I'm fine."

I tightened my arm around her. "Then I am, too."

Meg

AS SOON AS WE got home, Dustin bolted from the car and dashed into the house. I heard his bedroom door slam shut with a force that made me wince. My heart ached, knowing how overwhelmed he must feel. I turned to Evan, expecting to see judgment or frustration, but instead, there was just that same easy calmness in his eyes. Like a rock, that man. Others might think he was dull, but to me, he was... predictable. Trustworthy and sane and always right what I needed him to be. I just hoped he really felt the way he looked, because no one could really be that unruffled on the inside.

Without a word, Evan walked into the kitchen. I followed him, my feet heavy. What was he thinking by now? He was too nice to just leave me at the fairgrounds, and he was probably too nice to stop seeing me right away, but he couldn't want... this. Life with Dustin could be chaotic, but also miraculous. Dustin saw and felt things that no one else did, and he was a marvel to me. But that was because I knew him. I'd had no choice but to stick with him through all the hard things, and I saw the wonder in every day. Evan hadn't had a chance to see all that yet. Today, he just saw the hard.

I leaned against the counter, watching as he moved around the kitchen with a familiarity that surprised me. He reached for a glass and filled it with ice water, the clinking sound somehow soothing in the quiet of the kitchen.

He turned and handed me the glass. "Here," he said softly, "you look like you could use this."

I took the glass, feeling the coolness seep into my fingers. "Thank you," I murmured, taking a small sip and then holding the cold glass to my temple. The cold shock was refreshing after everything.

Evan leaned against the counter opposite me, his gaze thoughtful but not intrusive. "He'll be okay," he said, as if reading my thoughts. "He just needs some time to himself."

I nodded, fighting back the tears that threatened to spill. "I'm sorry the fair," I managed to say, "and about this. It was supposed to be a fun day, and you probably had no idea it could unravel like that. I don't know what I expected, but I didn't think it would be this hard."

Evan's expression softened. "You don't have to apologize, Meg. These things happen. Dustin's doing the best he can, and so are you."

I took another sip of water, the kindness in his voice washing over me. It was more than I could have hoped for—understanding, support, and no judgment. In that moment, I felt a glimmer of something rare and precious—the possibility of not having to face everything alone. Could it really be true? Evan was here, not just physically, but truly present in a way that made me believe that maybe I wasn't on my own.

That was a dangerous thought. Dangerous, because I could get addicted to it pretty easily. I didn't want Evan and me to become just about having someone around to help. I didn't want his pity, and I didn't want to reduce our... whatever this was... to just a connection based on mutual pain and survival.

"Evan, are you sure about this?"

His brow puckered, then he sauntered close and took the glass from my hand, setting it on the counter behind me. Then he slid his hands down my arms and hooked his fingers with mine. "Are you talking about what I think you're talking about?"

"What else?"

He frowned and nodded, his eyes growing unfocused. "It's hard, Meg. I still have days when I wake up thinking things are like they used to be, and I can't breathe. I see something that reminds me..." There was a sheen in his eyes, and he wetted his lips, then sniffed and blinked hard. "I'll always carry that. You don't stop loving someone just because they leave, but it doesn't mean you run out of room in your heart."

I squeezed his fingers. "But it also doesn't mean you have to grab the first person to come along. I've got... baggage," I finished with a weak smile. "There are much easier ways to try out the dating life again than to get involved with a mom with a special needs son."

"You think I was desperate?" A little sideways grin appeared, but didn't quite reach his eyes. "Meg, I wasn't looking to fall in love again. I wasn't trying to shake things up just to do something different. I just... well, you just kept being in my life, and finally, I realized how much I looked forward to seeing you whenever I'd get the chance. And lately, it's been your smile that keeps me company in the dark hours, and you know what? They're not so dark anymore. I like that. And I like *you*... well... more than 'like'." He lifted his eyes and locked them with mine, and there was something so hopeful and pleading in his look that it made my heart do a loud thump.

"But like you saw today, I'm not easy. I can't—"

"Meg." He lifted his hand to brush the backs of his knuckles over my cheek. "You're not going to scare me off, no matter how hard you try. Say no if you want, but unless you do that, I'm sticking around."

My mouth stretched—I couldn't stop smiling. "Are you sure about that, Evan Walker?"

His thumb strayed, caressing the ridge of my cheekbone, and his fingertips feathered over my jaw to the ticklish edge of my ear. "I'm nuts about you, Meg. I don't want to go anywhere, if you'll let me stay."

He was serious? I couldn't find any words—just found myself nodding, and laughing away those tears stinging my eyes. He lowered his head, and I slid my hands up his chest, letting him lean against them until his nose touched mine.

"You know what this means, don't you?" he murmured against my lips.

"What?"

"My family's going to lose their ever-loving minds."

I snickered and caught his shirt by the collar. "Let them. Come here, cowboy."

Evan

I 'D LOST TRACK OF the afternoon, and somehow, it blended into late evening. Dustin was utterly silent in his room. Meg had checked on him several times, but he kept saying he wanted to be left alone, and she thought that was the best thing for him. So, she and I ordered a pizza and did nothing more than just... talk.

Well... we did a little more than talking.

And I learned some things about Meg. She played the violin in school, used to fill in for a bluegrass band on the fiddle. She didn't play anymore because the sound set Dustin's teeth on edge, so she found a new way to feed the music in her soul by curating playlists of classical music for elementary teachers to play for their students. "Someday, I'll pick up my violin again," she sighed. "I'll probably sound awful, all out of tune."

I chuckled as I slipped my fingers through her hair. "I'd like to say I'd enjoy listening to you, but to be honest, I don't have an 'ear.' Can't tell if something's in tune or not. Guess I won't be of much help to you."

"Oh, that's better than you can imagine. Don't you see? A music lover wouldn't be able to stand it, I'd be offending his ears too badly!"

I shrugged. "Won't bother me at all."

"Good." She kissed me softly and drew back to smile at me. Then she came back for more.

A while later, we were still there, sitting there on the couch, with Meg's head resting on my shoulder and my hand still toying with her hair. I wasn't usually one to sit still very long anywhere. It didn't seem to matter what was happening or where I was—I always had to get up and do something useful. But just now, I didn't want to go anywhere. Maybe I was right where I belonged. We'd switched on the TV because Meg thought the noise would remind Dustin that there were people in the house, and he could choose to come out when he was ready, but we weren't really watching it. The movie blurred into the background, hardly holding a candle to the woman beside me. Her presence soothed the jagged edges of my solitude, filling spaces in me I didn't even realize were empty.

I shifted, trying to get comfortable on the couch that, despite its plush cushions, didn't quite accommodate my back. A thought crossed my mind, and I turned to look at her. "Is this the couch you got from Kelli and Marshall?"

"Yeah, it is. Why do you ask?"

A chuckle escaped me, soft enough not to jostle her too much. "I guess I've figured out why they were so keen to give it away. This thing has a knack for hitting all the wrong spots."

Meg's eyebrows knitted together ever so slightly. "Oh, I'm sorry. I've never really thought about it being uncomfortable. I was just happy it wasn't falling apart! Do you want a throw pillow or something?"

I considered her offer for a moment but then realized that there was something else I desired more. "The only thing that would make me more comfortable right now is this," I said softly before leaning in to kiss her.

The moment our lips met, I felt a rush of warmth and a sense of rightness. Holding Meg in my arms felt natural, as if she belonged there. The realization dawned on me, clear and bright—when I held Meg, my thoughts were solely of her. There was no effort needed to guide my heart; it had already leaped ahead, embracing feelings I hadn't thought possible again.

"Hey." She threaded her fingers through my hair. "You're pretty good at that."

I leaned back, grinning. "Always figured anything worth doing is worth doing right."

Meg laughed and pulled me close again, and I was lost. The softness of her, the way she met me just right and warmed me through, the way her hair felt against my lips, the...

"Oh, my... Dustin!" Meg lurched in my arms and sat up, tugging at the front of her shirt and brushing her hair back. "You can't sneak up on people like that, buddy!"

I sat up more slowly, and with a little more trepidation. Dustin was staring at me with an intensity that seemed to bore into my very soul. I smiled at him, but Dustin's gaze never wavered.

"Honey, are you okay?" Meg asked her son. "Look, I know we haven't talked about this, but Evan and I..." Dustin didn't seem to be listening. His eyes remained fixed on me, an unreadable expression on his face.

Finally, breaking the silence, he blinked and said, "Come see my carving."

It wasn't a question. It wasn't even rude—just an expectation, like he'd have been astonished if anyone wouldn't want to jump up and go look. Meg and I exchanged a quick, uncertain glance, then followed him to his room. The moment I stepped inside, my jaw almost hit the carpet. The carving was a revelation—a horse, its hindquarters defined in exquisite detail, muscles tense as if caught mid-rear. The tail whipped by an invisible wind, dirt particles seemed to fly off its hooves—it was a moment frozen in wood. An incomplete moment because all that was finished was the hindquarters. Everything in front of the flanks was still rough and raw, but the back was almost perfect.

"Dustin, this is incredible," I breathed.

Dustin looked from me to Meg and back again, his gaze lingering on our intertwined hands. Meg, sensing the need to shift the atmosphere, asked hesitantly, "Are you hungry, Dustin?"

His intense stare softened as he looked at me again. "I saw a pizza box. I like pizza. I had pizza with Evan once."

Meg's smile was a mix of relief and warmth. "I remember. We have more for you."

And so, we found ourselves gathered around the dining table, pulling apart the now-cold pizza and breadsticks. Dustin was in his element, his hands moving animatedly as he asked me about horses. His eyes sparkled with excitement, and every so often, he would pause to take a big bite of his pizza.

Underneath the table, Meg's hand sought mine. Our fingers intertwined discreetly, a silent communication that spoke volumes. This was more than just a simple dinner; it was a moment of connection, of understanding and acceptance. Meg's hand in mine under the table was like a warm anchor, grounding me in the present and giving me a glimpse of a future that was slowly taking shape.

Chapter Seventeen

Meg

I WAS SITTING ON the familiar bench at White Pines, my eyes following Dustin as he moved through his therapy session with Amber. The calm and focus he exhibited in these moments always filled me with a sense of pride and hope. Some days, I wasn't sure if I'd survive long enough for him to grow up and make it on his own. But it was days like this one when I got to see the little pinpricks of light poking through the veil, that made me believe that no matter what happened, my son really would be okay.

My phone buzzed, and I glanced down to see a message from Evan, saying he was on his way to watch Dustin. A small smile tugged at my lips; Evan's presence always made the day a little brighter. If someone had asked me six months ago what I thought of Evan Walker, I'd have said he was like a superhero to me—the kind of guy who could blaze through the fire and come out without even smelling like smoke. The kind you just sat back and watched in awe, because he was larger than life and too good to be true. But now, he was... he was...

He was the one who knew what it was to pray desperately for something and then learn to live with a different answer. He was the one who knew how to not back down when he stared into the face of the fight, but also how to gently choose the wiser path when necessary. And he was the one who could hold me even when I was afraid. No one—not John, not my parents, or any of my friends, no matter how well-meaning they were—no one made me feel as strong as Evan did when he just put his arms around me and kissed my hair.

And he was coming here today. Taking time off all the things he had to do at the ranch just to spend a few minutes with my son and me. I loved that man.

Before I could send a message back to him, Morgan plopped down beside me, her ever-present ball cap stained with sweat and a huge icy steel mug in her hand. "Hey, Meg. Dustin's doing great today, huh?"

"He is." I hesitated. "Morgan, about Dustin's outburst at the fair the other day... I'm really sorry. He just..."

Morgan waved her mug. "Don't worry about it. Actually, believe it or not, we got a new client because of that. This lady saw how calm Biz was and how much Dustin depended on him, and she brought her daughter out yesterday to meet the horses. Seems like there's always a silver lining, right?"

Her words eased some of the guilt that had been lingering since that day. "I'm just glad he's recovering well. And thank you for saying that," I said, feeling a weight lift off my shoulders.

Morgan leaned back, watching the pair in the arena. "Dustin's doing amazing, really. He's starting to adapt and express himself better all the time. It's remarkable to see."

I nodded, my gaze drifting back to my son. "That means the world to hear, Morgan. Thank you. It's all because of you, you know."

"Hah. Not in the least. He wouldn't even be here if you hadn't fought for him. He's doing well because he has you in his corner." She shrugged. "And because he's a pretty remarkable kid himself."

I always got a little choked up when she said things like that. I never felt like I deserved her praise for myself, but what she said and believed about Dustin... well, she was one of the people who lifted my chin and made me face truth when the lies started to feel so big. And the only words I had for her were a whispered "Thanks, Morgan."

We fell into a comfortable silence, watching the session, before I turned the conversation to her. "So, how are you feeling? With the pregnancy and everything?"

Morgan laughed, a hand drifting to her slightly rounded belly. "Oh, you know. Morning sickness is gone, and now I can't seem to stop eating! Between Kelli's daily takeout deliveries and Meryl's home cooking, I'm turning into a little pudgy mama. It looks like I'm showing already, but really, it's just a cheeseburger gut."

"Aw. I'm sure Cody thinks you're adorable."

"That's what he says. I think he's just afraid to get between me and my next meal."

Somehow, she caught me by surprise with that. It wasn't *that* funny, but I sputtered and laughed so hard that Dustin stopped what he was doing and stared at me until Amber encouraged him to keep going. Still chuckling, I wiped my eyes. "I don't know why I thought that was so funny, but I haven't laughed that hard in I can't remember how long."

"Sounds to me like you're overdue for a good laugh!" Morgan leaned back on the bench and tilted her head at me. "Mind if I say something kinda blunt?"

"Oh, dear. Can I stop you?"

She frowned and shook her head. "Probably not. You're a stuffer, Meg. You bottle everything up until you're fit to bust at the seams, and then you explode."

I raised my brows and shrugged. "Like I did at the fair? You're not wrong. I'm working on it, I really am. I guess I've had to keep a lid on things for so long..."

"It's not a criticism. I just wondered how things went after... well, you know."

"With Evan, you mean?"

"Yeah. You guys figured it out, I assume? Didn't scare the poor guy off?"

I hugged my arms across my chest and smiled, my eyes wandering to Dustin in the arena. "He's on his way here to watch, so... Wait a minute." I turned back to her with an accusing look. "You already knew, or you wouldn't be asking me that."

She shrugged. "Guilty as charged. I'm just glad to hear you've found a good guy who's tough enough to take you at your worst." Her voice dropped. "And by the way? You at your worst really isn't that bad."

I laughed. "Oh, I'm not so sure about that. I can be pretty savage when it comes to my kid."

Morgan leaned toward me, nudging me in the ribs and tilting her head toward the door, where a tall cowboy was just entering. "And you know what?" she whispered. "That guy there wouldn't want you any other way. You might think he's the one stepping in the gap for you, but I say it's really the other way around. You're good for him, Meg."

I blinked, staring at Evan as he made his hesitant way toward us, and a goofy smile started growing on my face. "You think?" I murmured back.

Morgan cocked backward in her chair and nodded, winking at my cowboy. "Mmm-hmm."

Evan took off his hat and started up the steps to the viewing area. "Am I interrupting something?"

"Nope." Morgan stood up. "I was just leaving. You two mind your manners, you hear? There are kids in the building."

A genuinely mystified look crossed Evan's features, but I was blushing furiously as Morgan left. "What was that about?" he asked.

"You don't want to know. Come here, you. I saved you a chair."

He shrugged and claimed the chair beside me, then leaned over to kiss me gently. "If you're offering, I won't refuse."

I tugged at the collar of his shirt as he sat back. "Thanks for coming. It means a lot to me."

His gaze was steady. "Thanks for wanting me."

I'll admit, that got me thinking for longer than I'd like to confess. Wanting him? Who *wouldn't* want Evan Walker? That was the silliest thing I ever heard. I didn't have anything to say to that, so I just gave him a funny look and let him lace his fingers through mine.

"Hey, you don't usually work tonight, do you?" he asked.

I nodded. "Not normally, but I am tonight. Filling in for someone who's out sick. Why?"

"Oh, no big deal." He adjusted the hat resting on his knee. "We've got that herd up in the mountains to bring down. I've been worried about how dry it is this year, so Dad and I decided today that we'd go up early and fetch them. Planning to leave at dawn tomorrow, and we'll be up there a couple of days."

I sagged. "Oh, no. I'd have liked to do something tonight before you go."

"That's okay." He flashed me a grin. "I'll come find you when I get back."

Evan

T HE PREDAWN LIGHT WAS just a brushstroke of color against the dark sky as I pulled the cinch tight on my horse. The cool morning air bit at my skin, a sharp contrast to the heat that would blaze over us when the sun came up. I swung into the saddle, feeling a buoyancy in my spirit that was a new addition to my usual contemplative mood. The last time I'd saddled up to make this ride, I'd been feeling a lot more somber. Watching Dad jaunting off with Meryl, Marshall and Kelli laughing as they rode together, and Luke with stars in his eyes when he watched Audrey... Jealousy wasn't quite the right word, but it had been hard to watch, knowing I'd probably lost forever that thing they were relishing.

But now... I grinned as I adjusted my hat and patted my colt's neck. Now, I was really looking forward to getting up

that mountain and back down again so I could hightail it over
to Meg's house for a little star-gazing of my own.

Around me, everyone else was bustling about, preparing
their horses. This time, it was Dad and Meryl, Dusty and
Jess, and Cody with his two assistants, Emily and Cole.
He'd thought it would be good for them to get out of the
training arena and out into the real world. And not just for
them, either—Emily was on Maserati, Cody was on Rust, his
twitchy sorrel futurity horse, and Cole was on Dexter, one of
the other hot three-year-olds they were showing this year.
A little honest sweat and mountain air was just what those
horses needed to take the edge off between shows.

And maybe take off the edge between the kids, too. Emily and Cole bickered over just about everything, including
whether to use splint boots on their horses in the mountains
and the right way to tie down their saddle bags. Cody was
scowling and shaking his head, and eventually, he just rode
over to the gate to wait for them there.

Everyone else was lost in their own pre-ride rituals. Normally, I'd be lost in my thoughts, too, but today was different. The playful, romantic banter between Dusty and Jess
caught my ear, and without thinking, I chimed in, teasing
them about how they'd only get to their private tent in the
mountains if we got this show on the road. Dusty blushed,
but Jess laughed proudly and gave the brim of her hat a jerk.
"Well, then, let's go!" she said.

As the sky lightened, we rode out, the mountains beckoning us with their age-old call. The ride to the cow camp
was always a long one, but today, it felt different—lighter,
somehow. I found myself engaging more, sharing stories and
listening to the others, genuinely enjoying the camaraderie.
Life was good. Family was good. And it might just be starting
to get a whole lot bigger and better.

We reached the camp as the afternoon sun cast long shadows of the trees across the streams. Setting up camp was
second nature to us—tents were pitched, a shielded cook fire
was kindled, and soon enough, the smell of coffee filled the
air.

"Looks like we'll have a clear day tomorrow," Dad commented. "Should make for easy driving."

I nodded in agreement, sipping my coffee. "Yeah, the calves have grown well over the summer. We should be able to move them along at a good pace."

After we bolted our coffee, Jess and Emily stayed to help Meryl stoke the coals for dinner in her Dutch ovens, while the rest of us swung back into the saddle to inspect the cattle a little closer. The calves were looking good—healthy and robust. We split into groups, methodically working through the herd, counting heads, checking for any injuries, strays from other ranches, and making sure our branding was intact. It was a job that required focus and attention to detail.

The work continued into the early evening, and as the sun began to set, casting a golden glow over the land, we regrouped at the camp. The mountains around us stood tall and silent, guardians of the land and the life it supported. Around the campfire, the night came alive with the sound of my family's laughter, the distant calls of the cattle, and the soft murmur of the wind. It was moments like this that I cherished—a reminder of the beauty and simplicity of ranch life. Next time I came to the mountains, I promised myself, I'd find a way to bring Meg with me.

I leaned back against a log, looking up at the stars beginning to twinkle in the night sky. A sense of peace settled over me, a feeling that had been elusive for so long. Life had taken on a new rhythm, a new meaning with Meg in it. The hardships of ranch life were still there, the aches of loss never entirely erased, but they seemed lighter now, more bearable.

I let out a contented sigh, the troubles of the past slowly fading into the background. Under the vast, starlit sky, I felt a deep sense of gratitude. For the land, for the life I led, and for the love that had unexpectedly come my way. It was a good life, a life I was thankful for every single day.

D AD AND MERYL WERE the last couple to call it a night. Everyone else had called it quits a while ago, but I always liked to be the last one to bed. I grunted my goodnights to them as Dad helped Meryl to her feet, and they trundled off to their tent together, then I poured a bucket of stream water over the fire. I hadn't pitched a tent for myself. It wasn't going to rain, and I wasn't up here with a wife—didn't need privacy—and I liked sprawling back on my bedroll to admire the dazzling blanket of stars spread overhead. But there was one thing I had to do before I could kick my boots off for the night.

I pulled Emma's sketchbook from my saddlebag, the bright pink cover worn and familiar under my fingers. My throat knotted a little as I made a cursory flip through the pages. The lantern light cast a warm glow on her sketches, illuminating the delicate lines and shadows of her work. For a seven-year-old, she'd really been pretty good. Even now, I didn't think my drawing could compare, but it would have to do. I'd promised, hadn't I? I'd finish what she started.

The camp was quieting down now, the night around me a symphony of subtle sounds—the gentle rustling of leaves, the distant hoot of an owl, and the soft murmur of the stream. The horses were grazing or snoozing quietly, and the last of the lanterns in the tents had been snuffed. It was in these serene moments that I felt closest to my little girl, enveloped in the peace of the wilderness she had so adored.

I paused before I walked off, making sure the campfire was soaked and cold so no sparks could set off the dry underbrush. This was a dangerous time of year to be having cookfires, and we couldn't take any chances. Once I was satisfied, I wandered deeper into the woods, lantern in hand, to a little crook in the stream that held a special memory for me. The rock Emma and I had often sat on to talk and draw was just as I remembered—solid, unchanging, a fixture in the ever-evolving landscape of life. Sitting there, I could almost feel her presence beside me, her youthful energy, and her insatiable curiosity about everything she saw.

Opening the sketchbook, I started at the beginning, my fingers caressing every one of Emma's drawings. Chipmunks and deer, new calves with their mamas, fish in the stream, and caterpillars on a leaf. Everything she saw had inspired joy and wonder, and it had let me see things through her eyes, if only just for a moment. Then, there was her last drawing—one of a big buckskin horse standing at the picket line, his nose in the water bucket, and her standing beside him with a brush.

I didn't even bother wiping the tears out of my eyes or stopping the gasping heaves in my chest. I'd forgotten she rode Biz on that last trip up here. Dad and Cody had taken her to a horse show the week before we left to muster cattle. Emma had ridden her four-year-old horse—just a baby himself—in the short stirrup class, and they won. Some of the kids her age were led by their parents, but Emma and Biz, green as they both were, didn't need that. They loped a slow pattern all by themselves, with him looking like he was ambling out to pasture and her beaming like a princess. *My* little princess.

As soon as we'd gotten home from the show, we started packing to head up into the mountains. Emma lobbied hard, and she and Anne had convinced me to let her ride that young gelding up here on her own. I was glad I'd said yes. What if I didn't have those memories of her? What if we hadn't filled every day like she'd filled this book? Or started to fill it, anyway.

That was why I was here now. I'd made her a promise after she left me that I'd keep looking for all the beauty in the world that she'd shown me in her short life. It was there all along, and I'd never even known some of those colors existed until she opened my eyes. But I hadn't done a very good job these last two years of trying to capture it. My drawings were dull and gray compared to hers.

I thumbed to the back, looking for my spot. There was only one page left in the book. Had I really filled the last ten pages on my own? It felt like an eternity had passed in those pages. The "rule" was that only the things seen on the trip into the mountains could find their way onto the page, so I'd tried to think of what she'd have noticed whenever I came here to sit down. But for the first time, I couldn't help but notice that my drawings were tinted with my grief, a stark contrast to the lively and joyous scenes Emma had captured. There was the dead deer we'd passed last fall. A dried-up stream. An empty bluebird nest. A sunset muted by a drizzling rainfall. Good grief, I'd been in a dark place when I chose those things to draw.

Tonight, I wanted to honor her memory differently. Emma would have found something joyful, so I would, too. And it wasn't as hard as it used to be.

I began to sketch, my pencil moving with purpose. I drew us, my family, together on the mountain trail—the laughter, the camaraderie, the love that had been present in every step we took that day. In my mind's eye, I saw each of their faces—the smiles, the jokes we shared, the easy banter that had flowed among us. This was the family Emma had loved, and I wanted to immortalize that joy in her book.

As a final touch, I added Emma beside me on her horse, just as I remembered her—full of life, leaning over toward me with her arms wrapped around my waist, her face radiant with the happiness of being part of our world. Drawing her was both painful and cathartic, each line a tribute to her enduring spirit in my life.

Tears blurred my vision as I finished. I wasn't a good artist, but somehow, tonight, even a stranger could have plucked up what flooded onto the page and declared that it looked like real life. I had just seen her so clearly, felt her so dearly, that the pencil seemed to move on its own.

I traced over her sweet little face one last time with my fingertips as I whispered to her, my voice breaking with the weight of my love and my loss. "I miss you, baby. Daddy's going to make it. I know that now, but I sure do miss you. Give your mama a kiss for me and tell her I'll always love you both, no matter what."

Shaking and shattered, I closed the sketchbook and blew out a trembling sigh. I wiped my eyes on the back of my sleeve, then nodded and smiled up to the moonlight splintering through the trees. I felt a profound sense of completion. It was as if I had closed the door on a chapter of my life filled with darkness and sorrow, and now, a new path lay open before me. My heart felt lighter, a sense of peace and acceptance washing over me. I had fulfilled my promise to Emma, and in doing so, I had found a way to let go of the pain while holding on to the love and the memories.

I stood up, the sketchbook securely tucked away, and made my way back to camp. The stars above shone brightly, a reminder of the vast and beautiful world that still awaited me. Emma's spirit, I knew, would always be a part of me, and so would Anne's. My heart would hold them forever.

But I had a big heart, with lots of room for more.

Chapter Eighteen

Meg

THEY PUT US ON the schedule! I'd been sipping my morning coffee, admiring a picture of the sunrise over the mountains that Evan had texted me yesterday before he rode out of cell range when the screen went dark, and a call from Dustin's speech therapist popped up. A cancellation, they said, and the therapist had reviewed Dustin's files—and probably the dozen emails I'd sent—and agreed to slide him in. That was, if I could get him to Pocatello by eleven.

My tutoring student had cancelled, so I could do that.

Probably.

Heaven must have been smiling on me today because we arrived ten minutes early—just in time to pay our bill. The *full* bill, because no check had arrived from John. Sigh. But we were here, and they were giving him a chance to prove that he'd grown... so long as I stayed in the room this time to help keep things from getting out of hand. They'd even assigned him to a new therapist—a grandmotherly figure named Mrs. Clark, who looked like she had been down the road a few times and lived to tell the tale. So, I'd make the best of it.

I sat in the corner, my heart pounding with hope and anxiety. Communication was his biggest hurdle, and I prayed the therapist... *got* it. Some people just don't. Some people try. But there are a handful in the world who are special, who can say the same words with the same inflection and facial expressions as other people, but there's something earnest deep inside of them that Dustin can see. *Please, please, let Mrs. Clark be one of those.*

"Okay, Dustin," she said, "let's just get to know each other a little." She held out a small, colorful stress ball. "I thought you might like this. It's squishy and fun to squeeze."

Dustin glanced at the ball and then away, disinterested. He fidgeted, avoiding eye contact, his gaze roaming the room.

Mrs. Clark didn't push it. She gently placed the ball on the desk and tried a different approach. "I've heard you like horses, Dustin. Do you have a favorite horse?"

He mumbled something under his breath, still not engaging, his hands clenching and unclenching at his sides.

Mrs. Clark nodded understandingly, not showing any sign of frustration. "That's okay, Dustin. Whenever you're ready to talk about the things you like, I'm here. Can you tell me how you're feeling right now?"

Dustin squirmed in his seat, his hands fiddling with the hem of his shirt. "I d-don't know," he mumbled, avoiding eye contact.

"It's okay, Dustin," I chimed in, trying to offer support. "Just like we practiced at home. Remember?"

Mrs. Clark nodded encouragingly. "That's right, Dustin. Just like you practiced with your mom. Are you happy, sad, anxious?"

He shrugged, his gaze flitting around the room. "A-anxious," he finally said, the word almost a whisper.

"I imagine you are," Mrs. Clark said softly,. "Can you tell me why you feel anxious?"

Dustin didn't respond immediately. His eyes darted around the room, landing on various objects—a stack of books, a colorful poster, a small plant on the windowsill. Then, his gaze fixed on the calendar hanging above Mrs. Clark's desk. It was a rodeo calendar, vibrant and filled with action-packed images. The picture for the current month showed a steer wrestler leaping from a speeding horse, his face a grimace of fierce effort with dirt and hooves flying behind him.

"Th-that's steer wrestling," Dustin murmured.

Mrs. Clark glanced over her shoulder. "Yes, that's right, Dustin. My daughter is a barrel racer, and she gave me that calendar. Do you like watching rodeos?" She pulled the push pin that was holding the calendar to her wall and offered it to him to look at.

Dustin's entire demeanor shifted. He stopped fidgeting and sat up straighter, his eyes locked on the calendar as he reached hungrily for it. "Evan used to steer wrestle," he said, a hint of awe in his voice.

"And Evan is..." Mrs. Clark leaned forward, her eyebrow edging upward. "A friend of yours? Someone you trust?"

Dustin swallowed. "Evan likes horses. I like Biz."

Mrs. Clark's eyes shifted to me for an instant, as if verifying the connection. I just nodded—yes, Dustin drew lines between seemingly random dots like that, and if he'd made some kind of link in his mind between Mrs. Clark's rodeo calendar and his friend Evan and his favorite horse Biz... well, maybe that meant he'd let her in.

Mrs. Clark smiled. "That's wonderful, Dustin. Let's talk more about horses and rodeos. I bet you know a lot about them. Who is Biz?"

And after that, she never got him to stop talking the whole rest of the session.

I WASN'T IMAGINING IT... there was a decided knot forming in my stomach, and not without good cause. I'd thought that John would be happy when I told him how well Dustin's session went. But he wasn't buying it.

"I thought you said they weren't putting him back on the schedule. He *hit* someone, Meg."

"No, he *tried* to..." I broke off. That didn't make it sound any better. "I talked to them quite a bit, and they said they were willing to try again. They had a cancellation today, and—"

"And now you want me to pay for it, is that right?"

I rolled my eyes. "That would be nice, but more than anything, I wanted to tell you how he did. I think you deserve to know."

"Look, Meg, I'm at work. Can this wait?"

I frowned and checked the calendar I had hanging on the wall. I sort of knew his work schedule, or at least, the schedule he'd given me six months ago. "I thought you were scheduled to be off by three on Thursdays. That's why I didn't call sooner."

He was quiet for a few seconds. "Okay, fine, I can talk for a minute, but make it quick. What do you want me to do? Throw a party because he sat through an appointment without losing his temper?"

I ground my teeth. "You really don't get it, do you? This was huge. Really, today was a great experience for him, and he needs to be able to follow up on it. And that means I need your support because I can't keep—"

"Explain to me why this therapist is any different from the others. Why should I believe this next time will be any different than the last?"

I took a deep breath, trying to stay calm. "This time, it was different because Dustin connected with Mrs. Clark over a cowboy calendar she had in her office. It reminded him of steer wrestling, which somehow led to Evan—"

"Evan? Who's Evan?" John interjected sharply, his tone shifting from skeptical to accusatory.

"Evan is... someone I've been seeing," I admitted, a nervous flutter in my stomach. I don't know why. It wasn't like he hadn't moved on, so why shouldn't I? "He's been really great with Dustin, and Dustin feels safe with him. He's even worked on the ranch with—"

"Wait a minute. So, you've got some guy I've never heard of spending time with our son? Alone? I don't like this, Meg. I need to know who this person is."

Frustration boiled inside me. "Evan is a kind, caring man. He's shown more support and understanding for Dustin in a month than you have in the last five years! He's been a positive influence in both our lives."

"That's not your call to make alone, Meg! I'm his father. I have a right to know about the people around my son."

I couldn't hold back my anger any longer. "You're his father in name only, John! You're engaged to someone else and haven't seen Dustin in months. You have no right to question my choices in my personal life."

There was a brief, tense silence before John spat out, "Fine. Do what you want. But I'm telling you, I'm not paying for anything extra. If this Evan is so great, maybe he can pick up the tab."

"That's not what this is about," I shot back hotly. "Yes, I need your help if he's going to keep doing the speech therapy, but more than anything, I'd like you to *care*. Dustin is doing better now because he's met more people who care about him, and it would be nice if his father wanted to be one of them!"

John's tone turned bitter. "Yeah, well, we'll see how long this Evan sticks around once he gets a real taste of what it's like with Dustin."

My heart sank. "You don't even know your own son anymore, John."

He hung up without another word, leaving me standing there, phone in hand, tears welling in my eyes. I slumped onto the couch, reeling with anger, pain, and helplessness, sobbing into the silence of the room.

Evan

I EASED BACK IN the saddle and just soaked in the view of the ranch sprawling out before me. The sight was always a welcome one, but this time, I could hear and even smell things that were still far off. Dear things—crickets behind the shed, the creaking of the old barn door, Meryl's chickens clucking around the yard, and Marshall's steaks on the grill. *Home.*

I drank in a sigh and patted my colt's neck. He'd earned a name on this long drive. A little goosey still, but he had guts and leg, plenty of bottom. I hadn't even been looking for a name, but this morning when we'd started out, he'd saved my butt by keeping his footing over a log that rolled up under him in the stream. And as I was praising him for a job well done, the name Strider just popped out of my mouth. Tough, hard-working, and able to roll with whatever the path sent his way.

I could learn a lot from this colt. *Roll along...* My gaze lingered on the house at the north end of our valley—the one I'd built for Anne. An idea flickered in my mind, one that seemed to make more sense the more I thought about it.

What if I offered to sell that house to Luke and Audrey? They could use a ready-made home, saving them the hassle of building from scratch. It was built for a family, and I'd be shocked if they didn't get started on a big one pretty quickly.

My share of the land would go with it—the choicest of all the ranch property since I'd been the oldest and Mom and Dad set it up that way. Luke would come out ahead in the deal, and in return, I'd swap Luke's land for mine.

That way, when I was ready, I'd have a fresh start in a new home, free from the ghosts of my past. It felt like the right step forward, a way to honor what had been while making room for what could be. If Luke and Audrey liked the idea.

As the ranch came closer into view, I watched my phone, waiting for the moment it would buzz back to life with cell service. As soon as it did, I typed a text to Meg. "Back from the drive. Went well. Hoping to see you soon." I had something kind of important I wanted to say to her... see what she thought of it.

The late afternoon sun was brutal as we dropped down out of the mountains. Heat radiated off the moisture from the irrigated pastures, creating a mirage-like effect across the whole valley. I plunged into the sorting pens with Dusty, Cody, and Cole, where cows and their calves fresh from the mountain jostled against the fence. While we worked there, maneuvering calves aside and getting them settled in for branding and weaning, everyone else peeled off to pick up whatever else needed to get done before nightfall.

It hadn't been muggy like this up on the mountain, but down here in the valley, the humidity was stifling. My shirt was sticking to me, and after I shut the gate on the last bunch we'd sorted, I paused and looked up at the sky. Streaks of red shot across the glaze of blue—a sunset worth taking pictures of, which meant the weather was changing. Clouds were building in the distance, dark and pregnant with rain. I fished out my phone again, checking the weather report. "Thunderstorm warning," it read, and I wasn't surprised.

Dusty side-passed his horse over, leaning close to peer over my shoulder at the phone screen. "Lighting weather. I figured. Looks like it's going to be a big one." He adjusted his hat. "Hope we at least get some rain with that lightning. We're way overdue."

I nodded and almost put my phone away, but then pulled it back out. Meg hadn't texted back yet. Maybe she was working. I could wait... but maybe I'd send her a quick picture because she said she liked my pictures. What should I...? Hmm. I squinted, tilted my camera, and shot an angle that got the back of Strider's head and a couple of calves standing close together, staring at my horse. There. A couple of quick taps, and the picture was on its way.

"I'm not gonna tell him, you tell him."

Luke's voice drifted over the noise of the herd, but when I swiveled in the saddle, I saw him and Marshall walking toward the barn. Probably looking for Dad.

"You're the one who spotted it," Marshall pointed out as they walked inside.

"Yeah, but you're the favorite. He'll think I'm making it up, but you know how to say it right."

I chuckled as my brothers wandered out of view, then swung down off my horse. "You did good today, bud," I murmured, patting his neck. "Earned some extra oats tonight." I loosened the latigo on my cinch and headed for the tack room, leading my tired horse behind.

I hadn't gotten twelve steps into the barn before I saw my brothers slowly coming to meet me, walking shoulder-to-shoulder with spooked looks on their faces. Luke was poking his tongue in his cheek and rubbing his jaw, and Marshall was fussing with his hat.

I pulled Strider's bridle and slid a halter on his head. "What's eatin' you two?"

Marshall looked at Luke, who backed away with his hands in the air. "I ain't tellin' him."

"Well, it's not *my* deal. Come on, you're the one who was feeding."

"What, did we get a bad batch of feed? Somebody colic?"

Marshall crossed his arms and stared at Luke. Luke blew out a sigh, rubbed his nose, and glanced over his shoulder. "It's Pistol. Stopped eating yesterday."

My face clouded. "What, like he didn't eat at all?"

"Not in about forty-eight hours. Lizzy even tried hand-feeding him. I checked him for colic, gave him some electrolytes and Banamine, even some of that magic gut supplement I give Two Bits, but..." He cleared his throat and shook his head.

I pulled my saddle off and carted it to the tack room, stewing in thought. Luke and Marshall were still standing around like cows waiting to be milked when I got back. "Is he drinking?" I asked.

"If you count the watermelon I fed him. He only ate about two bites. Man... you need to go look at him."

Absently, I passed Strider's lead rope to Marshall. "Yeah. I will. He was getting his Previcox, wasn't he? If he got really stoved up with pain, he might've lost his appetite. You didn't forget his meds?"

Luke shook his head. "Nope. I, uh... I called Doc earlier today." He swallowed. "You'd... better go look at him."

My boots scuffed the concrete aisle as I made my way down to Pistol's stall. I'd put him in a stall designed for a stallion—big, comfy box, with extra padded stall mats, a thick bed of fluffy shavings, and a huge sandy outside run. No pasture for Pistol anymore because Doc didn't want him out on grass that might trigger another founder episode. I'd tried to make him as happy and comfortable as possible, but when I slid open the stall door, my stomach sank with the recognition that everything I'd tried to do... was no longer enough.

Pistol was standing indoors, with his tail pointed into a fan. Head down, ears lax, lower lip drooping. A fly crawled across his face, and he didn't even shake his head. He did lift it slightly, however, when I said his name.

"Hey, partner," I murmured as I moved closer to him.

There was a decided flicker of recognition, but he let his head hang again. I ran my hand down the line of his mane, between his ears and over his poll, scooping up a handful of his scruffy old forelock. He never did have a pretty forelock, I remembered, with a little squeeze in my chest. Even in his prime, when he was getting buckets full of high-performance feed to fuel those record-setting runs he used to turn in, and his coat glowed like a polished sports car, his forelock had been a fat, short, fluffy wad of hair.

"Not feelin' it anymore, are you?" I asked as my hands stroked and tugged at his ears. He always used to like that, leaning his head over for an ear massage on each side. Now...

I moved a little, scratching his chin and easing that old head into my arms. This time, he did lean on me a little, the broad, flat forehead pressing into my chest as if leaning on me could take some of the weight off his feet. He dropped his jaw against my forearm and just let me hug his face, his muzzle twitching against my shirt like he used to when he was looking for a treat.

"I'm sorry, Evan," Doc's voice came through the bars of the stall.

I looked around. "I didn't know Luke had you come out. He just said he called."

Doc pushed his hat back on his head. "I examined him this morning. Thought I'd stop back by and talk to you if you were back." He nodded toward Pistol. "But I imagine he's the one you need to talk to."

I traced the lines of my old partner's face—those deepening sockets above his eyes, the lumps and bumps and long whiskers, and finally took a step back to look him in the eye.

And he told me what I needed to know. Life just hurt too much. I couldn't make him suffer through tomorrow with me just because I didn't want to say goodbye.

"It's not just a spell, is it, Doc?" I asked. "Just a bad day? He's gone off his feed when I left town before, and always bounced back."

Doc shook his head. "I ran blood work, Evan. His organs are giving up."

"Well. That's it, then. I can't ask him for any more than he's already given me."

"So... did you want to stick around?"

I swallowed and tugged at that puffy forelock again. "Yeah. I'll take him out to the yard, let him stand in the shade of the big pine tree on the lawn, and just stay with him. I owe him that much. But just wait a minute, will you, Doc?"

"I'll be out at my truck when you're ready."

I cradled Pistol's neck, stroking his jowls with one hand while I fished out my phone with the other. There was a text now from Meg.

—*Great picture! I missed you. Looking forward to seeing you, too.*

I didn't bother texting back. I just pressed call, hoping she wasn't at work. She picked up on the third ring.

"Evan, hi." Her voice sounded strange, like she was muffled or sick... or had been crying. "I was going to call you but..."

"Are you free?"

"Uh... yeah, I can be free." She cleared her throat, and I heard a door closing in the background. "Is everything okay?"

"Not really. Well... it would be a lot more okay if you were here. If you can make it."

"Evan, what's wrong?" Her voice had gone clear now. "Are you hurt?"

I shook my head, like she could see that over the phone, and scratched Pistol's neck. "I'm fine, but I have to do something I've been dreading. Not gonna be easy, I can tell you, but I have to. And... I'd really like it if you could be here when I have to put my horse down."

There was the faintest gasp from the other end, but she didn't come up with any silly apologies, no worthless moralizing or platitudes. I just heard the jingling of her keys. "I'm on my way."

Chapter Nineteen

Meg

"HE USED TO DANCE in the chute." Evan leaned back against the pine tree, tightening his arm around me as his head fell back against the rough bark. "Up on his hind legs till they opened the chute gate, his eyes all big and his nostrils flared, ready to storm the arena. He'd be gentle as a kitten and patient as an old owl on practice days. Sometimes, I wondered if he could even keep up, but he always knew when it was time to charge." Evan sniffed, and I looked up to see a smile reflected in the light of the full moon. "I'll never forget our last run."

I slid my hand across his leg to capture his, then squeezed his fingers tight. "Tell me."

His chest lifted under my cheek, and for a second, I wasn't sure he was going to. "It was in Denver. We'd been hot all year. Took a fall in practice the day before—our cow tried to run under the hazing horse, then bounced off and came straight for us. I was halfway out of the saddle already when he dodged, and I swear, Pistol tried to scoop me back into the seat. Lost his footing in the process, and we both took a tumble. But we were still game the next day for the real deal." He shook his head. "He was perfect. He knew how to rate a cow like no other horse I've been on. Put me right where I needed to be, and we came home with the buckle that day. And..." His brow creased as he studied the freshly turned earth mounded before us. "That was it. I retired that very afternoon."

I looked up at him. "You both retired on top of your game."

"Yeah," he nodded, a faraway look in his eyes. "Emma had just been born, and I didn't want to keep taking risks. I wanted both of us, me and Pistol, to come home sound and fit while we were still at our best."

"That must've been a hard decision."

"Not really. Bittersweet, maybe. I loved what we did, and I'd paid a lot of money for a finished horse that I only campaigned for a couple of years." He shrugged. "I could've sold him. Had a dozen offers, and he was fit enough, he could've stayed on top for five or six more years. Horses like that are perfect for young guys just getting started. But... Nah, it wouldn't've been right. I'd been starting to feel it after our runs. He still loved it, but he was getting bored. And he was my partner, so..." Evan drank in a sigh and nodded, more to himself than to me. "It wasn't a hard choice. He came home and turned into the best darned ranch horse I ever had. Won't be another like him."

"It sounds like he left quite a mark."

Evan chuckled softly, "The great ones always do." He kissed my hair gently, then took a deep breath, as if bracing himself for what he was about to say. "Speaking of making a mark..."

He paused, and something in his voice deepened. I heard his breathing change, and the back of my neck prickled with awareness. This was... different. "Meg, I feel like you've become a real part of my life. A part I want to keep. I know it might be too soon to talk about marriage, but I want you to know that I'm serious about being with you. I need to know what you feel."

His words hung there, thick with meaning. My heart started pounding harder. I wanted to grab hold of his words—of *him*, but all my fear and hope tangled together inside me, almost too big to voice. I looked down at our intertwined hands, and my breath caught as I struggled to find the right words.

"I know it's hard," he whispered against my hair. "It's terrifying, really."

I choked on a little laugh. "To put it mildly!"

"Look, I understand. We've both lost before, and setting yourself up to lose something that big again... well, I get it. And I don't want *us* to be about patching up the past, like some band-aid over our disappointments. I want more, and I want it with you."

I shook my head, struggling to find the right words. "It's not about my past, Evan," I started, my voice trembling. "It's not about the divorce or any of that. It's... it's something else."

He squeezed my hand. "What, all this?" He nodded at the land before us—that great wild life of his, with all its risks and rewards. The mound of fresh earth before us that represented the full circle of hope and loss. "Is this what worries you? All the stuff that comes with me? I know it's a lot. Always on the go, never sure of what's gonna come next, or—"

"It's not that, either. I'd take you, ranch or no ranch. I'd take you if you hadn't a penny to your name or if you wore a suit and tie every day. But I just don't know why you would want *me*."

Evan sat up a little, staring hard at me in the moonlight. "Meg, I don't understand."

"I'm terrified," I admitted, my voice barely above a whisper. "I'm scared of opening my heart fully, of letting you become a part of our family, and then... and then one day you might decide that being a step-dad to a special needs son is more than you bargained for. That kind of heartbreak... I don't know if I can handle it. And Dustin... it would be even harder on him."

Evan was quiet for a bit, his hand clenching mine, his jaw tight, and his expression unreadable. He leaned closer, his eyes more intense than I'd ever seen. "Meg, I wouldn't dream of hurting you or Dustin."

I studied him, searching his eyes for any hint of doubt. "Not on purpose. You could never. And I know you've said this before, and you even believe it. But how can you be so sure of what you'll want in a year? Ten years? You see how Dustin looks at you, how he associates you with safety and trust. He looks up to you more than he ever did his own father. How can I risk that? Unless you're truly sure, Evan, that you want both of us... I can't give you the answer you're looking for."

To my surprise, Evan sighed in relief, a soft chuckle escaping him. I was baffled by his reaction, but he just held me a little closer, letting me melt against his strong, broad chest. "Nothing could drive me away, Meg," he said softly as he folded me into his embrace. "I've faced my past to be honest with what I want in our relationship. And I want you both. I'm sure of that, more than anything."

He... he did? Really? I wiped a tear out of my eye—a happy tear, this time. Maybe there would be more of those to come. "You're sure?" I whispered again.

"Cross my heart." He bent down and kissed my nose. "And I'll do whatever it takes to prove it. You should never have to ask if I love you, Meg. I'll show you every day."

I smiled for real this time and slid my hand up his chest to cup his cheek. "You can start right now."

He liked that idea... I guess that was how I ended up pinned against that pine tree, holding my cowboy and learning to let him make me smile all the time.

Evan

U NDER THE PINE TREE, the world around us faded to nothing but Meg and me. I was lost in the feel of her lips, the warmth of her touch, when suddenly, a bright flash of lightning split the sky, followed by a resounding crack of thunder. We both jumped, and Meg shrieked in surprise.

"Well, isn't that something?" she teased. "Must be the real deal."

"I'm not arguing, but why do you say that?"

She grinned. "I've never kissed a man and had the heavens crack and thunder their approval."

"Hah. I think they're jealous," I said and leaned in for another soft kiss. But as another flash of lightning illuminated the yard, I stood up quickly, offering her a hand. "We better get inside. That storm's closer than I like."

Meg took my hand, and as she rose to her feet, the night air split with another brilliant flash, followed by an even louder clap of thunder. I wrapped my arm around her, pulling her close as I counted the seconds between the lightning and thunder. "Dang, that came up fast. No warning at all, and it's right on top of us. Let's head in before it gets worse."

Meg nodded, her earlier playfulness replaced by a sense of urgency as we hurried towards the house, the storm's intensity growing with each step we took. As we stepped into the ranch house, the sharp crack of thunder jolted through the walls, rattling the windows and sending a shiver down my spine. I glanced at Meg, noticing the worry etching her face as her eyes darted around the room. I put my hand on her arm and raised my voice. "Where's Dustin?"

Everyone was there, so many voices all together that I'm not sure how anyone even heard me, and I don't know who answered. "In the living room," someone called out, and I led Meg in that direction, our steps hurried and in sync.

As we rounded the corner, I saw him—Dustin, standing at the big picture window with Lizzy, both kids captivated by the storm outside. Seeing Dustin calm in the midst of the storm eased my worry. He seemed unfazed by the noise, probably because of the bright pink muffs over his ears.

Meg's shoulders visibly relaxed as she approached her son. "Where'd those come from?" she asked.

Lizzy piped up proudly, "They're mine. Luke gave them to me for target practice, and I thought Dustin would want them for the thunder."

"That was smart," I told her.

"I know," was her airy response. "He doesn't even care that they're pink." She turned back around at the next flash of lightning, and I saw her counting the seconds on her finger and showing Dustin how to do it. "Three seconds," she told him. "Wow."

"What does that mean?" he shouted over the muffled void in his ears.

She cupped her hands around her mouth. "Less than a mile away. Right, Luke?"

My brother stepped up to the window, squeezing Lizzy's shoulder. "Right, kiddo. This is a great window for watching the storm from, huh? Way better than our house in town. You can see the flashes over the mountains."

The mountains... exactly what I was worried about. Turning towards Meg, I caught her gaze. "You good?" I asked.

"Fine. Go do whatever you need to do." As I leaned in to kiss her, the chaos around us seemed to fade away, replaced by the warmth and reassurance of her presence. I feathered my fingers at her cheek, leaning in for one last endearment, then headed off to find my dad and his emergency scanner. Some folks might have never even seen one these days, but Dad listened to his religiously, and he usually knew what was going on as fast as the cops and fire departments did.

The dining room table was a patchwork of conversations and activities. Dad was hunched over the scanner, his bushy eyebrows scrunched together as the static-filled voices reported the storm's progress. Meryl sat beside him, her crochet needle flashing as quick as the lightning outside.

Jess walked in behind me, tousling her damp with a towel. I probably had a funny look on my face when I turned around because she looked kind of sheepish. "Hey, Evan. Power's out at our place."

"It is?" I turned around and looked at all the lights on in the house. "Are we running on generator, then?"

"Yeah. The power company turned off the grid when the storm started, and I was in the shower with shampoo in my hair when it cut out. Dusty and I hopped on the side-by-side and came up so I could rinse off. Thank goodness for the generator here!"

I nodded. "It's good for emergencies. What's everyone else still doing here, though?"

"*You* try sitting in that awful RV in a rain storm," Kelli said, gesturing towards Marshall with a playful glare. "It's only rained once since we moved into that thing, and it ruined one of my boxes of stuff."

Marshall snorted. "Trust me, sweetheart. We didn't lose anything."

She swatted his arm, but it looked a lot more like flirting than fighting. "I didn't tell you what was in there." She leaned close and whispered into his ear, and whatever it was, it made him blush like a cherry.

"Well, why didn't you say so?" he drawled. "We'd better do us some shopping."

"What we'd 'better' do is get a proper roof up over our heads before winter," his wife shot back, right before she kissed him.

"Aw, come on, Kel. It's just a tiny leak. Adds character, don't you think?"

"You'll think 'character' come winter when you're getting dripped on in bed."

I turned away from them, chuckling as I eased my way up to Dad's side. Cody and Morgan were nestled in a corner behind his chair, their expressions grave as they talked in low voices. But there was something in the way Cody rubbed Morgan's shoulder, and she held a protective hand over her stomach that made me melt deep inside.

Family just keeps on. It changes. Gets bigger and smaller, takes on different shapes, but the heart—I guess that was what Mom and Dad had built. That was the part that would keep on.

"Any rain yet?"

Dad glanced up as I pulled out a chair, his eyes briefly meeting mine before returning to the scanner. "No. But no major strikes, either. Just the usual warnings so far, but this storm's picking up. They're cutting off power to lots of places, just as a precaution."

"Those woods are dry as tinder."

"Yep. Ah, not to worry. Every year, we get these storm warnings, and usually, it's just a lot of talk. Still." Dad turned down the volume on the scanner and leaned back in his chair, stretching his arms out and letting one of them fall over Meryl's shoulders. He might have tried to look easy, but there was a tightness in his expression that I knew all too well. "I'm glad we got that herd down from the mountains early. Don't want to be out in this."

I shook my head. "Well, should we break out something to eat? Starving won't make the storm pass any faster."

Meryl pushed up from her seat. "I've got cold chicken we can warm up with the grill, and Dusty brought up some fresh corn on the cob from the garden."

"And I made a fresh batch of hot barbecue sauce last week," I added.

Marshall and Kelli were still teasing each other about something in the background, and pretty soon, he managed to drag Cody into it, and they were all laughing. That was right about when Luke walked in, fanning his hat over his face and calling to Audrey, "They're in here!" He gave Dusty a hard nudge in the shoulder. "Hey, you forgot to get the tractor under shelter. I just had to run out and move it."

"I had to rescue my dripping wife from the shower when the power cut out," Dusty argued. "What was your handicap?"

"Jess is a big girl. She could'a done fine without—"

"Alright, enough!" Dad growled at everyone. "If you're not listening to this scanner, go find somewhere else to make your racket!"

The room quieted down, a collective chuckle rippling through the family. Jess kissed Dusty on the cheek and flicked her towel at Luke playfully before heading out, and

Kelli leaned closer to Marshall, whispering something that made them both smile.

And I went to find Meg.

Meg

T HE SMELL OF BARBECUE wafted through the house, mingling with the sound of laughter and occasional thunderclaps. Blake passed around grilled chicken, joking, "Nothing like a storm to spice up a barbecue, huh?"

"That's not the storm." Jess was wiping her eyes and gulping the water between coughs. "Who made that barbecue sauce? I didn't know it had a handful of jalapenos in it. Stuff needs a hazmat label!"

Evan grinned as he tipped the bottle to pour it generously over his chicken. "That's my winter recipe. Warm ya from the inside out." He passed me the bottle next, but his hand tightened on it before I took it. "Might go easy on it, huh? A little goes a long way."

I just grinned and drizzled it over my chicken, then sliced off a chunk and popped it in my mouth. "Mmm. Just right."

That cowboy's smile could have lit up the Rockies. "Well, I'll be. Guess I won't have to worry about running you out of the house when I make it. You'll be eating it faster than I can get it bottled."

I nodded, quirking an eyebrow as I speared another piece of chicken. "You should sell this stuff. You could quit ranching and become a millionaire."

"And leave all this?" he asked with a teasing grin.

I shrugged and took another bite, savoring the savage tang of the homemade sauce. "Maybe not."

The glasses on the table rattled with another fierce roll of thunder, and everyone looked vaguely around, checking the windows for more lightning. "Well," Meryl said with a chuckle, "the good news is that if the generator dies, we won't need candles for light."

"Did the power company give an estimate of when they'll have us back on?" Marshall asked.

Evan and Dusty both pulled out their phones at the same time, opening the power company's app to check the outage details. But it was Dusty who answered first. "They're not saying, but I wouldn't look for them to turn us back on before the storm's over. They can't chance a pole getting struck and starting a forest fire. They got sued five or six years ago, remember that?"

The cowboys at the table all nodded and tucked into their dinner, but I was watching their wives. The only ones who didn't look at least a little uncomfortable were Meryl and Kelli. Audrey kept checking her watch and giving warning glances to Lizzy whenever her voice got too loud. Morgan wasn't eating—just staring absently out the window, rubbing her stomach. And Jess seemed preoccupied with a series of text messages to her dad, checking to make sure he was doing okay without power.

"Just invite him to come up," Dusty murmured to her after a while.

She shook her head. "He says he's fine, and he doesn't like driving in the lightning. I told him the car's a safe place to be, but he doesn't want to go anywhere."

Dusty rubbed her shoulders and leaned close to her ear. "Well, he'll be okay. He can take care of himself, angel."

Jess nodded and smiled at her husband, squeezing his other hand. "I know. I just want him to know he's welcome to come instead of having to be alone all the time."

My heart squeezed, watching them. They were just about the cutest couple ever, with the way they doted on each other. But, actually... My gaze rounded the table, and I realized that would actually be a pretty stiff contest in this family. Marshall and Kelli were like fire and gasoline, always bigger and brighter together than they were apart, and Luke and Audrey had somehow found their own likeness in a person who looked, on the surface, to be their exact opposite.

And Cody and Morgan... well, it's hard to out-cute a couple expecting their first baby, and those two were two halves of the same whole. There there was Blake and Meryl. All of them were just so sweet together. And here I sat beside Evan... almost as if I was really part of the family already.

And I couldn't think of any place in the world I'd rather be.

"What do you think, baby?" Cody wiped his mouth and started gathering up his silverware to stack it on his plate. "Shall we run home and check on stuff, or did you want to wait out the storm here?"

Morgan shifted in her chair, wincing at some little ache or pain. "I got all the horses under shelter before I came over, and we won't have power yet. We really need to get a generator."

"Sure, just as soon as I win another big check. Maybe I'll get lucky in Vegas this year."

"It ain't luck," Marshall said, banging his knife against a glass. "Maserati's better'n Five Iron. I've seen her work. You'll get it, bro. And that's not even to mention Rust. Colt's finally settling in and working like a house-a-fire."

Cody laughed. "Right. Well, anyway, we'll have to make do without that generator for right now. Not so bad being stuck here with good company, though," he said, glancing around the table with a smile as he reached for Morgan's hand to kiss it. "Are you finished? I'll take your plate to the kitchen."

And so, the evening wound down. The night sky lit up like a rock concert for hours, with cracks and rumbles that made my skin crawl when they were close. Most of us wandered into the living room to watch the storm with a glass of Meryl's ice-cold sweet tea and a fire in the wood stove to give us a little light.

I thought about going home. The ranch house was crowded, and I lived in town, where they hadn't cut the power. There was just no need for such precautions in the neighborhood—it was the houses up in the dry mountains that were the concern. I could get Dustin home, in his own bed, and maybe I could even invite Evan and some of the others to come, too.

But one look at Evan and I called off that idea. He'd been pacing behind his dad, listening to the scanner with a tight expression after dinner. Eventually, however, he came to sit on the couch next to me, but I think half his mind was still in the next room, trying to know whatever there was to know. If I asked, he would probably leave the ranch and see me home... and then he'd be miserable. And I'd just rather be with him, whatever he was going through, than to leave now.

But it was Dustin who really settled it for me. Most of the evening, he'd been watching the storm at the window with Lizzy, but he was tired now. He'd tried pulling the earmuffs off, but the first loud clap of thunder on his unshielded ears had made him change his mind. So, when Evan sat beside me on the couch, Dustin silently tucked himself into the corner on Evan's other side and fell asleep. Evan's arms wrapped naturally around us both, and soon, my head was pillowed on his shoulder as his steady breathing and the warmth of his arms lulled me to dreams.

Chapter Twenty

Evan

I STIRRED FROM A comfortable dream, momentarily disori-
ented as I woke. The soft weight of Meg's head resting on
my chest grounded me, and a smile tugged at my lips. Right
where she belonged. I gently kissed her forehead, savoring
the peaceful moment. She murmured something inaudible in
her sleep and snuggled closer, her breath warm and steady
against my skin.

Dustin lay curled under my other arm, snoring to beat
the band. I brushed a strand of hair from his forehead, and
I'm pretty sure my heart filled my whole ribcage, just seeing
him so relaxed and content. It was a rare and cherished
sight—the two people who had become my world, safe and
sound in my arms. I'd do anything to keep them there. But
the static I was hearing from the scanner, and the low voices
carrying from the dining room, meant something was up.

Reluctantly, I eased myself off the couch, careful not to
disturb them more than I had to. Dad and Marshall were
huddled over the table, holding a hushed debate. As I approached, Dad looked up and beckoned me over with a grave
expression. "Evan, there's been a fire spotted."

My heart sank. I was hoping those would give us a miss
this year. "Where?"

Marshall handed me his phone, displaying a live fire map
from the forest service. A red dot glowed ominously about

two miles north of our grazing boundary. "Right there," he said, pointing. "Still small, but they're keeping an eye on it."

I studied the map, zooming in and panning over the topography, trying to gauge the situation. The steady rain tapping against the window offered a glimmer of hope. "The rain should help keep it in check," I murmured, more to reassure myself than anything.

Dad's expression didn't change. He shook his head slowly, his eyes meeting mine. "That little rain will evaporate before it even hits, once a fire gets hot. And there's a 20 mph wind reported up on the mountain, blowing south."

That was what I was hoping not to hear. Rain or not, a wind like that could turn a small fire into an uncontrollable inferno, pushing it toward our land... and everything we held dear.

"What do you want to do?" I asked Dad.

He winced and put a hand over his chest. "Nothing yet. Forest service says they've got it under control."

"Yeah, we've heard that before," Marshall grumbled.

"We've got to move the cattle from the north pastures," I insisted, my finger tracing over the map. "Our pedigreed stock are up there, and they're sitting ducks if this thing spreads."

Marshall leaned over my shoulder. "We can bring them into the stockyard. They'll be pretty crowded for a few days, but there aren't any new calves to get stompled."

Dad blinked and nodded. "Fine. Might as well bring all the yearlings in close, too. The lower eighty? Pretty well shielded there."

"Yeah," Marshall agreed. "That well house we put in down there might come in real handy, keeping everything watered down."

"And don't forget the broodmares," Dad added. "Call your brothers, let's get moving."

I was about to counter his suggestion when Luke's voice came from behind me. "I'm here, what's the plan?" he asked, joining our huddled group.

I glanced at Luke and then back at Dad. "The brood-mares are on the south pastures. They should be okay for now. They've got the lake, and the pasture's bordered by a wide-open meadow that's all grazed down this late in the year. It's a natural firebreak. It's the cattle up north we need to worry about."

Marshall looked between us, his brow furrowed. "Do we need to call in Mitch, Brandon, and the others? Get more hands on deck?"

I paused, considering. Waking the crew in the middle of the night for what might be a false alarm was a tough call. "Let's not rouse everyone just yet," I decided. "We can start with what we have here."

Dad's breathing was irregular, and he was wincing like he did when he got heartburn after eating Luke's cabbage stew. A twinge passed over his face, and he nodded. "Fine. Focus on the northern pastures first. They're the most vulnerable, but at the first sign of anything, we pull those broodmares and foals in. We might need to fully evacuate them if we've got cattle filling up everything close to the house."

"We could put a trough and a round bale in the indoor arena," Luke suggested. "There's room for them all in there, but it'll be tight. Cody'll throw a fit about what all that stomping will do to his special arena sand, but I'd rather do that than lose twenty-five babies."

"I'd be worried about their lungs if it gets smoky," I mused. "Those foals aren't like the cows. They've got athletic careers ahead of them, and we can't afford smoke inhalation damage. Any ideas where we can take them?"

"The fairgrounds will open up," Luke said. "Like they did three years ago when that bad one came from the east."

"And we'd fill them half up with just our stock," Marshall said. "We've got connections. I say we leave the fairgrounds for folks who have just a few horses and nowhere else to go."

"I'll make some calls," Dad decided. "Can't wait till the last minute on something like that."

Luke nodded in agreement, his eyes scanning the phone map Marshall passed him. "Alright, let's get moving then. The sooner we start, the better. I already called Dusty."

"What about Cody?" Dad asked.

Luke hiked a thumb over his shoulder. "He just left. Morgan had an app on her phone that woke her up when the fire was spotted, so they headed out to button things down at White Pines. Said they'd be back to help out here if we need."

Dad glanced around at all of us and nodded. "Right. Let's saddle up."

Meg

I WAS DRIFTING IN and out of sleep, lulled by the sound of rain against the window, when Evan's gentle nudge stirred me awake. His voice was low, cautious not to disturb Dustin, as he explained the situation with the fire. My mind instantly shifted to alert mode, my thoughts racing to my son and how he would handle the disruption.

"Dustin... will all the commotion upset him?" I whispered.

Evan's eyes softened. "I can drive you both home if you'd prefer. You'll be safe here, but safer there."

I shook my head slightly. "No, I drove here, remember? I'd rather stay... maybe I can help somehow." The idea of leaving when there was a crisis unfolding didn't sit right with me. I needed to be here, even though I didn't know how to wrangle a herd or drive a stock trailer.

"There's not much to do, really. Just moving cows. Meryl, Kelli, and Jess might help, but we should manage. We're not even calling the hands in yet."

"How long will you be?"

"An hour or two, hopefully."

"I'll wait, then," I decided. "Especially if Audrey's staying here, too. I'll keep her company. Maybe she and I can make breakfast for when you all get back."

Evan grinned. "I like the sound of that. We can put Dustin in my room. He can sleep there quietly in case it gets noisy in the house, with all of us stomping through to get ready. Do you think he'll be okay waking up in a strange room with everything going on?"

"Where's Lizzy?"

"She's in Luke's old room, bedded down on the floor. I think Audrey's asleep, too. Luke didn't want to wake her."

After a moment of thought, I nodded. "Yes, let's do that. I'll stay close by."

Evan's tenderness as he carefully lifted Dustin, still deep in slumber, struck a chord in my heart. He carried him with such ease and care. Watching them, a warmth spread through me, a mixture of gratitude and affection. This man, who had come into our lives so unexpectedly, was now an integral part of our world, a source of comfort and strength. As he gently laid Dustin down in his bed, tucking him in with a softness that belied his rugged exterior, my heart swelled with an emotion that was both profound and terrifying.

Love.

Evan straightened to look at me, and swift concern crossed his features. He came to me and clasped my hands. "Hey. Are you okay?"

"Better than okay." I stood on my toes and kissed his cleft chin. "You'd better come back safe and sound to me, cowboy."

Evan chuckled. "Promise. Think he's warm enough?"

I slid a hand over Evan's chest, and he stepped away just enough for me to look at Dustin, crashed in the bed, and still sound asleep. "Maybe just a light blanket? He's generally a hot sleeper, but he likes the weight of something on top of him."

"I've got just the thing." He went to a drawer and pulled out a wadded quilt. It looked old and hand-made, scraps of different colors and fabrics worked into a beautiful prism pattern. And when he shook it out and tucked it over my son, I realized what it was.

"Did your mom make that?" I whispered.

Evan frowned as he turned back to me. "How did you know?"

"I... I saw the one Kelli had, and she told me the rest of you had one, too. Evan, that's... All that handwork, and it was from your mom! He's going to get it all rumpled. Are you sure you want to..."

"Quilts are for using," he said quietly. "And for family. My mom would be happier seeing Dustin curled up with it than seeing it balled up in a drawer. Hey, come here."

I let him draw me close and hook his hands together behind my waist. I leaned back just a little, reveling in his smile and his strong arms and the way he didn't let me go. "Whatever you're about to ask, I think the answer is yes."

"That's what I was hoping to hear." He pulled me closer for a kiss. "Stay with my family. It might seem like we've got it all handled, but there's always a place for one more to pitch in and pull on the yoke. We're stronger together, and I feel like you're part of us already. If you can put up with..." he chuckled and tipped his head toward the door when we heard Luke's voice outside, shouting for Dusty. "... all of that, then I'd sure love for you to stay."

I laughed and put a hand on his cheek. "I'd be honored, cowboy."

Evan leaned in for the kind of kiss that made me think there were more fires in this county than just on top of the mountains. He singed my nerves, scorched the hair on my scalp, and left me smoldering for more before he pulled back. "Gotta go, love. See you in an hour or two."

"I'm holding you to that."

"Hope so." He winked as he closed the door.

Evan

T HE NIGHT WAS THICK around us, the air heavy with the scent of wet earth and cattle. The moon was shrouded by clouds, so the only light was from the occasional flash of distant lightning, painting eerie shadows across the fields. If not for the light rain, it would be hot and stifling, even at three in the morning.

I squinted, counting the reflective glimmers of ear tags on the cows as we pushed them toward the stocker pens by the barns. Beside me, Dad and Marshall rode in silence, each lost in their own thoughts amidst the low moos and shuffling of hooves. Somewhere up ahead, Kelli and Meryl were riding point to make sure the cows had something to follow, while Luke, Dusty, and Jess had gone after the yearlings.

Strider moved out steadily, his head bobbing back and forth as he watched the herd. We were almost back to the corrals when I did a quick tally. "We're short about ten head," I muttered, scanning the dark horizon. "Twelve, to be exact."

Marshall pulled up beside me, his horse snorting softly. "You sure? Could be just mixed in deeper."

I shook my head, certain of my count. "No, I've been keeping track. They're missing. I'm going back to look for them."

"I'll come with you."

"I got it. Stick with Dad and the rest. You've got eighty head to get settled, so just make sure these are secure."

As they continued towards the corrals, I turned Strider around, heading back into the vast darkness of the fields. The sounds of the cattle faded behind me, replaced by the distant rumble of thunder. The storm had moved to the east, where, hopefully, it would crash against the mountain ranges and cool off. We sure didn't need any more lightning strikes.

My eyes adjusted to the dark, scanning the land for any sign of the missing cows. As I followed the creek through the darkness, guided by the sound of its rushing water, Strider grew increasingly fractious—trying to turn back, and once, he even whinnied for his buddies. He didn't like leaving the other horses just yet, but with a little encouragement and a reminder of what his job was, he moved out okay.

The path we were on tapered off, vanishing into the steep hillside, forcing us to cross the creek. Strider splashed through like a born and bred mountain cow pony, but once we hit the other side, he snorted sharply and stopped dead in his tracks, his whole body quivering. At first, I assumed it was just his greenness showing—he was still new to this kind of work, after all. But then, following his gaze, I saw what he was fixated on.

Under a tree, a short distance away, lay a cow—motionless and unmistakably lifeless. I guided Strider closer, though he danced sideways, reluctant to approach. Dismounting and tugging him by the rein, I flicked on my flashlight, its beam cutting through the darkness to reveal a grim scene. Several cows were huddled under the tree, all of them dead. Well... *that* wasn't what I'd been hoping to find.

Sweeping the flashlight's beam upwards, I noticed the tree itself was smoking, a large branch blown off, with an ominous glow emanating from a crack in the bark. A lightning strike. The cows had likely sought shelter under the tree, a fatal mistake during a storm.

I started counting the dead cows, a knot forming in my throat as the number grew. And then, right in the middle of them, I spotted our prize pedigreed bull—lifeless like the rest. A sense of loss washed over me; he wasn't just any bull, but a key part of our breeding program, irreplaceable and invaluable. Insurance couldn't make up for that loss.

Twelve head. All dropped in an instant by the hand of nature. I shook my head and mounted my horse. There was nothing I could do for them now; my focus had to shift to the living and the safety of the rest of the herd.

Meg

I PACED THE HOUSE for over an hour—peeking outside as if I could see where the riders were, and then wandering back to the bedroom to check on Dustin. He was sleeping like a rock, but it never occurred to me that I could get some rest, too. For one, I didn't feel right about curling up on the other side of Evan's bed. Just... felt a little presumptuous, somehow. But also, some part of me wanted to be useful in case anyone had to come back for any reason.

Around four-thirty, Audrey emerged from Luke's old bedroom, rubbing her eyes and tying a navy blue terry-cloth bathrobe around her waist that was about four sizes too big for her. "Have you been up all night?" she asked blearily.

"I couldn't sleep."

"Me either, but not for want of trying. Should we give up and brew a pot of coffee?"

"I'm up for that. I was thinking about starting some breakfast for them all when they get back. How long do you think they'll be?"

"Hopefully not much longer, and if I know Luke, his 'belly-button will be rubbing a hole in his backbone' by the time he gets back. Might as well have something ready when they hit the door."

The kitchen was a maze of unfamiliar cupboards and drawers. Audrey and I opened one after another, often in search of one thing but finding something entirely different. "This is what we get for trying to navigate a bachelor's kitchen," I muttered.

Audrey snorted as she rummaged through another cupboard. "I'd bet anything that Luke arranged everything haphazardly on purpose. It's his way of making sure he never has to cook. I just can't believe Meryl hasn't fixed it all by now."

"She probably learned her way around. Oh! That's where the coffee filters are. By the stock pot." I held them out with a wry look.

Audrey laughed and took one, passing me the spatula she'd just found so I could get started at the griddle. Despite struggling to find what we were looking for, we managed to whip up hotcakes, coffee, eggs, and bacon, and just in time for all the cows outside to start setting up a fuss. They were back, for sure, and about half an hour later, in they stumbled.

As everyone trudged in, tired and damp, I saw relief in their eyes at the sight of food. Evan came over, enveloping me in a warm, weary hug. "We lost some cows," he said softly. "Lightning strike."

"Oh, no! Very many?"

"Twelve, but they were some of our prize stock." He pulled back and ran a hand through his hair. "That will be a hard hit come next year when we don't have those up-and-coming young breeding cows."

"They didn't..." I shook my head. "They didn't suffer, did they?"

"They never even knew what happened. At least it was quick." He made a tight smile as his gaze swept the kitchen counter, all loaded with breakfast. "This is sure nice to come back in to, though. How did Dustin sleep in the strange room?"

"I don't think he even knows he's in a strange room yet."

Evan kissed my cheek. "I'll go check on him now. Think he'll be hungry?"

I shrugged. "'Hungry' doesn't always equate to 'want to eat' with Dustin, but I'm sure he is. He likes pancakes."

"So do I." He winked. "Be right back."

Turning back to the kitchen, I poured coffee for Blake, who looked like he needed it more than anyone. He was sagging in his chair at the table, only distantly paying attention to whatever Luke and Dusty were saying to him. He came to a little when I filled his cup, smiling up at me with a crinkle around his eyes that reminded me of his son. "Thanks."

I tilted my head to look at him. "Are you okay, Blake?"

"Yeah," he heaved a sigh. "Can't do those all-nighters like I used to."

"I was never good at them to begin with. Ready for breakfast?"

He nodded, and I went back to the kitchen to load up a plate for him and one for Meryl, who was upstairs putting dry clothes on. That was when Evan reappeared, his face pale, eyes wide with a panic I'd never seen in him. "Meg, Dustin's not in the room. He's missing."

Chapter Twenty-One

Evan

"YOU SURE HE'S NOT just down at the barn?" Luke was following me, grabbing his flashlight and his farm truck keys on the way out the door.

I glanced over my shoulder at him. "Meg never saw him leave the room, which means he probably went out the basement door that leads out back."

"What's your point?"

"Just that the most immediate path out of the backyard isn't out to the driveway and down to the barns. He might've gone down to the pond or out to the woods."

"Why would he do something like that?"

I shook my head. "I don't always know. Is Lizzy still sleeping?"

He shrugged. "I'd assume so." Then, his eyes narrowed, and he stepped back through the door into the house. "Hey, Audrey!" he called. "Can you check on..."

He never got to finish his sentence, though, because his wife was rushing to him, and I saw the look on her face over his shoulder. Luke said something low to her, and Audrey nodded, then Luke turned back to me, shaking his head. "So, uh... guess she's not still sleeping."

I frowned. "So they might have gone somewhere together. Well, that's good, at least."

"Good? Now we got two kids to track down."

"Yeah, and you probably know right where Lizzy's going to go. I haven't figured Dustin out yet—not sure anyone has. If he's with her, it'll be easier. So...?"

Luke rubbed his jaw, and when he dropped his hand, his face revealed a reluctant grimace. "You ain't gonna like it."

"I'll like something better than nothing. Where do you think she went?"

Luke cleared his throat and flicked his flashlight on, pointing it in the general direction of the trees. "Built herself a fort on the north side of the property. She probably went up there to rescue her stuff."

I scanned what I could see of the tree line. There was a bare scruff of a pink outline from the east, so dawn wasn't too far off. And the fire was still a safe distance away, according to Dusty's forest service map. The kids weren't in any real danger, and neither were we. "Well, let's go."

LUKE AND I WALKED about three hundred yards into the woods behind the ranch house, following an old deer trail that he said Lizzy used all the time. The early morning light was just beginning to penetrate the dense canopy of leaves, but not bright enough to cast shadows or even define the tree trunks. We still had to use our flashlights for a while.

As we approached Lizzy's fort, I shone my flash beam over it. This wasn't some clap-trap kid fort. It looked like an engineer had designed it and spent weeks at it. I could probably jump up and down on the roof, and it would hold. "Lizzy built this all by herself?" I asked, genuinely impressed.

Luke's chest puffed up a bit with pride. "Yeah, she used some of my tools and scrap lumber from Marshall and Dusty's houses. Kept her busy all summer. I'm pretty sure the thing is earthquake-proof."

"It looks like it," I huffed as I scanned the lines of its beams. I wondered if Dustin would enjoy having a private sanctuary like this, a place he could call his own. The idea of Meg and Dustin becoming my family was more real to me now than ever, and I liked the idea of giving Dustin the freedom to build something of his own. There was certainly enough room for him to do whatever he wanted. He might want more help than Lizzy did, but I'd be up for that. It would be a good way to spend time with him.

But as we got closer to the fort, we didn't hear the voices inside or see the kids' flashlights like we expected. Something was off. Luke checked inside, confirming what we already knew. "Doesn't look like she's been here at all," he said, sounding a little worried now.

"No? Well, where else would she go?"

"Search me. Maybe they turned back up already."

I tugged my phone out of my pocket to call Meg, but the trees were too thick. Nestled up against the hillside, out of sight of any cell towers, I wouldn't pick anything up 'til we got out of the woods. I followed Luke back out the trail, switching off my light as we got closer to the clearing where the morning light was seeping through the canopy.

As we emerged from the tree line, with the ranch houses visible in the distance, Luke suddenly stopped and sniffed the air. "Hey, do you smell that?"

I paused and inhaled deeply. There it was, unmistakable even amidst the fresh morning air—the acrid scent that makes every rancher's hair stand on end. "Smoke."

We exchanged a look. "That fire was nowhere close. I just looked at the update half an hour ago. It couldn't have moved that fast," Luke said.

"Unless there's another one. The lightning kept up for hours, and sometimes they don't spot the smoke right away."

"Can't be. It's just on the breeze from that other one. The smell carries for miles."

"All the same..." I checked my phone. Half a bar—probably not good enough service to get a call out yet. "I think we'd better find the kids. Pronto."

Meg

"**A**NYTHING HERE?" AUDREY'S VOICE echoed slightly in the dim tool shed as we peered into every corner. The shelves were cluttered with all sorts of ranch equipment, but no sign of Dustin or Lizzy.

I shook my head, feeling a tightness in my chest. "No, nothing." My voice sounded hollow in the small space. We stepped out, heading towards the shop, our boots crunching on the gravel path.

The shop was our next hope, but as the door creaked open, revealing an empty room, my hope faltered. The quietness was oppressive, twisting my anxiety into a ball in my stomach. I called out again, "Dustin! Lizzy!" My voice wavered.

Where would he go? He wouldn't leave Lizzy and strike off on his own, would he? And why would he just take off before dawn? Surely, there was some simple explanation. One thing I knew about my son was that when I reflected on the things he did, I could usually figure out the trail of thoughts and feelings that had led him there. Often, it was a spiderweb of interconnected emotions and associations, but when I got him to talk me through it, it made sense. Sort of.

But I didn't see how this one was going to make any sense at all. And now, with everyone operating on emergency mode and almost no sleep, it didn't seem to be the right time for piecing out any of Dustin's mysteries. A sob caught in my throat. I clasped my hand over my mouth, trying to muffle the sound.

Jess glanced at Audrey, then Audrey came to my side, her hand reassuring on my shoulder. "They're going to find them, Meg," she said softly. "Luke and Evan won't stop until they do."

I nodded, fighting back tears. "Thanks," I managed to whisper. "I'm sure Luke's right, and they went to Lizzy's fort. That makes the most sense, but..."

"But we had to look, you're right. Come on, I'm sure they'll be coming back to the house any minute," Jess said cheerfully.

As we reentered the house, everyone's eyes turned towards us, hope flickering in their expressions. Luke was sloshing down the last of a cup of coffee, and Evan was wiping his hands on a kitchen towel and stepping toward us. But as soon as they saw no kids standing with us in the doorway and the concern etched on our faces, the hope faded.

"Not down at the barn or in the shop or something?" Evan asked. I shook my head.

"We checked the fort," Luke said. "Lizzy's stuff is there—no sign they went to get it."

"You know," Jess volunteered, "we didn't check the bunkhouse. I didn't think they'd go in there, but I can go back down and—"

Just then, Blake and Dusty walked in from feeding and watering all the new cows in the pens. Blake was coughing lightly, and Dusty was staring at a report on his phone. "We've got a problem," Dusty announced. "New fire's been spotted. They reported it just after dawn, and it's much closer than the last."

"Yeah," Evan agreed. "We could smell it in the north field."

Blake took off his hat and sighed. "That's it, then. We need to start moving the broodmares and their foals. Can't risk them being caught if the fire spreads."

"Wait, Dad, we're still looking for the kids. We can't start rounding up horses until..." Evan stopped, then rounded on Luke with a funny look.

That was when Luke's eyes widened. "I bet..." Luke stuck out a finger, his thoughts scrolling across his face like a ticker tape. "I betcha Lizzy went down to round up them horses. With us out getting cattle brought in to safety, she'd have wanted to pitch in."

Audrey's face tightened. "That sounds like something Lizzy would do," she agreed heavily. "At a dead run, and probably on *your* horse."

"She'd better not've," Luke growled. "She'll get her fool neck broke."

"But it *does* sound like her," Audrey argued. "Because it sounds like something *you* would do first."

Luke rolled his eyes, but I was watching Evan. He was working his fingers into a worried fist and giving me a curious look. "Yes," I whispered, feeling a lump forming in my throat. "Dustin, too. He'd want to rescue Forge. It might not have been his idea, but if Lizzy suggested it, he'd go in an instant."

The room fell silent for a moment. Then, as if they'd choreographed it, all four brothers grabbed their hats.

Evan

T HE RHYTHMIC POUNDING OF hooves against the earth thrummed beneath me as Strider and I galloped alongside Luke and Two Bits. Our horses surged forward, their breaths coming in heavy, steamy gusts in the cool morning air. We weren't running in a brainless frenzy, but we sure weren't poking along, either. I was standing lightly in the saddle, letting my colt run as free an easy as he could as each stride ate up the distance towards the northeastern meadow where the broodmares grazed.

We were pretty sure that the kids did, in fact, head out this way. June Bug and Dozer were missing, and so were a couple of saddles. Luke started cussing when we figured it out, but then I caught him grinning and chuckling under his breath.

"Guess I taught her good," he'd muttered as he tightened his cinch on Two Bits. "She took my favorite saddle."

Luke and I rode in silence now, our focus laser-sharp on the task at hand. The meadow was a good distance away, and with every passing minute, my concern for Dustin and Lizzy grew. If they'd gone out to try moving the horses, we should see something by now. The herd moving back toward us, or at least two kids turning around because they couldn't find the mares. What if one of them had gotten hurt? Strider suddenly reached farther with each plunging leap, his muscles working beneath me as he picked up the tension in my gut.

Dusty and Marshall were hot on our heels, their conversation floating up to us intermittently over the sound of the galloping horses. "You got an idea where we can take the mares? We need to get them away from all this smoke," Marshall was saying.

Dusty's response came through the wind. "I've got a place in mind, but I need to make some calls. I'll check after we find the kids."

I nodded in agreement, even though they couldn't see it. Dustin and Lizzy came first. Everything else could wait.

The smell of smoke kept getting stronger, a bitter scent that scratched at the back of my throat. The sun was truly up now, casting a hazy, orange glow over the landscape. We'd seen fire seasons come and go over the years. Never got singed ourselves, but that heavy smog that blocked out the fresh air for tens of miles around and made the sun glare red like it was Judgment Day—you don't forget that. And it was happening again.

Not much farther now. We were over the rise that dropped down into the southern valley of our fields, and now about half a dozen thready stock trails spiderwebbed out before us. "Which way, Evan?" Marshall called. "You're the one who checks on the mares the most in the summer."

I'd already thought about that. They could be in the trees, sheltering from last night's rainfall, or filling their bellies in the meadow. But it was still early in the morning, and usually, the first thing the bunch did this time of day was head for water. "The lake," I shouted over my shoulder.

We didn't even break stride as we swept down over the low grass of the mares' grazing grounds. Marshall and Dusty weren't holding back now—they pulled up even with Luke and me, and the horses that should have been starting to feel winded all hit a surge of adrenaline. Two Bits started it, flaring his nostrils and plunging forward when Bay Rum tried to push his head in front. Dusty was up on my left on Kelli's mare—I guess he thought this would be too much for Duchess, and that was probably a good call. But Joy had legs for days, and she was running my three-year-old down like he was standing still. She even had enough left over for a playful buck mid-stride when she caught us.

"Ease up now," I called over the panting horses. "We gotta leave something in the tank for the ride back." That didn't slow my brothers down much, though. Marshall and Luke sat back a little, but the only way I could tell we'd slowed down at all was that my horse wasn't laboring so hard to keep up.

The lake was down in front of us now—about an eighth of a mile—but as soon as we rounded a stand of trees, we could tell the mares weren't here. Still, our horses needed water and a chance to blow after their hard run, so we slowed to a long trot and dropped down to the water's edge. Only a sip—we didn't need them getting a belly ache after that workout, but they'd need water before we got back.

Luke took his hat off and was using it to fan his face. "The meadow?"

I nodded. "Has to be. They won't be in the trees this time of day. Sure hope the kids figured that out."

"Lizzy's smart. She's been rounding up cows with me all summer. Ready?"

The others all checked their horses, and in a few seconds, we were off again. The lushest part of the meadow was around a stand of trees about half a mile away. We reached the edge, where the trees broke up, and I pulled Strider to a halt, scanning the area. There were the broodmares huddled together at the far end, their heads raised and ears pricked and alert. But there was no sign of Lizzy or Dustin.

"We'll split up," I called out to the others. "Cover more ground that way. Keep your eyes open and stay in contact."

With a nod from Luke and the others, we each set off in different directions, calling out for the kids as we went. The tension in my chest tightened with each unanswered call. We had to find them, and fast.

As we trotted down into the meadow, the rain's reprieve had given way to a hot wind gusting from the northwest, whipping through the grass and trees. Our horses' sides heaved from the effort, their breaths heavy in the growing heat.

Marshall, riding a few strides ahead, suddenly pulled up. "Look!" he shouted, pointing towards the north.

We all reined in, following his gaze to the hills where a menacing dance of flames flickered through the trees, about two miles away. This was more than just ominous smoke-spotting—this was fresh heat, and it was running unchecked and maybe still unspotted by the forest service. "No," I breathed. My worst fears—a wildfire, unpredictable and fast-moving, was threatening to engulf the very area we hoped to find Dustin and Lizzy.

"Call it in, Marshall. They'll need crews on that one if they haven't spotted it yet."

"On it," he replied, already holding his phone to his ear.

"Call while you ride. We need to hurry," I urged, "Those trees are like matchsticks. That fire can close in faster than we think." Without another word, each of our horses leapt into a gallop, fanning out to break and circle around the group of mares.

Then, out of the corner of my eye, I caught a glimpse of something familiar—the top of a straw hat just visible over a clump of brush. "There!" I shouted, pulling Strider to the left to check it out.

The others trailed behind me as I headed straight for the spot. My heart pounded in sync with Strider's hooves, each

beat a mix of fear and hope. As we neared the brush, I saw
him—Dustin, crouched down, his hat barely visible.

Relief flooded through me as I quickly dismounted, rushing over to him. "Dustin!" I called out. "Are you okay?" The
sound of the others approaching filled the air, but for that
moment, my entire world narrowed down to the sight of the
boy in front of me.

He turned, his mouth taut with frustration and his eyes
brimming with tears. He swiped his sleeve over his eyes and
refused to look up at me.

"What's going on?" I asked gently, dismounting and walking towards him.

Dustin's voice was raised, edged with the frustration of
being on the verge of a meltdown. "I can't get F-Forge to
follow me! I thought the others would follow him too!" he
cried. "He just w-won't do it! He keeps rearing up when I
pull on the rope."

I glanced over my shoulder at Luke, who was already beating his way through the herd to get to Lizzy. It looked like
she was playing ring-around-the-rosie with another mare
and foal—both ducking and dodging around each other and
the other horses every time Lizzy got close with a rope. So,
that was their plan. Try to lead a couple and see if the others
would follow.

"It was a good idea. It's better than trying to scare them
all, right?"

He sniffed again, and his voice was a broken growl. "We
tried that! Lizzy ran at them and told me to stop them from
going the wrong way, but they just wouldn't move at all.
They're stupid! It should have worked!"

I knelt down to his level. "Dustin, you're doing fine. You
were brave to try and save the horses. But herds don't usually
follow just one colt. They stick together. And I'm sorry to
tell you this, but a herd of horses doesn't move the same way
a herd of cows does. They're not intimidated by our saddle
horses, see?"

His eyes flickered with thought. "But we *told* them to
move. They know how to m-move, so they should... should do

it. You said June Bug led all the horses safely b..." he gulped, trying to catch his breath. "Back home once before, so she should do it again!"

"It's frustrating when they don't do what they know they should, isn't it?" I pointed up in the hills. "You know, they probably spotted that fire coming, and they're smart. They know that going that way would be dangerous. They just don't know that we have a safe way around that danger to get them to a better spot. They have their own kind of rules to keep safe, just like we do. Do you remember our rule, Dustin?"

He blinked, staring at the ground. "I always remember rules."

"Which one did you forget today?"

Dustin shook his head as his eyes widened. "I didn't forget. Lizzy knew where I was going. I told her, and she said she'd come."

I sat back on my heels. "This was your idea, not hers?"

He swiped his nose again and nodded. "I w-wanted to save Forge. You said he was sp-special, and..." He kicked the ground with his toe. "I wanted to show you that I could help. I know what needs to be done. I wanted to make sure he was safe."

Something tickled my heart right then. That... that was exactly what Emma would have done, if she'd been here. Risked hide and hair to brave the wild on her own, just to rescue one special horse and to prove her mettle. My eyes stung—maybe from the smoke, maybe from a bit of old cowboy pride trying to leak out.

"You're a good hand, Dustin," I said quietly, giving him a wink. "But you know, your mom is pretty worried. *I* know you're fine, but moms, you know, they want to know where their kids are."

"But I *told* Lizzy," he interjected quickly.

A chuckle escaped me. "Well, that's not quite what the rule meant. See, she's not a grownup, and she came with you instead of telling someone where you were. But right now, let's focus on getting these horses to safety. You can help lead Forge, and we'll all work together, like a team."

Dustin's eyes lit up at the mention of being part of the team. The frustration seemed to ebb away as he nodded vigorously. "Okay. I can do that. But he was rearing up before."

"I'm not surprised," I said, standing up and offering him a smile. "He doesn't know how to follow a lead rope yet, but how about we put a rope on Goldie—that's his mom. If you've got her, he'll stick right beside you. You lead Forge, and we'll guide the rest. Deal?"

He clenched his fists and nodded jerkily, staring hard at Goldie as his voice wavered again. "I *was* trying to help. It just never works right."

"Yeah, it did."

Dustin was starting to wave his fists together in agitation again, but he stopped himself and looked at me in some awe, his eyes fixed on my chest. "How?"

I put a hand on his shoulder, and he didn't flinch away. That there was a victory, and I lowered myself to peer directly at him under the brim of his hat. "You made me proud, Dustin. Not many have the guts to roll out of bed before dawn, brave the storm, and maybe a fire just to save an animal. That means you have heart and courage, and that's pretty special, whether it went the way you wanted it to or not."

He studied me gravely, and then the most remarkable thing happened. He locked eyes with me and smiled. "Okay."

Chapter Twenty-Two

Meg

I FOLLOWED MERYL INTO the living room, where she had gathered Jess, Audrey, and Kelli. Her fingers were laced in a tight knot, and she was glancing out the window every so often. "Girls, Blake's not saying as much, but this isn't my first rodeo. Those fires are getting close, and the guys are all worried about the livestock. They're not thinking about themselves yet, but we can."

Jess's voice trembled a little. "You think we'll have to completely evacuate?"

Meryl thinned her lips and put a hand on Jess's shoulder. "Maybe not, but now might be our only chance to think about what's truly important. Photos, keepsakes from their mom... things we can't replace. It'll probably come to nothing, but if things get bad all at once, those things will be the last of our concern. Might as well look to it now."

Kelli nodded, a pained twinge pulling at her mouth. "Guess I shouldn't worry about the stuff I have in storage. We're probably just grabbing what fits in the back of a pickup, right?"

"Less than that because the pickup beds will probably get loaded with equipment and feed and whatever they need to get the stock settled somewhere. Think the back *seat* of the truck for ourselves," Meryl replied with a grimace. "Not much room for a lifetime of treasures."

"The real treasures aren't things, though, are they?" I asked softly.

Meryl smiled. "They never are. You girls get started, and I'll pull some boxes down from the attic. I'm sure I still have some up there from when I moved all my clutter in a few months back."

I flew to Evan's room to make myself useful, but my heart was out on those sprawling pastures with my two guys. Had Evan found my son yet? Was he okay? I should have gone, but the guys meant to ride fast and hard to bring both kids and horses in quickly. I'd just get in the way.

Besides, Dustin seemed to feel almost as comfortable with Evan as he did with me. Dustin would run to Evan if he was scared and ready to be found. That didn't mean I could focus very well—not until my phone vibrated with a message from Evan:

-*Found them. Dustin and Lizzy are safe.*

I let out a breath I didn't realize I was holding and texted back a heart emoji. The rest, all the explanations and expressions of relief and admonitions not to take off again—those could all wait until they got back. Now, it was my turn to do something for Evan.

Determined, I started sifting through Evan's belongings. It felt intrusive, like I was wading into something that wasn't mine to see. How would he feel if he knew what I was doing? But there wasn't much choice—if his special mementos were going to be put somewhere safe, there might not be a "later" for him to do it himself. I held my breath as I pulled open drawers and searched the closet shelves.

A couple of changes of clothes—that would make sense. If they had to evacuate completely, it might be days before they could come back. I'd even heard of it taking weeks in bad cases. Second hat, clean socks, extra pair of boots, toothbrush... and then I got to the really personal stuff and had to fight with my conscience all over again.

There was a drawer in the top row of his dresser, too thin to hold things like jeans and shirts. I swallowed as I pulled it open. Right on top was a photo album—embossed white, with a centered picture inset in the cover of him and Anne. Good grief, they were just kids, cutting their wedding cake and laughing with icing smeared over their faces. Right below it was another album of Emma as a toddler, with some of her drawings tucked between the pages. Handling them felt like touching a part of Evan's heart.

Someday, maybe he'd show them to me on his own. For now, I'd just respect his privacy and pack them as safely as I could. I folded them between a couple of his shirts so they wouldn't get scuffed up in the box.

On his desk, I checked a stand of file folders for anything that looked important and found a few more drawings, each stroke a precious memory of Emma's young creativity. They were more than just paper and ink; they were fragments of Evan's soul, tied intricately to his daughter. I gently slid them into a manila envelope, ensuring they were safe, and added them to the box. Then, I spotted the most precious things.

I almost missed them, as they were tossed into a paperclip bin in his desk organizer, but the diamond glinted just a bit when I looked through the drawer, catching my eye. I hesitated before picking up Evan's and Anne's old wedding bands. He would definitely want these. I hefted them in my palm, my fingertips tracing the edges of the metal and trying to imagine all the love written there, as well as the shattering that must have happened the day he finally slipped that gold band off his finger.

I hadn't kept my ring. There was nothing sentimental about it anymore. I'd sold it, actually, and part of the proceeds went toward White Pines when they were getting off the ground. Nothing sentimental. It was just the most practical way I could think to give back to an organization that was giving my son the world.

But I was pretty sure Evan was at least a little sentimental about these rings. I found one of his handkerchiefs and tied it through the rings in a tight knot to keep them safe, and they went into the box. Someday, maybe Evan and I would talk about another set of rings, ones that belonged to us and our future, but if I had anything to do with it, these memories would be kept safe forever.

The last thing I made sure to grab was the quilt made by Evan's mom. It was all bunched up, like I'd worried that it might be, so I laid it flat and folded it reverently. Then I carefully placed everything in a box Meryl had brought in, carrying it to Evan's truck with a prayer in my heart. Hopefully, this box would be going back into the house in a few hours, and all this worry and preparing would come to nothing at all.

I stepped back into the house, my thoughts still lingering on the box of Evan's memories I had just placed in his truck. Kelli was in the kitchen whipping up some gourmet coffee for us, and I leaned against the counter to watch. "Hey, do you want to go out to the RV and grab anything? Just in case?"

Kelli glanced up, a half-smile on her face. "Honestly? Don't tell Marshall this, but there's not a thing in there that I can't do just fine with out. And I'd be happy if that rotting thing burnt to the ground."

I couldn't help but laugh. "Really? After all those boxes you insisted on packing?"

She leaned closer, lowering her voice. "Don't you *dare* tell Marshall I said that, okay?"

"Your secret's safe with me," I promised, still chuckling.

Our laughter was abruptly cut short by Meryl's frantic voice calling from outside. "Blake? *Blake!*"

Kelli and I exchanged a quick, worried glance before rushing out to the stable yard. My heart raced as we found Blake doubled over and clutching his chest, his face contorted in pain.

"Meryl, what happened?" I gasped, dropping to my knees beside her.

"He just collapsed," she sobbed. "We were packing feed out, and he grabbed his chest. Blake Walker, you look at me, you hear me?" She took his face in her hands and touched her forehead to his, shaking her head as the tears flowed. "You owe me a coffee, you crazy cowboy. Don't you dare quit on me!" But Blake's eyes were closed, and his body was terrifyingly still.

I knew CPR. It was required, working at the school. Audrey probably knew more, but she was still down in the basement and probably didn't even hear us. "Meryl," I shouted, trying to get her attention. "Mouth to mouth. Keep him breathing!" I positioned myself to help with CPR, counting the compressions as Meryl breathed for Blake.

Kelli, her hands shaking, was already on the phone with 911, her voice urgent as she relayed our location and the situation. "Please hurry!" she begged into the phone in between shouts for Jess and Audrey to come outside.

About thirty seconds in, I felt Blake's pulse and found it thready and weak. He still wasn't breathing on his own. I nodded to Meryl. "Keep going. He's going to be fine, Meryl."

She nodded and kept breathing for him, but the whole time, I was praying that I hadn't been lying to her. Blake *had* to be okay. I wouldn't let myself think anything different until help arrived.

Evan

I ENDED THE CALL, my knuckles still white on the phone. "Meryl's with Dad now. Doctors are running tests. It was definitely a heart attack, but they're hoping it wasn't too serious. Initial exams look optimistic, but it isn't good that he blacked out for a minute there. She says they're going to run a CT scan and maybe an MRI."

"I *told* him he ate like crap," Dusty grumbled, scrubbing his face with his hands. "Too much coffee and junk food."

I shook my head. "You won't change him one bit. Meryl said he sat up on the gurney and asked for steak and potatoes."

"Figures," Marshall said. "Are you going down there?"

"No. They've got a policy now, new in the last couple of years. One visitor per day, and Meryl's settled in to sit with him."

"That's malarkey!" Luke spat. "He just had a heart attack! I'll go down there and see my Dad whenever I darn well please. What do they think I'm gonna do, smuggle him french fries and ice cream?"

Marshall nodded in agreement, his jaw clenched. "Exactly. They can't stop us from seeing our own father. Maybe not all of us at once, but I'm not sitting at home waiting for a phone call."

I looked at my brothers, their faces etched with defiance and a hefty dose of worry. And as I stared them down, waiting for their hackles to drop, they all fell silent. "Dad wanted us to evacuate the stock. He's got the best doctors in the valley and his wife by his side, so we can't do anything more than that for him right now. He'd want us to finish the job." I saw their expressions soften. "It was the stress of this whole situation that brought this on. Knowing that everything's taken care of here will do his heart good. And, besides..." I nodded toward the driveway that led away from Walker Ranch and toward the town. "We won't be the only ones needing to move animals. Folks'll need help."

Luke was scratching his ear, but he tilted his head and shrugged. "Evan's right. What do we do first?"

"I think the horses are our first concern," I answered. "Cody and Morgan's place is to the south of town, so they're about as far from the fires as you can get around here. Cody said we could take all the broodmares and saddle horses and turn them out on their western grazing areas like we did last winter with the colts."

"What about the studs?" Luke asked. "We can't just have a bunch of studs running loose with the herds. If they don't kill each other first, all our ranch mares will be out of commission, and we'll have a whole slew of colts born in July next year."

"Yeah, that's a problem," I sighed. "Morgan opened up their indoor arena for local evacuees. The farm store donated the use of about a hundred stock panels, and they're already starting to haul them in to make some makeshift stalls. They'll throw up some temporary pens outside, too, but nothing I'd take five stallions to. Any ideas?"

"Jess's dad's place," Dusty offered. "He's only got... I think three stalls, but he's also got a pasture, a dry lot, and a round pen. That would work. We could even take Meryl's goats and chickens over there."

"Fine. Now, what about the show horses?" I asked. "I'll turn them out on the range if I have to, but I'm not too keen on putting a horse like Maserati out with a hundred-fifty other head. She's still scheduled to go to Fort Worth and Vegas this fall, and we don't need any lumps or bruises causing problems once this craziness is over. Rust is a stallion, so he'll go with the studs, but what about the others?"

Marshall crossed his arms and stared at Luke. "You know who to call."

Luke stuck out his chin. "What for?"

"Because the Langtons have about twenty open stalls, that's why," Marshall said. "Just because you and Gage butted heads last month at the team roping..."

I waved my hands. "We don't have time for this. Luke, call Ridgeview Ranch and see if they've got room for six horses in stalls. And mind your manners, now. Maybe ask for Cole—he works for us, right? Better yet, talk to Nora instead of one of her sons so we don't have you and Gage locking horns over the phone."

Luke heaved a sigh. "Fine."

"Fine." I scanned their faces. "Now, what about the cattle? We have, conservatively, eight hundred head to get moved, and that's not counting this year's calves. Where do we take them?"

"Some of them can get turned out at Cody's place with the saddle horses," Marshall suggested.

"We'll take the yearlings there," I decided. "I don't need a herd of bored ranch horses chasing our fat old mama cows into exhaustion just for the fun of it and making them abort their calves. The yearlings can handle it and stay out of the way. What about the rest?"

Dusty got a crooked grin and held up a finger. "I got an idea."

Meg

THROUGH THE DOORWAY FROM the next room, I found myself a quiet observer, listening intently to the Walker brothers strategizing. There was something profoundly admirable in the way Evan, typically so easy-going, transformed in these moments of crisis. His calm yet firm way of threading through the worry and confusion of the moment commanded respect. He'd stepped into his father's role like he'd been born to it, probably without even realizing he was doing it. It was a side of him I hadn't seen before—decisive, directed, yet not overbearing. His brothers contributed; every one of them adding his share to the pot. But it was Evan's guidance that shaped their plan, his suggestions quickly becoming collective decisions.

But the part that made me tear up was when I saw that beside each of the Walker men stood their wives. Kelli hugged the arm Marshall wrapped around her, nodding but not saying much. Jess and Dusty were looking at each other more than at anyone else, as if holding a silent conversation between themselves about how they would go about doing what was decided. And Audrey was... well, she was sitting on Luke's lap. It sounded odd to say it, but it didn't look strange or uncomfortable to anyone else. He was talking as much as the rest of them, and usually sounding pretty stubborn when he spoke, but the whole time, Audrey held one of his hands under the table while his other hand toyed absently with the long ends of her hair. From what I could see, her presence was what kept him mellow enough to think through the parts of the plan he didn't like.

As I watched, a mix of emotions stirred in my chest. There was pride, certainly, in seeing Evan in this light. This was a man who thought of others before himself, who could think clearly in a crisis, and who others looked to when they weren't sure of themselves. And somehow, he'd found something he liked about *me*. Who was I to contribute to all this? I'd stayed out of the room, on the periphery of this close-knit group, on the excuse of staying close to Dustin after his ordeal that morning. But the truth was, I wasn't sure of my place beside Evan yet. The closeness and shared purpose among the Walker family was something I'd never tasted before, and I didn't feel right pushing into the middle of it.

But one way or another, everyone around would be impacted by all the plans they were talking about. Outside this house, the town was waking up to the reality of the fires. My phone buzzed with notifications from local social media pages and emergency alerts. Neighbors were banding together, offering help to those on the northern outskirts, the area most threatened by the fires. A specialty media page had been created for local families needing help, and another for livestock transportation. Offers of shelter filled the community chats, coming from people for a hundred miles around. A retirement home's request for help evacuating to a facility in the next county was swiftly met, and their follow-up post gushed their gratitude for the overwhelming support.

I was still scrolling through the updates, taking in the flurry of activity, when Evan entered the room. He took my hands, his eyes searching mine, and something in me uncoiled. Whether I could be part of his world during this crisis or not, he was already all of mine.

"What can I do?" I asked. "Should I take supplies to Meryl at the hospital, help with the livestock, drive vehicles to safety? I've never driven a stock trailer, but if you need hands, I'll do anything."

Evan's expression softened. "I'm taking a load of horses to Cody and Morgan's place. I was hoping you'd come with me." He cocked his head toward the den, where Dustin was collapsed on the couch, asleep. "It would be the best place for him to go, too."

I studied his face, my heart swelling with the kinds of feelings I was only beginning to understand. How had this cowboy so easily taught me to feel things I'd never known before? And the fact that he really did want me at his side... well, that settled it. There was no other place for me. I leaned in, planting a gentle kiss on his lips. "I'm right here, cowboy."

Chapter Twenty-Three

Evan

I DROPPED THE PIN on the trailer door latch with a firm 'clunk' and made a final walk-around, ensuring everything was secure for the highway. The mares and foals shuffled and whinnied inside, but no one was squealing or kicking. That was a relief. Half these mares had never seen the inside of a trailer, being born and raised on the ranch with no reason to ever leave. Dusty and Jess were right behind me with another load, their trailer hitched and ready, and Brandon was just hooking up another trailer to take the rest of them. I checked each latch and hinge, my brain shifting into auto-pilot as I finished my pre-drive checks.

Satisfied, I climbed into the truck, the familiar scent of leather and dust greeting me as I tugged the belt over my chest. Meg and Dustin were already settled in, and as I started the engine, I spotted a huge box sitting next to Dustin in the back seat. I glanced at him in the mirror and asked, "What's in the box, Dustin?"

Meg shifted uncomfortably next to me, a flush of embarrassment coloring her cheeks. "I... uh, went through your room," she stammered slightly. "I grabbed some things that I thought might be important to you... in case you guys have to evacuate the house."

I blinked, pulling the gear shift into drive and pulling out onto the highway. "You did?"

Meg wouldn't look at me. She turned her head toward the passenger window, her fingers webbed through the hair at her forehead as she struggled to find the right words, her face turning a deeper shade of red. "I got you some clothes. You know... a few days' worth."

I glanced at the box again, the lid bulging against the contents. "That's a lot of clothes. Didn't know I owned that many."

She swallowed visibly. "There's some other stuff, too. Your wedding album. And some of Emma's drawings... and your mom's quilt." She paused, her voice barely above a whisper. "And your wedding rings." She looked away, clearly uncomfortable. "It was Meryl's suggestion, and there wasn't anyone else to do it."

Something warm was crawling through my chest, but I didn't have the words for it yet. I glanced over at her, and her face was a study in misery. "You grabbed all that?"

"I wasn't trying to be nosy. That stuff—you've never shared it with me, and I wouldn't have ever asked you to, not unless it was your idea first. I didn't go through the albums or anything—I just packed them. Really, I didn't mean to snoop through your private life, and—"

I reached across the cab, gently taking her hand to pause her flow of words. "Meg, you *are* my private life," I said, making sure to keep my voice steady and sincere. Of all the things I'd ever say to her, this might be one of the most important—one of the times I truly needed her to believe that I meant every word. "Everything you picked... those are just pieces of me, and you found all the right ones. I'd have wanted you to pick what you did, so when all the dust settles, I'll be able to share all of that with you."

She started breathing again. "Do you think there's anything I missed?"

I brought her hand to my lips, kissing it softly as I navigated the road, feeling her fingers tighten around mine. "If there is, it's not important enough to worry about. You thought of all the most precious things."

Meg exhaled, visibly relaxing, and managed a small, relieved smile. "Okay," she murmured. "I just... wanted to make sure you didn't lose them."

"They're just things, Meg." I squeezed her hand again, then tucked it close to my heart as I drove. "But what they remind me of will be right here, no matter what. And one of the things they'll always remind me of, for the rest of my life, is that you tried to save them for me."

Her face had faded from embarrassed scarlet to a pretty flush of pink, and a smile bloomed on her sweet mouth. "I'm just trying to return the favor, cowboy."

Meg

EVAN CLOSED THE GATE behind the last of the mares, letting them take off in the open range above White Pines. My phone wouldn't stop buzzing, and Evan's was going off, too. Evan was still watching the mares shuffling around, making sure the foals didn't get trampled, so I pulled mine out to check what was going on. It was almost completely red from all the local emergency alerts.

"Evan, look," I said, showing him the screen. "They're starting to close roads to outside traffic."

He took a quick glance, his expression turning grim. "Yeah, it's just to keep the sightseers and looters out," he assured me. "Residents can still get through for now. It's a safety thing."

Just then, Morgan's truck pulled up behind us. She hopped out and slammed the door, her face showing signs of fatigue and worry. "Hey, you two," she greeted, trying to muster a smile. "How are your girls settling in?"

"They'll be fine," Evan grunted. But he wasn't looking at the mares. He was scanning Morgan from head to foot, a crease of worry on his forehead.

"You okay, Morgan?" I asked. "You look beat."

She nodded, though her eyes betrayed her. "Just a bit tired. Got a dozen more trailers coming in from out of the area. I need to get back." She rested a hand over her expanding belly. "Cody's almost done helping them set panels, and then he was going to grab a stock trailer and come help you guys get cattle evacuated."

Evan shook his head and stepped up, placing his hand over Morgan's. "He's needed here. Lots of other folks with animals to tend to, and you need someone to help you keep things sane around here."

"I'll be fine. Really. I'll take it easy as soon as the worst is over."

"I'm going to call Cody and make sure you do that," Evan warned. "Won't have you hurtin' the baby over a bunch of cows."

Morgan squeezed his hand in both of hers and gave him a teary smile. "Thanks, Evan. I'll take care." She turned to Dustin, who was staring at Forge over the fence rail. "Hey, Dustin, you want to help me out here for a bit?"

Dustin's face lit up, and he nodded eagerly—not quite looking her in the eye, of course, but clearly making an effort to. "Yeah, I can help. I'm a ranch hand, right Evan?"

Evan nodded at my son with a wink. "You sure are."

"Great!" Morgan extended a hand, inviting him to hop into her truck. "Because I'll have lots more water buckets to keep filled. Think you can handle that?"

"Is Biz okay?"

Morgan laughed. "Biz is about the happiest I've ever seen him. He thinks everyone is here to visit him." She rested a hand on Dustin's shoulder—miraculously, he didn't seem to mind—and looked back at us. "Be careful out there, okay, you two?"

Evan nodded briskly. "Sure thing."

"I mean it." She gave me a pointed look. "Don't let him try to be the hero cowboy, saving the herd and the ranch. Don't let him take stupid risks over things that can be replaced."

I glanced at Evan and smiled. "I think he's got more sense than that."

"I know. But it makes me feel better to say it. Good luck."

Morgan started her truck and backed down the slope, just in time to get out of the way of Dusty and Jess as they pulled in with another trailer full of horses. Marshall was right behind him with a stock trailer loaded with yearling cows, and Evan said one of the ranch hands would be along soon after that.

There wasn't much more for me to do, so I got back in the truck, out of the way. About the time I closed the door, my phone rang. It was Cowboy Bill from Beaufort's. I frowned. Why would he be calling me? I wasn't on shift today, and I really didn't want to get called in. Not with all this going on.

"Hello?" I answered. Evan opened the truck door, and I looked up, holding my phone so he could hear the conversation as he got in.

"Meg? Hey, I really need your help if you can come in. We're swamped making lunches for evacuees and emergency responders."

"Lunches?" I asked. "What, like to-go orders?"

"You name it. The place is busting at the seams with folks needing a clean place to sit down, but I've also got crews calling in for meals they can have delivered. Are you busy? We really need a few more hands."

"Hang on just a minute." I muted the phone, turning to Evan. "I'd much rather help you. But realistically..."

"You can do lots more good there," he sighed. "I'd rather have you here, too, but I know you too well for that." He slid his fingers into the hair at the back of my head, pulling me close for a kiss as sweet as candy and hot as those blazing mountains. "You do what you need to do. Being apart for a little bit won't hurt us none—I'll be here waiting for you. And I promise I won't do anything stupid while you're gone."

I cupped his cheek with my free hand and unmuted the phone. "I can come. I'll be there as soon as I can."

Evan

D RIVING BACK TO THE ranch, I rolled my neck and squirmed a little in the truck seat. So this was what the weight of responsibility felt like. This was usually Dad's job, running the show, checking in with everyone. But I'd handle it, I guess. I plugged my phone in so the stereo could pick up my call and had it dial Meryl at the hospital. She answered after a couple of rings, her voice sounding weary and ragged.

"Hey, Meryl, it's Evan. How's Dad doing?"

"Oh, hi, Evan. Yes, things are fine here, thankfully," Meryl replied with a heavy sigh. "They did a CT scan, and there's no evidence of any lack of oxygen to his brain during the attack. The doctors are saying it was an NSTEMI heart attack."

"NSTEMI?" I furrowed my brow. "What's that?"

"Oh, hang on, I have to read it. Let me get my glasses." I heard her rustling some paper, then her voice came back. "Non-ST Elevation Myocardial Infrac... no... Infarction," she read out. "In English, they said it's a mild-ish type of heart attack, but it seems he probably won't need an angioplasty. Just some medication and a serious change in his diet."

"Dad'll hate that."

"I know. I'm going to need lots of prayer."

I laughed. "If anyone can make him toe the line, it's you. Dusty tried, and it didn't work. Hey, what's going on? Tons of noise in the background. Do you need to go?"

Meryl let out a groan. "Your father is charming the nurses. He's trying to convince them to give him more than just hospital food. And one of them might want to buy a horse—for top dollar, of course. You know Blake, always making friends."

I chuckled. That must mean Dad was in good spirits and up to his old hijinks. "Is he up for a quick chat? I'd like to talk to him."

"Let me check," Meryl said, her voice fading as she moved away from the phone.

There was a brief pause filled with muffled voices before Dad's familiar voice came on the line. "Evan, my boy! How's the ranch holding up? Need more help? Are you able to find places for everything?"

Hearing his voice made my whole body relax. He sounded like his usual self. "We're managing, Dad. Just moving the livestock to safer ground. We called in all the hands, and the neighbors let us use an extra stock trailer. Wyatt went to grab it so that will speed us up. We should have them all evacuated by middle of the afternoon. You concentrate on getting better, okay?"

"Ah, you know me. I'll be out of here hauling trailers by tomorrow. Keep my truck idling for me, will you?" His voice, though tired, carried that same determined tone I'd grown up listening to.

I laughed. "Don't worry, Dad. We've got it covered. You just be nice to your nurses. Don't you go givin' them a hard time."

We talked for a few more minutes—Dad swearing he'd be out helping us if Meryl hadn't chained him to his hospital bed and Meryl in the background laughing. I could almost *hear* her rolling her eyes over the phone. I promised to keep him updated, and I hung up. My dad was a fighter, but this was a reminder of how precious and fragile life could be.

And that was why I wasn't going to waste another minute of it. I'd told Meg that I wasn't in a hurry, but... well, that was yesterday. Today, I'd had a taste of life with her by my side, and that was how it ought to be forever. I wondered if she would take to that idea as quickly as I had.

I twisted my hands on the steering wheel, trying to look for the hills through the red-orange haze that had shrouded the valley. I couldn't see a thousand feet in front of me, from all the smoke refracting the sunlight. It looked about like I imagined hell would look, and the fires were just getting started. "Happy Armageddon Day!" had been the greeting in town when I'd dropped off Meg at the restaurant. Typical of our town—laughing in the face of danger.

I was almost back to the ranch now, so I called Luke to check in. He picked up on the second ring.

"Hey, Evan. Just dropped off the stallions at Jess's dad's place."

"They all settled in? No problems?"

"Nope. I got Lizzy helping me out, and we got it handled, huh, scamp?" I heard Lizzy chirping something in the background.

"Just Lizzy? Where's Audrey?"

"Meg called and said Cowboy Bill needed help at the restaurant. She loved his chili before she loved me, so I guess I'm playin' second fiddle."

"Hah. Where are you going next? Back to haul the show horses?"

"Cows. Switching trailers with Marshall... matter of fact, there he is now. Gotta go."

Switching trailers? Why waste all that time driving out of their way to meet up? I shook my head and shot a text to Marshall. His reply came several minutes later.

—Yearlings are all safe at Morgan's. Heading back for the show horses.

I raised an eyebrow. That didn't explain why Luke wasn't handling that. Wasn't he the one calling to make arrangements with the guys at Skyview, since he knew the Langtons better than the rest of us? I hit the voice button and dictated that question back to him.

Marshall replied almost instantly this time.

—Didn't want Gage Langton kicking Luke off the property.

Oh, brother. One of these days, Luke was going to have to quit being sore about Gage beating him at the roping jackpot last month. Shaking my head with a smirk, I dictated another message. "Alright, just making sure you've got everything you need."

As I pulled up to the ranch, Dusty was right behind me, hauling another stock trailer. I stepped out to meet him. "Thought Jess was with you," I said. "What happened to her?"

"Man, you won't believe it. The forest service called. Said they had a brush truck broken down on the highway and they couldn't get their own mechanic there fast enough. Jess was the only one to pick up the phone, and they offered her a whopping pile of cash to come get it running."

"Wow." I whistled. "What about her tools and everything?"

Dusty chucked a thumb over his shoulder. "Her dad's meeting her with those. Stinks, because I don't like to think of her out there taking risks, with all that."

I grinned and punched my little brother in the shoulder. "You mean with all those firefighters checking out your wife, right?"

He shook his head, but the look on his face was too proud to smother. "I'm not worried about that. Jed'll keep her safe, and she won't give any of them the time of day. So, what are we hauling next? The pedigreed cows?"

"If we have somewhere to take them. What was that place you mentioned earlier? Did you make that call you were talking about?"

He grinned, holding up his phone. "Sure did. Austen Conrad. Remember him?"

I narrowed my eyes, wary of anything involving Austen. "The creep? He lied to me once. Why would you want to deal with him?"

"Because he's got eighty acres sitting empty. And he owes me one. Helped him sell his cattle when he left, and I never did see a dime for my trouble. He can't get anyone to buy or lease the property from him, it's not being used, and I figure it can hold the rest of our stock for a short stint."

I considered it for a moment. "Well, we don't have many options. Let's get these cows loaded and moved."

Chapter Twenty-Four

Meg

I'D NEVER SEEN THE Beaufort's kitchen so slammed. I think everyone who had ever worked there, plus a few strays like Audrey, had turned up to pass out lunches. She and I were lined up with a few others at a row of tables at the edge of the kitchen, taking hot food and assembling to-go lunches as fast as our hands could manage. Cowboy Bill had turned his establishment into a hub of activity, offering free meals to the firefighting and rescue teams, as well as a safe place to sit down, grab a meal, and recharge their phones to families who had been forced to evacuate their homes. The air was thick with the smell of cooking and a sense of urgent camaraderie.

Beaufort's party room had been transformed into a makeshift dispatch center, buzzing with the coordinated efforts of fire and rescue crews. And the empty gravel lot across the street was full of horse trailers—an impromptu dispatch waiting zone for neighbors who had trailers and were waiting for evacuation calls to come in. Goats, llamas, sheep, pigs—just about every kind of farm animal was getting pulled away from the fire's teeth by local volunteers.

Audrey paused for a second to stretch her back before grabbing another takeout box to fill. "How's Dustin holding up through all this?" she asked, her voice barely rising above the kitchen's din.

I paused, a warm smile spreading across my face as I pulled out my phone to show her the pictures Morgan had texted me earlier. "He's doing amazing," I replied, my voice thick with pride. "Morgan sent me these pictures of him helping out."

One picture showed Dustin dragging a heavy hose down the makeshift aisle of stalls at White Pines, where all the evacuated livestock were being kept. In another, he was holding a horse's lead rope with laser concentration as Doc Burns checked the animal for stress colic. There were others, too—all of Dustin up to his elbows in the manic work of keeping over a hundred refugee horses safe and comfortable.

Audrey squinted at the screen as she scrolled through the pictures. "Wow! That's incredible!"

"Isn't it? She said he's not just following directions—he's actually seeing what needs to be done and just handling it. That's always been hard for him, you know? Context isn't his strong suit—seeing the bigger picture and deciding what to do next. It's like he's found his stride in all this chaos."

Audrey beamed at me. "That's wonderful, Meg. He's an amazing kid, and he's in good hands with Morgan."

I nodded. "He really is. I can't tell you how proud and... and how *grateful* I am. It's moments like these that show you what someone's really made of, isn't it?"

"And who you can count on when it matters most." Audrey bit her lip as she shot me a hesitant grin. "Nothing quite like family to lean on in a crisis."

I arched a brow. "'Family' already, huh?"

Audrey's smile about split her face, and she shrugged as she wrapped a sandwich and grabbed a chip bag for the box. "Yeah, family. You don't think any of us are letting you guys get away, do you?"

I fisted a hand at my hip. "Audrey Walker, I never figured you for a matchmaker. Kelli? Absolutely, but not you."

"Oh, come on, Meg. There isn't a soul in town who hasn't noticed how Evan crawled out of his shell this summer. You gave him back a piece of himself that was missing."

I sighed, smiling a little, as I put my phone away and got back to work. "No, I didn't. No one can give him that back. But maybe I helped him learn to grow something new. I know he did that for me."

Audrey paused, her brow crinkling a little as she cocked her head at me. "Well, whatever it is, it's beautiful to see."

That choked me up a little, and it was even hard to smile back at her with my throat all tight and my eyes threatening to sting. "Thanks, Audrey."

Evan

THE LATE AFTERNOON SUN cast long shadows across the ranch as I made my final rounds, ensuring that all was secure and that no animals were left behind. Wyatt had just rolled out with the last load of cow/calf pairs, and my brothers had turned up right behind him to find nothing left to load but some feed. I had a flatbed of alfalfa loaded up on the big semi-trailer, but we had animals all over the country at this point, so my brothers and I hand-loaded more bales and grain sacks into their stock trailers to get us through the evacuation. A week, two weeks? It was anyone's guess how long it might be before fire crews let people back into their properties.

Once they dropped off the feed, my brothers would turn their attention to our neighbors. Whoever still needed to evacuate, they'd get all the help they needed. Dust clouds billowed in the distance as Luke and Dusty drove away, the last of the stock trailers disappearing down the road. A deep sense of unease settled over me; the ranch had never felt so empty and vulnerable.

As I was locking the main barn door, a fire command truck rolled up the driveway, and the chief stepped out. He approached me with a grim expression, his eyes scanning the property. "You the owner?"

I showed him the keys to my barn door. "Just locking up."

He nodded and heaved a weary sigh. "Gotta check. Empty properties tend to attract all kinds of trouble."

"I'm well aware. We're all good here. Is there a problem?"

"I'm going door to door to ensure everyone's evacuated. Also, I'd like to take a look around. Is that the dwelling up there?" He pointed up the driveway to the ranch house.

"One of them. We have three other houses on the property... well, two of them aren't finished. Why?"

He took off his peaked cap and ran a hand through his sweat-stained hair. "I'd like to walk around it, if you don't mind. We're assessing which properties can be defended against the fire."

I paused, my hand still on the lock. "Defended? Can you explain that?"

The chief gestured towards the dense woods bordering our land. "Some properties are too close to the forest, or the ground's too dry, among other factors. We try to protect what we can, but we have to consider the safety of our crews first. In some cases, defending a property might be too risky."

I felt a lump form in my throat. The thought of losing the ranch to the fire was a reality I hadn't fully prepared for. And I knew what the chief would find when he walked around our place: houses too close to the woods, too spread out from each other, driveways too long for an escape. We had access to water, but that was about all we had going for us if things got bad.

"I understand," I said, trying to keep my voice steady. "Help yourself. We've moved all our livestock. I'm the last one here, about to head out. Just one more thing I need to do, and I'm on my way."

"You'll need to hurry. We're closing the roads to residents soon. The fire's spreading faster than we anticipated."

"I'll be out in a few minutes. Thanks for the heads up."

The chief returned to his truck and started up the drive-way, and I took one last look around the ranch. I hadn't told him the full truth, because I hadn't planned on leaving "in a few minutes." To stall a little, I walked over to the biggest hay barns in the main yard and took some pictures of the size of our stacks. That could come in handy if we should have to file an insurance claim. Crazy as it sounded, the hay was now the most valuable resource on the property, even more than the houses. And that didn't even cover the last cutting, still growing out there in the fields.

The chief drove back down the driveway a few minutes later, and he rolled down his window to put his head out. "Don't be long. I'm supposed to see that everyone is out, but you said you were on your way, so I won't run you off. Just hurry, sir."

I nodded and waved. "Will do." And then I walked the other way.

There was one last thing I could do. It might take me a while, but I could keep an eye on the fire and pull out before it got bad. I didn't plan on taking stupid risks, but if I cut some fire breaks now, around the barns and houses, I might be able to save them. We'd kept the fields irrigated, so the pastures right around the houses weren't dry tinder like the forest. All I needed to do was fetch our big field plow and turn some earth over—a single pass around each building ought to do it.

I jingled my keys in my pocket and glanced back at the semi-truck loaded with hay that I was supposed to drive out of there. Meg would be waiting for me. I'd promised to head straight to Beaufort's when I was done, but this... this was important. Insurance would pay market value for whatever we lost in a fire—in fact, the agent had called me earlier, just checking to make sure we knew they'd cover us.

But insurance couldn't replace everything. We'd still be set back by years. We'd lose hay that we needed to survive the winter. Lose buildings where our animals were sheltered. Might have to sell out and start over. This might save the ranch, and my family's future.

I pushed my hat down tighter on my head and ran for the shop where we parked the plow.

Meg

"I CAN'T FEEL MY feet." Audrey was stretching her toes out under the table and wincing.

"Maybe if you didn't wear three-inch heels?" I suggested. "I don't know how you walk in those things."

She grinned. "Toes of iron. Most of the time. Besides, they were the first things I grabbed when I was running out the door." She rolled her neck and worked at a knot in her shoulders. "I'll have to get back to my house and find something better."

"What was that, baby?" Luke walked up behind Audrey and started massaging her shoulders for her, bending down to plant a kiss on her cheek as he did so.

She grabbed his hand and turned her face up to kiss him back. "There you guys are! I was starting to wonder if you'd be hauling trailers all night."

"Nah." He pulled up a chair beside her and kicked another out for Lizzy. "Everyone was on top of it, so stuff's quieting down for now. It'll get worse about two in the morning."

I wrinkled my brow. "Why is that?"

"Because." Luke reached across the table and pulled apart a piece of cheesy bread that Cowboy Bill had given us to snack on while we took a break. "The smart folks saw this coming and got their critters evacuated way early. You don't sit on your thumbs when you have livestock because if you wait till you get an official evac order, it's too late to get your animals out. Plus, there won't be anywhere to go by the time you think to do something about it. So, them that think ahead are already taken care of. It's the ones who don't think they need to worry yet who'll be putting out emergency cries for help in the middle of the night, when the fire is at their back door."

"And you'll go, of course," Audrey said, wrapping her hand over his and shaking her head with a knowing smile. "Red-eyed from going forty hours without sleep and shaking from three quad shots of coffee."

"'Course I will. You know me, always up for a little thrill-seeking."

She snorted and rolled her eyes at me. "Right."

"Have you seen Evan yet?" I asked. It was six in the evening, and the restaurant was getting even more busy, filled with the hum of conversations and the clatter of kitchenware.

Luke shook his head. "He had a flatbed of hay he was dropping off up at High Line Ranch, last thing I saw. He's probably hauling hay for some neighbors 'bout now."

I nodded. That made sense. My eyes roved the restaurant, searching the sea of familiar faces, but the one that made my heart stand still wasn't there. Jess and her dad had arrived an hour earlier, and both had jumped in to help clear tables or deliver lunches to fire crews. Kelli was out somewhere doing the same thing with coffee, trying to help all those guys stay awake for their long night.

I picked a little more at the cheesy bread and gestured to Lizzy that she could have some if she wanted. "Did you guys have some fun adventures moving livestock?"

She brightened. "Yeah, there was this one big fat sheep, he looked like this." She blew out her cheeks and held her arms aloft, mimicking a round gut. "He just wouldn't move, like he was glued to the ground, so Luke had to pick him up and carry him with his legs all sticking out! He said some bad words, too."

Luke nudged her. "No need tellin' anyone about that. Tell her about the pig."

"Oh! And there was this pot-bellied pig at the same house, and the lady who owned him said he would kick and squeal if I tried to carry him like a dog, like this..." She held her arms in a cradle shape. "So she told me to carry him upside down, and he just went..." She knocked her head back, her eyes rolling in her head and her tongue lolling.

Luke was laughing at Audrey's raised brow over the spectacle. "She's not exaggerating. I got a picture. Wanna see?" He broke his phone out and passed it to Audrey.

"Hey, guys." Marshall and Dusty walked up behind us, their hats hanging from limp hands and their faces haggard. There weren't many spare chairs in the restaurant, so Luke grabbed Audrey—I think he enjoyed it when she squeaked in surprise—and pulled her into his lap to nuzzle her cheek and wrap his arms around her. Lizzy moved over onto the bench beside me to make room for Dusty, and Marshall sank into Audrey's old seat. Both looked like they wouldn't be moving again anytime soon.

"Is there anything to eat?" Marshall asked hopefully.

I started to get up. "I'll ask for something for you. Porterhouse, right? I'm not sure if we can get something that elaborate right now, but—"

"No, don't worry about it." He blew out a sigh and swiped up one of the last pieces of cheesy bread. "I'll get something in a minute. I need to call Dad."

While Marshall dialed his phone, Dusty propped his elbow on the table and leaned his head on his hand. "When will Jess be back, any idea? She said she was running meals up the highway to the fire crew's staging area."

"Not long, I don't think."

He nodded. "I'll wait for her and figure out something to eat."

Marshall had Meryl on the phone now, and the rest of us paused to listen, hoping for good news.

"Yeah," he confirmed. "Everything's out, including all the neighbors. What? No, Dusty made a call, got them over to Austen Conrad's old place. Yeah, broodmares are all up at Cody's. Oh, the stallions? Jess's dad's house... yeah, that was lucky. Hmm? No, Evan didn't want the broody cows up at Cody's gettin' chased by the horses, so he said to take them... Wait a minute, what did you say?" His face scrunched in confusion as he listened to the other end of the line.

"Huh, Evan hasn't called yet?" he said, more to himself than anyone else. "Weird. Well, are you doing okay? You're not giving Meryl a hard time, are you? Oh, they said that? Yeah, well, maybe you should listen. Yeah, we're at Beaufort's right now... no, I'm not gonna smuggle you a pulled pork sandwich. You behave yourself now, y'hear?"

After a few more nods and murmurs, he hung up and turned to us. "Dad's doing okay. They're keeping him for observation. But... has anyone seen Evan? He should've checked in by now."

A ripple of concern passed through the group. I felt a knot form in my stomach. Evan had said he'd be here after making sure the ranch was secure before moving on to help the community. Glancing at my phone, I realized he hadn't messaged or called.

I tried to keep my voice steady as I dialed his number, my fingers trembling slightly. The phone rang and rang, but there was no answer. I tried again, hoping he'd pick up, but it went straight to voicemail. It was probably nothing... a lot going on, I reminded myself. He was probably in the middle of something. But for eight hours straight? I hadn't seen him since ten that morning, and it wasn't like Evan not to let me know he was okay.

"He's not answering," I said, my voice shaking a little.

Dusty narrowed his eyes. "Hang on. I can track his location." He broke out his phone and tapped the screen a few times. Then, his face crunched as he squinted at the screen. "That's funny. Must not be updating. Unless..." He tapped it to refresh, then shook his head. "According to this, he's still up at the ranch. In the northern pasture, to be exact." Dusty looked up, scanning the table. "You don't think..."

Marshall growled. Luke swore—earning a scalding look from his wife. And I...

I started praying.

Evan

I PUSHED THE TRACTOR to its limits, jamming gears and dragging our high-speed disc to cut a twenty-nine-foot swath of turned earth around the ranch buildings. I'd secured the main horse barns, the hay lofts, and the main ranch house. Now, Dusty's half-finished house lay behind me, a barrier of churned soil circling it like a castle moat.

The tractor rumbled beneath me as I headed toward Marshall's house. I paused briefly, wiping sweat and soot from my brow, to check the latest fire report on my phone. The glowing screen displayed a map, a menacing red line inching closer. I believed it, too. It was getting harder and harder to breathe.

Should I cut out and leave now? I zoomed the fire map, and then my phone screen froze and blacked out.

I sighed and tossed it down on the floorboards. I knew I should have grabbed a charging cord out of the truck. Now, I couldn't even call anyone—not that I'd wanted to earlier. If I'd told any of my brothers what I was doing, they'd have been on the phone all at once, bullying me into quitting and high-tailing it out of there.

But I wasn't stupid. I knew the property was good for just a little longer. The road getting out of there might be another matter, but so far, I was okay. I'd been tuning in on the tractor's radio to the local dispatch from the fire crews. I should have time, if I hurried. A decision loomed before me, a gamble with time and safety. My house, the one I built for Anne, still stood vulnerable, directly in the path of the encroaching fire. If there was any chance to save it, now was the moment. I could swing back and circle around Marshall's RV and framed trusses when I was done, but my house, set against the northern edge of our grazing meadows, was right in the fire's teeth.

I revved the engine, the tractor lurching forward as I set off across the fields. The smoke was growing thicker, a haze that blurred the landscape and stung my eyes. Each breath was a battle against the acrid air that filled my lungs, making me cough and gasp for cleaner air. A little longer, and I'd be out.

My house came into view, a stark silhouette against the backdrop of smoke and ember-lit sky. It was eerie, with the evil red haze hanging in the air, making everything look desiccated and abandoned. I almost couldn't recognize the place just because of the dead-feeling smoke in the air, how different it made everything feel. I hesitated, my hands tightening on the steering wheel. That house was once a monument to a life I once envisioned. Now, it was just another abandoned structure at the mercy of the raging fire.

But it was more than that—it was a part of me, a chapter of my life etched in timber and stone. I couldn't just let it burn without trying. With a deep breath that made me cough, I jerked the tractor forward.

I dropped the disc and started along the edge of the driveway, forming a teardrop shape around the front yard and to the corner of that pretty little white picket fence. I'd built the first summer we lived in the house, right after I hung the porch swing where we used to while away the summer evenings, gazing at the stars. I started to curve around the side of the house when the disc plow screeched to a halt.

"What in blazes?" I pulled the tractor out of gear and clambered down, my lungs burning from the smoke, and a flurry of expletives poured from my mouth. There was a whole row of broken disc blades, twisted and useless from striking an underground boulder at that speed. What was I thinking? I remembered that stupid thing now that I'd hit it. I'd tried to drive a hitching post pole down through this rock once, but it was a monster—several feet wide and lurking just under the surface of the pasture grass, where no one would suspect it. And I'd just bent up our disc plow trying to run over it at Mach three.

Panting, I stared at the house, each detail a stark reminder of the dreams Anne and I had woven together. Frustration surged through me, a primal scream building against the fire consuming the last piece of my past. I ripped off my hat, flinging it like a frisbee at the front door, but it fell short of even clearing the fence. I couldn't seem to even get that right! I yanked the tractor keys from the ignition and lobbed them next... and they sailed against a window, crashing through the glass and shattering it everywhere.

I don't remember the last time I lost my temper. I'm not sure if I ever had. Even when I got the call that Mom had passed in the hospital. Or the hideous day a few years later when that police officer showed up in the barn, looking for me after I'd come in from the fields. I didn't scream or swear, I didn't break things or punch my fist through a wall. It wasn't that I didn't want to or didn't have a reason. The rage had just never boiled over that hot, because crippling grief was always stronger.

But not this time. I wrenched my fingers through my hair and thundered at those reddened heavens, dropping to my knees and raving as I had never done in my life. *"Why?"* I kept repeating. "Why this, why now?"

It wasn't like I was asking for much. I knew I couldn't get back what had been taken—I'd made my peace with that, hadn't I? All I'd wanted was to protect, to honor, and to cherish. And I couldn't even do that! I leaped to my feet and barged up the steps of the house, slamming the door open and tearing through the halls into that bedroom where the keys had landed.

And that was when I stopped dead.

I don't believe in ghosts. But imagination is a pretty powerful thing. Love lingers, it speaks, and it has a face and voice all its own. And in that moment, I swear, it spoke to me as I stood there heaving and staring at our old bed.

At the memory of Anne, sitting there with her legs crossed and arms splayed back on my mom's quilt, smiling at me like she did the day she told me she was expecting Emma.

"Oh, God," I breathed, the prayer barely a choked gasp on my lips. "I can't do this. Don't make me..."

"Evan." Anne was shaking her head gently, a tear at the edge of her eye, but her smile was everything I remembered—sweet and whole and warm and oh, so gentle. "Why are you still here?"

I blinked. Shook myself a little. Anne had vanished, the patchwork quilt was gone, and now all that filled the room was just a hot, parching wind blowing in through that broken window. "Anne?"

But of course, she couldn't answer. She wasn't there—hadn't been for two years. I had even stopped thinking I could hear her voice in the dead of night. Stopped waking from those nightmares where I was running after the car, trying to pull it back from the intersection and put out the flames. So why would I have imagined her so clearly now?

I swallowed and stepped closer to that window, looking out at the ember haze, when something tickled my neck. I turned around, staring once more at that empty room. And as God is my witness, I heard Anne's voice again, clear as the last day I'd kissed her on the porch. "Let go, Evan."

I thought I *had* let go. I was sure I had! How else could I be so happy when I was with Meg? How else could I be imagining a new life, a life I was looking forward to with joy and hope? But...

Well, I was still here. Still haunted every time I stepped over that threshold. And if I was honest with myself, the reason I was still racing the fire—after the barns and everything that kept our ranch alive were surrounded by a freshly tilled break—wasn't to protect property. There was nothing left in this house for me that insurance couldn't replace—nothing but shadows and memories that I'd do better to put away, so they couldn't keep plucking at me.

I bent and picked up the tractor keys, fingering them as they tumbled in my hand and staring at the glint of the metal.

My boots crunched on the shattered glass as I moved slowly back toward the door. "Anne," I murmured. "You said it. I believe it. And... you're right. It's time."

But the echo of Anne's voice had faded. She didn't answer back, and maybe she never would again. Instead, I could see, as if she was right there in front of me, Meg's beautiful face. Meg, welcoming me into her arms and sharing her hurts and hopes, letting me trust her with all of me.

And Meg's voice, so clear and full of life. Her words from earlier that day resonated in my heart, reminding me of the promise I made. "Come back to me, cowboy," she'd pleaded. "Promise me, because I love you, and I'll be waiting." And I'd promised. With everything in me, I'd sworn to be hers, and never to look back again.

Yeah. That was where I belonged—there, where I was loved and understood, where I felt hope and excitement for the future for the first time in too long. Not here in the past. And so, I walked out of that house, and I closed the door behind me. It was time to go.

Chapter Twenty-Five

Meg

"CAN'T YOU DRIVE ANY faster?" Luke grumbled. "Gramma Chandler could outpace you in her wheelchair."

"Grandma Chandler's been dead over twenty years," Marshall shot back.

"That's my point. Come on, does this thing even *have* a gas pedal?"

Marshall punched his older brother in the shoulder as he drove. "Can't hardly see ten paces in front of me. What do you want me to do, drive off the cliff?"

"That cliff's in the same place it always was. Do you want me to drive?"

"Guys!" I interrupted from the back seat, holding my phone to my ear. "Seriously? Please, I'm trying to hear."

"Sorry," Luke mumbled, crossing his arms and settling back into his seat.

Marshall's cheek ticked as he glanced at me in the rearview mirror. "Sorry. Still not answering?"

The call beeped out right then, and I hung up and shook my head. "It's going straight to voicemail. Do you think the phone is dead?"

"Probably. He might not have taken a charging cord with him. Wasn't he driving the semi?"

"Yeah," Luke agreed. "He was supposed to deliver that load of hay out to High Line, but Dusty just went out there, and Evan hasn't been there yet."

"So…" I shook my head. "How does that tracking work if the phone is dead?"

"Last known location, far as I know," Luke said. "Right, Marshall? It can't do anything if the phone's dead, right?"

Marshall shrugged. "Search me. I just know how to make calls. Oh, hold up. Roadblock."

I craned my neck to see over Marshall's shoulder, and I could just make out a cavvy of vehicles gathered on either side of the road. "They aren't going to let us through?"

Marshall rolled down his window, but it wasn't a fire marshal or a sheriff or anyone in uniform who walked up. It was just a regular-looking guy, and he was eyeing us up and down. He glanced at me in the back seat, took a long look at Luke, then nodded to Marshall. "You live around here?"

Marshall flipped out his driver's license. "Walker Ranch. Not here to cause trouble."

The cowboy glanced at Marshall's ID and narrowed his eyes. "Fire department's shutting down access to all the properties."

"I know, but we're looking for my brother. Last location shows him still at the ranch, so we gotta check."

"You should call the authorities, son. They're not letting anyone in up—"

"Hang on," Luke interrupted. "Isn't that Bud Wilkins over there in the pickup?"

The cowboy looked over his shoulder. "What about him?"

Marshall leaned out the window and cupped his hands around his mouth. "Bud! Get over here!"

I was still lost. What was with this guy? Why was he blocking the road? Didn't he understand we needed to get through?

The guy Marshall had called sauntered over and thumbed his hat off his forehead. "Well, Marshall. Luke. What brings you two miscreants up here?"

Marshall gestured to the guy who'd stopped us. "Tell this ya-hoo that we're not up here looting houses. We just came up to fetch Evan—think he might be in trouble."

Bud Wilkins' face clouded. "Evan?" He stepped back and called to his friends. "Let 'em pass!" Then he tipped his hat to Marshall. "Good luck. Better hurry."

"What was all that about?" I demanded as Marshall rolled up the window and drove through the roadblock.

"Aw... you know," Marshall said. "Few years back, there was a fire down in the next county. They had looters and all kinds of troublemakers out tearing up properties when folks evacuated. Some were even starting more fires, just to make trouble. These guys are just makin' sure that doesn't happen here."

"But... that's illegal. They can't just be vigilantes and stop people on the road! Can't they go to jail for that?"

Luke shrugged. "If anyone cared to lock 'em up. I think most folks are happy to feel their neighbors are lookin' out for them. If you notice, they didn't technically have a barricade across the road. Just guys waving you down, see? It's gray area. Besides, they're not the roadblock we have to worry about. Where did Jess say they'd set up when she was leaving?"

Marshall glanced at me in the rearview mirror. "I don't remember, but it's moving down the mountain. Don't worry, I'll make 'em let us through."

Evan

I LEAPED DOWN FROM the tractor, dumping it unceremoniously in the middle of the driveway. No time to park it neatly in the barn. Smoke swirled around me like a thick, choking fog, its acrid scent filling my nostrils. The air felt like an oven and smelled like the nastiest campfire I'd ever been around. It was well past time to high-tail it.

All that was left was to get that semi-trailer full of hay out of here. I jumped up to the truck, yanked open the door, and climbed up into the cab. My hands were trembling slightly as I inserted the key into the ignition. I couldn't get out of here and back where I belonged fast enough, and I started twisting the key as quick as it would turn. But the only sound was the hollow click of a dead battery.

What the devil? I tried it again, but nothing, and I slammed my fist against the steering wheel. I'd planned it all out! Where did I go wrong? And then, like a bolt of lightning, it struck me—the auxiliary had been on during the hectic loading, hours earlier. We'd been using the winch, and I'd told Brandon to hit the road. I'd be right behind him... except I hadn't. It had been a small oversight with huge consequences. Now, hours later, the battery was completely drained, leaving me stranded.

I hit the steering wheel again, begging *something* to work. Even if it was just the horn! My phone was out of juice, my ride was dead, and I was alone, with no other transportation and no immediate way to call for help. A quick glance confirmed what I already knew—everyone's personal vehicles were gone, including mine. I was effectively stranded.

Frustration and panic rose in me as I fiddled with the controls, my mind racing through possibilities.

The only source of electricity on the whole property was the generator at the house, but it was too far to be of any use. I let out a heavy breath, feeling the weight of isolation. The barn's landline, once a reliable backup, was a casualty of technological upgrades and was now useless without power. I hopped down from the cab and started pacing, rubbing my jaw and staring at that lifeless hulk. Waiting for help wasn't an option; the roads would be closed by now. The fire was moving too fast, and I had lingered too long. My only chance was to make a break for it.

Maybe... not *every* vehicle was gone. I sprinted toward the barn and yanked open the door. A smaller Kubota tractor we used for toting the hay from one field to the next. Slow, but it would get me out of there. A behemoth swather that would take up the whole road. I counted on down the line, but what I was really looking for was something zippy, nimble, and fast. Something to get me around blockades and over whatever obstacles might have fallen across the road in the mayhem. And at the end of the row, I found it—Dad's side-by-side ATV. The keys were even in it—a small mercy. I jumped in, turned the key, and the engine roared to life. Music to my ears.

As I steered the ATV out of the driveway, I glanced back at the ranch—my family's legacy, the land I loved. My heart ached at the thought of leaving it to the mercy of the flames, but I had to. Meg, Dustin, my brothers, and Dad—they were my true legacy, the ones I needed to return to.

Meg

"OH. SO THAT'S WHERE the roadblock is." Marshall growled and shot the gear shift into park, slamming his shoulders against the back of his seat and glowering out the window. "Looks like this is as far as we go."

"Like heck," Luke spat. "Show them your ID. They can't keep you out of your own property. It's not like we're going back to save Dad's tie collection. This is Evan we're talking about!"

But it was no good. Marshall did his best, showing his ID and explaining in his most reasonable voice that his brother was up at the ranch, possibly in need of help. But the officers wouldn't budge. "We'll radio the sheriff to check on your property," one of them said, but it was cold comfort. They didn't know Evan, or where to look on the ranch for him if he was in trouble. And they wouldn't let us through, no matter how much we pleaded.

I felt a surge of frustration, a fierce urge to just get out and march up the mountain myself. Luke was muttering a string of curses and gesticulating through the glass at anyone who happened to glance his way. Marshall, usually the calm one, looked strained to breaking.

Then, as if things couldn't get any worse, Marshall pointed ahead, around the bend of the road. And then, even he started swearing. Sometimes, there just aren't words big enough for that kind of calamity.

My eyes followed his gesture, and what I saw made my heart seize. Fire was encroaching dangerously close to the highway, not a quarter mile from us. Flames leaped and danced hot against the sweltering air, with sparks flying over the pavement. A helicopter flew over our heads and dipped low above the flames, dumping water from the river onto the blaze, but it was a losing battle. The fire was moving faster than anyone could contain.

My phone slipped from my fingers, clattering to the floor of the truck. All attempts to call Evan again were forgotten. Panic swelled within me, threatening to overwhelm my senses. The thought that Evan might be trapped up there, alone and in danger, was too much.

"We have to do something! Can't you ask them to radio someone to check the ranch while we wait here?" I cried. What could we do, faced with an unstoppable force of nature and a blockade that refused to budge? There *had* to be something I could do! But all I could do was watch and wait, hopelessly trapped on the wrong side of the line.

Marshall had his head out the window again, talking fast to a kid who looked barely old enough to shave, but who wore a gold badge on his chest. "Look, sir, I understand your dilemma, but you have to go. Now," the kid said. "My chief just radioed that we have to move the blockade down the mountain—it's too hot here. I have officers who need to clear out."

"Well, where's that dad-blamed sheriff?" Luke hollered over the helicopter noise. "We'll wait to hear back from him before we clear out."

I just sat there shaking, feeling numb—cold and feverish at the same time, trying not to let tears spill over. Evan *had* to be safe somewhere! He promised he wouldn't take risks, wouldn't be caught... He *promised* he'd come back to me.

"The sheriff's on his way down now," the young officer barked back at Luke. "And you'd better not be here when he gets here. We're moving this whole unit down the mountain."

"Please, just let us wait for the sheriff!" I begged. "Just let us talk to him and make sure—"

But the lad walked away, waving for his superior to come run us off. Marshall's hand was on the gear shift, his eyes seeking mine in the rearview. "I'm sure Evan's okay," he said. "Maybe he's already out."

"Can't we call the sheriff dispatch ourselves?" I asked. "You heard them—they said an officer was still up there, and they were just waiting on him to come down before moving everything out. Could we find out who it is and ask him to check?"

"Probably Wyatt," Luke muttered. "He doesn't like me. Doubt he'll be much help."

"But..." And then, as if by magic, we could see flashing lights appearing around the bend up ahead. We could barely make them out through the smog. Difficult to tell what kind of emergency vehicle they belonged to, but the crew had said they were only waiting on one sheriff...

Marshall stuck his head out the window and was arguing with yet another officer. "Come on, just let us talk to Wyatt. I can see him, right there! Fine, we'll turn around as soon as we talk to him. No, sir, I don't want any trouble. I just need... yes, I'll get turned around now, and we won't block the escape route. Fine." He rolled the window up, growling as loudly as Luke, and nosed the pickup to the side of the highway to start turning it to face back downhill. All I could do was strain to turn around, my eyes fixed on what I could see of the road behind us.

The sheriff's car popped back into view a few seconds later, closer now, and I could make out the green and white markings all over the hood. The lights made a hazy glow as the sirens wailed and the car drew closer. I had taken my seat belt off now, and was standing up on my knees in the back seat, peering out the back window, hoping for a glimpse of the sheriff's face. Did he look grim? Urgent? Had he stopped at Walker Ranch when they radioed in that we were trying to get there?

But before I could get the answer to any of those questions, I saw *him*. The familiar face in the passenger seat, the face of the man I loved. My breath hitched, and my hands flew to my mouth, muffling a shriek of joy. "Evan!"

"What?" Luke and Marshall's heads snapped around, but I didn't bother explaining. I was jumping out and leaping into the middle of the road, flagging down the sheriff.

The car skidded to a halt, the sheriff's door opening first. He stepped out, shaking his fist. "What in tarnation you tryin' to do, lady? I almost hit you!"

And then Evan stepped out—his face streaked with dust and sweat, his clothes dark with soot, and a smile as big as the sunrise... and everything was right. Relief flooded through me, so intense it was almost physical. He was safe, alive, and he was scooping me up in his arms, lacing his fingers through my hair and around my back, and murmuring that he loved me, and all he'd wanted to do was to find me.

"Walker, is she with you?" Sheriff Wyatt had his hands on his hips, his eyes narrowed at me. Then, something behind me caught his attention, and he raised a brow at the guys in the pickup. "I might've known. Pick up one of you careening down the highway in an ATV with no tail lights and running on a flat tire, stumble into the rest of you tryin' to get through a roadblock. Those rules aren't made just to be broken, you know."

Evan set me back on my feet, kissing my forehead and snaking his arm around my waist. I pillowed my cheek on his shoulder, pulling as tight to him as I could. "Sorry, Wyatt. Thanks for the lift. Not sure I'd've made it out, even if I hadn't popped that tire."

"You wouldn't have. That side-by-side isn't made to do forty-five on the highway." Wyatt shook his head at Evan, his expression somewhere between disgust and grudging amusement. "One thing about it, no one can say you lot aren't a chip off the old block." His face softened and he sighed. "Give Blake my best, will you? And get yourselves out of here so we can get these crews to safety."

Evan's hand found mine. "Yessir. We're on our way."

Epilogue

Evan
Three weeks later

"Going to be an early winter," I said, my eye on the sky. Already, they were heavy with a silver glaze, threatening rain and wind and change. There were still some fires up there, somewhere, but it sounded like they were all under control at last. And with the weather changing, they'd simmer down quick.

"You can tell that just from looking at the clouds?" Meg jogged her horse to catch up with Strider as she scanned the gray-blue beyond the mountain range.

"Nah. Dad's Almanac said so."

She gaped at me for a second, then broke into a laugh. "You don't really put any stock in those superstitious old things, do you?"

"Why not? This year, we were supposed to have a fast, hot summer and wildfires. Was that wrong?"

She puckered her lips and shook her head, her eyebrow arched. "Lucky guess."

I shrugged. "If you say so. But lookit that." I reached down and brushed my colt's neck backward, displaying the start of his winter coat. "I always say you can set your calendar by the horses getting their winter hair in, and this is about two weeks early."

She was still looking at me skeptically. "So if it's going to be an early winter, does that mean we'll get enough snowpack to keep us from drying out so badly next summer?"

I grinned. "Now you're talking like a rancher."

"Maybe because I'm marrying one. Trying to keep up with you is a full-time job."

I rode my horse closer to her and turned over the hand that held her reins—the hand that wore that sparkling new diamond I'd given her last month. "I'm tame compared to the rest of my family."

She laughed and switched hands on her reins so I could cup her left hand to my face, turning her palm over and planting a kiss in the middle. "I don't know how Meryl and Audrey do it, to be honest."

"Lots of prayer would be my guess." I threaded my fingers through hers, and we just rode, side by side—our hands laced and our horses swinging their heads in a long, easy stride. This was peace. This was everything my heart could want—the woman I loved and the world before us.

"Wow." Meg sighed as we rounded a stand of trees, and her gaze lit on the blackened hillside bordering the broodmare pasture. "It never fails to astonish me, how close it got."

"Hmm." She was right. The fire had scorched across our pastures, incinerated a few fences, torched a couple of our field hay barns and nearly all our last cutting. Marshall had lost his new trusses and his RV—a thing for which his wife was not in the least sorry. And I had lost my house.

But everything I'd cut a firebreak around was still standing. In some places, the earth was black all the way to the tilled soil, where the flames died out. The ranch house, the barns, and just enough hay to survive the winter—it was all safe, and we'd only lost a dozen cattle in the lightning strike.

But better than that, thanks to our community's quick thinking and everyone pitching in together, not one single human life had been lost in the inferno that almost swallowed our town.

"Evan, promise me one thing."

I turned back to Meg, and my smile faded at the serious look on her face. "What is it?"

"Promise me you won't do anything that crazy again."

I tightened my hand in hers. "Promise, love. There's nothing here that's worth risking what I might've lost."

"Good. Because I'd like to keep you around."

I leaned across the space between our horses and kissed her. "Me too."

The broodmares were in sight now, and Dustin was trotting on ahead of us on June Bug. This had become our afternoon routine, once we got the okay to move back home. We were out for over a week while crews battled back the blaze, and it was a few more days after that before we got all the stock re-settled. But as soon as we got them all home, Meg and Dustin and I made it our jobs to go out and look at the foals. We were well into September and Meg and Dustin had started back in school by now, but I was waiting for them with saddled horses as soon as they got home.

"Look at that one, Dustin." I pointed to a strong-looking bay colt, bucking and playing, leading the others in a chase. "That feller there is a born leader."

Dustin leaned forward in his saddle, his gaze following my gesture, then cutting away without even commenting on the handsome bay. I should have known he'd only have eyes for one colt, and that was the palomino nibbling the toes of his boots and trying to get attention. Forge was his horse now—I couldn't see any way around it. A kid who risks his life to save a horse deserves that much.

What that meant for the competitive athletic career we'd planned for that handsome colt—well, time would tell. Maybe Dustin would start learning under Cody and show the horse himself. Or maybe he'd just be a trail pony and a friend—any of that was fine with me. I was just proud to be able to give the colt to him, and to see the way the kid's eyes lit up whenever he talked about his horse.

Dustin was petting the little white tuft of hair poking up between the colt's ears, and I thought he'd forgotten all about Meg and me even standing there, until he asked, "When do we start working with them?"

"Soon, Dustin," I replied, watching the foals play. "We'd have brought them in to start weaning and gentling them at the end of August, but we have to finish building a new fence around the field we usually put the babies in. I'm thinking early next week. You about ready?"

"I was already ready. I'm just *waiting*."

I chuckled and squeezed Meg's hand. "I know the feeling, bud." Waiting... that was what I was doing now. Meg and I were getting married in four more days, and I was counting them off by the second. And after that, we'd decided that we'd start trying to have more kids.

I knew what I wanted, I had a plan and dreams to work toward. Everything was in place, and now it was just a matter of time and doing. Because I don't know a better recipe for satisfaction in life than having a dream you never stop building. Having to learn patience in the waiting just means you've got something good to look forward to, and I had everything my heart could want.

"Hey, Dustin," I said. "We're going to ride on a little farther. Do you want to come or wait here?"

He finally looked away from the colt. "I can stay?"

"Sure, you can stay. I know you know the rules."

He didn't bother answering, but the fact that he immediately turned his attention back to Forge was all I needed to know. Meg and I rode on, over the rise and down the next gulley. I had something I wanted to show her.

She stopped as the charred bit of land came into view. I caught an uncertain look in her eye, and I tugged at her hand. "Come on."

Meg nudged her horse forward again, and together, we rode around the blackened site of the house that had once been my home. All that was left now was the concrete foundation—everything else, we'd already scraped off and hauled away. "It looks so different," she murmured.

"Yeah. So, I had an inspector out today."

She turned to look at me. "And?"

"And he said the foundation is solid. The fires didn't damage it."

Her eyes brightened. "Really? So we can start making plans to build?"

"Only if you want to." I got off and looped my rein around the hitching rail—a welded steel pipe, so it was one of the few things that hadn't burned up. Meg followed, and I held out my hand to walk around the foundation with her. "We'll need to look at different floor plans to see what we like. Might be that this foundation won't serve what we want, and we bulldoze it and start over."

She turned around, scanning the layout of the remaining concrete footings. "You know what, Evan?"

"What?"

"I think it's perfect, just as it is. We don't need to root out everything. We can build on what we have."

"You're sure?"

She smiled and wrapped her arms around my neck, smiling up at me. "Yeah. I don't want to erase the past. I just want a future with you—right here, where I belong."

I slid my hands into the pockets of her jeans and pulled her close, her fingers plowing through my hair and her body pressed against mine. "Good, because that's my way of thinking, too."

Meg

I RESTED MY HEAD against my cowboy's chest, listening to his heart beating strong and steady under that flannel shirt. Never in my life had I felt so safe and protected. Wanted. And understood.

I'd fought that battle all my life, without even realizing that I was fighting. Never had anyone seen my soul, met me in my struggle, and stepped into it with me. It's the curse of my personality, I suppose—I was always focused on surviving whatever was in front of me, trying to make it look like I was okay for my son's sake. And people just assumed I was fine.

But Evan was the one person to look at my "fine" and see the heart of the battle. And he wasn't afraid of the hard. He was strong enough to face it with me, and gentle enough to wipe my tears when it wasn't "fine" anymore. And he was the one who lifted my head and showed me a tomorrow that I could hope for.

"Hey," he murmured into my hair after a few minutes, "there's something else I want to show you."

I lifted my head and let him take me by the hand. "What is it?"

"Check this out." He led me across the foundation to what used to be the backyard. "There was a stand of maple hardwoods behind the house, and they didn't burn as hot and fast as the pines. They're still dead, but the wood is hardly charred on the inside."

"So?"

"So, I was thinking I'd cut them up for Dustin. Or he can carve them right where they stand, if he wants. I've seen that before—it's like a permanent sculpture. They look pretty cool, but they're huge. Think he'd want to work on something that big?"

I smiled, remembering that surprise Dustin had brought in the car for Evan. "I think he might."

"Well, I'll ask him. That ought to be enough wood to keep him busy for a while. But hey, we'd better go, huh?"

Hand in hand, he led me back to the horses, and we swung into the saddles together. A little while later, we'd collected Dustin and were on our way up to the ranch house for dinner.

Cody usually went home when he was done working colts for the day, but today, he'd stayed around to help Marshall set up his new RV. This time, they were parking it next to the ranch house, and Kelli and Morgan had been busy all afternoon getting dishes and groceries stocked into it. This RV was twice the size of the one Marshall had brought home from the auction, and nicer than any house I'd ever lived in. Which was a good thing, because it looked like they'd be spending the winter in it.

"Hey, Meg!" Audrey greeted me as we turned our horses back out into the pasture. She was just stepping out of her car, still wearing her scrubs, and tying her hair back behind the nape of her neck. "Have a nice ride?"

"We did." I stepped down from the saddle, and Evan took my horse. He and Dustin would unsaddle them and rub them down together—it was their little routine. "What are you doing up here today? I thought you'd be making Lizzy start her homework."

"Plenty of time for that later. Luke said he wanted to do a cookout with everyone tonight while the weather was still nice. Supposed to start raining later this week, according to the almanac."

I chuckled. "You buy into that thing, too?"

She stopped and pushed her sunglasses up into her hair. "I've learned not to question it. If the guys say the weather is changing, I figure they know what they're talking about."

"Well, you might be right." Evan called my name from across the barnyard, asking if I was ready to head up to the house. "I'll meet you inside," I called back.

And then I waited for my son, wondering if he'd remember the thing he wanted to get out of the car for Evan.

He did.

I found Evan inside, washing his hands at the sink. Dustin lingered at the door, his arms full of his wrapped bundle and his eyes hesitantly popping up now and again, waiting for Evan to notice him. Evan turned around with a smile for me, then he caught wind that something was up and looked at Dustin.

"What do you have there, son?" he asked.

Dustin swallowed and turned around, leading us to the dining room table without a word. Evan raised his brows at me, but I smiled without a word of explanation. This was

Dustin's secret to spill, not mine. Evan just shrugged, slipped his hand to the small of my back, and walked me into the dining room. "What's going on?" he asked.

"It's for you." Dustin tugged the sheet away and then stepped behind us, so people wouldn't be staring at him. But nobody would even think of staring at him anyway because the sculpture gracing the center of the dining room table took their breaths away. It made my heart stop a little every time I looked at it, and I'd seen it unfold bit by bit as he carved it.

Evan's face drained of all color, and I heard his breath catch. "Dustin... is that...?"

"It's Biz," he replied quickly, staring at his shoes. "And Emma."

Evan put a hand to his mouth, his eyes brimming with swift tears. Everyone else had found their way inside now, and no one was saying a word. Evan stepped haltingly toward the table, shaking his head in wonder. It truly was remarkable as a piece of art, but it was more than that. It was a moment in precious time, frozen to be remembered forever in wood that looked warm and vibrant and alive.

Biz was captured in the middle of a reining slide stop, like he used to do when he was showing. His hindquarters bulged with muscle, his mane and tail flying as his front feet peddled the flying sand that Dustin had somehow managed to capture in the wood. And sitting on his back with a proud laugh, her face turned up to the heavens and her arms reaching up to the sky, was Emma—just as she had looked that last day I said goodbye to her at school.

"How did you..." Evan began, his voice hushed.

"You gave me his pictures. But... but they weren't *right* on their own, until... until I saw the drawing." Dustin's gaze was shuffling from the floor to Evan's chest.

To others, he might have looked unhappy—uncertain, even, if anyone would like his work. But I knew him well enough to know that he was bursting with pride and the hope that Evan would understand what he meant by the gesture, and all those feelings were so big he couldn't force himself to meet anyone's gaze. He was twisting his hands in the hem of his shirt, glancing to the side, and he shrugged. "Biz is *every*one's horse, but... but he was Emma's first. So... so she... she had to be there."

"I don't know what to say," Evan whispered. He glanced back at me, his eyes alight and so full of love. That was it for me—I burst into happy sobs, my hands clasped over my mouth. He reached for my waist and tugged me close so he could press a kiss to my forehead. But then he let go and walked over to my son. He crouched on one knee, so he had to look up into Dustin's face, and just waited for my son to meet his gaze.

"Thank you," Evan said, in words that sounded like they came from the depths of his soul. "What you captured—it's bigger than words, Dustin. I can see your feelings there, and they're just like mine."

Dustin quit fumbling with his shirt and gave Evan a lop-sided grin... just like the one Evan liked to use on me to make me melt. "Did... did I get it right?"

"Yeah, you did, son. You have a gift—you *are* a gift. I want you to know how much it means to me that you chose to share it with me."

Dustin's smile widened, and he looked at me. "And with Mom. You can't forget Mom."

Evan set his arm on his knee and turned around to grin at me. "Never. You and your mom are my whole world."

Blake chose that moment to clear his throat. "Well, now..." He was tapping his chest, clearing his throat again. "That's... that's something, Dustin."

"Blake?" Meryl asked suspiciously. "You aren't having chest pains, are you?"

"Me? No, my stomach's growling. Is supper ready yet?"

"Dad!" Dusty hissed. "You're interrupting."

Evan stood up, his hand on my son's shoulder. "That's okay. We don't care to be the center of attention anyway, do we, Dustin?"

Dustin leaned into Evan's hand as he shook his head. "Can... can we eat now?"

My eyes widened. Dustin was *asking* to eat? This was new. We weren't even having spaghetti or pizza! Evan's eyes touched mine, and he just smiled. "Yeah. Let's bring the food in and say grace."

"That's what I'm talking about. Steak and corn on the cob," Blake said, rubbing his hands together and smacking his lips. "Can't beat 'em."

"Not for you," Meryl informed him. "You get chicken breast and green salad."

"But I took my medicine today," he complained.

"That doesn't mean you're bulletproof, cowboy," she scolded. "And I, for one, would like to keep you around. Luke, you can set that platter here. And Dusty and Marshall, can you fetch us a few more chairs? Cody, help me put another leaf in the table. We're going to need it!"

Marshall returned from the living room a minute later, toting a couple of chairs. He set them both down behind us, and Evan grinned, grabbing them and sliding one toward me. "Have a seat, soon-to-be Meg Walker?"

I wrapped my arms around his neck and kissed his chin. "I don't mind if I do."

He slid my chair in under me, and as the Walker family—*all* of us—gathered around the table, I took my place beside my cowboy. He clasped my hand, the one wearing his promise that he'd be mine and I'd be his for the rest of our days, and leaned over to kiss my cheek. "Looks like we're going to need to build us a *big* house, love."

I squeezed his hand back. "I'll build anything with you, cowboy."

K EEP READING FOR A preview of Cole and Emily's story in *A Rival for the Cowboy!*

Bonus Epilogue

THIS CHRISTMAS VIGNETTE WAS sent out to my newsletter subscribers, but it's such a sweet ending to the series that I've made it available for a free download, anytime and anywhere. _**Snap up this little epilogue**_ to wrap up the whole series and enjoy your favorite couples as they look forward to their growing families!

Keep reading for a preview of Cole and Emily's story in _**A Rival for the Cowboy!**_

From our hearts to yours

T HANK YOU FOR SPENDING a little time with the family at Walker Ranch.

I hope you've enjoyed getting to know everyone. I'd love it if you would share this family with your friends so they can experience life on the ranch with these swoony cowboys and sassy cowgirls. As with all my books, I have enabled lending to make it easier to share. If you leave a review for *A Heart for the Cowboy* on Amazon, Goodreads, Book Bub or your own blog, I would love to read it! Email me the link at <u>TheCowgirlWrites@TessThornton.com</u>

Would you like to read Blake Walker's romance? Dive into Blake and Meryl's story, and stay up to date on upcoming releases and sales by <u>**joining my newsletter**</u>

And now, keep reading for a sneak preview of Cole and Emily's story!

More from Tess Thornton

<u>**The Walker Ranch Series**</u>
A Home for the Cowboy
Cody and Morgan's Story
A Second Chance for the Cowboy
Marshall and Kelli's Story
A Winter Surprise for the Cowboy
*Blake and Meryl's Story
An Angel for the Cowboy
Dusty and Jess's Story
Taming the Cowboy
Luke and Audrey's Story
A Heart for the Cowboy
Evan and Meg's Story
A Winter Surprise for the Cowboy is a Free Novella
available only to newsletter subscribers

<u>**The Ridgeview Brothers Ranch Series**</u>
Coming in 2024...
A Rival for the Cowboy
Cole and Emily's Story
A Crossroads for the Cowboy
Chase & Kate's Story

A Christmas Wish for the Cowboy
Trent & Lauren's Story
A Match for the Cowboy
Gage & Amber's Story
A Partner for the Cowboy
A Cowboy Buddy Book featuring Luke Walker and Gage
Langton

A Rival for the Cowboy

Cole

MY GLOVE WAS STICKY with nervous sweat inside when
I tugged it off to adjust my reins. I wiped my palm
on my jeans, swallowed, and rubbed a quick circle on Lynx's
neck.

"Easy, girl," I muttered. My voice was gravelly, so I cleared
my throat and tried again. "Easy now."

Wasn't doing much good. The bay filly's head was up, and
she was hopping from one front foot to the other, jigging
sideways and chomping the bit. I kept having to bump her
back into line with my leg. Rookie horse, rookie rider—we
made quite the pair.

Far as I could tell, Lynx was the only horse in the whole
warm-up pen acting half-crazy. Everyone else looked bored,
just moseying along the rail, loose-rein and casual. Mean-
while, I was clinging to the filly's side like a twitchy jockey,
trying to keep my butt glued in the saddle while she spooked
at her own shadow. I jerked my hat lower and prayed no one
was laughing too loud. Time to head into the main arena for
our pattern.

A couple riders gave me sympathetic glances when we
went by. They'd all been here before, showing young horses
for the first time. But when I passed the row of bleachers
against the fence where Emily sat with her eyes glued to the
ring steward, I made sure to stare straight ahead.

Last thing I needed was Little Miss Perfect watching me get publicly humiliated. She already made me look bad enough.

We circled around to take our place at the gate to start our pattern, number 213 pinned neatly on both sides of my saddle blanket. Far as Lynx cared, it might as well have been a "REJECT" stamp on my rear.

I kept catching myself rolling my eyes skyward, and it took some effort to level my head. Wasn't the horse's fault she was wound up, I scolded myself. Barely three years old, first time off the ranch, four hundred-mile haul, new routines. I was lucky Cody even trusted me to show her.

I blew out a breath that fluttered my lips and focused on relaxing my own muscles. That usually helped get a young horse to settle, too. But then Lynx jumped and swung her butt toward the rail, and I almost came out of the saddle. So much for that idea.

From his vantage point leaning on the fence by the gate, my boss Cody was probably laughing at me. Or worse, trying real hard not to. This year was my shot to prove myself after barely eking out of the rookie ranks last fall with just a top-ten finish in a local jackpot show. Cody kept saying I had potential, that horses took to me well. All I knew was Copper sure took to Emily in a hurry, and now I was battling an uncertain filly determined to run me into the dirt.

The crackly loudspeaker had announced the first two riders, and then it was us. "Number 213, Cole Langton aboard Playin it Smart, bred and owned by Walker Ranch, shown by Cody Haskins."

I peeled Lynx away from the rail and aimed us for the center. Every step in, she jigged and spooked worse with the clapping and whistles urging us on. I gritted my teeth and murmured soothing phrases that were as much for me as they were for her.

Far as patterns went, it wasn't a tough one. I coiled my glove tighter into my rein hand and touched my heel to Lynx's side. Time for this green broke filly's first dance.

As my old man always used to say, go big or go home...

We tipped down the center of the arena, Lynx's hooves pounding an uneven cadence. I steadied my reins, sat deep, and tried for that illusion of graceful control.

First stop was decent. The filly hunkered quick as I cued, skidding fifteen feet or so. I kept her still for the count, though she fought me, head flung up and neck arched. The four spins we sort of fumbled through, hopping more than pivoting clean. But soon as I touched my spur, Lynx broke forward, eager to move those fresh legs.

I had to smile. However wacky she felt under me, she sure wanted to work. I shaped a fast circle to the right, big and round as I could make it in the confined space. She offered to change leads a stride early, but I held her straight until my marker. Her second lead change flowed better, and I almost sighed in relief.

Then came the left lead circles, and that's when things unraveled. We overshot our first turn, Lynx's shoulder bulging out. My reins rasped as I corrected too quick, and she threw her head, stiffening up. I tried easing her back around, keeping my legs soft, but now she wanted to gape her mouth and pretend she didn't know what I was asking.

"Easy," I whispered, hating the desperate thread in my tone. The filly wasn't quite right yet. She needed another year to bake, and I was rushing her too much...

I had to remember to ride her like the greenie she was. Shouldn't expect she'd be anywhere close to Copper's level yet. They were the same age, but she'd been smaller, hotter, and she was behind him by a good four months. Might as well be a year. Hardest thing now was keeping my own jumpy nerves from frazzling us both.

We finally swung onto the last required pass down center. It wasn't pretty, what with Lynx still distracted and poking along. But if we scratched out one decent sliding stop to polish off the run, maybe no one would notice too much.

Fifty feet from the far end, I sat deeper and let the reins slip. The filly perked and drove forward willingly. I smiled in front of my gritted teeth.

"That's my girl, easy now..." I adjusted my hat as the filly's feet shifted under me. Almost done. Now to let her sit a second and blow before I signaled the gate crew that...

Crap. They'd taken my hand on my hat as a cue. My grin froze as Lynx's ears pricked wildly right as her hips coiled under. Her stride bolted unevenly, and I caught a flash of white barreling at the closed arena gate.

Oh, blast. They were opening it up, already letting our cow in.

"Steady!" I yelped, but Lynx was already hopping sideways, shying from the gate crew rattling their levers and pulleys. She skipped again as the panels squeaked apart, making the gap for her worst nightmare to come bolting out.

I should have felt her tensing, knew she wasn't ready. If I'd just gotten her a little more broke back at home... Taken a second before trying to keep my fool hat in place...

No time for should-haves. I had a half second to get this filly back under me. As the black cow made its dart toward freedom, I gripped hard with my knees and threw everything I had into cutting Lynx to the left to head off our cow.

Big mistake.

Her slide went from controlled to a panicked scramble. We plowed past the end marker in a spray of dirty chalk. Lynx was still trying to spin away from the cow while I hauled the reins sideways. Our turnaround was sloppy, missing the backup a good ten feet. And then, the black baldy split right by us. Too slow, too slow! I wheeled her about and asked her to jog quietly, letting her catch up without getting too excited.

The cow was wandering by then, clueless to the wreck its entry had caused. Jaw tight, I just tried getting us to the gate without any more trouble. But when I asked the filly to jog, she ignored me completely. She wanted out of there just as bad I suddenly did.

I guess I couldn't blame her. The cow work was a bust before we even boxed the dumb critter. Wasn't the horse—it was me pushing too much gas and not riding the horse under me, but the horse I wanted her to be. I should have backed her off from trouble right when I felt it gather.

As we passed Cody, I stared hard at Lynx's ear and tried not to imagine the look on his face. Didn't matter. Show was over for us. I patted the filly's neck anyway as we exited the loud arena.

"Good girl," I muttered, swallowing the frustrated break in my voice. "We'll get 'em next time."

If Cody even let me leg up on one of his prospects again after that disaster...

Emily

I PRESSED MY LIPS to keep them from drawing into a thin line. Squinting against the glare, I watched Cole circle to line up his entry. Even from my perch halfway up the bleachers, I could read the tension singing through the young filly he rode. She had talent and try—I'd seen that myself back home in practice runs - but this atmosphere overwhelmed her.

And maybe Cole too, from the desperate set to his shoulders. I sighed softly. Of course, Cody would trust him with a prospect here. Never mind that more consistent riders—heck even half our students back home—would have shown Lynx off better after all the hours I'd put into exercising her. If Cole wanted to play with the big boys, today would test what he was really made of. My toes curled as I ticked through the pattern in my head, anticipating each mistake before they happened.

The filly overshot her first stop by a good eighteen feet, likely from Cole cuing too quick, then second-guessing himself. His timing worsened on the spins, and Lynx just looked baffled. At least when I'd been that green as an exhibitor, I'd drilled at home. I didn't have hundreds of eyes tracking each error, because Cody fixed all my mistakes in the schooling arena through patient repetition.

I drew a short breath as Lynx bobbled again—Cole was seesawing up there, letting the atmosphere eat him instead of riding calm through her trouble. The filly was a sweet goer for all her greenness, but I knew how quickly that could sour if she got the wrong idea of what showing was about. Risky giving her to someone without seasoning.

Jaw tight, I watched Cole throw a panicked yank sideways right as their cow burst free for its suicidal bolt across the arena. A sharp whistle slipped through my clenched teeth—he was going to undo months of patient training if he couldn't ride smarter. As their pattern ran long and tortured, other riders lined up along the rail for their crack at the boxing class. Lots of shaking heads and a few chuckles. Cole didn't stand a chance in the placings. Sympathy twinged for the burning cheeks Cole hid under his hat brim against the eyes of the world he was so hungry to impress.

I blew out an exasperated huff as they made their shambling exit. Disappointing, but at least no real harm done yet if Cody could get Cole back to basics at home before permanent damage set in. Though for his pride, the blistering defeat was likely hurt enough. I hoped Lynx hadn't lost her spark for the game—she deserved far better partners to nurture that blistering talent she had.

With a last patronizing head shake, I rose to follow, mentally cataloging the skills we apparently still needed some tough love to drill. If Cole hoped to ride with Cody, he had plenty yet to learn.

I found Cole at Lynx's stall, at the end of the row draped with red curtains and boasting the big Lazy W brand. The rest of our show string were napping or eating, but Lynx was dripping sweat and in need of a good rub-down and cool-out before she got turned loose. Cole was yanking roughly at the cinch, ears crimson. My steps slowed. Maybe now wasn't the best moment to review his ride. But he spun right as I scuffed my boot in the dirt, immediately on the attack.

"Come to tell me more ways I screwed it up? Saves Cody the trouble."

I rocked back slightly, blinking. "Just making sure you're okay. Rough ride for anyone—"

"I don't need your sympathy." He gave Lynx's girth another jerk, pulling it completely loose, and slung the sweat-soaked cinch up over the saddle. The filly shifted, eyes rimmed in concern my way. "Shouldn't you be getting high and mighty Copper pretty for his victory parade?"

The dig flushed my neck with embarrassment on behalf of the horse. "That's unfair, Cole. You know Copper and I have worked hard. I just meant—"

"Go bother someone else." He spun his saddle down off Lynx's back, slinging it angrily across his shoulder. "Don't you have better things to do?"

The dismissal slammed me back a step. I threw a bewildered look at Cody, who stood stone-faced outside his stall holding his champion horse Rust. He shook his head once, tired disappointment hanging off him.

Cole was already stomping off. I almost called out to stop him, hating leaving things ragged between any member of our team. But Cody subtly waved me off before leading Rust toward the warm-up pen. Handling Cole fell on his shoulders. I had my own stuff to worry about.

I patted Lynx's shoulder in sympathy. "He doesn't really mean it," I whispered in her flickering ear. If only excuses could heal the harm of careless tempers. With a sad glance after Cole, I turned slowly toward Copper's stall. Winning suddenly felt far less important than guarding each step we took to get there.

I slipped inside and greeted the gentlemanly stallion with a finger tracing that perfectly round star in the center of his forehead. "Are you ready for your turn, big guy?" I slipped a halter on him and smiled as he immediately nosed at my shoulder for an apple slice I didn't have. "You goof," I laughed, giving his golden neck a hug in apology. Copper flattened an ear coyly my way, gentlemanly as ever. Hard to believe such a clownish lug was actually a thickly muscled stallion who had taken his trial run in the breeding shed just last month. I kept scratching his silky hide as I moved to tie him in the corner of his stall before fetching his saddle. He leaned into every rub, eyes blinking sweetly shut in bliss.

We made quite the pair—both of us craving connection like water in the desert. Only I couldn't afford Copper's friendly manners slipping. He was still a stallion, and this was April—the time of year when even the best-mannered studs tend to lose their marbles. Too much rode on this show going perfectly, and with Cody trusting me to help season one of his best horses... well, I wasn't taking any chances. Copper had to mind his manners.

As I hefted the saddle pad and custom leather onto his back, Cole trudged back from the wash rack with a soggy Lynx in tow, his patented scowl dug deep. I paused to offer congratulations on surviving their trial by fire, but Copper chose that moment to wheel and nip affectionately at my hat.

"Copper!" I gasped, jerking away with a frown. The stallion snapped upright, clearly shocked by my sharp tone. Behind him, Cole shook his head and led Lynx on with an exaggerated eye roll.

Heat flooded my cheeks. Now Cole would think that single nip meant Copper was getting dangerous or disrespectful. And there wasn't time before our class to clarify that the sweet stallion simply forgot himself for a moment. We'd school a little harder on his ground manners. I wanted to rub his nose in apology for snapping at him, but that was the last thing I should do to discourage him getting a little too friendly.

"You're okay," I murmured. "We got this." Cole's disgust still nettled, but I shoved it roughly aside. Champions rode for themselves and their horses—not to please bitter critics. And that was what I aimed to be—a champion. I had the best coach in the country and, in my opinion, the best colt this side of anywhere. It was just a matter of time.

G ET YOUR COPY OF Cole and Emily's story and find out how these rivals find love in *A Rival for the Cowboy!*